I0671064

Spear of the Sigilla

Songs of Sevria
Volume 1

Patrick Basil

Cover art by germancreative
Map by Vitor Nunes

Spear of the Sigilla

Patrick Basil

Table of Contents

Chapter 1	*1*
Chapter 2	*8*
Chapter 3	*15*
Chapter 4	*23*
Chapter 5	*29*
Chapter 6	*36*
Chapter 7	*42*
Chapter 8	*50*
Chapter 9	*57*
Chapter 10	*64*
Chapter 11	*70*
Chapter 12	*77*
Chapter 13	*83*
Chapter 14	*89*
Chapter 15	*96*
Chapter 16	*102*
Chapter 17	*108*
Chapter 18	*114*
Chapter 19	*120*
Chapter 20	*126*
Chapter 21	*132*
Chapter 22	*138*
Chapter 23	*144*
Chapter 24	*150*
Chapter 25	*156*
Chapter 26	*164*
Chapter 27	*171*
Chapter 28	*177*
Chapter 29	*184*
Chapter 30	*190*

Spear of the Sigilla

Chapter 31	*199*
Chapter 32	*205*
Chapter 33	*212*
Chapter 34	*218*
Chapter 35	*223*
Chapter 36	*229*
Chapter 37	*235*
Chapter 38	*242*
Chapter 39	*250*
Chapter 40	*256*
Chapter 41	*263*
Chapter 42	*269*
Chapter 43	*275*
Epilogue	*281*
Glossary	*282*
Bibliography	*284*
Chapter 1	*285*

Patrick Basil

For my wife and my children,

without your support

Sevria would still be a pencil sketch.

Spear of the Sigilla

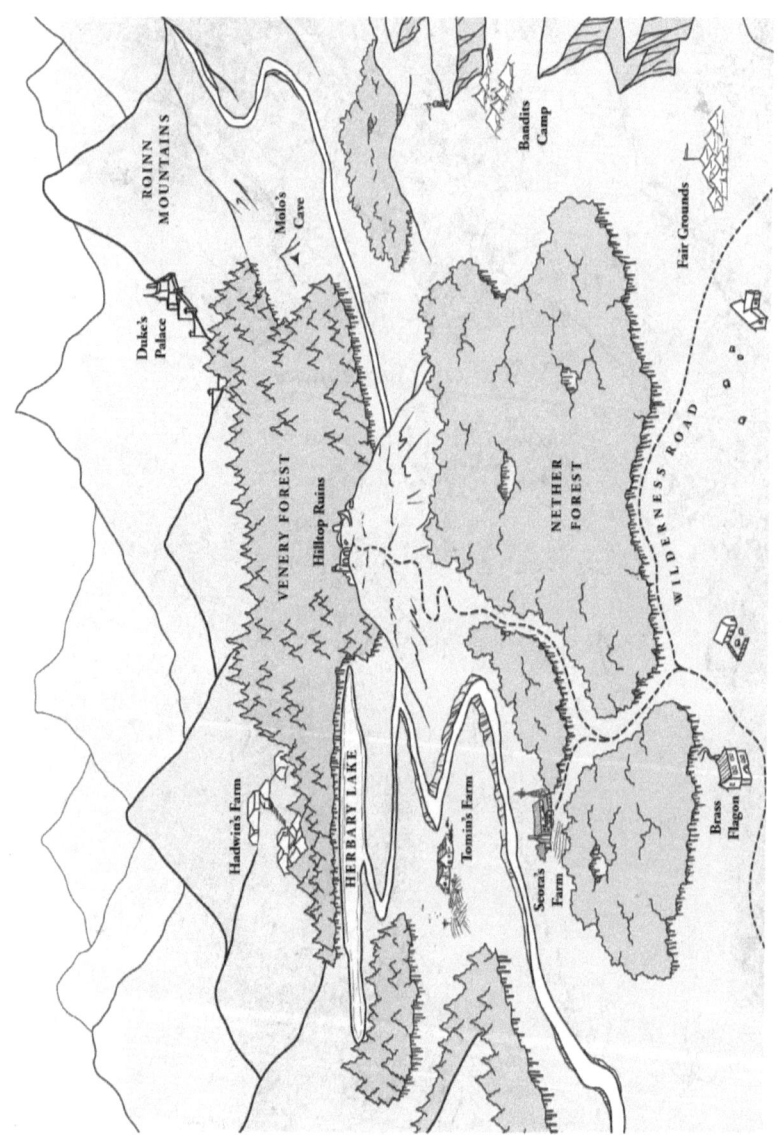

Chapter 1

Rinn woke with a start in unfamiliar surroundings. She had fallen asleep in the back of the wagon again, sprawled out on the sheets of canvas covering her family's worldly belongings. Not that there were very many belongings or very much family, just her and her father, Marshal. The pair had been travelling for months, meandering across uncultivated grasslands and through strange forests. Their wagon followed a meager trail that wandered far from the safety of the wide Imperial Roads.

Rinn rubbed her eyes and made a number of little noises as she stirred. The fragrance of wildflowers danced on the warm afternoon breeze, daring her to raise her head and look around. She saw movement nearby, her father unhitching the horse from the wagon.

"Good. You're awake." He smiled. Rinn felt her father did not smile enough. Back in the Empire, before they left, he laughed and joked at every opportunity. On the road, he barely spoke. He sat in the driver's seat for hours with his sword on his lap scanning the countryside like a bird of prey. Rinn always imagined her father as being birdlike, with his long skinny nose and tiny pointed beard on his chin. His olive complexion and slicked-back black hair were the opposite to Rinn's own pale skin and tangled mop of blond curls.

Rinn lifted her head to see colorful fields stretching out all around her. The wagon rested on a hilltop covered in brilliant blooms and tall slender grasses. Lush forests draped across nearby hills and billowy clouds chased each other across an azure sky. Rinn rubbed her eyes once more.

"Am I dreaming?" She asked.

"No." Her father reassured. "This is our new home."

Rinn leaped off the wagon and wobbled a few steps until her legs fully awoke. Then she dashed off into the meadow in unbridled joy, brushing her hands across the flower tops as she ran. She circled the hilltop three times, laughing as she went. She sped past their horse Bayard, patting him on the side, he raised his head from grazing and whinnied in protest.

At the highest point on the hill Rinn found a massive pile of grey stones. She picked her way up the rocks, careful not to tear her favorite dress, a dappled green frock with flowers sewn into the hem. From her vantage at the top of the pile she could see the entire countryside—a sprawling valley of forests and fields. A narrow, serpentine river wound its way south around the hillside. Gray craggy rocks poked through the forested hills to the west, like misshapen sentinels keeping watch over the land. To the north the scene was framed against a backdrop of jagged snow-capped mountains.

"Be careful up there." Her father called out, depositing an armload of canvases and poles at the foot of the stones.

"Daddy." Rinn shouted from her perch. "This place is amazing. Are we really going to live here?"

"Yes, we are." He answered with a bit of hesitation.

"It's so beautiful." Rinn beamed. "Where is our house?"

Marshal glanced briefly at the pile of stones and then returned to the wagon to grab another load of poles. Bewildered, Rinn looked down from her perch and slowly the outline of a building began to emerge—a rectangle of crumbling stone walls with several side rooms. The ruined building had no windows, no roof. Vines and weeds obscured most of the structure and gangly trees grew inside the living space. A square pile of rocks leaning against one wall resembled a dilapidated chimney, and the opening in another wall might have been a door. Rinn clambered down the rocky ruins and sprinted to her father.

"We can't live here!" She waved her hands wildly. "This isn't a house. It's just a bunch of broken rocks."

Marshal set down the load he was carrying and placed his calloused hands on Rinn's shoulders. He summoned his softest, kindest voice. "Rinn, this is our new home. This is a nice, safe place, far from trouble. It may not look like much, but with some work, we can fix it. I'm sure this was a beautiful home once."

Rinn started to cry big, soggy tears, like a runny-nosed six-year-old, not a girl of thirteen. The stress of traveling for months across wild, strange lands, sleeping in the back of a wagon, eating dried food, all with the hopes of seeing her new house overwhelmed her. She withered to the ground sobbing uncontrollably. Her father knelt in the grass beside her and cradled her head in his lap. He stroked her curls and spoke kind words as she wailed. Quite some time passed until the waves of emotion receded. After Rinn's nose was wiped and her eyes dried, her father stood her up and escorted her to the wagon. He handed her a small hand axe.

"This will help take your mind off things." He pointed to the ruins. "Do you think you can cut down some little trees? Quite a few of them are growing inside our house."

Rinn pushed up her sleeves and stomped off with her little axe. She mercilessly assaulted the saplings growing inside the ruins, yelling at them each time she chopped. "No trees inside the house!" She tossed the broken twigs out the gaping holes where windows once stood. "Go play outside!" Her father laughed to himself as he watched. He returned to his task fastening ropes to wooden poles. Rinn soon needed to rest, murdering little trees was exhausting. She wandered outside to her father and plopped down on a rock to catch her breath. "What are you doing?" She huffed.

"I'm setting up my old tent." He proudly assessed his work, a carefully laid-out canvas with sixteen wooden stakes. "I used this when I was in the Legion. There's enough room for ten soldiers inside. It should be more than big enough for the two of us." He poked Rinn's sweaty nose.

Rinn frowned. "We're going to live in a tent?"

"For a bit, until we can get the house ready. It's actually quite comfortable inside." Rinn did not look pleased. Marshal stroked the thin fuzz on his chin. "What do you think you've been sleeping on this whole time?" Rinn tried to recall the journey, but memories of her old house in Viburna came instead. She vividly pictured her upstairs bedroom window and the bright lights of the nearby city market. She imagined the burbling fountain in the small courtyard behind her house and could almost feel the warmth of the kitchen hearth. Tears started to well at the corners of her eyes.

"I don't want to live in a tent." Rinn dropped her little axe and wiped her face. Violent waves of sniffles overcame her.

"It's only for a while." Her father held her close. "Until I can fashion a roof for us. And maybe a few windows. Possibly a door or two." Rinn started to sniffle-laugh. Her father joined along.

::

The tent nestled snuggly inside the ruins, in a square room just off the main hall. The center of the house was left open, like a private courtyard surrounded by stone walls. Marshal dug a fire pit in the courtyard and lined it with rocks. Rinn piled butchered saplings in the fire ring along with dry grass for kindling. Marshal added a pinch of fire salts. After a few moments they crackled and burst into a cheery flame. For the first time in many nights, Rinn enjoyed a hot meal. She did not mind the blandness of beans and millet, so long as she did not have to eat dried rations once again. After dinner, cots and bedrolls were arranged inside the tent. Rinn had her own private nook, flanked by canvas tent flaps. She changed out of her sweaty travel clothes into a clean nightshirt and readied herself for bed.

Rinn poked her head out of her nook. "Shouldn't we say our evening prayers?"

"I don't think the Imperial gods can hear us out here." Her father casually chuckled. Seeing Rinn's troubled expression he quickly recanted. "Well, we are surrounded by nature, so I guess we could offer a prayer to Lucus."

"Great. The god of forests is my favorite." Rinn closed her eyes and clasped her hands as she recited the six-line homage to Lucus. Marshal stumbled on the words as he attempted to follow along. After the prayer, Rinn eagerly climbed into her new bed and Marshal tucked her in, kissing her on the forehead.

"Good night, Rinn." He smiled.

"Good night, Daddy." She happily snuggled deep into her bedroll.

It did not take long for Marshal to drift off to sleep, but Rinn stayed awake for quite some time, distracted by the unfamiliar sounds of chirping insects and distant animal calls. Sleep finally overtook her, and in her dreams she relived her last night in Viburna. From her bedroom she could hear hammering on the door of her house. She snuck downstairs and spied her father speaking with a figure in long, black robes. His face was hidden by a large cowl, and he spoke in urgent, hushed tones. By the next morning, her house had been sold, and everything they owned had been packed onto a wagon heading out of town. It could have been his garments or curious gestures, but something about the man made Rinn believe he was a priest.

Outside the tent, in the darkness of night, quiet feet stalked the hillside. They slipped past the sleeping horse and explored the stony ruins. A furry nose sniffed at the smoldering campfire and the empty cooking pot. The horse snorted in his sleep startling the skittish prowler who raced off into the night.

::

The next morning, Rinn woke to the smells of breakfast cooking. She stiffly crawled out of the tent pulling on a woolen shift against the chill. Her father sat on a small stool near the campfire, drinking his morning ale and stirring a small pot.

"Good morning. Did you sleep well?" Marshal asked dishing out a bowl full of porridge for her. Rinn nodded her bramble of blond hair and accepted the warm bowl. He pointed with his half-empty mug. "Supposedly, there's an inn about a half-day's ride south. We'll travel there tomorrow to replenish our supplies. We ate most of our food on the journey here."

Rinn sat down on a blanket near her father and blew on her porridge to cool it. "Daddy, why did we have to leave home in the first place?"

"This again?" Marshal swirled the ale in his mug and finished it before he answered. "The Imperial cities are not a good place for us right now. It's safer out here in the countryside where no one's looking for us."

"Who'd be looking for us?" Rinn furrowed her eyebrows. "We didn't do anything wrong."

Marshal gently mussed her tangled hair. "No, we didn't. But the world is a complicated place."

"What's wrong with it?" Rinn asked, sipping her porridge.

Her father tried to explain. "Ever since the last emperor died, the politics of the Sevrian Empire have spiraled out of control. Power-hungry politicians fight for control of the government, and the Legions gather in the west, preparing for war. Rebellion is brewing in the streets. Sevria is not a nice place for anyone, especially young girls."

"That's just dumb." Rinn rolled her eyes. She drew circles in her porridge with her finger. "That stupid emperor died a long time ago. I don't see why it matters anymore."

"I know this whole thing doesn't make much sense, but I promise I will explain it better when you're older." He reassured her.

"My birthday is coming soon." Rinn raised a finger. "I'll be fourteen."

"Yes, you will." Her father agreed. "You'll practically be a grown-up." He refilled his ale and drank, silently staring off at the sunrise. Rinn had seen him like this many times, lost in memories of the past.

"You're thinking about Mother again, aren't you?" Rinn did not like it when her father retreated into the past.

Marshal returned from his reverie and took Rinn's hand. "Years ago, your mother and I agreed to give you a special present when you came of age. On your next birthday, we'll eat sweetbreads and celebrate with presents. But today, we have work to do, so finish up and get dressed. We have trees to kill!" Rinn smiled and devoured her breakfast.

Chapter 2

Rinn worked all morning pulling weeds while her father chopped through brush and small trees. Their horse Bayard was left to explore the hilltop freely, he was trained not to wander. Once the overgrowth around the stones had been cleared, the shape of the ruined house started to emerge—a generous structure built around a large feast hall. The design seemed strange to Rinn who was used to square Imperial houses built around open central courtyards. Her father explained that houses this far north were enclosed under large roofs to protect them from severe winter storms that ravaged the land. Rinn had only ever seen snow flurries once and they did not last very long.

After lunch, Rinn and her father explored the countryside. Riding together on horseback, Marshal pointed out areas that would be good for foraging and hunting. They paused at a river bank to rest and water their horse. Rinn found a line of berry bushes growing by the water's edge, with odd, oblong, blue berries. Her father assured her they were safe to eat, so she sampled one. The berry started off sour followed by a burst of sweetness that made Rinn giggle. She packed Bayard's saddlebags full with them, occasionally feeding the horse a handful. On the way back to the ruins, Marshal spotted several birds' nests and recovered yellow, speckled eggs from them.

Around dusk, Marshal strung his bow and ventured into the forest to hunt. Rinn waited alone in the wild, unfamiliar place, stoking the campfire to fend off the twilight gloom. A flock of noisy, oversized birds circled overhead and made Rinn feel uneasy. She retreated into the tent, whispering prayers to Parma, the god of protection. The campfire burned lower and lower until it was a heap of dimly glowing coals. Rinn worried that her father would never return, and she would be left alone in the wilderness to die. In her imagination she was being chased through the forest by ravenous beasts with murderous teeth and razor-like claws. Rinn drew her knees up and hugged them tightly, fighting tears.

When her father burst through the tent flaps, Rinn screamed. She ran over and locked her arms around him, vowing to never let him go away again. She wanted to be mad at him for taking so long, but when she saw the rabbits he caught, the prospect of freshly cooked meat melted her anger. On closer inspection, they were not exactly rabbits, but something similar with long bushy tails, like a squirrel with large hind legs. Marshal pelted the animals and set the meat to cook over the campfire. The smell of roasting almost-rabbit made Rinn's stomach grumble.

Grease rolled down Rinn's chin as she tore away bits of meat. "It's so good." Her father nodded in agreement, mouth full. They rounded off their meal with handfuls of oblong berries. After finishing his last bits of meat, Marshal wiped his hands and made an announcement.

"I think we had a visitor last night." His voice was unreasonably calm.

"A what?" Rinn scanned the campsite wide-eyed. "Who?"

"Not sure." Marshal poked at the fire, adding a bit more wood. "But something has been snooping around our campsite."

"Something?" Rinn cowered close to her father. "Like an animal?"

"Possibly." Her father admitted. "It barely left any tracks, and what I could see, I didn't recognize."

"Is it dangerous?" Rinn scooted closer to her father. "Are there dragons out here?"

"I don't think so." Her father chuckled. He put his arm around her with confident calm. "Don't worry about it.

Bayard is trained to alert us if anything dangerous approaches the camp." Rinn peered into the absolute darkness of the wilderness beyond the ruins. She gripped her father even more tightly. Marshal mussed her hair. "You don't have to be afraid. I have a plan."

Before bed, Marshal placed a few bird eggs and a handful of berries in a small pouch and hung it outside on a wooden stake. He made sure the drawstrings were tied in a tight knot and then turned in for the evening. Rinn attempted to sleep, but terrifying images of fanged creatures lurking around their campsite haunted her thoughts. She lay awake half the night jumping at every noise she heard.

In the morning, Marshal sat at a small table inside the tent drinking a bit of morning ale while Rinn slept in her porridge. He made an announcement. "Our visitor came again last night." Rinn startled awake and shot her father a panicked look, bits of porridge dripping from her face. He chuckled as he wiped her off. "It's okay. I don't think it means us any harm. Whatever it was, it took the eggs and left. It was probably just hungry."

"Was it some kind of animal?" Rinn wiped porridge from her face.

"An animal would have torn open the bag. Whatever this was, it untied the knot, took out the eggs, and left the bag behind. Quite a polite little thief."

Marshal postponed their trip to the inn until this business with the night time visitor was sorted out. Rinn was assigned chores of cleaning, weeding, and fetching water while Marshal chopped wood for the roof. Over the next few nights, different bits of food were left in the bag for their guest. Even though Marshal kept close watch, the thief always managed to slip in and out unseen. Apparently, it was a picky eater; eggs and bits of cooked meat were always taken, but vegetables and berries were left untouched. After several nights of anxious waiting, Rinn's curiosity boiled over. The next night, she feigned sleep and slipped out of her bedroll after she heard her father's soft snoring. She situated herself behind a low rock at one end of the ruins. She camouflaged herself under a large blanket and watched the food-filled pouch. The vast starry sky stretched out before her. In the city, the nights were not so dark nor noisy. A long time passed and Rinn struggled against the lullaby of cricket songs, nearly dozing off several times. Finally, she glimpsed a shape moving in the night, a vague outline in the dim moonlight soundlessly creeping toward the food pouch. In her hiding spot, Rinn tried to stifle her rapid breathing as she watched a strange furry paw remove the pouch and untie the knotted strings. The visitor sniffed the contents of the bag and hung it back on the wooden post. The dark shape vanished into the night. Rinn stayed hidden beneath her blanket for a while before she stirred. She stretched her cramped arms and legs and began to stand. A feline face appeared inches from her own.

"Do you have any more eggs?" It asked in a childlike voice. Rinn screamed, and the visitor winced, covering her furry ears with her paws.

::

The thief sat on the floor of the tent, happily eating eggs and licking out their shells. She was covered in tawny fur caked with dirt. Large triangular ears sprouted from her head and long white whiskers from her cheeks. She wore nothing but a filthy, torn shirt that barely covered her torso. Finishing the eggs, she began to sniff around the tent. She walked on her hind legs balanced by her bushy tail. Even though she was covered in fur, Rinn could see the emaciated frame of the feline girl. She appeared younger than Rinn, and stood a whole head shorter in height, if you did not count her ears. The girl pawed through the bedrolls and blankets, opened each basket and box, and thoroughly explored every corner of the tent. Marshal intercepted her when she nearly tipped over their chamber pot.

Rinn tugged on her father's tunic. "Daddy, can I keep her?"

"I'm not a pet!" The feline girl protested, folding her ears down, her tail swishing madly. Rinn hid behind her father, and he scowled at her rudeness.

"Rinn did not mean to offend you. I am called Marshal, and this is my daughter." He extended his hand in greeting. The feline girl sniffed at it and then continued her exploration of the tent. Marshal asked. "What is your name?"

"I don't have one." The girl complained.

Marshal raised an eyebrow. "Where did you come from?"

"The forest." The little girl licked her paws and methodically rubbed her ears. "But your food smelled so good, I had to come out of hiding to try it." She continued cleaning herself.

"You were hiding?" Marshal asked innocently. The girl nodded. "Who were you hiding from?"

"Bad men." The girl gave her ears several more passes and then switched to cleaning her whiskers. "I don't want to talk about it."

"You don't have to." Marshal stepped away and studied the odd girl as she moved. Rinn tugged at his sleeve.

"What are we going to do?" Rinn whispered in his ear.

"She seems harmless enough." Marshal shrugged.

Rinn insisted in a loud whisper. "She's all alone. We can't send her back into the forest." She balled her hands into fists. "What if those bad men come after her again?"

Marshal grumbled. "Okay, we can let her stay the night." He turned to the visitor. "Would you like to stay with us for the night? We're happy to share our food with you." Marshal's voice was filled with honesty and concern.

"Sure." The little feline girl smiled revealing two tiny, little fangs. Rinn squealed happily and clapped her hands.

"Let's try getting you cleaned up a bit, maybe find you some better clothes." Marshal handed Rinn a grooming brush normally used on their horse and motioned her toward the visitor. Rinn timidly approached her with the brush.

"What's that?" The feline girl asked, sniffing the strange object.

"Sit down, and I'll show you." Rinn suggested. The little girl dropped down on her haunches, just like a cat. Rinn gently brushed the fur on the back of her neck, scraping away the dirt. The little girl squinted her eyes and bobbed her head in pleasure. She lifted her chin, so it could be brushed, too. Rinn stroked carefully through the reddish-brown fur, smoothing out the kinks and detangling the knots. The feline girl hummed a happy tune to herself as Rinn worked. Marshal rummaged through their clothes and found a dress Rinn had outgrown. Rinn helped the feline girl out of her filthy, torn shirt and into the dress. It fit her well enough, cinched with a belt; but her fluffy tail bunched up the skirt. A slit had to be cut in back to accommodate it. The feline girl stumbled on the hems of her dress as she walked. Rinn wondered if she had ever worn a dress before. Marshal tried to fit the new girl with shoes, but nothing designed for human feet would cover her long back paws.

By the time the wardrobe was sorted out, the first rays of dawn were streaking across the sky. Marshal hurried the girls off to get some sleep before the day began in earnest. Rinn climbed into her bedroll and Marshal tucked the new girl into his. Within moments the feline girl was sleeping blissfully under the blankets. Marshal watched over the sleepers like a sentry.

::

That afternoon, the girls frolicked through the hilltop wildflowers like sisters. Nearby, Marshal chopped timber, always keeping a watchful eye on them. Rinn dragged the new girl down the hillside to visit the river. She picked cattails and chased her new friend with them. The feline girl squealed and laughed as she ran. Rinn kicked off her shoes and tiptoed through the shallows. Her friend stayed a comfortable distance away from the water.

"Dad's going to make fishing poles, so we can catch fish here." Rinn splashed with her feet.

"I like fish." The feline girl acknowledged. She pointed a paw across the river. "What's that?"

Rinn squinted to see a strange rock sitting on the opposite shore. It was the size of a large melon with a purple eye crudely painted upon it. "That's odd." Rinn stepped out of the water. "I wonder whose rock that is?"

"It's creepy." The girl shuddered.

"It's certainly weird. Let's go tell my Dad." She took the little girl by the paw and ran up the hill. Breathlessly, they told Marshal all about the unusual rock. They dragged him down to the river banks to investigate, but by the time they returned the unusual stone had vanished. Marshal scratched the thin beard on his chin.

"Maybe you girls should stay closer to the house." He escorted them back to the campsite, warily eyeing the far shore as they went.

Chapter 3

"Daddy, you have to let her stay." Rinn pleaded with her father in the courtyard outside their tent. The feline girl was sleeping inside. "You should hear the horrible stories she tells. They had her locked up in chains. They beat her. They barely fed her. It's no wonder she ran away."

Marshal listened carefully and considered for a moment before he answered. "I will do what I can to help her, but we don't know anything about who she is or where she came from. We don't even know what she is."

"She's a little girl, and she needs our help." Rinn stomped her foot.

"Alright, alright." Marshal acquiesced. "She can stay for now. But she's going to have to earn her keep." A small head covered in tawny fur poked out from the tent flaps, little ears perking up hopefully.

"I know you're not sleeping." Marshal rolled his eyes. "You might as well come out." The feline girl crawled out of the tent meekly and stood before him, paws behind her back. Marshal mustered his sternest voice. "I know you don't have anywhere to go and this is not much of a house, but you can stay here with us if you want."

"I can stay?" the girl asked, bouncing in place, her tail wagging madly.

Marshal smirked and quickly regained his composure. "You can stay until we find out who you are and where you belong. But if you stay, you are going to have to mind what I say and do your share of the daily chores. I won't treat you any differently than I do my own daughter."

"I'm your daughter?" Big tears welled up in the little girl's eyes and she sprang forward, grappling Marshal in a two-arm and two-leg hug. Even her tail wrapped around him. Rinn could swear she heard purring. Caught off guard, Marshal patted the girl on the head which only made her snuggle in harder.

"Okay, enough." A red-faced Marshal peeled the girl off himself and set her down. "If you are going to stay with us, you're going to need a name. Are you sure you don't remember anything?"

The feline girl shook her head and twiddled her paws. "I had a name, but no one could pronounce it, so I forgot. I haven't heard it in a very long time."

Marshal took all this in and then posed the question. "Well, what do you want to be called?" She shrugged her shoulders.

"How about Macka?" Rinn suggested. The girl scrunched her nose and shook her head. "Felis is a good name." The girl stuck out her tongue and shook her head vigorously. "Tigris?" Again, the girl refused. She peered at Marshal expectantly. He scratched the thin fuzz on his chin.

"We could call her 'Catherine'." He offered.

"'CATherine'? Really, Dad?" Rinn palmed her forehead. "That's just stupid."

"I like it." The feline girl admitted.

"Really?" Both Rinn and her father asked in surprised unison.

"Sure." The girl slowly mouthed the name Catherine, putting extra emphasis on the first syllable. She rolled the 'r' with a little trill, rocking back and forth on her haunches as she repeated the name.

"You can't be serious!" A flustered Rinn exclaimed, hands on her hips. "That was a joke. Dad, tell her you're not serious."

"But I like it." The feline's tawny fur bristled as she argued.

Marshal stepped in, placing a hand between the girls. "Okay, enough you two." He knelt down before the feline girl. "You can change your mind if you want to, but you do need a name. Are you sure you want us to call you 'Catherine'?"

"Yes." Replied Catherine.

"Well, Catherine, tomorrow we're going to an inn." Marshal declared. Rinn bounced up and down excitedly, the feline girl looked lost.

"What's an inn?" asked Catherine.

::

Marshal rose early to prepare the horse and wagon for the journey. He estimated that the inn would be a half day's ride south, a direction they had not traveled. Their flight from Sevria had taken them deep into the Rustic Lands, a vast unconquered wilderness beyond the great Imperial Vallum. Rinn had not seen any cities or towns, just scattered rural homesteads and the occasional small village. The Rustic citizens seemed very poor and were delighted when her father purchased supplies with Imperial coins.

In the beginning, Catherine was apprehensive about journeying through the wilderness, but Marshal reassured her they would be safe. When she learned that she could ride in the back of the wagon with Rinn, her mood brightened. Marshal also promised to buy her fresh meat once they reached the inn. Together they deconstructed the tent and packed all their belongings onto the wagon, covering it with the tent canvas. Marshal fed and watered Bayard while Rinn gave him a good brushing. Catherine kept a conspicuous distance away from the horse.

"You don't have to be afraid of Bayard." Rinn brushed in long strokes. "He is a gentle horse. He won't hurt you."

"I'm not scared!" Catherine complained. "I just don't trust him." The horse whinnied, and Catherine skittishly jumped behind Rinn. She laughed at the feline girl. Soft morning sun peaked over the hills as they departed. Marshal mounted the driver's seat, and the girls sat on the tail board dangling their feet off the end. They chatted endlessly as the wagon rumbled down the hillside into the southern forests. Marshal followed a broken path crowded with tree trunks and overgrown bramble. The wagon stopped frequently so fallen limbs and brush could be cleared from the trail. Rinn did not mind the delays, she was enjoying having a friend to talk with. She barely noticed her surroundings growing steadily darker. Overhead, the dense canopy of leaves loomed like a storm cloud, casting the forest into a dim twilight. Tree trunks rose like columns to the darkening sky. Rinn became aware of her unsettling surroundings. It reminded her of the Great Temple of Aedis, with its endless rows of alabaster pillars. She visited the temple once when she was five and got turned around in the forest of white stone. Rinn remembered feeling so small and lost in that temple, just like she felt now.

"Daddy, I don't like it here." Rinn scooted to the front of the wagon to be closer to her father, and Catherine joined her.

"There are bad people here." Her feline tail swished, and her ears darted.

"You've been here before?" Marshal's eyes scanned the twilight forest. He unsheathed the longsword sitting on his lap.

Catherine nodded yes. "I was running from the boat men." She curled up into a ball, wrapping her tail around herself.

"Boat men? You mean sailors?" Marshal puzzled. "Were you in Sevria?" Catherine looked at him without understanding. He rephrased his question. "Have you ever been to the Empire? Lots of walls, many guards?" Catherine shook her head no. Marshal stammered. "Where did you come from? The nearest ocean lies beyond the deadly Roinn Mountains. Cat, how long have you been on your own?"

"Most of my life." Catherine sniffed.

"Oh child, I am so sorry. I wish we could have found you sooner." He pulled her onto his lap and gave her a hug—she barely weighed anything. Not wanting to be left out, Rinn crawled onto the driver's bench next to him, and Marshal put an arm around her, too. During this tender exchange, the first bandit jumped down from the trees. He landed in the back of the wagon, two short swords readied for attack. Cat hissed immediately, buying Marshal the precious seconds he needed to react. As the redheaded ruffian lunged, Marshal careened sideways throwing Rinn and Cat to the floorboard. He parried a second attack with the sword from his lap and countered with a thrust through the bandit's sword arm. Howling in pain, the bandit dropped his rusty weapon. The horse whinnied and bucked, tossing Marshal and the bandit from the driver's bench.

Marshal rolled into a ready stance, keeping ahold of his sword. In a quick glance, he saw four other bandits emerging from the trees. They appeared to be siblings, all with similar short stature and matching bright red hair. They wore motley bits of leather armor and brandished poor-quality weapons caked in rust. Rinn lay in a panic on the floorboard of the driver's bench with Cat crouching nearby, claws out. The four bandits circled around Marshal with weapons drawn. The first bandit, nursing a wounded arm, cursed and reached for the girls in the wagon.

"Stay away from them." Marshal demanded. He feigned and attack at one of the bandits and then kicked him squarely in the chest. The other three closed in, separating Marshal from the girls in the wagon.

"We got a fighter." One of the bandits called out, a female, though she had the same build and hair cut as her mates. Marshal continued his attack, trying to get back to the wagon. The injured bandit climbed onto the driver's bench and saw the crouching Catherine, fur fluffed out and tail whipping furiously.

"It's a Grimalkin." The pock-marked bandit cursed, making a sign.

"I'm not a Grimalkin. I'm angry!" Cat hissed and launched forward. She raked the bandit's face with her claws and kicked off his chest. The bandit reeled and clutched his bleeding face. Rinn lay on the floor board, her heart pounding out of her chest. The bandit's sword had landed just beyond her fingertips. She stretched out her hand to grab it. As Marshal clashed with the brigands, he paused long enough to see Rinn reaching for the short sword.

"Rinn, no!" He called out too late. Rinn's hands wrapped around the hilt of the sword and she held the weapon protectively between her and the injured ruffian. A metallic smell permeated the air and the rust on the surface of the short sword fell away like dust, leaving behind a shining silvery blade. The weapon glowed faintly in Rinn's hands with a pale green light. The injured bandit slashed with his remaining sword, trying to knock the weapon out of Rinn's hands. She lifted her shining blade in defense, and with a hideous sound, it sliced cleanly through the bandit's own sword. Both the bandit and Rinn were startled as the severed tip of the bandit's sword felt to the ground. Marshal used the confusion to break through the line of attackers and make his way to the wagon. Rinn climbed down from the driver's bench and joined him. Cat followed.

"Hanley." The brigand leader called out. "Don't just stand there. Get that horse." Rinn stared in amazement at the severed end of the bandit's sword lying on the ground. Marshal motioned for her and Catherine to get behind him. The injured bandit cursed as he fumbled with a knife trying to cut the horse free using only his uninjured hand. Bayard bucked and nipped.

"She ain't coming, Egan." He complained.

"Useless." Egan pushed the female bandit next to him toward the horse. "Grale, go help him."

Marshal calmly called the bandit leader out. "Egan, you should take your men and leave." Marshal spun his sword in his hand. "We are not the easy prey you were hoping for."

Egan spat on the ground. "I ain't leaving empty handed."

Marshal bantered casually. "Times may be tough, but banditry is not the answer. The penalty for horse theft is hanging."

"This ain't the Imperium, fool." Egan shook his rusty sword in anger. "These are Clanmorris' lands. We take what we want, and I want your horse."

Marshal clenched his jaw and glowered at the bandit leader. "Pick one." He challenged. "Pick which of your men you want me to kill first." The bandits retreated behind their leader. Marshal stood calmly, long sword ready, gaze determined. On his right Catherine snarled, and on his left Rinn clutched her odd, glowing blade. The bandits began to hem and haw, mumbling to each other.

Hanley held out his injured arm and touched the claw marks on his face. "We should go." He said in a low voice.

Egan fumed. "It's one man and two little girls."

"That's an Imperial sword." Grale pointed out. "He's got a soldier's stance. He's Legion trained."

"And we don't even know what that thing is." Hanley pointed to Catherine, who hissed back at him. Egan studied the situation and considered the horse once more. With a loud snort, he turned to his crew.

"Come on, lads." He barked. "These three ain't worth our time." He leveled a stare at Marshal. "We will meet again, Legion." The bandits melted into the forest. Rinn's heart was still galloping when her father took her forcefully by the hand.

"Drop that sword." He ordered.

"Why?" Rinn asked. She liked the idea of having a weapon to protect herself, Cat had her claws and her father carried a sword. Rinn wondered why she should be left defenseless. "I want to keep it."

"Do as I say, girl, before someone else sees it." Marshal's tone was overly harsh. "We need to bury it." Rinn reluctantly let the sword fall to the ground. Marshal kicked it to the side of the road. He dug a shallow hole with his hands and scooted the sword inside. He summoned Rinn and solemnly commanded. "Say exactly these words: 'An-for-letan'."

"What?" Rinn did not understand the bizarre language. Her father repeated them once again, slowly, insisting she say them. Something inside Rinn did not want to.

"These are your mother's words." He begged, a tear streaking down his stern face. Rinn tried her best to say the words, her father coached her when she misspoke. Once the phrase was correctly said, the sword lost its silver luster and crumbled into dirt. Marshal hastily covered the hole and set several stones upon it, like a miniature tomb. Behind the wagon, Cat sucked on her paw as she watched the events unfold. Marshal barricaded the girls in the back of the wagon and drove it down the broken trail at an unsafe speed. "The inn should be close." He called out. "We can reach it in less than an hour."

The girls sat in stunned silence as the wagon sped through the forest. Rinn flexed her fingers, remembering the feel of the short sword in her hand. In her head, she heard herself repeating those strange words over and over again.

Chapter 4

R inn flopped down in the hay on the barn floor. She had finished brushing down Bayard, and the tension from the earlier attack still hung heavily over her. Catherine lazily batted a mouse back and forth, it squeaked in protest. She asked Rinn. "Why did your Dad make you bury that sword?"

"I don't know." Rinn vividly remembered the feel of the weapon in her hand and the sound it made as it sliced through her opponent's blade. She thought back to her peaceful life in the Imperium. Her father worked as a guard at the local market, patrolling in his black uniform. Every day he strapped on a sword, and Rinn was never allowed to handle it. When his work shift was over, he locked it away in a wooden trunk. Most of the boys in the city began training with swords at the age of seven. It was common to see girls sparring with wooden swords alongside the boys. Rinn was never allowed to participate—she realized now her father had never told her why.

Marshal found the two girls sitting silently in the barn and beckoned for them to come inside for lunch. They shuffled to the inn, a large wooden and daub building with a tarnished sign hanging outside with a picture of a brass flagon. Rinn entered and had to let her eyes adjust to the darkness of the taproom. Cat rushed past her, drawn by the smell of food. Marshal led them to a long trestle table near the hearth. Dying embers from the fire illuminated one end of the room. A pleasant auburn-haired woman carrying several wooden bowls met them at the table.

"So sorry for the mess." She wiped off the table and set food and a basket of trenchers down. "We don't get many lunch guests." She hastily braided her mane of auburn hair and wiped her apron clean. She introduced herself as Muireen, her round, pretty face bursting with pink freckles as she smiled. The girls sat down at the table, and Catherine immediately stuck both paws into the bowl of stew.

"Cat, manners." Marshal chastised. He showed her how to scoop up the stew using a bread trencher and eat it without dirtying her paws.

"Quite an energetic girl." The barmaid laughed, hesitating slightly before saying the word girl.

"She is unique." Marshal nodded. "I think this might be the first time she's eaten at a tavern."

"Is that so?" Muireen leaned over the table, nearly spilling out of her corset as she filled Marshal's mug. "Would she care to hear some music? Our bard is loitering in the kitchen, disturbing the cooks." Rinn chewed her food slowly, stomach knotting up as she watched the woman flirt with her father.

"If it wouldn't be too much trouble." Marshal pleasantly replied. With a wink and a grin, Muireen strutted off to the kitchen. The trio ate in silence. Rinn wanted to ask her father about the sword she had to bury and the strange words he made her say, but this did not seem the right time or place. Marshal's ale tankard was refilled twice before the bard finally emerged from the kitchen. He walked slowly, purposefully, like the master of a grand parade no one could see. He wore an embroidered purple tunic draped over his slender frame. His impossibly thin legs were wrapped in boots laced all the way up his thighs. His long nose and pointed ears suggested some sort of mixed elven heritage. In his arms he cradled a strange wooden box with push buttons and levers. He took his place on a stool near the hearth. With one hand he rotated a crank on the instrument while the fingers of his other hand flitted across highly decorated buttons. Haunting music filled the room.

"Is that a magic box?" Rinn asked her father.

"No. It's an elfish instrument, called a symphonia." Marshal hushed the girls. "Listen, he's going to sing." In a high-pitched voice rich with vibrato, the bard spun tales of valorous knights from glorious days long past. He sang the ballad of Mantell and Owen, fearless heroes who battled the dragons that once terrorized the lands. Rinn was so enthralled by the story of the brave knights that she stopped eating altogether. In the end, the fearsome beasts were subdued and pushed back into the Pernic Sea. The bard ended his performance with a lilting instrumental piece played on his mysterious box.

"Here." Marshal gave each girl a small Imperial coin. "Put that in the bard's hat." The girls shyly walked up to the musician, who weaved melodies on his symphonia. Rinn and Cat dropped their coins into his hat, and the bard nodded politely. As they walked away his eyes followed the feline girl intently. On their way back to the table, Catherine pulled on Rinn's sleeve and whispered.

"Look over there." She discretely pointed her paw to a gigantic man sitting in a dark corner. "That's the rock we saw by the river." To Rinn's surprise, on the table in front of him rested a round stone with a crude purple eye painted on it. The two girls hurried past and sat down nervously.

"Daddy, I think we need to go." Rinn tugged on her father's tunic. Marshal drained his tankard as the bard played his final notes.

"I agree." He stood and stretched. "It's gotten later than I was hoping. Let's get back to the wagon and head out." He settled his tab with Muireen, whose eyes lit up at the sight of his Imperial silver.

"The trade caravans always prefer Imperial coins." Muireen dropped the coins into a metal strongbox. "I can buy quality wares with these. If you need anything else, please let me know." She leaned across the bar with a longing expression. Rinn folded her arms in disgust.

"I do need a few things for the homestead." Marshal replied playfully. As her father bantered with the barmaid, Rinn nervously kept an eye on the giant man with the strange rock. She was certain he was watching her. Eventually, Marshal completed his transaction and escorted the girls to the stable. Rinn was glad to be out of the taproom, away from the creepy man and his rock. Marshal tipped the stable boy for watching their wagon and hitched Bayard up. Cat still refused to get near the horse. Muireen arrived with a load of dry goods, two firkins of ale, and a pair of chickens in a cage. Cat was excited to see the chickens, but Marshal explained they were not for eating. Cat grumbled, until she learned that these chickens would lay eggs.

After the wagon was loaded, Muireen held onto Marshal's arm. "Looking forward to doing business with you again." Rinn bit her bottom lip as she pulled her father away from the overly-affectionate woman. The trio boarded the wagon and headed out. Bayard plodded down the broken trail heading north. Lumbering along the side of the path was the huge man with the strange stone. Marshal pulled the wagon up alongside him.

"Are you headed north?" Marshal asked casually.

"I am." The giant man replied. He stood a head taller than Bayard, who was not a small horse. His beard was wide and untamed, his shirt stained and unkempt, but his head was shaved perfectly smooth. He carried a heavy pack over his left shoulder and his unnatural rock in his right hand. Rinn could swear the purple eye was pointed right at her.

"We're also headed north." Marshal smiled pleasantly to the fellow. "Care for a ride?" He gestured to an empty spot on the bench near him. The big man thought for a moment and then climbed aboard, nearly tipping the wagon over in the process. Rinn barely had enough time to grab the sidebars as the cart heaved, and Cat dug in with her claws and hissed. The giant man settled into the driver's bench, setting his pack at his feet and his round rock beside him. Marshal flicked the reins and the horse plodded onward, straining against the extra weight. They rode in silence until they were some distance from the inn.

Marshal spoke first. "If you are looking for work, I could use a man with your talents."

"My talents?" The big man raised an oversized eyebrow.

Keeping his eyes trained on the road ahead, Marshal confessed. "I was at Brigantum. I've seen what you can do, Primus Molossus."

The large man rubbed his hand idly on his round rock. "You are older than you appear. I did not know you served in the Migalian Wars. I recognized you from your time at the palace, Theodric." Marshal clenched his jaw and gripped the reins, and after several hard breaths he finally spoke.

"I go by 'Marshal' now." He never took his eyes from the road ahead.

"You're a long way from home, Marshal." Molossus peered over his shoulder at the two girls who were feigning disinterest but intently eavesdropping. He leaned close to Marshal and whispered. "You should not have brought her here."

Marshal stole a glance at his daughter. "What do you mean?"

"The Margot." Molossus growled lowly. "You should never have taken her to the inn. That bard recognized her, it won't be long before someone comes looking for her."

"Cat?" Marshal seemed stunned.

"You call her 'Cat'? Of all the stupidest things! You don't even know what she is." Molossus picked up his rock and set it in his lap. "She's a Margot, a rarity stolen from across the eastern seas. Her kind are trained as slaves, warriors, concubines. Kings and Emperors spend fortunes to have their own Margot. Fiercely loyal, incredible fighters, and highly skilled in the bedroom." Molossus trailed off. Rinn and Cat looked at each other in confusion. Molossus broke the prolonged silence. "How did you come by her?"

"She came to us." Marshal admitted.

"By the Forge! The hands of the gods at work." Molossus shifted his rock as he spoke.

"The gods and I are not on the best terms." Marshal refuted. "All I know is we found a little lost girl who was hungry, and we had food. I don't think the gods had any hand in this."

"Be on your guard, Theodric." The big man spoke gravely. "Her value cannot be counted. Her captors will surely come for her."

"My name is Marshal now." He grumbled. The horse plodded slowly towards the ominous forest. In the back of the wagon, two girls whispered quietly amongst themselves. Rinn mouthed the word Margot.

Chapter 5

The wagon came to a halt, jostling Rinn and Cat in back. Seven redheaded bandits blocked the narrow forest road ahead. Rinn recognized some of the ruffians from her journey to the inn, but they had been joined by several burlier men with better armor. As the travelers approached, the bandit gang readied their swords and spears. Rinn and Cat hid behind grain sacks and Bayard gave a nervous nicker.

"These boys gave me some trouble on the way in." Marshal kept tight hold of the reins, his sword in his lap.

"Pshaw." Molo waved a dismissive hand. "Keep driving." The cart lumbered forwards. When the bandits caught sight of the oversized passenger, they began to whisper to each other, and one by one they slunk back into the forest.

"They certainly know you." Marshal whistled his endorsement. "Who are they?"

"Clanmorris boys." Molo explained. "They ran anything that looks like law and order out of this area years ago. No one knows their true numbers, but they turn up everywhere. I suspect they have a hidden base somewhere in the mountains."

"What happened to the wilderness dukes?" Marshal snapped the reins.   "A few dukes are still holed up in their fortresses, but most have died off or were driven out." The girls left their hiding places and moved closer to the front of the wagon.

"Are we safe?" Rinn scanned the area anxiously.

"Perfectly." Marshal grinned. "Thanks to our new friend."

"I didn't do anything." The giant man huffed. A small paw behind him crept toward the round rock sitting on the driver's bench. Molo turned to the feline girl who froze mid-reach, he lowered his massive brow and slowly shook his head. "Clive is not a toy, little cat."

The heavily loaded wagon travelled slowly, and the travelers did not arrive at the hilltop ruins until almost evening. Marshal and Molossus busied themselves reassembling the military tent while Rinn and Cat slept in the bed of the wagon. Bayard drank deeply from a makeshift horse trough. Marshal attempted to persuade Molo to stay as they worked. "I was serious about hiring you. I can pay you a fair wage."

"I don't have much need for Imperial coin out here." The big man confessed, setting another tent pole. "But, if you can still hunt, I'd be willing to work for a steady supply of freshly caught game."

"That sounds fair." Marshal agreed. "But, be warned: you may have to fight Cat for it." An enormous grin cracked across Molo's face, and his entire body shook with laughter until his bald head turned red. The ruckus woke the sleeping girls. Marshal escorted the drowsy pair inside the tent and asked the giant man to join them. He introduced his friend. "Girls, this is Uncle Molo." Molossus raised a curious eyebrow. "He will be helping us while we rebuild the house." Rinn regarded the giant man with apprehension, but her father reassured her. "Molo's an old colleague. We served together in the Legion years ago."

Cat blurted out. "Are you a giant?"

"Don't be rude." Rinn shushed.

"Actually, she's right." Molossus confessed. "I am quarter giant. They are mostly unknown in this part of the world."

"You smell like giant." Cat scrunched up her nose, and Molo eyed her suspiciously. The group unloaded the contents of the wagon into the tent before darkness fell. Molo showed Cat how to tie down the rain flaps, and Cat turned out to be surprisingly adept at tying and untying knots. Bedrolls were laid out inside the tent for the girls. Marshal offered one to Molo, but he declined, insisting that his home was not far away. With a promise to return in the morning, he took his leave.

After he was gone, Rinn mustered the courage to ask her father about the events that had been troubling her. "Daddy. What were those strange words you made me say?"

Marshal sat on the floor near his daughter. "It's an ancient language not entirely unlike our own."

"But what did it mean?" Rinn insisted, squeezing her hands.

"I think it means, 'I give this back'." Marshal squinted as he thought.

"You think?" Rinn puzzled. "How can you speak a language if you don't know what it means?"

"Your mother only taught me a few phrases." Marshal sighed long and low, full of melancholy. "It's all I know."

"My mom spoke a different language?" Rinn compared her own pale skin color with her father's amber complexion. "Was she a foreigner?"

"Not at all." Marshal laughed out loud at the question. "Do you remember your history from school?"

"Yes." Rinn sat up in her bedroll. "The nine gods led the tribes of people to Edera, the undiscovered continent." She recited her lessons perfectly. "The goddess Aedis guided the first Emperor Sevrius to a holy site where he built the temple which became the heart of the new empire." She beamed proudly.

"You were taught well." Marshal acknowledged. "But you only heard half the story. Did you know that people were already living here when the nine tribes arrived?"

"Really?" Rinn's eyes popped open.

"Yes." Marshal continued. "The Sevrians drove them from their homes. Those native people spoke an ancient tongue, the one you used today."

"What happened to them?" Rinn wondered aloud.

"Most of them died off or were mixed into the nine tribes." Marshal admitted wistfully. "But some are still around, hiding in plain sight." He tucked her into her bedroll. "The hour is late, time for bed. We have a long workday tomorrow." He kissed her forehead and closed the tent flap. Rinn laid in her bedroll, staring into the darkness for quite some time. Cat snored softly nearby snuggled under warm blankets. Rinn tried to imagine her mother as a primitive huntress stalking through the wilds in animal furs. Somehow, she knew this could not be further from the truth.

::

Construction of the new roof took twelve days, hastened by giant-labor. The first task was repairing the dilapidated walls. Rinn and Cat mixed batches of mortar, while Molossus and Marshal carefully fit worked stones into gaps in the decaying walls. Next, Molo harvested wood for the roof, downing small trees in single swings of his massive axe. Marshal hewed off the larger limbs, and Rinn and Cat snipped off small side branches. Molo hoisted the logs and Marshal guided them into place. Once the roof was set, Marshal sprinkled it with sealing salts, creating a water-tight barrier. The ruins finally began to resemble a livable house, and Rinn started to unconsciously refer to it as her home. The girls selected a room off the kitchen for their new bedroom and covered the floor with hay. Marshal and Molo crafted simple wooden furniture for the house—tables, stools, and three beds. The tent was left standing until doors and windows could be fashioned.

Now that she was eating regularly, Cat's frame had filled out. Her tawny fur glistened like amber in the noonday sun and her pink nose was wet and shiny. During a midday break, Cat asked Rinn a question. "What's a Margot?" Rinn recalled the conversation her father and Molo had on the trip back from the inn. She remembered the giant using the word, but she was not entirely sure what it meant.

"Why don't we ask Uncle Molo?" She suggested.

"Nope." Cat looked around suspiciously as she whispered. "I don't like that creepy rock he carries. It watches me."

"It's just a rock." Rinn shrugged indifferently. She saw Molo and her father eating lunch on a flat boulder, the strange stone was nestled in the grass nearby. Rinn realized that its purple eye was pointed directly at her.

"It's not normal." Cat shuddered. "Did you know he talks to it? He calls it Clive." Rinn did not really have a response to that. The two finished their lunch and played in the yard behind the house, Rinn weaved headbands while Cat stomped on wildflowers. Rinn missed many things about her Imperial home in Viburna, but the peaceful, quiet country life had its own appeal. For the first time, she felt like she could get used to living here.

::

The bandits came the next day, eight strong, armed with swords and spears. Molossus readied his axe and Marshal his blade.

"Girls, stay inside and don't come out." Marshal ordered.

"This flimsy door wouldn't stop anyone." Molo opened and closed the hastily fashioned door.

"True." Marshal conceded, adjusting his swordbelt. "We'll just have to make sure they won't get close enough to try."

The brigand leader was a short, stocky man with red hair. Rinn recognized him from the attack on the way to the inn, he was the one they called Egan. He was accompanied by Hanley, still nursing an injured hand and scratches on his face.

Egan approached Marshal antagonizing him with his sword. "You." He barked. "You're trespassing on Clanmorris lands. Leave now or die." For the benefit of the other bandits he added. "But your belongings can stay here—we'll look after them for you." His fellow ruffians laughed.

Marshal leaned his head to Molo and sighed. "I'll take the leader, you can have the rest."

"Sounds fair." Molo twirled his oversized axe.

Their boldness stunned Egan, but only for a moment. He urged his men into action, calling out in a loud voice, "Farrah, farrah!" Egan engaged Marshal in complex swordplay, forcing him back with a flurry of attacks. Marshal assumed a defensive stance, surprised by the ruffian's skill with a blade. He parried carefully, waiting for an opening. The remaining bandits surrounded Molo, harassing him with spears and ropes, like cattlemen wrangling a wild bull. The giant swatted at their spears with his axe and dodged to avoid their ropes. Hanley and Grale slipped away from the action and maneuvered around the house. Marshal tried to disengage from the bandit leader, but Egan blocked his way.

"We're not finished here." He pressed forward with precision. Marshal parried and circled, desperate to get to the house. Hanley and Grale kicked in the flimsy door and found two surprised girls crouched near a window. Cat arched her back and hissed.

"Grimalkin!" Hanley threw up his hands when he saw the feline girl. He lingered in the doorway, unsure of what to do. "It's that damned monster."

Cat rose up to her full height and bared her claws, the fur on her back bristled and her ears flattened out. "I am not a monster. I am a girl." A barrage of claws rained down on the unfortunate bandits, raking them both across their arms and face. They tried to fight off the angry Margot, but the bandits ended up running from the house screaming.

"She's a little girl with claws." Rinn yelled out the door after them.

Outside, Marshal still danced with the bandit leader as Molo wrestled with the remaining raiders. Several lay at his feet, victims of the flat of his broad axe or a blow to the head from Clive. Inside the house, Rinn spied her father's weapons trunk in the corner. A part of her wanted to reach in and grab a sword to beat back the thugs who were invading her home; however, she knew her father would be angry with her. So, she waited, trusting that he and Molo could defeat these ruffians. Eventually, the noise of the fighting outside died down. Rinn peered out the broken doorway and saw her father and Molo standing over the bodies of three unconscious men.

"Where did the bandits go?" Rinn cautiously stepped into the open, Cat following closely behind.

"They got what they wanted and left." Molo flipped over one of the unconscious raiders with his foot.

"They took Bayard and most of our supplies." Marshal cursed as he sheathed his sword.

"This was a well-run siege." Molo commented picking Clive up from the ground.

"Did they take my chickens?" Cat asked anxiously, her tail twitching.

"Yes, little cat, the chickens are gone." Molo answered solemnly.

Dismay on Cat's face contorted into rage. Her fur stood on end and she flexed her claws, crying out in a loud voice. "My chickens! I'll kill them—every single one of them."

Chapter 6

Rinn peeked out her bedroom window, which had no glass or frame, just a thin blanket over the opening. Outside, three unconscious bandits had been bound together and secured to a post. Molo splashed a bucket of water over them, and the three men groggily came to their senses, struggling against their bonds. Molo sat in plain view on a large rock, Clive resting in the grass at his feet, its purple eye fixed on the bandits.

"Struggle all you want." Molo spoke nonchalantly as he rummaged through a canvas sack. "Won't do you any good. Our little cat has a way with knots." He pulled out several apples, swallowing each one whole without chewing. The bandits nervously eyed each other. "Marshal will be here soon to decide your fate. Pray that he is more merciful that I am— I would have tossed you in a grave long ago." The giant downed several more whole apples and then left.

Marshal appeared soon after, dressed in his military uniform. His hair was combed, and his thin beard trimmed, the medals on this uniform clinked as he paced back and forth in full view of the bandits. "Prisoners. I accuse you of the crimes of raiding, violence against civilians including children, and horse-theft, which alone is grounds for execution. However, I am willing to show mercy in exchange for information. Your clansmen cleverly engaged us in battle while others robbed our stores. That was smart. But they left you behind, which was not. Now, answer my questions, or I shall have my companion crush your heads."

The bandits poured out everything they knew. They depicted Clanmorris as a vast, extended family scattered across the Rustic Lands. The clan members kept the ancient gods, honoring their feast days and traditions. All clansmen swore fealty to a single ruler, called Aosta. The three bandits did not know much about this shadowy figure. Marshal pushed them for more information about the clan's numbers and military capabilities, but the men knew very little.

Rinn, who had been watching the scene unfold, began to wonder if these three were actually clan members. On closer inspection, she saw red paint in their hair. These men looked nothing like Egan or Hanley, and the equipment and clothing they wore were of the lowest quality. Marshal learned what he could and then cut their bonds. Before he released them, he impressed upon them that his mercy was at its end—further incursions on his property would cost them their lives. The bandits scampered down the hillside and faded into the forest.

After they left, Rinn confronted her father. "Why did you let them go?"

"They were unimportant." Marshal walked around the property assessing the damage.

"I know they weren't real clansmen, but they were criminals. They should have been punished." Rinn crossed her arms and frowned, Cat strolled beside her, imitating her.

"Those three were victims, just like us." Marshal contended. "They didn't have the brains to plan an operation like this. They only did what they were told. The real criminals are their leaders. And someday, our paths will cross again."

The remainder of the afternoon was spent clearing debris and taking stock of what was stolen. Rinn and Cat picked up pieces of the smashed kitchen door, while Marshal and Molossus sorted through the remaining foodstuffs. The giant man sighed. "They did not leave you with much. What will you eat?"

"We'll have to make another trip to the inn." Marshal confessed somberly.

"That will be difficult without a horse." Molo pointed out. Marshal nodded grimly. Molo plucked Clive from the ground and set him in the crook of his arm. "I have some food stored up that I could bring over. If you regularly catch enough meat, it could last us the winter."

Marshal touched the big man's arm. "Thank you, my friend."

"We'd best be quick about it." Molo urged. "The winters here are unpredictable. Early snows are not uncommon."

The mention of snow piqued Rinn's attention. "It almost never snows in Viburna."

"You're lucky." Cat shivered. "Snow is horrible." Her fur shook as she wrapped her arms around herself.

"I wouldn't mind seeing snow." Rinn tried to imagine the countryside blanketed in white. "I bet the hills would be beautiful covered in snow."

"Snow may be pretty." Molo admonished. "But the bitter cold that comes with it can kill you, freezing you to the bone. Winter is made to be endured, not enjoyed."

"Don't be so harsh." Marshal rebuked. "Rinn will learn soon enough."

Marshal and the girls spent the next few days repairing the property, while Molossus hauled supplies from his home. Apparently, he lived across the river in a hidden cave, but he refused to allow anyone to accompany him to his refuge. After dinner, the men drank what was left of the ale and started swapping stories about their soldiering days. Rinn mustered the courage to ask Molo a question. "What is that stone you carry?"

Molo looked down at the rock resting beside him. "You mean Clive?"

"See!" Cat jumped. "I told you he calls it 'Clive'." Marshal reclined and waited with interest to hear the explanation. Molo rubbed his hand over the smooth rock, careful not to touch the purple eye.

"I've been out in these Rustic Lands for some time now. I found Clive near the river. He made the perfect tool, round for crushing and hard for hammering, so I carried him everywhere. He was so useful he just became part of me, like a soldier's sword or a blacksmith's hammer. Somewhere along the way I must have painted that eye on him. Now, I just can't imagine not having him with me." While he spoke, Cat crept up quietly and tried to touch the rock. Molo glared at her. "I wish you would stop, little cat."

"Where's the harm?" Marshal teased.

"Would you let her handle your sword?" Molo protested with a scowl.

"Probably not." Marshal admitted, hand on the hilt of his sword.

"About that." Molo stood up and stretched, trying to change the subject. With his arms extended, he could easily reach the ceiling. "This place needs better defenses."

"I was thinking about a wooden palisade." Marshal offered.

"That'd be a good start." Molo nodded in agreement. "But we're going to need help."

"Where can we find workers out here?" Marshal raised an inquiring eyebrow.

"There're more people living in the wilderness than you'd believe." Molo rinsed his mug and set it on the table. "Most people live in seclusion. But there are a few farmhouses not far down the river. We should pay them a visit." Marshal agreed to see them tomorrow. Molo waved his good-byes and headed out into the darkness. Marshal tidied the room and tucked the girls in for the night.

::

Molo led Marshal, Rinn, and Cat down the rocky riverbanks, flanked by sparsely wooded hills. Molo carried Clive like a compass, turning him left and right as they walked. Rinn noticed small streams draining into the meandering river. It grew wider and faster as they traveled. After an hour of walking and one rest stop for the girls, Marshal spotted a ramshackle house not far from the water's edge. Marshal chose Rinn to accompany him, leaving Molo and Cat to wait at the riverbank. Rinn felt pity as she approached the house, even though she lived in a half falling-apart stone ruin, this house was worse. Threadbare walls barely supported the sagging roof, which was patched with wads of cloth and clumps of moss. Marshal gently tapped on the thin, poorly-fit door. Rinn worried it would fall right into the house if he knocked much harder. After a few moments of silence, a raspy voice called out from behind the flimsy door. "Go away. We don't want your protection."

Marshal smiled to himself. "We aren't here to rob you. My name is Marsal and this is my daughter Rinn. We want your help." The door cracked open and a wrinkled face with an oversized nose appeared. Rinn had never seen a head so large, except on Molossus. However, this man stood no taller than her shoulders with a cleanly shaven face and unkempt hair. Rinn had seen dwarves in the Imperial cities, but she had never actually talked to one.

"Speak your piece." The little man blurted out.

"As I said, my name is Marshal." He inclined his head politely. "I have recently moved in to the ruins upriver."

"Bags! Are you mad?" The dwarf coughed.

"Maybe." Marshal admitted. "But I have money and I am willing to pay for supplies and labor." He produced a black leather pouch and shook the coins inside. The little man considered the proposition.

"Wait here. I'll get the master." He turned and left Rinn and Marshal standing at the doorway. Rinn peaked inside the house, which looked worse than the exterior. It smelled like a tavern floor with garbage and bits of broken furniture scattered about. Rinn shied away from the noxious odor, but her father stood resolute. After some time, a middle-aged man stumbled to the doorway. His disheveled, graying hair was covered in filth and his unruly beard stuck out in unflattering directions.

"What's this I hear about you living in the hilltop ruins?" The man's speech was slurred, and he leaned heavily on the dwarf as if he was a cane. The small man supported him without expression. Looking down Rinn saw the metal band wrapped around the dwarf's right leg, aghast when she realized it was a slave shackle. In the Imperium servants were commonplace, but outright slavery was illegal. The sight of the twisted metal band on the dwarf's ankle turned Rinn's stomach. As her father talked with the drunk, her blood began to boil—she hated this horrible man more than she hated the bandits that attacked her house. She made a private vow to rescue this poor dwarf.

"Agreed." The drunken man slurred.

"Very good, Tomin. I will be back in the morning." Marshal shook the man's unsteady hand. He took Rinn by the shoulder and walked away from the house. On her way back to the riverside, Rinn uncorked her anger.

"Why would you deal with that horrid man." Her voice cracked.

Marshal breathed. "I know. House dwarfs were outlawed years ago. But we need food and Tomin apparently has chickens and cows. So, for now we have to put up with him."

"We can't leave that poor dwarf locked up in there." Rinn balled her hands into fists. "That place was disgusting. Let's go back and get him. You could beat that old drunk easily."

"I could, but slave shackles are enchanted and can't be removed. Only another slaver can release him. If I took that dwarf too far away from his master, he would likely die." Marshal bent down and held both of his daughter's hands in his own. "Don't worry. We'll find a way to help him when the time is right."

Marshal related to Molossus all that happened at the ramshackle house, including the enslaved dwarf. Molossus had to restrain Cat from charging directly in, full of murderous intent. He carried the bellicose ball of fur as they traveled up the river toward home. On the trip, Rinn memorized every landmark, vowing to return someday to free the poor, enslaved dwarf.

Chapter 7

Marshal and Molo left early in the morning to trade with the drunken farmer Tomin. Rinn and Cat were left by themselves, given strict instructions not to leave the house. Rinn tried to busy herself with chores but she could not stop thinking about the poor mistreated dwarf.

"I'm going back." Rinn confided to Cat. "I'm going to rescue him."

"Who?" Cat cocked one ear up and another down.

"The house dwarf." Rinn whispered. "That awful drunk keeps him locked up in that a horrible house."

"I tried to sneak down there last night." Cat confessed. "But when I opened the door, Clive was waiting for me." She frowned with her whiskers and ears hanging low.

"What is it with you and that rock?" Rinn raised her hands in frustration.

"It watches me." Cat buried her head in her paws.

"It's just a rock." Rinn admonished. She was bored and becoming irritated. She rummaged through her room for anything that could occupy her time. Cat walked to the front door and unlatched it. Rinn called out. "We're not supposed to go outside, Cat."

Defiantly, Cat threw the door open. Sitting on the ground outside was the purple-eyed stone, staring directly at them. "See." She pointed to Clive with her paw excitedly. "Look!"

Rinn stared at the rock, wondering why Molossus had left it behind. The watching eye was giving her chills. She jumped up and shut the door. "Okay. That was weird." Cat paced inside the room, sucking her paw.

Rinn spent the rest of the morning trying to take Cat's mind off the watching stone. She offered her every distraction she knew, but Cat had no interest in cooking or sewing or dress up. Instead Cat paced around the house, peeking into containers and sniffing for mice. For their protection, empty window openings had been boarded up, which made the inside of the house dark, even in the middle of the day. Rinn stayed close to the fireplace where there was some light, but Cat was unaffected by the darkness. She explored every corner, discovering nothing.

Cat pried away one of the window boards and slithered outside. Rinn heard the commotion and rushed over to investigate. Bright light from the open window poured into the room. Rinn stood on her tiptoes, trying to see out. Cat's furry head appeared in the window, startling Rinn. "Cat. Don't do that."

"Come see what I found." Cat clung to the window sill.

"Cat!" Rinn cried out, her chest thumping rapidly. "We aren't supposed to be outside. Get back in here before we both get in trouble."

"You need to see this." Cat blinked as she dropped out of site. Rinn stomped over to the door and threw it open, outside Clive stared at her. Rinn gingerly stepped over the rock and dashed down the side of the house, keeping close to the walls, doing her best to stay out of sight. She found Cat at the far end of the house, digging at the foundation stones. "Get back inside right now." Rinn ordered.

"Something's under here." Cat scraped away at the ground furiously. Rinn bent down to investigate, tracing the dirt with her fingers, feeling the outline of something buried just below the surface. Together they gradually unearthed a large rectangular stone, cracked down the middle. With a mighty effort, they shifted the two halves apart. Beyond, a dark passageway led down into the unknown. Cat squirmed into the space and disappeared.

"Wait, Cat." Rinn cried out in a panic.

At first, Rinn heard nothing, then from out of the hole, Cat's small voice echoed. "It's really dark down here." Rinn crouched near the side of the house, sure that her father would come home at any moment. She knotted the folds of her dress as she called into the hole, begging for Cat to return. It seemed like forever, but Cat's head finally resurfaced. "There's a really big room down there, and it's super creepy. You should come see it." She wriggled her way out of the hole, her dress and fur smeared with dirt and spiderwebs. Rinn dragged her back inside, insisting she change out of her filthy clothes. Rinn stripped her down and scrubbed her with soap and water while Cat squirmed. The rest of the morning was spent brushing the tangles out of Cat's fur while the little Margot happily hummed to herself. By the time Marshal and Molossus returned, the two girls were sitting innocently by the fire as if they had an uneventful morning. It took Cat seconds to betray them.

"Come see what I found." She darted outside to the hole behind the house. She started to wiggle into the crevice, only to be deftly fished out by Molossus. Marshal peered down into the emptiness.

"This is curious. Molo, would you mind moving those stones while I fetch a lantern?" Molo set Cat down, placing Clive right next to her. Cat crossed her arms and legs and wrapped her tail around herself in protest. Molo lifted the large stones from the ground, revealing a hidden staircase descending into the darkness. Marshal returned with a lit lantern.

"It's some sort of cellar." Molo tossed the flat rock into the yard.

"That's odd. Why seal it off?" Marshal led the way into the darkness with the lantern. Molo followed behind, ducking as he went. Rinn crept down the first few stairs before her nerve gave out. She waited anxiously with Clive and the pouting Cat. Several times Cat extended a paw to touch the round stone, but she backed off at the last second. Eventually, Marshal and Molo re-emerged from the staircase.

"It's an old cellar." Marshal dusted himself off. "Nothing exciting or dangerous down there."

"I wonder why it was concealed?" Molo bent down to retrieve Clive. Once the rock was removed, the pouting Margot raced off. Marshal raised an eyebrow at her strange behavior, but Molo just shrugged indifferently.

Marshal shined the lantern down the cellar steps. "This could be a safe place for the girls to hide if we get attacked again."

"They can't hide forever." Molo observed as he walked away.

"I know." Marshal said to himself.

::

"Here they come." Rinn pointed to the group ascending the hill. Marshal and Molo had traveled further down river and found a farming family with neatly tilled fields. Marshal hired the two oldest boys to help harvest lumber.

"They look pretty small." Cat remarked.

"Cat, next to Uncle Molo, everyone looks small." Rinn rolled her eyes.

Marshal arrived with the two teenage boys and introduced them. "Rinn, Cat, this is Bos and Lutra, sons of Seoras. They will be helping us out for a few days." Bos was a thickly built teen with short ash brown hair and the wispy beginnings of a beard. He smiled politely. Lutra was thinner and shorter with a long face and straight hair. He stared wide-eyed at Cat. Marshal headed to the work table. "I'll get some axes and show you where to work."

Marshal led the boys to the edge of the forest and taught them how to select tall, straight trees with narrow trunks no wider than two hands. Bos was proficient with his axe and mowed through the growth at the edge of the forest. Lutra wielded his axe with less strength and skill, but he selected his trees more carefully. They both worked hard, unless Cat was nearby, and then Lutra's axe swings became slower and less precise, Marshal had to prod him several times to keep working. Molo dragged the felled trees to the house where the girls clipped off the small side branches. Marshal himself worked at digging trenches for the palisade wall. By noon, a significant pile of lumber had accumulated.

The girls placed lunch on an outdoor work table. The weary laborers welcomed the meal. Bos ate so heartily he impressed even Molo. Lutra ate sparingly, never taking his eyes off Cat, who did not seem to notice. Molo finally set Clive on the table in front of the young teen, distracting him. After the meal Marshal rose from the table and stretched.

"Let's set a few posts and then call it a day." He led the workers to the woodpile. The girls stayed behind to clear the table. The men held the palisade posts as the boys backfilled the trench with clay and dirt. They had set the first five when a high-pitched shriek echoed through the forest. Molo and Marshal looked at each other.

"It can't be." Marshal said gravely.

"Bobs." Molossus gripped a fence post like a club.

"Boys, get back." Marshal commanded. "Girls, into the house. Now!" Rinn watched in awe as four enormous bird-like creatures burst from the tree line. The monstrous birds stood nearly as tall as Molo and walked on long scaly legs with wicked three-toed claws. Their bodies were covered in thick iridescent feathers of green and blue. An oversized orange beak dominated their heads. They strutted forward, dragging their long-feathered tails behind them. The largest bird spread its wings, which seemed too small for flight, and let out a shrill cry. The pack advanced, bobbing their heads up and down as they walked.

Marshal ran to fetch his sword from the worktable. "Boys!" Before he could say more the creatures attacked. Molo swung one of the palisade posts, unexpectedly catching the lead bird off-guard. It skidded across the yard. Marshal charged two other birds, keeping them at bay with skillful swordplay. The fourth bird charged Lutra, who desperately tried to back away. Before the bird could strike, Bos planted his axe into the bird's beak. The creature squawked loudly and swatted Bos away with his claws, flinging him limply across the yard. Lutra scampered to his fallen brother, cradling his bleeding head. The feathered monster raised up for the kill, Molo and Marshal were too far away to stop the strike. At the last moment, a violent ball of fur and claws flew at the bird. Cat wrapped her arms and legs around the monster's neck biting and tearing her way into the thick feathers. The bird danced around trying to dislodge the painful pest.

Rinn watched in disbelief as her hillside turned into a battleground. Marshal impaled one creature with his sword as Molossus grappled another in his oversized arms, prying open its beak to an unnatural angle. Cat desperately hung on to the thrashing bird near the fallen Bos as Lutra watched helplessly. Fear gripped Rinn when she saw the lead bird rise, the one Molo had knocked away. It shook out its feathers and squawked. It stalked toward the defenseless brothers. Rinn had no time to think, she grabbed the closest thing she could find, a long-handled spade her father had been using. With a yell, she rushed the bird, holding her shovel like a lance.

Time slowed for Rinn, and the familiar electric smell sizzled through the air as the black iron tip of the spade crumbled away until it was a shining metallic edge burning with a pale green light. Rinn charged the creature as it reared up to strike, slamming the silvery spade into one side of its torso and out the other. The monster gurgled and fell with a thud. Molo crushed his bird's beak like a walnut, and Marshal impaled it through the chest. The two men moved to finish off the remaining bird, still trying to extricate itself from the tenacious Margot. They moved together and within moments, the bird was down. Cat continued to bite and claw even after the animal was dead.

Molossus viewed the creature Rinn had impaled and laid a solemn hand on Marshal's shoulder. "We need to talk." Marshal looked at his daughter and hung his head low as he nodded. The carnage Rinn had inflicted was unbelievable, a massive hole gouged through the bird's midsection. Rinn sat on the ground stunned, staring at the glowing spade in her hands. She tossed it away in revulsion and started to cry. Marshal lifted her into his arms and carried her back into the house. Molo assessed Bos' head wound, while Lutra gawked at the feline girl still furiously assaulting the dead bird.

::

Rinn was supposed to be asleep, but she lay awake on her bedroll. In the next room she could hear her father and Uncle Molo arguing.

"Are you out of your mind?" The giant strained to speak in hushed tones, but emotion overwhelmed him. "You took the Sigillum out of the Empire."

"That bloodline died out years ago." Marshal responded flatly.

"I know what I saw." Molo countered. A silence fell between the two men. "By the gods, you're actually her father. You wouldn't have gone to these lengths if you weren't."

"Yes." Marshal's words were filled with anguish. "She's my daughter."

"Once the Curia finds out, they will send armies for her." Molo took a long drink and paused. "Well, I guess this explains the Margot."

"Cat?" Marshal's voice seemed piqued with interest.

"Their race has always had a special bond with the Sigilla. It's one of the reasons kings always wanted to possess one for themselves—to legitimize their reign." Molo paced around the room. "Who else knows?"

"Just one other, a priest." Marshal answered.

"A priest? You should know better than to trust the Church." Molo hmphed, slamming down his mug.

"This one is different." Marshal made his final reply and the two men left. Rinn lay in her bed awake, thinking about everything she overheard.

Next to her, a small feline voice asked. "What's a Sigilla?"

"I don't know, Cat." Rinn felt lost in an ocean of questions. Her life in the Empire had been simple, almost routine. Out here in the wilderness, nothing made any sense.

Chapter 8

The next morning, Rinn found her father and Molo at the site of the battle. They were plucking feathers from the bird carcasses with pliers and collecting them in large wicker baskets. Rinn ambled up and gave her best what're-you-doing expression, though the horrific smell made her want to leave. Her father held up an iridescent blue plume the length of his forearm. "Bob feathers are as strong as tempered steel."

"What are these things?" Rinn pinched her nose in disgust.

"A breed of feathered dragon." Molo answered. "I don't know what their real name is, but in the Legion, we called 'em Bobs, on account of how they walk." He imitated a bobbing motion with his head.

Marshal flipped over another carcass. "The Legion was tasked with clearing out Bob nests. An entire war was fought over them. Bobs are dangerous pests." He pried more feathers away and laid them in the basket. "They were supposedly hunted to extinction." Rinn delicately picked out a feather, it was nearly weightless, yet completely unbendable.

"This is a type of dragon?" Rinn turned the feather over in her hand examining it. It glistened green and blue like lizard scales or dragonfly wings.

"It was." Molo dropped several more feathers into the basket. "You know, I have never heard of anyone killing a dragon with a shovel before." Molo laughed as Rinn shot him a petulant glare.

Cat strolled in at exactly that moment. "Rinn the dragon-slayer." She sang repeatedly as she danced around. Rinn scowled and stomped off, Cat trailing after her.

::

Bos and Lutra stayed home to recover from the attack. Rinn was not sure they if they would ever come back. But after several days, they walked up the hill, axes in hand. Rinn ran out to greet them.

"Good morning." Rinn shook, giddy with excitement.

"Hiya, Rinn." Bos wore a bandage on his head, but he seemed otherwise in good health.

"Hi." Lutra waved. He looked around as if he had lost something. "Is Cat here?"

"She's out with Uncle Molo." Rinn replied. "They are searching for the monster nests. Apparently, Cat has an excellent nose for finding things." Lutra hung his head and sighed. Rinn tried to think of something to placate him. "She should be back soon."

"Come on, Bos. Let's go cut some trees." Lutra urged morosely.

Cat and Molo returned around midday. They found the Bobs' nest, it had been charred by fire. Molo suspected the dragons were driven from their home and herded in the direction of the hilltop. Marshal cursed the redheaded clansmen, and promised that a day of reckoning would come. Bos ate his lunch with Marshal and Molo, probing them about life in the Legion. Lutra ate in silence, trying his best to watch Cat without being too obvious. Rinn teased Cat about Lutra, but the feline girl was oblivious to the attention of teenage boys.

::

The long workday ended, and the boys left for home. Rinn cleaned up the dinner dishes as Marshal and Molo finished their mugs. Rinn summoned the courage to ask her father about the strange things that had been happening.

"What is a Sigilla?" She blurted out.

Molossus stood, picked up Clive and Cat, and headed for the door. "We'll be outside." The giant carried the squirming Margot away. Marshal crossed the room and set his mug in the wash basin.

"Sit down, Rinn." Once again, his eyes were filled with that familiar, distant sadness. "This was supposed to wait until your birthday."

"It's less than a month away." Rinn protested.

"True." Marshal shifted uneasily in his chair. "Consider this an early present." He spoke slowly and solemnly. "Sigilla are the protectors of the Empire, granted special powers by the gods. Many of the Sevrian Emperors were aided by the skills of the Sigilla."

"I've never heard of them." Rinn confessed.

"Very few have." Marshal continued. "Sigilla were vital instruments when the Empire was young and fragile. As the centuries passed, the Empire came to rely more on the might of its Legions. The Sigilla became unneeded and unwanted. They were pushed out and kept hidden. The last Sigillum died and the bloodline was thought to be lost."

"Was mother a Sigilla?" Rinn hesitated as she said the word, her clear blue eyes locked on her father.

"Yes." He conceded, unable to meet her gaze any longer. "Your mother was a Sigillum."

Rinn chewed her lip as she assembled the story. "So, mother had me before she died and the Sigilla bloodline was passed on, but no one knew it."

"No." Marshal choked on the words. "Your mother died first."

A cold chill shook Rinn. "She died giving birth to me?" Rinn gulped back bile.

"No, your mother died years before you were born." Tears streamed down Marshal's face, cracked with emotion.

"That doesn't make any sense. How is that even possible?" Rinn's voice was barely a whisper. Her father would not speak about it any longer.

::

A wall of awkward silence rose between Rinn and her father over the next few days. Work on the palisade wall continued as planned, but Rinn was not asked to help. She spent most of her time wandering around the property alone. She searched for the shovel she had used to slay the Bob, but it was not to be found, most likely buried with the bird corpses. Rinn tried everything to distract herself from confused thoughts about her mother, she even explored the dark cellar using an oil lamp. She wasted most of an afternoon down there sifting through dusty crates of ancient supplies: empty glass bottles, moldy sacks of grain, and dry clay urns. Cat eventually found her and dragged her outside.

"Here she is." Cat reported to Molossus.

The giant set Clive on a nearby boulder and addressed the girls. "Starting today, your father has charged me with teaching you the art of combat." The big man paced with his hands behind his back, like an army general. "Even with these protective walls around us, there is still significant danger. At any time, you could come face to face with Clanmorris raiders or worse. You need to learn how to defend yourself. Rinn, I am going to be working with you today. Cat, you will spar with Marshal." Cat bounced up and down happily on her haunches. Rinn frowned internally, wondering if she was somehow being punished. Molo seemed to read her thoughts. "Your father is a speed fighter and a good match for Cat. You are a power fighter. I will teach you to hone that power and direct it."

As a scrawny thirteen-year-old, Rinn did not exactly feel powerful. Even though she did not understand his reasoning, she followed him to the yard where her father was waiting with a wooden sword. He wore a lightweight leather cuirass.

Two padded cloth vests were waiting for the girls. Rinn struggled to get into hers, but Cat had even more difficulty. Rinn had to help her wiggle into the tight-fitting vest. Rinn noticed that Cat had lost her childish frame and had hints of feminine curves. Once the girls were appropriately dressed, Molo motioned Cat forward.

"Okay, little cat. Go ahead and attack. Don't worry, you won't hurt him."

A wide smile broke across Cat's face. She hunched over, tail pumping furiously, the blacks of her eyes widened, and her whiskers twitched. Without warning she sprang forward, pouncing on Marshal at full speed. He easily intercepted her with the flat of his blade and flung her sideways. She landed on four feet and circled around him, looking for an opening. She launched again, hoping to catch him on his vulnerable side, but Marshal pivoted and tossed Cat away once more. She prowled low to the ground, wiggling her tail and behind. She hurtled forward, missing Marshal completely, he tried to block her, but she had already flown past him. She rebounded off a nearby tree trunk and caught Marshal squarely on his torso sending him to the ground. She sat proudly on his chest and licked his face repeatedly.

"That was fun." She kneaded his chest with her paws. Marshal wiped his face and rolled out from under her.

"You're getting slow, old man." Molo chastised, helping up his friend. He escorted Rinn to a separate part of the yard. "We will practice with wooden weapons. From what I remember, Sigillum magic only works on metal." Molo selected a wooden sword from a satchel he was carrying and handed it to Rinn. She swished the sword around in the air awkwardly. Molo selected the same weapon for himself, it looked like a dagger in his oversized hands.

"Okay, go ahead and swing at me." Molo motioned with his offhand, and Rinn advanced hesitantly, batting her sword at Molo's weapon, the impact knocked the sword from her own hand. Embarrassed, she bent down to pick it up. "Don't hold it so tightly." Molo instructed. Rinn tried clumsily to strike several more times before Molo finally took the sword away from her. "I don't think this is working." He handed her a wooden spear. "Try this, instead."

Rinn gripped the spear tightly. She remembered the feel of the shovel in her hands as she charged the feathered dragon. She stepped forward and jabbed at Molo. He actually stepped back and deflected her blow with his sword. The big man burst into laughter. "That's much more like it." The two practiced sparring with wooden weapons until it was almost night. Exhausted, Rinn and Cat ate a brief supper and then collapsed onto their beds.

::

Marshal took Cat into the forests to hunt. She was an excellent tracker, but she had the bad habit of immediately eating everything she caught. Marshal was trying to teach her restraint, so they could store food up for the winter. Rinn accompanied Molo to the riverside, where he taught her the patient art of fishing. Rinn found it boring and frustrating; somehow, Molo had a pile of plump fish and Rinn had only caught a few fingerlings. Sensing her frustration, Molo relieved her of her pole and gave her a fishing spear with a small metal barb on its end. He watched intently as Rinn took hold of it. No magic activated, the barb was just a barb. Rinn straddled two rocks and stabbed fish as they swam by, usually missing. Aiming at underwater targets was difficult at first, but once she got the feel for it, Rinn showed some skill, easily outpacing Molo and his less efficient fishing pole.

Molo and Rinn met up with Marshal and Cat as they returned from their hunt. "You two certainly did well." Molo eyed the line of freshly caught game slung over Marshal's shoulder: six almost-rabbits and ten odd-colored forest birds.

"It's easy when your hunting partner can smell game miles away." Marshal patted Cat on the head who grinned with closed eyes. Marshal inspected the baskets of freshly caught fish, Cat drooled over their contents. "You did well yourself, that's quite a catch."

Molo laughed. "Your daughter is half crane. You should see her in action with that spear. She's a natural fisher."

Marshal regarded Rinn with a newfound respect. "Maybe I should take her hunting with me next time."

Molo wrapped a big arm around the girl. "Forget it. She stays with me." The two men argued playfully the entire way home.

Chapter 9

R inn accompanied her father to Tomin's farm. A steady trade had grown between her hilltop and the drunk. Molo fashioned a raft they could pull up and down the river to compensate for their lack of horse. Marshal loaded it with fresh timber and smoked fish to exchange for milk and eggs. Rinn rode on the raft as it glided downstream, maneuvering it around rocks and tangles of river weeds with a long pole. Marshal jogged along the riverbank guiding the raft with a rope. When they arrived, Marshal tied the raft to a convenient tree on the riverbank. They approached the ramshackle house, and Marshal carefully knocked on the door. "It's Marshal and Rinn. We're here to trade."

The house did look less dismal than the last time Rinn visited. The worst parts of the roof had been patched with fresh timber and the front door seemed new. The house dwarf appeared and set two baskets of eggs and an urn of milk on the porch. Marshal made an offer of smoked fish and a fresh supply of lumber. The dwarf agreed and tromped off to collect the wood, Rinn followed him to the riverbank.

"I'm Rinn." She tried to be cheerful. "What's your name?" The dwarf lifted a load of timber from the raft, completely ignoring her. Rinn followed him anyway. She whispered to him. "I can help you."

The dwarf trudged on. "If you want to help, carry some wood." Rinn sheepishly went back and picked up a few small boards and hurried after him.

"I can get you out of here." Rinn whispered. The dwarf deposited his wood along the side of the house and returned for more. Rinn dropped her few boards and pursued him. "I'm serious. I can do it."

The dwarf abruptly faced the girl, possibly trying to intimidate her, but he was a head shorter than Rinn and standing downhill. "You think you can buy me like a new toy, girl?" He huffed. "I don't want to be your plaything. I'm fine right where I am. Now, go away." The dwarf spit and stomped off.

Rinn's pride was hurt, but she was undaunted. She called after him. "I can take that thing off your leg." The dwarf stopped midstride. "At least, I think I can." The dwarf shook his head and headed back for a second load of wood. Rinn wanted to follow, but her father called her away.

::

The palisade wall was completed, and construction began on a new building, a house for Molo. Stones were laid for the foundation with timber walls above. The late summer heat gave way to autumn breezes and patches of yellow, red, and orange began to appear in the forest. Most days, Bos and Lutra remained at home to help their family bring in the fall harvest. Rinn missed their company. She was moping around the house one cool evening, when her father made an exciting announcement.

"Tomorrow, in honor of Rinn's birthday, we're going to a harvest fair." He raised his mug with a smile. Rinn clapped happily.

Cat leaned in close and whispered to Rinn. "What's a harvest fair?"

Rinn bubbled with excitement. "A huge gathering a people to celebrate the end of the harvest season. There will be merchants, food, jugglers, acrobats, and musicians. It will end with a big parade and dedications to Imber, the goddess of rain."

"Not this time." Corrected Marshal. "We're not in Sevria anymore—the Imperial gods aren't worshipped out here. Molossus says this fair is dedicated to Samria, one of the rustic gods."

"Rustic gods?" Rinn cocked an eyebrow.

Molo explained. "The Imperial gods don't answer the prayers of the wilderness people, so they pray to their own gods. Some people claim they were the original gods of this land before the founding of the Empire. Samria is the goddess of harvests along with her brother Boldyn, the god of fire."

"We heard about the fair from Seoras, Bos and Lutra's father." Marshal sat down and began sharpening his sword with a stone. "This fair coincided nicely with your birthday, so I thought it might be a fun diversion. It's about a three-hour journey away, so we'll have to leave early in the morning."

"I've never been to a fair." Cat added, ears perky.

"You're going to love it." Rinn replied with dreamy eyes.

::

Rinn and Cat rode in the bed of the wagon as Molossus pulled them along the dirt road like a horse. The effort did not seem to bother the giant man, but he was overly sensitive to Marshal's playful jokes. Several times Marshal offered to help pull the cart, but Molo shrugged him off. The girls amused themselves with games and chatted about everything they would see at the fair. As their destination drew closer, they encountered groups of travelers headed in the same direction. A few exchanged greetings, but most were put off by the sight of a large man being used as a draft animal.

The dusty road passed through a valley of orchards, and the strong aroma of apples filled the air. The orchards gave way to a lowland cradled between two river forks. The open field blossomed with hundreds of colorful tents and temporary buildings. Streams of visitors trickled into the fairground, crowding its improvised streets with humans, dwarves, and members of the more exotic races. Merchants peddled goods of every kind: produce, baked goods, carved wood, forged iron, glittering jewelry, colorful textiles, candles, and magical trinkets. Entertainers performed on small wooden stages erected throughout the fairground. Children ran everywhere, chasing each other with wooden swords.

Molo stopped to let his passengers take in the view. After a few moments, Marshal playfully swatted him with a short leather riding crop. Molo shot him a venomous glare and trudged forward with the wagon. He deposited the cart alongside many others, lined up beneath shady trees. Marshal retrieved a bag from the back of the cart and produced a crimson robe with a full hood.

"Here, Cat." He said, handing the robe to her. "Put this on." Cat took the robe with a frown. "It's for your safety, in case there are any slavers out here." Rinn helped fasten the robe around Cat's neck and pulled the hood over her ears and face. Marshal nodded approvingly. "I borrowed it from Seoras. Apparently, Bos and Lutra have a little brother who's about your size." Cat sniffed the robe thoroughly. It covered her fairly well, except for her tail which liked to peek out every so often.

Marshal escorted the girls through the crowds to the merchant booths, while Molossus pursued his own errands. Rinn ogled the chaos and commotion of the fairgrounds: hawkers calling out to passers-by, street musicians playing for coins, jugglers and acrobats performing death-defying acts. Cat wanted to touch every shiny thing she passed, but Rinn restrained her. Marshal led the girls to a less crowded area with long weathered-wood tables. "We should get some food first."

"Food!" Cat squealed happily. The two girls sat across from each other at the table while Marshal procured their meal. They kicked their legs and giggled at all the unusual people passing by, Rinn swore she saw an orc. Marshal returned with oversized drumsticks and sweet breads.

"Happy birthday, Rinn." He took a seat and passed out the food. Grease dribbled down Rinn's chin as she devoured her drumstick. Cat ate like a carnivore, noisily chewing on the bone.

"Catherine? Is that you?" A familiar voice broke through the crowd. Two teenage boys waved and walked over, Marshal rose protectively. Bos and Lutra were dressed in colorful tunics edged with fancy embroidery. Lutra tried to peek at Cat's face under the cowl of her robe, but she shied away. "I didn't know you were coming to the fair."

"We just got here." Marshal stepped in front of Cat, trying to draw attention away from her. "Did you come with your family?"

Bos answered. "Our parents are at merchant's row with our little brother." The burly teen waved his hand to the far end of the fairground.

Lutra tried to bypass Marshal and talk to Cat. "There's an acting troupe about to perform. Do you want to watch the show with us?"

Rinn's eyes lit up. "Daddy, can we go watch the play? I haven't seen actors in such a long time." She tugged at his sleeve, but Marshal held up a protective hand.

"The stage is close by." Bos offered. "We'll keep close watch over them."

"Okay." Marshal acquiesced. "But I will accompany you." Lutra and Bos exchanged cross looks, but agreed anyway. Marshal escorted the girls to the dirt gallery below the stage where the audience was milling in eager expectation of the performance. Marshal maneuvered to the side of the stage and found a place where the girls could see, Bos and Lutra idled nearby. With a bright explosion and a puff of smoke, a team of acrobats burst onto the stage, jumping and tumbling over each other. The crowd responded with hoots and applause. Marshal eyed the audience nervously, his hand resting on his sword hilt.

Mummers took the stage next, hidden behind elaborate masks, acting out skits of bravery, wit, and romance. Comical stories of famous Imperial heroes getting duped by simple farmwives and clever shepherds. The audience cheered every time an Imperial soldier was paddled on the behind or knocked off stage. Rinn could not help but laugh at the silly antics, but she also felt the sting of having her childhood heroes mocked. At one point, Cat convulsed with laughter so hard her tail swished out from under her robe. Marshal, who never broke a smile, quickly tucked it back beneath the hem.

"Cat." He whispered. "Calm your tail."

"I can't help it." She complained. Between skits, single performers came out to entertain the audience while the players changed costumes and backdrops. During one exchange, a single musician took the stage with an unusual instrument.

"Hey!" Rinn pointed to the musician. "That's the bard we heard at the tavern." She energetically waved at him. The elfish musician never turned his head, but his eyes found Rinn and then her robed friend. A smile crossed his face as he played.

"It's time to go." Marshal gathered up Rinn and Cat and ushered the girls away. They protested, wanting to stay and watch the rest of the performance. Bos and Lutra both pleaded for a bit more time together, but Marshal would not be dissuaded. He dragged the girls through the crowded streets, holding their arms tightly. At one intersection, Marshal hesitated and urgently pushed Rinn and Cat into a dressmaker's tent. Through the tent flaps, Rinn could see a gang of redheads passing by, brandishing clubs and swords.

"Why are they here?" Rinn whispered to her father.

"Quiet." He admonished privately. Marshal absently began to rummage through the merchandise. "These dresses are nice." He spoke loudly. "Which one would you like for your birthday?" A heavy-set shopkeeper came over to eagerly peddle her goods. The dressmaker tried to entice Rinn with different gaudy patterns and styles, all of which she refused. She did take a liking to a modest orange dress with a decorated felt bodice. Rinn was escorted behind a curtain, where several young women helped her into the dress and tailored the fit. Cat busied herself playing with balls of colored yarn, tangling one so irreparably that Marshal ended up having to buy it for her. Finally, Rinn emerged in her new dress, feeling like a princess. Marshal paid for the birthday present with Imperial coin, which the shopkeeper eagerly accepted. Marshal thanked her and hurried the girls out the back flaps of the tent. He led them behind the merchant stalls, away from the fairgrounds to where the wagons were parked. He moved cautiously up and down the rows until he found his own wagon.

"Where is that damnable giant when you need him?" Marshal muttered to himself. He stowed their belongings in the wagon bed and urged the girls to climb aboard. Abruptly, he spun around and drew his sword. A lone man stood before him, lanky and sinewy, completely wrapped in tight, black cloth, like a corpse prepared for burial. Rinn could only see the man's brown and red eyes peeking through the black wrappings.

The stranger lifted a black, serrated sword and pointed to Cat. "That thing is coming with me."

Chapter 10

The afternoon sun hung low in the sky. The stranger's shadow stretched across the dirt field. Empty wagons were lined up in neat rows, their owners making merry at the fairgrounds. The unknown assailant slowly walked toward Cat. Rinn grabbed her and crawled beneath the wagon.

Marshal interposed himself between the stranger and the girls. "She stays with us." Marshal assumed a defensive position, circling slightly to his left, trying to move the sun out from behind the approaching man. The stranger matched his movements, keeping the sun behind him. In his off hand, he held out a length of twisted black metal. Rinn gasped when she saw it, an open slave shackle.

"That thing does not belong to you." The stranger's voice was low and coarse, like someone suffering from chronic disease. "Move aside before you get killed." Cat hissed at the villain and his horrible metal shackle.

"She doesn't seem to want to go with you." Marshal cocked his head sideways, with a grin. "I'm not surprised. Your manners are terrible, and frankly, you smell awful."

In the blink of an eye, the cloth-wrapped man lunged forward, aiming a lethal thrust at Marshal's midsection. Had he not been expecting it, Marshal would have certainly been skewered. Instead, he managed to block the savage attack and stay on his feet. The man slipped past him and grabbed Cat by the neck. She scratched and kicked desperately, only making him squeeze tighter. Marshal rained steel down upon the stranger, but he countered every attack without losing his grip on Cat. Rinn clung to Cat's other arm, desperately trying to pull her away, but the stranger was unmoved. Marshal scored a lucky strike on the man, ripping away the black cloth from his arm. His skin was entirely covered in intricate tattoos. The stranger growled, but would not release his prey. With a brutal swing he knocked Marshal off his feet and sent his sword scattering across the hard-packed ground.

The assailant pushed Rinn away and flipped Cat upside down, clamping the metal shackle around her leg. A circle of runes engraved into the band activated and began to glow blue. Cat howled out in terror and fought back as hard as she could, but the tattooed man held her fast. He unceremoniously flung her over his shoulder like a sack of grain and turned to leave. In his way stood a girl, barely fourteen-years-old, wielding her father's sword, its blade bathed in a soft glow of green light.

"Out of my way, insect." The stranger's raspy voice mingled with the sounds of Cat's screams.

"Give me back my sister." Rinn yelled at the man.

A groggy Marshal reached out from the ground where he lay, nursing a head wound. "Rinn, no." It was too late, Rinn charged the stranger, swinging her father's sword in a large clumsy arc. The stranger casually brushed her stroke aside, but with a horrible sound, Rinn's blade cleaved cleanly through his own serrated weapon. Rinn flailed wildly, lashing out at the man multiple times, across his face and torso, sending showers of green sparks each time. Ribbons of black garb peeled away and fluttered to the ground. Beneath them was a gaunt, pale man, every inch of his skin was covered in a patchwork of intricate tattoos the color of clotted blood. Where Rinn's sword made contact, faint green lines were fading from view. The wiry man considered the severed end of his sword.

"Well, isn't this interesting." The man tossed aside his wasted sword hilt and pulled out a serrated black dagger, dropping Cat. He advanced toward Rinn as Marshal struggled to stand. Rinn shook as she held her father's sword. "That's quite a talent you have, little witch. You'll make a nice prize."

Unexpectedly, the tattooed man tumbled forward, struck from behind with brutal force. He lay on the ground unmoving, and next to him, Clive rolled to a stop.

"Clive!" Cat screamed with delight, hugging the rock. Rinn dropped her sword and ran to her injured father. Molossus walked into view and helped steady Marshal as he staggered. Blood trickled down the left side of his face. He reached out to his daughter, hugging her tightly.

Molo bent over and tried to pry Cat away from his rock. "You can let go now, little cat."

"What is that thing?" Rinn grimaced at the fallen man.

Molossus shoved the unmoving body with his foot and stared at the intricate tattoos. "Not all monsters look like beasts. Sometimes, the worst creatures start off as men. We need to leave. Now." He collected Cat and Clive, wrestling the rock away from the overly affectionate feline and set them both in the back of the wagon. Rinn supported her father as he took several wobbly steps to retrieve his sword.

"Get us out of here." Marshal weakly climbed into the wagon bed and collapsed. Molo hoisted the yoke and pulled away from the fairgrounds in a quick march. Rinn watched as the crumpled figure in black shrank out of view, never moving. In the wagon bed, Cat cried as she bit and chewed on the metal shackle encircling her leg, ripping out chunks of fur in frustration. Rinn put a calming hand on her shoulder.

"Cat, do you trust your big sister?" Cat looked up at Rinn with huge soggy eyes, whiskers pointing straight down. She nodded meekly. Rinn reached for her father's sword, its silver blade still glowing a faint green. "Hold still." Rinn delicately slid the blade beneath the metal shackle, keeping the flat against Cat's leg. Rinn quietly said a prayer, not to any deity in particular, just an expression of her wish to help Cat. The green light intensified, flooding the back of the wagon, and with a flick, Rinn sliced through the woven metal band around Cat's leg. Blue runes sparked and angrily fizzled out as the shackle fell away. Freed from her bonds, Cat threw her arms around Rinn, tackling her in a warm hug. Molo, who felt the wagon shift, turned around to investigate.

"Everyone okay back there?" He called to them.

"Never better." Rinn did her best to conceal her excitement. Cat squeezed her one last time before letting go. She licked her leg, smoothing the fur over the place where the shackle had been.

"What was that weird green light?" Cat asked between licks.

Rinn turned the sword over in her hand, studying the green edge. "It's a kind of magic. Father called it Sigillum."

"No one can break a slave manacle." Cat stopped grooming to sit by her sister and examine the sword. "How did you do it?" She tried to touch the blade, but Rinn batted her paw away.

"Careful. This magic must be pretty dangerous. My father does not want me to use it." Rinn remembered hearing her father call out to her during the battle. Her father's groggy voice interrupted.

"Your father wants you safe." Marshal sat up slowly holding his head.

"Then teach me how to use this power." Rinn set the sword down.

"I can't." Marshal admitted through heavy eyelids. "I don't know how. Only your grandmother knew the full extent of these abilities, and she refused to teach us much. Just a few words."

"But there must be someone out there who knows." Rinn's hands balled up into fists. "A wizard or something."

"You misunderstand, Rinn." Marshal leaned back against a grain sack. "This is not magic. Sigillum powers are a divine blessing. You need to find a priest."

"A priest?" Rinn was flush with frustration and excitement.

"It won't be easy." Marshal laid back, closing his eyes. "The Curia declared all Sigilla to be enemies, to be hunted down and killed."

"Is that what happened to my mother?" Rinn inquired anxiously.

"Yes, she was killed by the Curia." Marshal mumbled as he dozed off. "Twice." Rinn stared at him, bewildered. The wagon rattled down the dirt road, heading north, away from the fairgrounds.

::

Marshal stayed in bed several days recovering from his injuries, leaving Rinn and Cat with very little to do other than housework. Rinn palmed a small knife from the kitchen one afternoon and snuck away with Cat to the riverbank. She showed Cat the small knife and tried to practice her magic. Cat watched curiously as Rinn unsuccessfully tried to summon the green glowing light.

"I can't do it." Rinn complained, about ready to throw the knife into the river.

"Can't do what?" Cat asked, picking the cotton out of cattails and littering it all over the ground.

"I'm trying to make this knife glow." Rinn insisted.

"Did you ask it nicely?" Cat pondered.

Feeling like a fool, Rinn spoke to the small blade. "Would you please turn silver with a nice green glow." Nothing happened. Rinn glowered at Cat.

"Maybe it only works with swords?" Cat suggested.

Rinn shook her head. "Molo thinks it will work with anything metal. I just need to figure out how I did it before."

"What were you doing when it happened?" Cat selected another cattail to mutilate. Rinn thought about the question. Each time she summoned her power, she had been trying to protect someone, either from bandits, weird bird-dragons, or that terrifying slaver. Rinn held the knife and pictured protecting Cat from a giant bear about to attack. Dutifully, the knife sizzled with green energy as the dull metal fell away like powder, revealing a bright silver blade. Rinn bounced with joy, she felt like she had just opened the lock to a treasure chest.

"I can do it." She held up the glowing knife in triumph.

Cat came over to investigate. "How sharp is it?" She reached out to touch the blade, but Rinn yanked it away.

"Careful." Rinn cautioned. "We don't know what it can do." She carefully carried the blade to a fist-sized rock on the riverbank. She sliced through the stone with a grinding noise, as effortlessly as cutting water. Cat picked up the neatly sliced stone halves and sniffed them. Rinn experimented on different rocks, shells, and even dead branches, but she did not find anything the knife could not cut. After about an hour, the knife began to lose its glow. Eventually, the metal blade decayed into rust and crumbled away. Rinn tossed the worthless knife handle into the river and hurried back to the house with Cat, never noticing Clive hiding in the brush nearby.

Chapter 11

I mprovements to the house and work on extending the palisade wall neared completion. New, stronger doors had been built for the entrance and additional furniture added. Now that harvest season was over, Bos and Lutra returned regularly to help out. Construction on a new home for Molossus began, including a large outdoor forge with a covered wooden workbench. Marshal wanted to keep the windows boarded up for the winter, but Rinn suggested creating window panes from the empty bottles in the cellar. Molo was familiar with the process of using cullet, crushed shards of broken glass, heated and reshaped into new forms. Rinn and Cat took turns playfully pulverizing glass bottles with hammers. The boys carried the powder to Molo's forge where it was heated and shaped into flat panes. Molo used large padded gloves when he handled the glowing glass. Even though the window panes were not transparent, when installed they completely changed the atmosphere inside the house. The interior rooms became bright and cheerful and in desperate need of cleaning.

As the days grew cooler, Rinn and Cat spent more time near the warmth of the forge. Cat stole one of Molo's oversized gloves and ran around with it on her head. Molo was panting with exhaustion by the time he caught her. Marshal hunted most mornings, exploring new areas around the hilltop. In the afternoons he smoked meat and hung the skins out to dry. Winter food stores were stacked in the cellar. Molo taught Bos and Lutra how to mix mortar and set stones, and together they worked on building a stout chimney for his forge.

One busy morning, a newcomer came to call, a beardless man in his forties, wearing the clothes of a farmer. He carried no weapons, just a walking stick. Marshal was away hunting, so Molossus strolled down the hill to greet the man. "Hail." He called out across the lawn. Rinn and Cat watched the exchange from within the palisade wall.

The farmer gawked at the giant man. "Hail, good sir. I'm Arlin." The farmer tried to sound impressive, but he was road weary. "My brother is Hadwin, he runs the farm north of Herbary Lake."

"Well met, Arlin. I am Molossus. Come up to the house and tell me what brings you this far south." He motioned to the top of the hill. With its new roof and glass windows, the stone house looked impressive from a distance, the formidable palisade wall enclosing the property added to the effect. The farmer whistled in admiration as he approached. Rinn and Cat whispered as they watched the newcomer. Molo offered him water and a bench near the forge, Arlin thanked the giant man profusely. Molo removed his smith's apron and sat down on the worktable, resting Clive in his lap. "Herbary Lake is about a half day's walk from here."

"That's right." The farmer gestured with his hands as he spoke. "Like I was telling, my brother runs the farm there, nearly twenty fields in all. We'd closed most of the paddocks for winter, but a nest of grashels moved in."

Molossus winced. "Oh, I hate those things."

The farmer pleaded. "We heard you have some fighting men here. Those pests need to be removed before winter sets in. We can pay—we have plenty of foodstuffs and wines."

Molo rolled Clive in his hand as he considered the offer. "Our hunter, Marshal, is out right now."

"I'd like to meet this hunter." The farmer's expression brightened.

"Sure." Molo conceded. "I'll bring him in three days' time. Please, rest, eat, and drink before you journey home." He barked at the two spying girls to go fetch some food from the house.

"You have my thanks." The farmer bowed his head.

::

After the evening meal, Rinn and Cat cleaned dishes while Molo tried to convince Marshal to hunt grashels. "This Arlin seemed pretty desperate. He offered to pay us in food and wine. I think we should at least look into it."

Marshal furrowed his brow as he listened. "I don't like leaving the girls alone while we go soldiering."

"Bring them with us." Molo shrugged. "Rinn could use practice with her spear."

"Take the girls grashel hunting?" Marshal threw his bow and arrows into the wooden trunk and locked it. "Are you daft? Men get killed by grashels."

"Careless and drunk men, maybe." Molo countered.

Marshal exhaled deeply. "The whole reason I came out here was to keep her safe. The last thing I want is to drag her into unnecessary danger."

"She's a Sigillum." Molo placed a large hand on Marshal's shoulder. "Fighting is in her blood. Besides, there's more than enough danger out here. You can't keep her safe forever."

"I know I can't." Marshal sighed. "But is it wrong to want to try."

::

Rinn, Cat, Marshal and Molo departed for Arlin's farm two days later. Rinn trekked uncomfortably in her new clothes. Her father had fashioned doeskin trousers for both her and Cat, which he called their hunting clothes. Cat immediately took to her new supple pants, bouncing and tumbling around the yard. Rinn was accustomed to only wearing dresses and felt the pants left her lower half too exposed. She refused to wear them when the farm boys were around. Marshal also crafted tight-fitting vests for the girls from a thick leather material. These wool-lined vests provided warmth and protection when worn over a tunic, but again Rinn found them too immodest. She was still developing, and she preferred her budding body shape hidden under the loose folds of a tunic, not accentuated by a tight vest. As she walked, she clutched her cloak tightly around her, trying to conceal her embarrassing outfit.

"Are you cold?" Her father marched second in line, behind Molossus.

"A bit." Rinn pouted.

The four party members carried long spears, which Molo called pilum. Marshal was surprised when Rinn took hold of her spear, the strange magic did not activate. Rinn clutched her pilum like a walking stick, and Molo slung his own oversized spear over his shoulder. Marshal carried Cat's weapon, she was constantly leaving it behind every time she ventured off to investigate some interesting rock or bug along the path. They followed a well-worn animal trace leading north into the highlands at the foot of the mountains.

Molossus pushed through a tangle of brush and the party stumbled onto the banks of a wide, blue lake overgrown with lush green plants. Ignoring the cool autumn weather, stubborn blue and white flowers blossomed along the water's edge. Molo pointed to a small clearing ahead. "We'll stop here to rest and refill our waterskins." Rinn stretched out on the lakeshore while Cat frolicked into the underbrush. Molo called out to her as he settled down. "Save your energy for the hunt, little cat. Come get some water."

Cat did not respond. Rinn looked around, but Cat was nowhere to be seen. Molo called out again, Marshal and Rinn joining in, their three voices echoing across the vast lake. The feline girl did not reply. Marshal took the lead. "We'll split up and search. Keep your guard up, we don't know what's out here." He motioned for Molo to move west down the lakeshore, while he and Rinn travelled east. Molo held Clive above his head and pointed him different directions as he walked. Marshal searched the ground for tracks while Rinn nervously followed behind. She held her spear tightly as terrifying images of the tattooed man filled her head. She vividly recalled Cat's screams when the metal shackle was strapped to her leg. Rinn's palms started to sweat and her spear rattled. Her father calmed her shaking hands. "We'll find her."

From deep in the foliage Molo bellowed out Cat's name. Rinn and Marshal sprinted in his direction. When they arrived, they found Molo standing over the feline girl. She was stretched out in a green leafy field, blindly rubbing her back and face against the plants. Marshal plucked a green sprig and sniffed it. "Catmint." He announced. Rinn stifled a laugh.

Molo cursed as he hoisted the girl by the scruff of her neck. Cat jerked to attention, surprised. Molo dragged her back to the lakeshore, giving her a verbal flogging the entire way. Cat desperately struggled to get back to the mint field, but Molo would not let her go. Rinn secretly picked several handfuls of the plants and stuffed them in a pouch before heading back.

::

Hadwin lived in a long timber house with a large thatched roof on a vast upland plain. The building had been added onto so many times, it was hard to imagine what the original structure may have looked like. The multi-roomed complex sprawled across the property along with orderly rows of chicken coops, several large barns, and a collection of apiaries. A dozen men hauled hay and wood into nearby barns. Women and children scurried around the property with baskets of eggs and pitchers of milk. Arlin rushed out to greet the party, accompanied by a shorter, broader man with brown hair—clearly his older sibling. Arlin made the introductions. "Thank you for coming. This is my brother, Hadwin." He turned to his brother. "Molossus and Marshal from the hilltop."

"Well met." Marshal struck his chest once, a common Imperial salutation.

"An Imperial soldier." Hadwin chuckled. "Exactly what we're needing. Do you have any experience fighting beasts?"

"Some." Marshal remarked. Molo suppressed a cough.

Hadwin explained the situation: on the outskirts of the furthest fields, a colony of grashels moved into the soft soil. Molo explained to Rinn that grashels are venomous animals about the size of a large fox and covered with spiny needles. They burrow underground, leaving their backs partially exposed. The poison in their needles stuns unfortunate animals, which they eat. Grashel poison is not strong enough to kill a man, but the needles can penetrate a farmer's boot and cause painful welts that take weeks to heal.

Arlin led the party to the outer fields, opening and closing the gates of the wooden fences that neatly divided the farmland. Crops had been harvested, leaving behind aisles of broken wheat stalks and withered vines. Cat danced around, jittery with excitement. "This is going to be great." She bounced up and down, rubbing her paws.

"It won't be, if you get stung, little cat." Molossus put a hand on her head to quiet her, but her tail would not be still.

Rinn questioned her father. "Are these things really so bad?"

Marshal gave a wry smile. "You're about to find out."

::

"Go!" Molo signaled, and Cat sprinted across the field. She slid to a stop before a lumpy mound and thwacked it with a long stick. A shrieking ball of needles and teeth burst from the ground. Cat dashed back to the waiting party with the angry grashel in pursuit. It streaked toward the hunters on four stumpy legs, Rinn readied her spear to skewer the pest.

"Steady now." Marshal squinted as Cat sped past the waiting spear wall. Rinn gripped her weapon tightly as the grashel impaled itself on her pilum with a sickening shriek.

It shivered once and then stopped moving. Marshal gave it a second jab, just to be sure.

Cat circled back. "Did we get it?"

"Yes, Cat." Marshal patted her on the head. "Good job." She sat on her haunches and purred happily, squinting her eyes. Rinn saw the green-yellow blood on the end of her spear, and her stomach turned. She held her breath to keep from getting sick. The creature she had dispatched was certainly ugly, covered in poisonous spines, but killing did not come naturally to Rinn, even when it was something as hideous as this. She shuddered as she pulled her spear out of the creature's limp body.

"Are you going to be okay?" Molo leaned over and looked her in the face. Rinn nodded briefly, biting her lips and holding her breath to keep from retching. Molo remarked something to Marshal, but Rinn did not hear it, because Cat sped by shouting.

"I'm getting another one." She bounded across the field. Rinn's eyes went wide and her spear shook violently in her hands.

Chapter 12

A dark, crisp night lingered on Hadwin's property. Inside the farmhouse, all was bright and cheery, warmed by the fires of a dozen hearths. The weary grashel hunters had been invited to stay the night and were treated to a generous feast. Rinn's mouth watered at the sight of all the food set out for them: roast geese, cured hams, vegetable stews, and sweetbreads of every sort. Hadwin and his wife Morven took their seats in the center of the room and invited the hunters to sit with them. Farmworkers and their families crowded into the main hall until every seat was taken. Children frolicked in the aisles and babies were passed from lap to lap. It was a joyful atmosphere full of laughter and heady conversation, but the noise in the dining hall was daunting to Rinn. She had been raised an only child, unaccustomed to large, social gatherings.

Hadwin stood and lifted his glass. "A heartfelt welcome to our valiant grashel hunters." The entire room cheered in appreciation, beating their mugs on the tables. "These brave warriors cleared each and every pest from the outer fields, so we can plant this spring without worry." Again, the crowd beat their mugs and raised their voices for the visiting warriors. Rinn blushed at the attention. The day had been grueling work, she personally killed over thirty of the venomous pests. Even though her arms and back were exhausted from the day's labors, her mind was restless, occupied with uncertainty. Once everyone had started eating, she posed a question to her father.

"Why didn't my magic work today?" She tried to ask casually. He nearly choked on his food.

"Quiet." Her father managed, coughing. "We can talk about this some other time." He smiled at his hosts, who exchanged puzzled looks.

"I was just curious." Rinn sulked, picking at her food. The question still gnawed at her. She spent the entire day engaged in combat, the grashels were not very big nor bright, but they were plenty aggressive and covered in poisonous quills. Rinn had expected her spear tip to glow or turn silver, but it never did. She felt threated each time one of the creatures raced toward her, but her powers never manifested. Rinn could not understand why.

On the bench next to her, Cat was soaking in the joys of a hearty feast. She was the center of attention for the younger girls and boys, who either wanted to pet her soft fur or see her extend and retract her claws. The adults occupied themselves with serious drinking and mindless conversation. Even though Rinn sat in a room packed with people, she began to feel very alone. She had been the one who actually killed most of the grashels, but she was getting almost none of the attention. The experience had been terrifying, it took every bit of her courage to repeatedly let those venomous beasts charge her. No one understood how difficult the day had been for her. Quietly, Rinn excused herself from the table, and wound her way through the maze-like house until she found a door leading outside. She slumped down on the ground leaning against the cold exterior of the house. Alone in the night, the crisp air bit through her leather clothes. Her cloak was inside, but she refused to go back to get it. She wrapped her arms around her knees and fought back tears as she shivered in the dark. A round rock rolled over and stopped in front of her, its purple eye trained perfectly on her.

Sniffing, Rinn looked up. "Hello, Clive." Molossus walked into view and draped his heavy fur mantle over her shivering frame. Saying nothing, he sat down beside her and leaned against the wall. He waited for her to talk first.

"I just don't understand him." Rinn finally blurted out.

"Your father?" Molo left the question hanging.

"He won't tell me anything about my powers." Rinn balled her hands into fists. "It's like he doesn't want me to ever use it. I can't help it—sometimes it just happens. And sometimes it doesn't." She scowled and exhaled sharply, her steamy breath visible in the cold air. "It's like he's afraid of it."

"He is." Molo rolled Clive around with his foot. "He's afraid for you. If the Curia found out what you can do, they would hunt you down and kill you."

"Why?" Rinn pleaded for an explanation, tugging at the big man's tunic.

"You are living proof that the Curia aren't the real rulers of Sevria." Rinn seemed confused, so Molo explained. "For nearly five hundred years, the Empire has been ruled by a single leader, an emperor. A council of nine men advised the emperors for centuries, the Curia. But the last Sevrian emperor, Tarandus, passed away without any heir. Many came forward, claiming to be the legitimate ruler of the Empire, but without proof. Ultimately, the Curia took it upon themselves to rule in the emperor's place."

"But what does that have to do with me?" Rinn begged, desperate to understand.

"You have the abilities of the Sigilla, the emperor's personal defender." Molo shifted so he could see Rinn more easily. "If you exist, then there must be an emperor out there somewhere. The Curia don't want to lose the power they worked so hard to usurp."

"That's stupid." Rinn complained. "Let the Curia rule the Empire, I don't care. I just want to be left alone."

"It's not that simple." Molo rubbed his oversized hands. "The Empire is a mess. The Curia are selfish and abusive. Civil war is coming—if it hasn't already started, and millions of people who live in Sevria are going to be affected, needlessly suffering. Many will die on the battlefield, more will succumb to famine or disease. If you could stop all that, wouldn't you want to?"

Rinn wanted to help, but all those problems seemed too much for her to handle. She was only fourteen, how could she stop a war? She only wanted to keep her sister Cat safe and live a quiet life in her hilltop home. The rest of the world would have to take care of itself.

Molo drew a small knife from his belt. "I once met emperor Tarandus himself. He gifted me this knife." In his hands, the blade seemed ridiculously small. He reverently handed the knife to Rinn. She examined it in the dim light, turning it over in her chilled hands. The knife was very light and elaborately decorated, its handle trimmed with fancy runes and tiny gems.

Rinn questioned as she handed the small knife back to Molo. "The last Emperor died forty years ago."

The big man chuckled. "Would you believe that I am almost ninety years old? It's the giant blood in me." He stroked the wild hair that was his beard. "I actually don't know how long I'll be around. Some giants live for hundreds of years." Rinn started to shiver, so the big man pulled her close, putting his massive, warm arm around her. "I remember your father when he was young, always cautious, always careful. It's kept him alive all these years. He likes everything orderly and in control. But some things can't be controlled, no matter how hard you try."

Rinn listened as Molo told her stories about her father as a young guard in the Imperial palace. Questions burned inside her, questions that needed answers. An opportunity like this would not easily present itself, so Rinn summon the courage and bravely asked. "Uncle Molo, did you know my mother?"

"Only a bit." Molo confided. "I knew your grandmother better."

"You knew my grandmother?" Rinn sat up in surprise.

"She was a remarkable woman. They called her Virago, the warrior. When the last Emperor died without a male heir, the Curia fought against the Legions for control of the Empire.

Your grandmother sided with the generals. She fought the Curia for many years. Eventually, she was captured and killed." He hung his head in sorrow, or maybe shame.

Rinn's head swum. "I've never heard of her. She's never mentioned in my history lessons."

"Of course not." Molo stated plainly. "She was a Sigillum."

::

The next morning, after being fed and graciously thanked once more, the party departed. They journeyed home laden with foodstuffs from Hadwin's farm. Molossus hauled two large wine barrels on his back. Rinn thought he looked like a giant beetle. "This would be much easier with a horse." Marshal jabbed at the big man. Molo grunted and kept walking. Progress was slow, and they had to stop and rest frequently. As they passed Herbary Lake, Cat pouted, wanted to frolic in the catmint again, but Marshal pressed on. By the time they arrived home, it was well after dinner. Bos and Lutra, who had been watching the hilltop in their absence, came out to greet everyone. Bos relieved Rinn of her packs and Lutra did the same for Cat. The two girls flopped down on the grass, exhausted.

"How did the hunting go?" Lutra inquired.

"The girls did quite well." Marshal lifted his chin proudly.

"How many did you kill, Cat?" Lutra asked.

Cat sat up. "I didn't kill any. I chased them." She had a twinkle in her eyes and her tail wagged furiously. She pointed a paw at her adoptive sister. "Rinn did most of the killing." Bos raised an eyebrow at Rinn, who turned bright red and hid her face in the hood of her cloak. As the boys carried the foodstuffs into the house, Lutra shot one last backward glance at Cat as he left.

Rinn turned to her feline sister. "Did you have a good time?"

"I sure did." Cat's little fangs poked out as she grinned. "We should go back again."

"You're not afraid of anything, are you?" Rinn took Cat by the paw and led her back to the house.

"Nope." Cat beamed. "Nothing." But, in her head, Rinn could still hear the sounds of Cat's screams when the tattooed man wrapped the black slave shackle around her leg. Rinn hated seeing her like that, helpless and afraid. In the cold evening air, her resolve intensified; she would not stand to see anyone suffer that way, trapped in the bonds of slavery. Tomorrow, she and Cat would slip away. There was a dwarf who needed her help and she would not stop until he was free.

Chapter 13

An early morning frost covered hilltop, painting everything in soft shades of white and gray. Rinn quietly unlocked the palisade gate and cracked it open barely a handsbreadth. She squeezed through the opening with Cat on her heels. Rinn was wrapped in a warm fur cloak concealing the long knife she pilfered from her father's weapons trunk. The girls slinked past Molo's forge, Clive sat in the window of the house watching them. Cat made a face at the rock as they crept past. The pair sprinted down the hillside all the way to the riverbank. Rinn knew that if she followed the river south, she would find Tomin's house.

"Where are we going?" Cat seemed eager to be out adventuring.

"We're going to Tomin's farm to free that dwarf." Rinn confided. "I can't stop thinking about him and the horrible conditions he's living in."

"Are we going to fight?" Cat's eyes sparkled in the predawn mist.

"No." Rinn admonished her adoptive sister. "Not unless we have to. I'm going to remove his leg iron, like I did with you. He'll be free to do whatever he wants."

"What if he wants to kill us?" Cat pondered, paw to chin.

Rinn was astounded by the question. She never stopped to consider what the dwarf would do once he was freed. She assumed he would just go home. But he would have no money and no way to travel and winter weather was about to move in. She did not know where he would live or how he would earn money. As she walked along the riverbank, her resolve weakened, but the image of the pitiful dwarf living in squalor shook away her doubts. Rinn marched on, certain she was doing the right thing.

Rinn and Cat followed the river down to the low country where Tomin's house squatted near the riverbank. Cat sniffed at the air, and stopped. "Something's not right."

"What is it?" Rinn asked, fingering her father's knife.

"I don't know." Cat stared off in the distance. Rinn warily scanned the area, deciding it would be safest to keep moving. As they turned a bend in the river, they spotted the farmhouse, burnt to the ground. Cat covered her mouth with her paws in shock. Rinn sprinted to the stinking wreckage of the farmhouse. The dilapidated building was a smoldering shell, ash and cinders swirled in the morning breeze. Rinn stepped through the gap where the front door had once been into the black, greasy smear that used to be a building. The broken furniture and piles of trash were charred beyond recognition. Rinn covered her nose with the hem of her cloak and started picking through the remains. Cat remained outside, refusing to touch the foul-smelling ash.

"We have to find them." Rinn haphazardly overturned half-burnt boards and sifted through ash piles desperately looking for survivors. Cat half-heartedly poked at the burnt timbers. Rinn's search found no one, alive nor dead. She left the wreckage of the house covered in ash and melancholy. The farm animals behind the house were missing, obviously stolen. Rinn knew who was to blame, the damnable Clanmorris, and they would pay.

"Wait." Cat's ears lifted, and she started to sniff at the air again. She followed her nose, and Rinn followed Cat. They crossed the yard beyond the cow pasture to a chicken coop.

"Cat. We don't have time for this." Rinn put her hands on her hips.

Cat ignored her and opened the door to the triangular chicken coop. She wiggled inside, tail and all.

"Catherine." Rinn yelled. "Get out here this instant." Rinn heard a scraping and groaning noise coming from inside the coop. Cat shimmied out backwards, struggling to pull the body of Tomin the drunk. He was heavily burnt, but still breathed. The dwarf crawled out after him, blackened and sporting a large gash on his nose. Rinn helped Cat drag the farmer into the open, amazed he was alive.

"I couldn't leave him." The downcast dwarf looked at the ground in misery. Rinn stepped over to the smelly, filthy dwarf and threw her arms around him, crying tears of joy. The dwarf boggled at the gesture. Rinn squeezed once more and released him. She reached to her belt and drew her knife, the dwarf put up his hands defensively. "Wait, I didn't do this."

"I know, Clanmorris did." Rinn responded, she held her blade at arm's length. "Tell me your name."

The dwarf frowned, a deep furrow forming in his brow. He growled harshly. "I am called Lump-nose."

Rinn shook her head and smiled genuinely. "Your real name."

The dwarf grudgingly answered. "Felsic."

Rinn gripped her knife tightly. "I am Rinn. I release you from your bonds of slavery, Felsic." Rinn closed her eyes and tried to recall what she did when she freed Cat. She remembered a sort of prayer, not to any of the gods she had learned about in the Empire, just a call for aid. This dwarf was in need, like Cat had been in need, and Rinn desperately wanted to help. Light flashed off the edge of her knife as the familiar metallic smell permeated the area. The dull metal melted away like a fine powder leaving behind a glowing silver blade, tinged with green. Rinn lowered the blade to the black shackle encircling the dwarf's leg and sliced down through the braided metal band. The shackle resisted, Rinn felt like she was carving through tough sinew, but it eventually gave way, and the metal band fell to the ground. The dwarf reached down and felt his leg, free of the shackle. Disbelief washed over his face.

"How? Only the Khuraak can remove a ginj." A slow anger built up inside him. "You're a slaver."

"No, I'm not." Rinn backed away defensively. "I don't even know what a ginj is?" Rinn asked in confusion. Cat gestured to her leg, and Rinn realized it must be the name of the slave shackle. "I don't know why, but my power can cut through slave shackles. I freed my sister that way." Cat wanted to clarify Rinn's statement, but Rinn shushed her. "You're no longer a slave, Felsic, but your old master is dying. If we can get him to the hilltop, my father can treat his burns."

"We can't drag him all the way home." Cat rocked nervously on her haunches. A large shadowy figure stepped out from behind the wreckage of the burnt house.

"I'll carry him." The giant man announced. Rinn watched Molossus approach and her stomach fell, she knew she was caught. Seeing the giant, Felsic raised his hands defensively. Even Cat shrunk to the ground, her paws covering her head. Fear washed over Rinn, her father would be furious, her punishment would be severe. Molo said nothing as he carefully picked up the injured farmer. He tapped Cat on the head. She tried to disarm the giant with innocent, kitten-like eyes. Molo held out a large round rock with an eyeball on it. "Carry Clive." He commanded. Cat eagerly reached out to grab the stone with delight, nearly dropping it to the ground. Undaunted by its unexpected weight, she bounced happily after the giant, lugging her new plaything.

Rinn motioned to Felsic. "Come on, let's go home." Grudgingly, he trailed behind her. They followed the river north, back to the hilltop. Along the way Rinn rehearsed several plausible stories to tell her father. When they arrived, he was waiting solemnly at the palisade gate. Molossus entered first carrying his wounded cargo, and Cat meekly snuck by carrying Clive. Marshal stopped Rinn and stared her down in silence. Rinn desperately wanted to blurt out her entire explanation, but she could not find the words. She hated feeling so small, especially for helping people in need.

Her father pointed to the house, and Rinn obeyed, head held low like a beaten dog. The dwarf watched in amazement. Marshal inhaled deeply and put a hand to his forehead. He motioned to the dwarf to come inside, too.

Inside, Molo sent Cat to fetch a bucket of clean water while he tore the burned man's clothes away. Cat planted Clive on the kitchen table and hurried off. Marshal stormed inside, ripping into his daughter. "Are you out of your mind?" Rinn shrank back in fear.

"Leave her be." Molossus interrupted.

"She snuck out in the middle of the night to go gods-know-where." Marshal's face was bright red as he yelled. Even the dwarf was taken aback. "She's never leaving this house again."

"She's not to blame." Molo tended to the injured man while he spoke. "She was under a godspell."

"A what?" Marshal was dumbfounded as he turned from his daughter to the giant man.

"The gods have a hand in this. How else could she have known about the attack?" Molo peeled away layers of burnt clothing from the injured farmer who moaned in pain.

"What attack?" Marshal stared at the burnt man, seeming to notice him for the first time.

"Tomin's farm was burnt to the ground last night." Molo received a bucket of water from Cat and began to clean the wounded flesh. "He was left for dead, but this good dwarf dragged him to safety. Rinn found them half-dead hiding in a chicken coop." Cat tried to speak up, but Molo shushed her. He fixed his eyes on Marshal. "This is the gods' will at work. If she hadn't left when she did, this man would have died."

The silent dwarf nodded in agreement.

Marshal slumped down into a chair and reached for his mug. "Her mother is going to kill me." He took a long drink of wine to calm his nerves. Rinn felt a wave of relief, having dodged a harsh punishment, but the weight of Molo's statements started to sink in. She deliberated in her head:

had the gods really controlled her actions? Rinn did not want to think so. She wanted to free the dwarf the first time she met him. She had decided exactly when to leave—the gods did not make her do anything. She may have said a small prayer when she cut the dwarf's shackle, but she did so voluntarily. Rinn did not think of herself as the gods' plaything.

Marshal sat in his chair, drinking while Molossus bandaged the burned man's wounds. Cat returned with a second bucket of water and plucked Clive off the table. Rinn was quietly lost in her own thoughts. The bewildered dwarf finally spoke up, waving his stubby arms. "Could someone tell me what's going on here?"

Marshal filled his mug a third time and poured one for the dwarf. "Here, take it. I think we all need a drink." The dwarf accepted the mug, but he was too agitated to drink. He pointed to Rinn.

"That girl sliced through my ginj like it was paper." The wine in the mug spilled as the dwarf ranted. "That's not possible, those enchantments are unbreakable. I demand to know how she did it."

Marshal and Molossus exchanged glances. Marshal answered. "There are mysteries about her even we don't understand."

"Who is she?" Felsic stared accusingly at Rinn.

"She's my daughter." Marshal drained his mug wearily.

Chapter 14

Marshal and Molossus curtained off a corner of the main room for Tomin. Burns covered his upper torso, arms, and face, but with treatment they were improving. Molo taught Rinn how to wash the wounds and apply new dressings, a job she detested but did anyway. The ailing man would occasionally sit up to ask for alcohol, but Marshal only gave him water and small bites of food. The days grew colder, and morning frosts lingered long into the afternoon. Bos and Lutra remained at home most days to help winterize the family farm. Rinn and Cat had long boring spans with little to do except chores.

"Let's go play." Cat stretched out on the floor. Rinn sat down on the cold stones next to her. Rinn had not worn her traveling clothes since their hunting excursion, but Cat preferred her tight-fitting leather pants and vest and rarely wore anything else.

"What do you want to do?" Rinn quizzed, retying the ribbon holding her mop of curly hair. In the past few months, Rinn's blond frocks had grown past her shoulders, making her appear a little more mature. Or at least she thought so. Cat's fur also seemed to be growing, not getting longer, but getting thicker as the winter months approached.

"We could catch mice?" Cat offered with a gleam in her eyes.

"You've already caught every mouse on this hill." Rinn laughed. It was midday and sunlight from the brownish window panes bathed Rinn and Cat's room in a hazy light, the gray stone walls appeared plain and dirty. Rinn noticed how drab and boring the inside of the house looked. "We should paint."

Rinn jumped up and hauled Cat off the floor. Standing side by side, Rinn was surprised to see how much her feline friend had grown in only a few months. Rinn had been several hands taller than Cat when they found her, but now only a few fingers separated them. Rinn wondered if it was the fluffiness in Cat's fur making her seem taller.

Rinn spotted her father in the kitchen, fletching new arrows for hunting. "Daddy, we are going berry picking." Rinn pulled two cloaks off their wall pegs.

Marshal looked up from his task. "Don't travel too far and stay away from the forest. And be home before it gets dark." Rinn half-expected him to come along as their escort and guard. Instead, he offered some advice. "There are hawthorn bushes to the north near the river. Their branches are plenty thorny, but they should still have berries. Just don't eat the seeds." He helped them find baskets. He also handed Rinn a belt and a long knife similar to the one she had swiped previously. "Take these along." He added. "As a precaution." Rinn was surprised but accepted the weapon.

Rinn and Cat bounded across the hillside, swinging their baskets. Warm sunshine made the girls forget about the chill in the air. They found the hawthorn bushes easily, they were the only patches of color in the brown, late-autumn landscape. Rinn and Cat carefully teased the bright red berries from the thorny bush tangles. It did not take long to fill two baskets to overflowing. Cat playfully stuck berries on the tips of her claws and chased Rinn around the bushes. The two laughed and panted, their breath visible in the frosty air. They hefted their baskets and headed back, never knowing that they were being watched.

At home, Rinn and Cat warmed up by the hearth whose fire burned continuously during these cold autumn days. Rinn fished out a large pot and dumped the berries into it. She added several pitchers of water and swung the pot over the fire. She left it to cook, occasionally returning to stir it with a long wooden ladle. Her father came over to investigate.

"Making jelly?" He peeked into the pot.

"No." Rinn fussed over her cooking. "I'm making paint."

"That much? Are you going to paint the whole house?" Marshal smirked.

"Cat and I want to decorate our room." Rinn hooked the boiling pot away from the fire and stirred it.

"You won't need all of that for one room." Marshal squinted as he thought. "I'll make you a deal: you use half of the berries for paint, and I'll make the rest into jelly for dinner."

"Jelly takes forever." Rinn complained.

"Nah." Marshal waved his hand. "It's so cold outside the jelly will set up in no time." Rinn agreed and her father strained the mixture and divided it into equal batches. Rinn added flour to her portion and mixed it into paste. Marshal added sugar to his and cooked it a bit further. After her paint had cooled, Rinn brought it to her room and showed it to Cat. She demonstrated how to dip paint brushes made of crushed twigs into the mixture and apply it to the walls. Cat handled the long thin brushes with great difficulty. She finally gave up and stuck both paws into the paint and smothered the walls in pawprints, squealing in delight as she spread pawprint polka-dots everywhere.

Rinn painted meticulously, artfully drawing warriors and maidens standing atop castle walls. Winged horses flew in the sky while menacing dragons slithered near the floor. Her monotone mural filled up much of one wall. Anywhere Rinn did not draw, Cat filled the blank space with her pawprints. After dinner, the girls stayed awake painting late into the night, fueled by the sugar buzz from Marshal's hawthorn jelly. The next morning, he found them sleeping on the floor in their paint stained clothes. Seeing the wall-sized mural they had created, he let them sleep in.

::

"I'm really impressed with the pictures you girls drew." Marshal took another helping of the meat that reminded Rinn of venison. Everyone sat around the table enjoying lunch. Tomin joined them for the first time, his recovery progressing nicely. He gripped a spoon in his bandaged hand and fed himself soup.

Cat rocked in her chair. "Isn't our painting great? Rinn drew all the people. I made all the dots." She held up her paws, still stained rosy red.

"I'm most impressed with the animals around the fireplace." Marshal added.

"What animals?" Rinn cocked her head sideways. Both girls slipped off their chairs and inspected the fireplace. Marching from the floor to the mantle, a miniature menagerie of forest animals pranced, flapped, and strutted up and down. A wreath of painted foliage wove itself around the mantle extending up to a beaming sun painted above the hearth. The realism and intricacy of the figures amazed Rinn. "I didn't draw this."

All the heads at the table turned to each other, except one, which was staring at the floor. Marshal posed the question. "Felsic, did you draw those pictures?"

Felsic never raised his eyes. "I hated to see good paint go to waste." Molo inspected the artwork carefully. Even Tomin limped over to see his former servant's creations, gawking at the tiny parade of animals. A broad smile broke across Molo's face. He placed a very large hand on the dwarf's back.

"Tomorrow, you're coming with me to the forge." Molo's smile was truly terrifying. "I haven't worked with a Dverg in ages."

"Dverg?" Rinn inquired.

"There are many races of dwarves." Marshal leaned in and whispered. "The Dverg are gifted artists. It's a wonder that one should end up as a slave." Felsic shrank away from the attention, trying to silently eat his meal. Rinn regarded the dwarf in a different light. When she lived in the Imperium, dwarf goods were always for sale at the marketplace. The dwarf merchants traveled in caravans and kept to themselves—Imperial citizens never associated with them. But Rinn had always been bothered by the fact that dwarves could make such wonderful crafts and still live in abject poverty. Officially, slavery was not legal in the empire, but it was common knowledge that the very wealthy forced dwarves to work on their massive estates.

After dinner, Felsic found Rinn in her bedroom. He handed her several paint brushes, delicately crafted with soft bristles. "I never had a chance to thank you, for what you did." He hesitated as he spoke. Rinn graciously accepted the brushes, thumbing the soft bristles absently. They felt strangely familiar. Unexpectedly, Felsic reached out and grabbed Rinn's hands. "I do not know what power you used to free me—but I beseech you, good lady, free my brother." The dwarf knelt down on the floor, not a far distance for him to travel. He begged Rinn. "My brother was sold into slavery just as I was. He's somewhere in these very uplands. If we could find him, you could break the spell that binds him."

Rinn reeled back from the dwarf's request. Rescuing someone from a mostly passed out drunk was easy, but Rinn had no idea where Felsic's brother was or who held him captive. She wanted to help, but common sensibility and self-preservation restrained her.

"Please, my lady, save my brother." The dwarf lay prostate at her feet. Rinn did not know what to do. She wanted to help, but she did not know how.

"When do we leave?" Marshal interrupted, leaning against the doorframe. Surprise and hope played across Rinn's face. She rushed over and hugged her father. The dwarf rose, tears flowing down his enormous face. Pulling out a handkerchief, he blew his giant nose with a sound that rattled the walls.

::

"It has been six years since I last saw my brother." Felsic recounted his story over breakfast the next morning. He described how he and his brother were captured by Kuhraaki slavers who raided the western coasts of Murstein. The pair were smuggled across the Egesian Sea to Sevria, bound for the Imperial slave markets. Rinn listened, but all the strange place names confused her. Felsic continued his tale. When the slave trade route broke down, and the brothers were hastily auctioned off to merchants traveling down the Desolate Coast.

Felsic had no idea who held his brother, but he remembered the insignia of the soldier who bought him. He drew the design using a stick of charcoal on the tabletop, Marshal recognized the insignia—it belonged to one of the wilderness dukes. He reassured the dwarf that he would help him find his brother, Felsic hugged him so tightly that both their faces turned red. Rinn had never seen a dwarf so happy.

::

Winter was looming and with more mouths to feed, Marshal tried to stretch what food they did have. Seoras was willing to sell food from his farm at reasonable prices, his harvests had been plentiful, and his grain stores were overflowing. He was happy to be rid of the excess, he did not want to attract the attention of Clanmorris. Bos and Lutra made regular deliveries in an old donkey cart, trading grains and vegetables for fresh fish and animal pelts. Rinn helped carry the heavy sacks to the cellar. Once Molo's forge was operable, the boys occasionally brought items that needed smithing. They often stayed and watched Molo and Felsic work. Bos tried his hand at hammering iron, with some success. Lutra followed Catherine around most of the time, trying to win her affection, without much success.

Marshal decided to journey to the tavern through the southern forest. He loaded an a-frame sled with furs and a few artistic pieces Felsic had crafted. Rinn worried as she watched him depart. She wanted to go with him, to protect him in case he ran into any bandits, but he assured her that he would travel faster on his own, and speed was his safest option. It did not keep Rinn from fretting the entire day while he was away. He returned that evening with a sled full of foodstuffs and two firkins of ale.

Molo and Rinn fished every day, bundled in warm furs against the cold. Marshal and Cat hunted in the afternoon, keeping the household with a fresh supply of meat. Along with root vegetables and dried grain from the farm, they had a reasonable diet. Now that Molo's house was complete, construction began on a wooden watchtower. Bos and Lutra helped chop trees and Marshal mixed a batch of sealing salts to weatherproof the support beams. In just a few days, a rickety tower soared over the palisade walls. Cat raced up and down the structure like a squirrel, happy to have a new playground. Seoras showed up one day himself, to see the house and the progress being made. Rinn proudly toured him around the property, her own private fortress on a hill. A funny thought struck her: now that she was used to the wilderness, she was happier living here than in her tiny house back in the Imperium.

Chapter 15

C at scurried across the roof of the rickety watch tower, chasing invisible foes. Rinn reluctantly climbed the wobbly ladder to her, the wooden tower swaying with each step. Reaching the top, she clung tightly to the railing. Cat's upside-down head appeared from above.

"Hi." Cat flipped down onto the platform floor. "What are you doing up here?"

"Looking for you." Rinn would not relinquish her death grip on the railing. Cat rocked happily on the pads of her feet, the movement shook the tower terribly, and Rinn thought she was going to be sick. Rinn tried to calm her adoptive sister. "Cat, stop moving. I have a question." Cat sat down on her haunches and pointed her ears forward. Rinn reached into the pouch around her waist and pulled out the paintbrushes Felsic had given her. Cat nodded her head and smiled, showing her two little fangs. The bristles were the same colors as Cat's fur. "I thought so. This is your hair, isn't?"

"Guilty!" Cat pointed a claw to herself with a feline laugh.

"You and the dwarf are working together." Rinn squinted.

"I like him. He's funny." Cat curled up on the tower floor. "I heard him pacing around the other night. We had so much extra paint, so I offered him some. He said he didn't have any brushes, but we fixed that."

"Sounds like you had a good time." Rinn finally realized just how spectacular the view from the tower was. Strategically placed at the highest point on the hill, the observation platform afforded an unobstructed view of the entire landscape. Rinn could see the sparse evergreen forest to the north that was her father's favorite hunting ground. To the east a dense hardwood forest stretched off into the distance, slowly shedding its autumn leaves. Beyond lay a broken, rocky land leading up into the mountains. To the west, a winding river snaked north and south. Rinn could see a caravan of tiny people plodding along its banks. Smoke was visible off in the distance. "Something's wrong." Rinn told Cat to go fetch her father. Cat bolted down the tower at a dizzying speed, Rinn had to avert her eyes.

Close to midday, the refugees from Seoras' farm arrived. Marshal and Molo ushered them through the gate. The weary farm workers wore ripped and burnt clothes that reeked of smoke. Rinn ran up to Bos and Lutra with Cat close behind.

"What happened?" Rinn saw bruises and cuts on the farm boys. Lutra limped slowly and did not even raise his head to look at Cat.

"Clanmorris." Bos uttered with absolute hatred. "They attacked our farm, burned everything. Mom's hurt. Most of the animals were killed or stolen."

Rinn gasped. "That's what happened at Tomin's farm. What's going on?"

::

Marshal assembled the injured in the main hall, laid out on tables, cots, or the floor. Seoras sustained a gash to his shoulder, but his wife, a rotund woman named Gallina, suffered the worst injury, a long, deep cut to her thigh. Many of the farm hands suffered burns and one had an arrow wound to his upper arm. Even Bos and Lutra's younger brother Kelan had been injured, holding his left arm painfully. Molossus went straight to work on Gallina's leg. Seoras held his wife's hand as the giant cleaned the wound, Clive watching from an adjacent table. Felsic stood behind Molo, assisting the oversized surgeon. Even though Molo's hands were enormous, he cleaned and stitched the gash with the careful skill of an artisan. Marshal took little Kelan aside and made a splint for his broken arm.

"They came in the middle of the night." Seoras lamented as his shoulder wound was being sewn up. "With fire and swords they came, burning my home and slaughtering my animals." Tears of rage flowed freely. "Those monsters tried to kill us." He buried his face in his good arm and sobbed bitterly.

Rinn sided up to her father. "This is what happened at Tomin's place." Her father nodded once, completely emotionless as he worked. Rinn grabbed his hand. "Daddy, are we going to be attacked, too?"

He said nothing.

Everyone worked to help each other. Even Tomin, the recovering drunk, used his experience at being a patient to help care for the burned. Rinn boiled water and prepared herbs while Cat tore strips of cloth for bandages. Once all the wounded were treated, the commotion in the main hall settled down. Cat curled up in a ball in front of the fireplace, and Rinn rested her head in her arms on a table in the kitchen, exhausted. Marshal nursed a mug of ale, staring blankly into the fireplace. Molossus entered, drying his hands with a towel.

"What's your plan?" He poured himself a drink.

"My plan?" Marshal swallowed. "I'm not the soldier of rank here."

"No. But you are the tactician." Molo locked eyes with Marshal. "So, come up with a plan." Marshal sighed and finished off his mug. With a gentle shake he roused his sleeping daughter. She sat up, tangles of blond hair falling in her face.

"Rinn, tell me everything you remember about the attack on Tomin's farm." He systematically questioned everyone in the house. He even listened to little Kelan, the nine-year-old with his arm in a sling. He reconvened with Molo and Rinn in the kitchen later that afternoon. Lutra was assigned watch duty in the rickety tower, and Cat kept him distracted. Bos and the able-bodied farmhands guarded the palisade entrance with spears. The few animals that came with the refugees were moved inside the palisade walls. Marshal roughly sketched the property on the kitchen tabletop with a piece of charcoal.

"We sit on high ground, reasonably protected." Marshal added marks for terrain as he spoke. "The clan seems to use the same methods each time they attack, so we should know what to expect. They will come at night. They'll first use fire to scare the animals and burn the buildings. Riders on horseback will corral anyone attempting to escape. Our only safe option is to hide."

Molo scratched his mess of a beard. "Something doesn't add up. They steal cattle and horses alright, but they don't loot the buildings. They burn them down, valuables included. They aren't raiding, it's almost as if they are looking for something."

"Or someone." Marshal corrected. "I think the clansmen are being used. I don't know by who, but I have my suspicions."

Rinn's eyes widened. "You don't mean?" She covered her mouth to keep from speaking aloud what she feared to say.

"Yes." Marshal stood soldier straight, unwavering. "These aren't simple bandits. These are raiding parties, and I think they are looking for Cat."

Molo growled like a bear. "That tattooed monstrosity is behind this."

Terrifying memories jostled Rinn, the lamenting screams Cat made when the tattooed villain shackled her. Rinn relived her anger and vicious sword strike which should have cut the man in two, but instead had almost no effect. Rinn felt so small and helpless, a little girl in a room full of adults. She backed up against a wall and trembled, hugging herself.

Marshal stood and in a loud voice addressed everyone in the main hall. "Clanmorris has preyed on innocent farmers and their families long enough. They have yet to meet organized resistance." He planted his knife into the table for emphasis. "They are certain to show up here, and we will make them regret it." The room shook with cheering and applause.

::

Hilltop prepared for war. Able-bodied farmhands mended and strengthened the palisade wall. Men and women crafted rudimentary weapons, armor, and shields. Molossus and Felsic presented Rinn with a gift, a vest made from braided bob feathers. It shimmered in the sun with rippling shades of iridescent blue and green. Molo had not been able to work the material effectively, but Felsic skillfully weaved the steel-like barbs into a fabric, and Molo forged it into a wearable armor. Rinn tried the vest on, sliding it over her dress. The armor was lighter than cloth, but it moved like a rusty door hinge. She guessed it would take time to get used to it. She hung the armor on a peg in her room and joined her father in the main hall.

Molo and Felsic sat at a trestle table opposite Marshal. "How do you plan to protect little Cat?" The Margot slept soundly, curled up in her usual spot in front of the fireplace.

"The cellar has only one entrance, Cat will be safest there. I won't risk her in general melee." Marshal motioned to the sleeping ball of fur.

"Good plan." Molo nodded. "How do we defend the house against fire attacks?"

A devious smile broke across Marshal's face. "We turn it back on them." The dangerous glint in his eyes frightened Rinn, the whole situation sent a chill through her. She fought against feathered dragons and grashels, even defended Cat from the tattooed villain. But the thought of killing people, actual people, even the idiotic clansmen, churned Rinn's stomach. She listened as her father described the recipe for a flammable concoction: fire salts, cooking oil, grain alcohol, and tree resin. Molo ventured out to collect pine tree sap, and Rinn was tasked with heating a large batches of cooking oil.

She stirred the pot mechanically, trying not the think about what she was making, or how it would be used.

::

Rinn left the kitchen stinking of the awful liquid she helped create. She met Cat as she scampered down the watch tower. Rinn hoped her cheerful sister would help lighten her mood. She called out a greeting. Cat turned and Rinn saw huge tears in her eyes. The feline girl rushed to her and grabbed onto her tightly.

"Lutra saw him." Cat sobbed, shaking with tears.

Rinn struggled to console her hysterical sister. "Who? Who did he see?"

Cat's whiskers hung low, and tears dribbled down them like dew. "When they attacked, he saw him." She buried her head in Rinn's shoulder. "Yallakh. He's coming for me."

"Who's Yallakh?" Rinn questioned.

"The tattooed man." Cat squeaked.

"Dad thought he might be behind this." Cat nodded her head into Rinn's shoulder. Rinn held her sister close. Rage boiled away her fear, and her hands longed to hold a spear. She swore to protect Cat, even if she had to kill every red-headed bandit and the tattooed man herself.

Chapter 16

T he attack came at night, just as Marshal had predicted. Lutra signaled from the watch tower and the homestead came alive. Rinn had slept fitfully, the strange conversation she had with her father the night before haunted her dreams. They had spoken privately in his bedroom. She remembered sitting on his bed full of anxiety, like a child about to be scolded. He sat on a stool opposite her, equally as uncomfortable.

"Rinn. I need you to fight." The resolution in his voice was betrayed by the regret in his eyes. "This may be hard to understand, but you're the one who rescued Cat. You insisted we take her in. Now, her captors are coming for her. You also rescued Tomin and Felsic after their home was burned to the ground." Marshal had to take several breaths to hold back the emotion that threatened to overwhelm him. "Right now, we need a Sigillum—a protector. That is what you do, it's who you are. I should never ask this of you, but I need your help."

Marshal's sheathed sword leaned in the corner, Marshal reached for it and drew the blade. The metal of the sword had been burned away leaving a charred and crumbling ruin behind. This was the sword Rinn used against the tattooed man, and now it was worthless. Her father had always loved that sword, a memento from his soldiering days.

Marshal touched the ruined blade. "Your power burns through metal much faster than your mother's ever did. She did not fight often, but when she did, her acies could last for weeks."

"Achious?" Rinn stumbled over the odd word.

"Acies—reverent blade." Marshal tried to explain.

"I don't understand." Rinn's frustration soured her voice.

"I know." Marshal returned the sword to its sheath and he sat down on the bed next to his daughter. "This is not magic, not like the sorcerers use. This power is a divine blessing."

"A blessing? Which god did this to me?" Rinn felt like a rabbit trapped in a snare. "Was it Sidus? Or Parma, the guardian god?"

"Doubtful." Marshal awkwardly tried to hold his daughter's hands. "I have seen your mother's acies carve through a Parma shield wall." Rinn was stunned. Parma soldiers were supposed to be unstoppable, their enchanted shields unbreakable. "This is not the work of Imperial gods we know."

"Who, then? Who is doing this to me?" Hot tears blurred Rinn's vision.

"I don't know." Marshal admitted, hugging his daughter close. "I never told you about your mother's abilities, because every blessing comes with a cost. I wanted you to live out your life without the burden of these powers. But you are who you are—someone who can't sit by and watch people suffer. You are a protector. And now we need you and your abilities."

"I'm not a fighter." Rinn sulked. Her father mussed her hair.

"You are more like your mother than you know. She taught me a few words, and I was supposed to pass them on to you when you were ready." Marshal rose from his chair and stretched his arms. "Well, if I'm asking you for help, then you must be ready." Rinn looked at him expectedly.

"Well?" She demanded. "Tell me already!"

"Yes, my lady." He bowed graciously.

::

Rinn gathered with the others in the courtyard behind the palisade gate. Everyone had been issued weapons made by Molo and Felsic. Marshal had sent scavengers to scrounge all the metal they could from remains of Tomin's farm. Rinn hefted a well-balanced spear with a long iron tip. Molo even showed her how to throw it, but cautioned her against it, because it was the only weapon she had. Her father taught her the word to summon her acies power willingly. Rinn held off saying it, knowing that her weapon would last at most a few hours before it turned to ash. In her head she recited the new words her father taught her, trying to determine how to use them. Her father was confident she would know when the time was right.

Molo stepped through the crowd cursing. "Rinn. Where's your armor?" Rinn realized she was still wearing her everyday clothes. Everyone else in the courtyard sported some sort of protection: leather chest guards, shoulder pads, or metal helmets. She would have laughed at their motley appearance if she was not so embarrassed herself, showing up to a battle in a dress. Cat arrived wearing her sparring vest and hunting pants. She handed Molo Rinn's dragon feather vest. The giant hmphed. "At least someone here has some sense." He strapped the iridescent armor onto Rinn, tugging firmly on the straps. Rinn shrieked at the tightness. "Little cat, get back in that cellar." He shooed the feline away. "And stay there."

Marshal strode into the courtyard with orders for everyone. "Clanmorris will be here soon. Our tower guard counted about twenty men, some on horseback." The refugees shuffled nervously. "If we work together, we can get through this. The clansmen will start by threatening us. Don't yell back. We want them to think we're scared. Next, they'll assault the palisade wall with fire. We have a surprise ready for them. Once that fails, they'll try to breech the gate. This's where we must stand and defend ourselves. They outnumber us, but they can only come through a few at a time. It'll be just like grashel hunting." He winked at his daughter. "We'll catch them off-guard as they charge." Marshal called out to Catherine as she walked away. "Cat, your duty is to remain safe. Your refuge is the cellar. Stay there until the fighting is over." She nodded her feline head as she descended the stairs. Marshal addressed the rest of the crowd. "Leave most of the fighting to Molo and myself. Defend yourselves if you must, but no heroics. Be safe and live to see tomorrow."

In the distance, war cries mingled with the sound of horses' hooves. Everyone in the courtyard moved to their assigned positions. Lutra scampered down the watch tower, leaving Clive behind in his place. Marshal climbed onto the roof of the stone house, readying his bow. Raiders burst out of the forest line and riders galloped around the hilltop in a battle frenzy, hooting and yelling. From beyond the palisade wall, a mocking voice derided the feeble refugees. Rinn could not see much in the dark, but she recognized the arrogant snarl of Egan, the bandit leader. He shouted a stream of insults and threats.

"Your flimsy fence won't do you any good. Come out like good little sheep before we come in slaughtering." Egan howled like an alpha wolf calling his pack. "These murderous bastards won't wait long." The night was filled with the roar of bandit raiders, mocking and laughing the home's meager defenses. Rinn wrapped her hands around her pilum and repeated in her head one of the new words her father taught her. She focused on the gate—her job was to stick anything that tried to come through. To her right, Bos hefted a one-handed axe and a wooden shield. Tomin and two farmhands flanked her left with swords and shields. Felsic and Molo crouched near the palisade wall armed with urns filled with Marshal's gruesome concoction. Seoras remained inside the stone house with his injured wife, injured son, and the other refugees who were not fit to fight. He was the absolute last line of defense if all went poorly.

A single flaming arrow sailed across the roof of the house. Rinn could see the silhouette of her father, and so could the bandits. Egan shouted to the figure on the roof. "Come down and open that gate before you get yourself and your family killed."

"I want my horse back." Marshal taunted from the rooftop.

"Kill him." Egan signaled to several men on horseback around him. They loosed multiple volleys of flaming arrows at the house. Shooting into the dark at an elevation, none of their arrows came close to hitting Marshal, though a few stuck into the roof timbers. Marshal stamped them out and then launched a few shots of his own. The bandits were well-lit, stationary targets on horseback, easy pickings for an experienced bowman. Two of the mounted archers fell from their saddles stuck with arrows. The rest retreated out of range.

An incensed Egan barked orders to his men (from a safe distance away). "Burn it down, lads." Raiders on foot with torches advanced to the palisade. They gathered at a vulnerable place in the palisade wall, one in which Molo had removed a few timbers to make it appear damaged and weak. They moved to set the wooden posts aflame. Molo reached over the wall with one hand and spiked a pottery urn on the ground at their feet. Pungent vapors oozed from the broken urn and quickly ignited, bathing everyone in fire. Screaming redheads batted their arms and legs trying to extinguish the flames. To add to the confusion, Marshal picked off another horse archer with his bow. Felsic doused any burning palisade poles with muddy water. Stubbornly, several of the bandits attempted to burn the palisade wall a second time, only to meet with another volley of flammable liquid courtesy of Molo.

The bandits quickly abandoned their fire tactic and assembled outside the palisade gate. Egan shouted new orders and Rinn could hear axes biting into the hinges of the gate. For the briefest moment, she was impressed that the bandits were smart enough to chop through the hinges and not the door itself. As the stout gate began to buckle and fall, Rinn filled her pilum with the will to protect her friends and family, especially Cat. A metallic smell filled the air as the black iron of the weapon turned bright silver and flared with a brilliant green light. Tomin and the farmhands gawked at

Rinn, Bos stepped uneasily away from her. Rinn stood resolute as the first bandit rushed headlong through open gate. In her mind, she tried to picture grashels charging at her and not people. She plunged her pilum into the chest of the first bandit, feeling no resistance. The spear drove straight through the man, exiting out his back. The bandit never uttered a word, he merely fell forward, dead. Rinn spun her glowing spear tip in a figure eight, just as Molo had drilled into her, freeing her weapon from the dead bandit's body. She fought back tears and braced for the next attack.

Three bandits fell to Rinn's unnatural strikes, but more stampeded through the gate. Soon, Bos, Tomin, and the farmhands were engaged in a pitched melee as clansmen poured into the courtyard. Molo and Felsic joined in the fray. A bandit who was getting the better of Tomin was struck in the chest by a thrown Clive. Felsic beat his smithing hammer at the bandit's unprotected legs while Molo swung an over-sized club at their heads. Rinn backed up to appraise the combat in progress. The bandits had stopped pouring through the open gate and were actually being pushed back. Molo, Felsic, and Bos overpowered their foes, while Tomin and the farmhands were at least holding their own. A surge of hope lifted Rinn, until she saw the figures on the rooftop—her father and the tattooed man locked in deadly combat.

Chapter 17

R inn watched helplessly as her father fought for his life on the roof of her hilltop home. She could not see the tattoos covering his attacker's body, but she recognized him. His tall, lithe frame was draped in cloth ribbons, like a mummy, and he moved his sword with unnatural speed and strength. Marshal retreated as he parried one vicious attack after another, trying to keep space between himself and the murderous slaver. But he was running out of roof. Rinn hefted her pilum spear to throw it; however, she knew she had no chance of hitting the tattooed man at such a great distance.

"Yallakh!" A shrill voice broke through the crisp night air. The rooftop combatants paused, and both turned to see a lone feline girl standing defiantly in the courtyard. "I'm right here, demon." Cat flexed her claws. With impossible grace, the tattooed man leaped from the rooftop and hurtled downward. He landed in a graceful crouch and rose to his full height. Without fear or hesitation, Rinn wedged herself between Cat and the sinister swordsman. She trained the glowing edge of her pilum at the villain.

"Out of my way, tiny witch." The evil man hissed like a snake.

"You cannot have my sister." Rinn's resolution made the tip of her weapon glow even more fiercely. Cat poked her head out from behind Rinn and bared her fangs at the awful man.

"Sister?" Yallakh cackled. "That thing doesn't belong to you, selfish speck. You don't even know what it is."

"She's my family, and you cannot have her." Rinn braced herself for an attack. In her mind, she felt a word echoing, ready to be released.

"Suit yourself." The tattooed man slashed an efficient path through Rinn, but not before she could whisper the word her father taught her.

"Beorgan."

As soon as the word left her lips, the air around her crackled. Yallakh's wicked sword bent against an invisible wall with a violent sizzle. Rinn and Cat were bathed in the green light of a dome-like barrier, a woven tapestry of translucent triangles and swirls. Rinn marveled at the beauty of the intricate design, she could not believe she was capable of creating something so beautiful. The tattooed man struck the green wall several more times in frustration, further mangling his sword. He finally threw down his worthless weapon and reached out to the barrier with his tattooed hands, the patterns rippled at his touch. Rinn and Cat stepped away slowly, the domed shield moved with them.

"What is this magic?" The tattooed man studied the impediment, engrossed in curiosity. The shield almost seemed to stick to his fingers when he pulled them away. While his attention was distracted, Rinn took the chance to strike, thrusting her pilum at his midsection, tearing away the bandages that wrapped around him. Yallakh dodged backwards, but Rinn had clearly made contact, there was a green line crossing his abdomen. He reached down and felt his stomach. "You little minx."

Rinn advanced again, forcing the man to fall back a few steps. She did not see fear in his eyes, just cold calculation. He paced around her barrier like an animal trapped inside a cage. Rinn knew she could not best him in combat, but she had an idea. She herded him towards the cellar door. Cat stayed close as the two moved across the yard in unison, the barrier moving with them. Rinn kept the villain at bay with the point of her pilum, but he took every opportunity to press against the barrier, bending it.

Molo crept up behind the villain, impressing Rinn that someone so large could move so stealthily. The ink-covered fiend was not fooled, he spun around drew two daggers and faced the giant. Molo raised Clive in his right hand, focusing his purple eye directly on the tattooed man. Transfixed by the stone, Yallakh dropped to his knees, his wicked knives falling from his hands. Rinn swore she saw Clive blink. The tattoos covering the fiend's body rippled like water. Yallakh held his head in his hands and let out a feral scream. Even in agony, he could not tear his eyes away from the round stone.

"You've been very naughty." Molo lifted the screaming man and tossed him down the stairs into the cellar. The shield around Rinn and Cat dissipated into a cloud of green mist. Molo hauled several enormous rocks from the yard and stacked them over the cellar entrance like a burial cairn. Rinn surveyed the courtyard, looking for more bandits, but it was eerily empty.

"Where did everyone go?" Rinn asked Bos and Lutra who were standing a short distance away.

"They all fled." Bos hesitated, backing up a bit. "When you conjured that thing." He could barely finish his sentence.

"Rinn. That was awesome." Cat threw her arms around her adoptive sister and rubbed cheeks with her. Cat's whiskers tickled Rinn. "Yallakh didn't stand a chance."

Lutra was aghast. "You know him?" Everyone stared at Cat. Even Marshal, who had climbed down from the roof. Felsic waddled over with Molo and waited for her to answer. Cat drew circles in the ground with her back paw.

"Cat?" Marshal insisted.

"Yes, I know him." Cat spoke to the ground, eyes downcast. "He's a hunter for the Khuraak."

Felsic dropped his hammer. "You escaped from the Slave Nation?"

Lutra bit his bottom lip. "Cat was a slave?" He reached out to touch her, but she was some distance away. The situation deteriorated into idle prattle as everyone involved in the skirmish discussed this. The numerous conversations made Rinn's head spin. Frustrated, she raised her voice.

"Hold On!" She barked at the crowd. "Who are the Khuraak?"

Marshal hushed the crowd with a gesture. "The Khuraak are a seafaring people." He spoke dispassionately, like a military instructor. "They come from lands beyond the Egesian Sea."

"The Egesian Sea?" Rinn grimaced. "Isn't it supposed to be full of monsters and pirates?"

"The Khuraak are the monsters and pirates, Rinn." Molo explained, brushing off Clive. "They probably sent the hunter to find and retrieve Cat."

"But the sea is so far away." Rinn raised her eyebrows. "How did they find her all the way out here?"

"Yallakh can find anything." Cat muttered absently.

Marshal recounted his own theory. "Do you remember the bard we met at the inn? I think he recognized Cat. He had probably seen a Margot before and knew someone would be looking for her." Lutra mouthed the word Margot. Marshal continued. "He likely sold the information to Clanmorris who encountered the hunter. That might explain why the clansmen and the hunter were working together, attacking farms in the area. They were looking for Cat."

Rinn silently vowed to never trust bards again. Inside she was torn, by rescuing Cat, she had caused so much suffering. But she could not abandon her feline sister. The idea of sending her back into slavery was unimaginable. Rinn would fight for her sister, but the cost of freedom suddenly terrified her.

"Will the slavers come here?" Bos directed the question to Marshal. Marshal thought for a moment before answering.

"The Khuraak do not travel well overland." Marshal deduced. "It would be impossible for them to cross the Roinn Mountains in large numbers. They're sailors, not soldiers."

Molo stared at the boulders piled over the cellar entrance. "They must have trusted this Yallakh implicitly, to send him off alone after such a valuable prize."

"Yallakh never fails." Cat muttered.

Molo shoved Clive under his arm. "Well, if he never fails that should buy us some time. The slavers will wait for him to report back."

"The first snows of winter will fall soon." Marshal added, scanning the skies as if he could see the snow far, far away.

"That'll make Cat even harder to track." Molo smiled.

"So, what do we do now?" Rinn planted the butt of her pilum in the ground. The iron tip no longer glowed green and was already starting to crumble into metallic ash.

"We'll offer shelter to everyone who has been affected by these attacks. We'll help them make it through winter. If we pool our resources, we can survive this." Marshal checked on everyone involved in the fighting. For the farmers, the combat ended quickly with only minor injuries. The bandits were not so lucky, seven of their number laid dead, three outside the palisade and four more at the gate. Marshal arranged for graves to be dug near the bottom of the hill. Rinn watched in misery as the bodies of the dead were dragged away, consumed by the knowledge that she herself had killed half of them.

::

After a day of hard labor, the residents of Hilltop gathered in the stone house for a celebratory feast. Seoras raised a mug to honor Rinn's bravery against the bandits and the terrible tattooed man. Rinn did not know how to handle praise, especially when most of the farmers were clearly afraid of her and her powers. Roasted musk deer was paraded in by Molo and Felsic, still on the spit. Rinn had seen deer in Sevria, but this one had long fangs instead of antlers. Marshal carved the meat and served all the guests. Everyone ate and drank merrily, except Tomin, who was left to watch over their cellar guest. A charitable soul brought him food, but neglected his request for ale. Inside the warm feast hall, Arlin produced a small fife and played a lively song. Dancers quickly filled the floor. Cat spun around in circles with Lutra, and even little Kelan bounced along, merrily ignoring his broken arm. Rinn was astonished to see how people could enjoy themselves so soon after losing their homes and livelihood.

Once the festivities began to die down, Molo and Felsic approached Marshal and Rinn in the kitchen. Molo opened the conversation. "If we are going to continue to fight, we are going to need better weapons and armor."

"You know where to get them?" Marshal inquired with great interest.

"I do." Felsic briefly glanced at Rinn. "The Dukes of the Wild. Molo thinks he knows where my brother is. We can rescue him and get supplies at the same time."

Molo folded his arms. "I know the insignia of the man who bought Felsic's brother. He's known as the Mountain Duke, holed up in his cliffside fortress. It'll be a tough journey, and I don't think he'll part with his property easily."

Marshal tilted his head and smirked. "It can't hurt to ask."

Chapter 18

Rinn's boots crunched through the snow. She wore traveling pants under her heaviest dress and a thick woolen cloak on top of that and she was still shivering. When the snow first started to fall, Rinn thought it was beautiful, blanketing the countryside in pure white. But after two days of travel through the frozen landscape, Rinn had as much love for snow as Cat did. Her hands and feet were numb, and her nose never stopped running. Felsic led Marshal, Bos, Cat and Rinn northeast, beyond the charred remains of several burned down farmhouses. Molo stayed behind at Hilltop to watch over the prisoner and organize the refugees. New temporary houses were planned, and extensions to the palisade wall would be needed to accommodate the growing community.

When night fell, Marshal showed everyone how to find tree wells, areas under thick pine trees where the snow did not fall. They slept in these hollows, wrapped in bedrolls covered with warm blankets. Cat and Rinn shared a bedroll under a large pine. Even though Cat's fur was wet from the snow, Rinn hugged her tightly, feeling warmth in her hands and feet for the first time that day. Marshal and Felsic alternated night watches, though nothing seemed to be moving in this silent world of ice.

The next day, the party continued their trek through the snowfields, heading further north, higher up into the mountains. The constant cold nibbled away at Rinn's sanity, the glare off the endless white blinded her vision. She lost track of time, marching lifelessly through the snowy highlands. Rinn began to forget what warmth felt like. She tried to recall sunny days laying in fields of wildflowers, but she could not seem to picture it correctly. When she was just about to scream, Felsic pointed off in the distance.

"There." He announced. Perched on a rocky crest between two mountain peaks, stood a solitary, stone fortress. Two squat, square towers flanked a large walled compound made of the same stone as the mountains themselves. A massive iron gate dominated the entrance. Driven snow and ice covered the arched stone bridge leading to the fortress. As they approached, Rinn wondered if they could reach the fortress at all. Felsic seemed undaunted, climbing onto the icy snow bank, proceeding to the great iron door as if he were walking on solid ground. As Rinn watched him ascend, she realized that no guards patrolled the walls, no one hailed from the windows above the gate. From the outside, the fortress appeared to be an empty shell.

Felsic reached the gate, partially buried in ice. He clambered up the snowdrift until he could reach a second story window. Struggling, he managed to somehow squeeze through the narrow opening. He reappeared at the top of the tower and threw down a length of rope. The rest of the party scaled the ice wall using the rope, except Cat, who climbed up in her own unique way. Strong winds buffeted Rinn as she neared the top. From the walkway over the gate, she could see the entire low country, giant forests dotting the snow-covered plains like patches of brown moss. Lakes were capped by a veneer of ice which glistened in the midday sun. Rinn thought she could almost see the Vallum, the sprawling stone wall that marked the eastern boundary of the Sevrian Empire.

Marshal ushered the party into a tower door and down a flight of stone stairs. He navigated through a series of complex winding hallways connecting the buildings. Rinn was happy to be out of the bitter mountain winds, but the rooms she moved through made her uneasy. Fully furnished living quarters were draped in cobwebs as thick as blankets. She waded through a carpet of thick dust as she walked. She felt like she was wandering through a mausoleum. The other members of the party seemed just as unsettled.

Bos whispered to Marshal. "Have you been here before?"

Marshal waved a hand. "These Imperial forts are all built the same. The Legion values consistency over creativity." He led them into an armory hall lined with stacks of shields and rows of spears. Weapon racks in the center of the room held hundreds of swords and daggers, all dusty with disuse. Rinn had never seen so many weapons in one place. She carefully tiptoed past the racks, trying not to think about the destruction these weapons could wreak in the hands of a trained army. Cat noisily knocked over a row of spears, and Bos and Felsic shushed her while they tried to set things right. Marshal motioned for them to be quiet as he led the party on.

They entered warmer parts of the fortress, with swept flagstone floors and polished furniture. The inviting smell of burning firewood permeated the hallway. Rinn was filled with an unquenchable desire to sit by a nice, warm fire. Cat sniffed at the air and she slinked behind Marshal. "Someone is coming." She pointed her paw down a dark corridor. Footsteps echoed in the stillness. Everyone except Marshal drew their weapons. A dwarf appeared, carrying a lamp.

"The Duke will see you now." Rinn saw a familiar black metal shackle peeking above the dwarf's right boot. Only the briefest glance passed between Felsic and their dwarf escort. He led the party to a large eating hall furnished with orderly rows of wooden tables. Everyone had their weapons confiscated and placed in a large chest outside the hall. They were escorted to the far end of the room, where an elderly man sat on a high-backed chair, eating in solitude. Two dwarves stood at attention on the wall behind him, brandishing short poleaxes. Rinn's party was brought before the dining man. Rinn had never seen anyone look so old, wrinkles upon wrinkles buried his eyebrows and drooped from his cheeks. His hair and skin were ashen gray, and gray rings clouded the brown of his eyes.

The escort dwarf announced. "Lord Duke Kapros."

"Ave, Lord Duke." Marshal saluted with his right hand. "Equis Marshal Amali at your service."

"Spare me, Equis." The Duke bit into a mountain plum, its juices running down the sides of his mouth. "We have no need for horsemen in the mountains."

"My apologies, good Duke." Marshal backed up gracefully. "We are living as simple farmers and huntsmen in these rustic lands. But recently, our homes have been plundered by raiding slavers."

"What business is that of mine?" The Duke drank from a silver goblet, his shaky hands spilling much of the wine onto his white shirt.

"The Khuraak invade our lands. We beseech your help. We just need the means to defend ourselves." Marshal bowed with his hands out in supplication.

"You want to take what is rightfully mine. You pack of thieves." The old Duke snarled. "Emperor Tarandrus bestowed this fortress upon me himself. Virago dined in these very halls." Rinn remembered Molo calling her grandmother that. The elderly man rose up, knocking over his goblet. Red wine poured off the side of the table. "Everything in this fortress belongs to me. Me! You will not have any of it." The dwarves came to clean up the mess and escort the elderly man out. As the duke tottered out of the room, holding onto two dwarves for support, his tone softened. "I give you leave to stay the night, out of the cold. But be gone in the morning."

::

Rinn and the others huddled around a small fireplace. They were given quarter in an unfurnished room not far from the kitchen with a dwarf guardian standing watch outside. Rinn was relieved to be out of the cold, but she did not like the idea of being imprisoned. Cat scratched at the cold stone walls and pined miserably. Bos huddled in one corner under a blanket, he occasionally glanced at Rinn before he returned to his brooding. Rinn cowered beneath her cloak, while Felsic and Marshal discussed quietly.

"That was my brother, the one who escorted us in." Felsic divulged. "We have to free him."

"He didn't seem to recognize you." Marshal lamented. "Are you sure he's not under some sort of spell."

"Nonsense." Felsic snarled. "You've never been a slave. You've never lived without hope. His will's been broken. Once he knows we can free him, he'll snap out of it."

"We can't do much without weapons." Marshal leaned in closer. "Rinn needs metal." He realized Rinn was staring directly at him. She marched over and inserted herself into the conversation.

"If you are going to talk about me, you might as well tell me what's going on." She plopped down next to her father. "I may be able to help."

"We want to free Felsic's brother." Marshal admitted. "But they confiscated our weapons. If we could just get our hands on a knife."

"Cat could steal one." Rinn shrugged. "There were plenty of knives back in the armory." Her father and the dwarf stared at each other, dumbstruck by the obvious answer.

Marshal called over to the sprawling feline. "Cat, are you bored?"

"Yessss." She rolled around on the stone floor languidly.

"Want to sneak around and steal something?" Rinn asked.

Two feline ears perked up and Cat shot into a sitting position. "Really?" Her eyes sparkled with life. Rinn explained the situation. The eager feline wanted to depart immediately, but Marshal convinced her to wait until night after everyone went to sleep. When all was quiet, Rinn watched as Cat snuck soundlessly out the door. As she padded past the guard, she seemed to disappear completely into the shadows. The dwarven guard never noticed her leave. Rinn waited, stirring the dying embers in the fireplace to pass the time. She was anxious for Cat to return, but also weary from the three days of arduous travel. Eventually fatigue overtook her and she fell asleep against a wall. She dreamed of the fortress in its heyday, filled with soldiers, hosting grand feasts. The old duke appeared much younger, full of vigor. Rinn laughed and danced with the soldiers and even the younger duke himself. She could see the joy in his eyes. Rinn woke with a start. It was just before dawn, and she saw Cat sitting on her father's lap. He was patting her head, and she purred proudly, a pile of knives on the floor at his feet.

Chapter 19

Marshal casually walked out into the stone hallway, a dagger neatly concealed beneath his heavy winter cloak. Felsic and Bos followed closely behind him, Rinn and Cat brought up the rear. Two dwarves with long axes waited to escort their guests to the exit—neither dwarf was Felsic's brother.

"We were wondering about our weapons." Marshal asked leisurely.

"They will remain here with the Duke." The brown-bearded dwarf spoke indifferently. His eyes were lifeless as he motioned to the doorway.

Marshal argued to get his weapons back, but the dwarf ignored him. Without warning, Marshal drew his knife and Bos seized the distracted dwarf from behind. Together they wrestled away his axe. Felsic kept the second guard at bay with his knife while Rinn and Cat dashed past them into the dim hallway. Rinn ran down the empty corridors, trying to remember the way back to the dining hall. Each time Rinn hesitated, Cat pointed out the correct path. The two girls finally reached the main hall and searched for any sign of the Duke, but he was not there. Rinn crossed the large room with her knife drawn. Cat followed close behind with her claws out. Four doors exited the dining hall and Rinn did not know which one to take. She decided to wait for her father. The sounds of scuffling and shouting echoed down the corridors. Rinn prepared for the worst, repeating in her head the summoning word for her protective barrier. Marshal, Bos, and Felsic burst through a doorway.

"Hurry!" Marshal beckoned as he ran down the hall. "The Duke is in his living quarters. We'll corner him there."

"What then?" Rinn tried to ask the question, but her father disappeared through another doorway. She had no choice but to follow. Rinn kept her knife out as she ran, she would have felt more secure with a spear, but the knife will have to do. She immediately felt guilty for feeling so warlike, she came to help a dwarf, not kill him. There had to be a way to end this peacefully. Cat called out to Rinn who was lagging behind, lost in her thoughts. She hurried to catch up. Together they entered an elaborately furnished sitting room, brightly lit with gold candelabra. Fine marble statuary and richly woven tapestries lined the walls. Duke Kapros hid behind an ornately carved chair. Five dwarven guards with axes protected him. The cowering Duke hurled insults. "This is treason. The Imperial Legion will hunt you down. Death to thieves."

Marshal took a step forward, carrying himself like a military commander. "I am Equis Theodric Amali, and I find you, Duke Kapros, in dereliction of your duties. For the crime of refusing to aid Imperial citizens in need, you are to be removed from your post."

"Be quiet, Equis." The Duke threatened from behind his chair. He shook an ancient bony fist in the air. "You and your rag-tag band of hoodlums have no authority here. Now, get out before I have you all killed."

Marshal grinned. "You are right. I have no authority over you. But she does." Marshal presented a startled Rinn. He put his hand on her shoulders and whispered into her ear. "Go ahead, Rinn. You know what to do." He stepped back, leaving Rinn alone to confront five armed dwarves and one angry Duke. Rinn was confused and scared, she did not want to fight, she did not want to kill anyone. The elderly Duke was stubborn and had certainly treated her poorly, but she did not think he needed to die. She remembered that one of the dwarfs protecting the Duke was Felsic's brother, who she came to rescue. She did not want to hurt him, she wanted to protect him. A realization struck her, she knew what to do.

Rinn walked forward and the Duke heeded her with a hateful gaze. Rinn raised her hand and spoke a single word. "Beorgan." Instantly, the barrier dome surrounded her, bathing the room in green light. Beautiful swirls of light and glowing green triangles played in the intricate, transparent dome. The dwarves retreated from its brilliance. Bos shielded his eyes instinctively. The Duke was drawn from his hiding place, his mouth hanging open as he fell to his knees. He covered his eyes in the folds of his robe.

"Forgive me. Please, forgive me." He fell forward on the ground, sobbing. "I did not know. Forgive me. Forgive me. Forgive me."

Marshal spoke in a commanding voice. "This is the grand-daughter of Virago. The blood of the Sigilla flows within her."

"The Sigilla were supposed to be dead." The pitiful Duke cried. "How was I supposed to know?"

"There are powers even death itself cannot conquer." Marshal countered. With a softness in his expression, he addressed his daughter. "Go ahead, Rinn. Finish your duty." Tears welled up in Rinn's eyes as she suppressed her inner joy. The shield wall evaporated and Rinn skipped forward excitedly, Cat following close behind. Rinn approached the dwarf Felsic pointed out as his brother and drew her knife.

"What is your name?" She asked the confused dwarf.

"I am Mafic." The rotund dwarf answered defensively.

"Mafic, brother of Felsic. I am Rinn." She raised her knife and rust and corrosion fell away from the blade until it shimmered a bright silver. "I hereby release you from your bonds." She knelt down and severed the black iron shackle around his ankle. It sizzled spitefully as it fell to the ground. Rinn rose, satisfied. Mafic's axe dropped from his hand. The dwarf laughed so loud, it startled Rinn and her companions. Mafic laughed and laughed until he was red in the face and could barely breathe. He rushed forward and picked up his brother, spinning him in circles. Felsic embraced him in return, tears in his eyes. Rinn squeezed Cat's paw as she watched the brothers' joyful reunion.

The four other dwarves threw down their weapons and knelt before Rinn. Without a word she happily severed each of their shackles while Cat clapped her paws gleefully. The Duke sat in his chair watching in disbelief. When he saw Rinn and Cat together, he was awestruck. Bewildered, he quietly begged a question of Marshal. "Is that a Margot?"

"Yes. It is." Marshal beamed.

"Gods preserve us." The Duke shuddered. "That little girl could destroy all of Sevria."

"No, I think she's going to save it." Marshal said proudly.

::

Rinn was bundled up in her new furs for the trip home. Duke Kapros had a sudden spree of generosity, offering any number of gifts to the party. Marshal was given leave to take whatever weapons and armor he desired from the supply rooms. Dwarven winter cloaks were given to Rinn, Cat, and Felsic. Marshal and Bos chose heavily padded Imperial gambesons, a snugly fitting jacket designed to be worn under armor. Marshal expertly strapped four tall shields together into a sled, which he loaded with weapons. Rinn selected five of her favorite pilum spears and added them to the pile. Food and water for the return trip was stacked on top.

Rinn learned that the Legion had abandoned this fortress years ago, leaving only the Duke and his dwarven slaves. Rinn severed the shackles of all the dwarves that lived here. Five dwarves elected to follow Rinn, aside from the boisterous Mafic, who had yet to stop laughing. A few dwarves elected to remain to care for the elderly Duke, who had not been a harsh master. Kapros did not object to the dwarves who chose to leave, he considered it an honor to have them accompany such an esteemed guest. The Duke met the travelers at the main gate as they prepared to depart. With a bowed head, he held out a small cloth-wrapped package for Rinn.

"Please do not think poorly of this old man." He set the present into her small hands. "I intended to give this to your grandmother, but when the time came, I lost courage. Now, maybe I can make up for that regret."

Rinn unwrapped the delicate bundle. Inside she found an exquisite necklace of finely worked gold set with deep green gemstones. Hanging from the chain was a gold leaf pendant folded into tiny swirls and triangles, a miniature replica of Rinn's own barrier shield. Rinn nearly dropped the necklace in shock. She stammered as she attempted to rewrap it. "I can't accept this, it's too valuable." She tried to hand the priceless item back to the elderly Duke, but her father subtly shook his head. Rinn winced and accepted the present, clutching the necklace to her chest. She fumbled to find the right words. "I have never before received such a fine gift. I don't know how to thank you."

The wrinkles on the ancient Duke's face squeezed together as he smiled. "By accepting my present, you've helped an old man to live out his last days in peace." Rinn hugged the duke, nearly toppling him over. Cat watched the scene awkwardly. The dwarves who chose to accompany Rinn arrived with their personal belongings stuffed into stout leather backpacks. Marshal gave the Duke a formal military salute and the party took their leave, dragging the shield-sled laden with supplies behind them. Rinn knew she had a three-day journey through frigid snow and biting wind, but she had never felt warmer. She had freed Felsic's brother and brought joy to an elderly duke, and no one had been hurt.

::

The party traveled south, out of the highlands. Rinn wore the necklace at all times for fear of losing it. She fingered the pendant absently as she walked. Cat bounded through the snows playfully, still basking in the excitement of the last few days. Mafic laughed and joked with Marshal and his brother. The other dwarves kept to themselves, solemn and somber. They had a leaner and more muscular build than Felsic and his brother. Rinn tried to engage them in conversation, but these dwarves always answered in short, curt responses. She asked her father about it, but he explained that they had been through quite an ordeal and it may take some time for them to adjust. Rinn reminded herself to keep track of them back at Hilltop.

Uncomfortable questions bothered Rinn as she trekked through the wet snow. She had broken the dwarves' bonds of slavery, but she had no idea what to do now. She did not know where the dwarves would live or what they would do. She did not even know if there was enough food to keep everyone fed through the coming winter months. Rinn's head ached worrying about the ramifications of her choices. She held onto one certainty, one reassuring fact, freeing the dwarves had been the right thing to do.

Chapter 20

Rinn spotted her hilltop home in the distance, a welcome sight after three tiring days of winter travel. But as she drew nearer, she realized something was not right, the compound was a beehive of activity. Strangers entered and exited the main gate, unfamiliar men chopped wood at the forest's edge. Marshal and Rinn exchanged wary glances. Rinn spotted someone she recognized, Lutra crunching through the snow coming out to greet them. He was wrapped in a woolen cloak with thick boots and gloves. Marshal questioned him. "What's going on here?"

"Welcome back." Lutra stammered in the cold air. "Apparently the Clanmorris boys made a mess of many farms in the area. When word got out that there was a safe place to stay the winter, people started pouring in."

"These are all refugees?" Marshal marveled at the number of displaced people. "Incredible."

"I see you brought a few more." Lutra gestured to the dwarves accompanying the party.

"I guess we did." Marshal admitted.

"I'll go get Molo. He can help you unload." Lutra darted off, but not without first waving a quick greeting to Cat— unfortunately, she was not paying attention. Marshal and Bos dragged the shield-sled through the gate into the ever-expanding compound. The dwarves gawked at their new surroundings.

"So many people." One of them marveled.

"Glorious!" Mafic smiled broadly, squeezing one arm around his brother's shoulder. He proudly strolled through the compound chattering and pointing at everything he saw. The other dwarves timidly followed behind, never saying a word. Road-weary, Rinn shuffled into her house and collapsed onto her bed. Cat curled up next to her and in moments the two were fast asleep.

::

At dinner, Rinn squeezed onto a bench next to her father. The main hall of her house was packed with refugees, tired faces of farmers and their families. Outside bitter winds raced over the hilltop, but inside the house was a furnace fueled by the body heat of so many visitors. Rinn recognized some of the people in the room, Hadwin's family along with workers from his farm, but many faces were new to her. Men, women, and children crowded at tables and across the floor, eating in common. The refugees wore simple winter clothes, and many nursed injuries. The dwarves huddled together in one corner, talking among themselves. The roar of idle chatter filled the room.

"It certainly is lively." Marshal yelled above the ruckus. Rinn replied with a forced smile. She remembered enjoying the crowded marketplace streets in her hometown of Viburna, but the stench of so many bodies gathered in one room was making it hard to breathe. She wanted to slip away and eat her food in the privacy of her room. Cat squeezed next to Rinn, her feline ears folded back against the noise.

Molo sat on his customary tree-stump stool draining a bowl of porridge. "They came from all over. Word of our stand against the clansmen spread quickly."

"I had no idea there would be so many refugees." Marshal stared into his empty ale mug. "We're going to have to set up some rules before this gets out of hand."

"It's your house, Lord Marshal." Molo grinned mockingly.

"I was afraid you'd say that." Marshal flubbed his lips and set down his empty mug. He climbed onto the bench and tried to speak over the crowd, but no one paid him any heed. He gave Molo an expectant look.

The giant man rose to his full height and bellowed out. "Quiet!"

A hush immediately fell over the room and all heads turned to Marshal, standing on the bench. "Thank you." Marshal nodded to Molo. "And thank you friends for sharing a meal with us today. I know many of you have lost your homes and livelihoods, some have even lost loved ones. I'm happy to welcome you to our hilltop. I am known as Marshal, and I open my home to you. But if we want to survive this winter, we're going to have to work together."

The crowd listened as Marshal outlined some basic household rules. Rinn took the opportunity to slip away with her food bowl, crossing through the kitchen to grab her winter cloak. Outside, she crunched through the snow to the watchtower, cradling her food bowl to warm her hands. Even though it was early evening, it was as dark as midnight outside. A quarter moon, the one that could be seen, slipped in and out of wispy, silver clouds. A solitary figure sat high in the watch tower, playing a lonely tune on a wooden flute.

Cat appeared, startling Rinn. "What're you doing?" Rinn was stunned at how silently Cat could move in the darkness. She did not even leave pawprints in the newly fallen snow. Rinn looked down at the food bowl she had dropped in surprise.

"Cat! Don't scare me like that." Rinn bent over and tried to scoop her stew back into her bowl, but it was already a mess of snow and mud.

"Sorry." Cat fumbled her paws. "I was bored, and I saw you sneak out." Her tail flitted across the snow. Rinn dumped the useless contents of her bowl onto the ground. She bemoaned the loss of her dinner, but it was impossible to stay mad at Cat for very long, she did not mean any harm.

"I came out to get some air." Rinn pulled her cloak tightly around her shoulders. "What do you want to do?"

Cat's little fangs showed as she grinned. "We could pester Lutra." Rinn looked up at the rickety watch tower swaying in the evening breeze. That was the last place she wanted to go.

"Let's go back inside and find a nice fire." Rinn took ahold of Cat's paw, which felt like a warm winter glove. The two girls skipped through the snow back to the house, occasionally stopping for snowball fights. The commotion inside the main hall was dying down, and people were starting to settle for the night. Rinn and Cat passed Tomin, sitting on the large pile of rocks behind the house, eating the last bits of his dinner. Tomin was not an attractive man, his face had been horribly scarred by burns, but since she last saw him he had at least bathed and cut his beard. Rinn sat down next to him. "Didn't you go to the meeting?" Cat sniffed at the rocks.

"No." Tomin patted the pile beneath him. "I'm on guard duty."

With a grimace Rinn hopped away from the stones. She had forgotten all about the tattooed man. "Is that slaver still down there? Is he even alive?"

"Master Molo thinks he is." Tomin shifted uncomfortably on his seat.

"Yallakh's still down there. I can smell him." Cat raised a paw to her nose. "He smells like death. I hope he rots down there."

Rinn pushed Cat away. "I don't want a dead guy living beneath my house." Tomin raised an eyebrow at her odd choice of words. "I didn't mean living, I meant to say dead. Not dead, buried. Alive." Rinn growled and stomped off in frustration. She headed back to the kitchen to get more food. On the way, she could not stop thinking about the man in the cellar. He had been left alone in the darkness this entire time, nine days. Rinn would have killed him without hesitation to defend Cat, but now that he was a prisoner, she did not know what to do. He was a terrible person, a monster, but starving him to death in a cellar seemed impossibly cruel. She tried not to think about it as she washed out her bowl and dished herself another serving of stew. She squeezed back into her spot on the bench near her father, listlessly eating her dinner. With each bite she was reminded of the man slowly starving below her. Marshal was discussing housing specifics with a few heads of the farming families, they took turns voicing their needs and concerns. Rinn silently finished her dinner and shuffled back to her room, knowing she would not be able to get any sleep that night.

::

"We can't leave him down there." Rinn blocked the door as her father tried to leave for his early morning hunt. He was outfitted in warm furs and carried his curved bow and a quiver packed with barbed arrows.

"Who?" Marshal inquired absently, eager to leave.

"Yallakh. He's still trapped in the cellar." Fury burned in Rinn's eyes. Her hands were balled up in fists. Marshal stroked the wispy hairs of his thin beard.

"I think you need to talk with Molo about him. He knows some things you need to hear." Marshal nodded in satisfaction and headed out into the cold. Rinn retreated back to her room, stepping around all the refugees sleeping in her house. Families gathered in groups, sharing bedrolls and blankets. The main room was warm and safe, although it smelled terribly, like too many unwashed undergarments. Rinn changed into her heaviest outfit and headed outside, storming directly to Molo's forge. Smoke rose from the chimney as the big man pounded out metal on a massive anvil. Bos and another teenage boy assisted him.

"Morning, Rinn." Molo spoke between hammer blows. He introduced the new boy, a tall teen with long black hair. "This is Calder, Hadwin's oldest son." The boy briefly looked up from tending the forge, but never said anything. Molo asked. "What can I do for you?"

"My Dad told me to ask you about Yallakh." Rinn furrowed her eyebrows and pursed her lips, putting on a serious face to mask her fears. Molo handed his hammer to Bos and directed the boys what to do. He escorted Rinn a few steps away from the forge.

"What's this about?" Molo bent over to face Rinn, his expression sour. She was only half his full height, and he was very intimidating when he was upset.

"I want to know about Yallakh." Rinn squeaked.

"What about him?" Molo demanded, wiping his hands.

Rinn wanted to leave, forget about the conversation, but she could not let it go. "He still down in our cellar."

"Of course, he is." Molo seemed very satisfied.

"What's going to happen to him?" Rinn was not getting the answers she wanted. "I asked my father and he told me to talk to you."

"He did?" Molo scrunched his oversized eyebrows. "I think you'd better come inside. We'll need a private place to talk, there are things about that man that no one else needs to know." Molo opened the door to his new home and ushered Rinn inside.

Chapter 21

Rinn had never been inside of Molo's new house, and she had to stifle a laugh. The giant lived with Felsic and the house had been outfitted with two of everything, one massive and one miniature. A huge table sat against the far wall with a ridiculously tall chair, and next to it a stubby table with its own squat chair. Rinn took a seat at the smaller table. The chair was plenty wide but a bit too short for her. Rinn noticed that the short table legs had been decorated in carvings of trees and animals, clearly Felsic's handiwork. Rinn imagined in time, all the hardwood furniture in the room would be crawling with his creations.

Molo sat down on his huge chair, filling a mug with water. "Your father told me to tell you about Yallakh." He picked up Clive and set him on the table in front of himself. "Are you sure you want to know? It's not a pretty story."

"Yes." Rinn was taken aback by the question. She already knew the tattooed man was a slaver and a murderer. She doubted there could be much worse. "I need to know."

"Let me explain some things first." He rotated the rock on the table. "As you've probably figured out, Clive is not just a rock. I can see things with him—right now I see Cat on the roof trying to eavesdrop." Rinn looked up at the ceiling amazed. She did not understand how Molo could see Cat through the solid roof, but she believed him, it sounded exactly like something Cat would do.

"How does that work?" Rinn squinted at the ceiling.

"Clive doesn't see ordinary objects, just people, or more accurately, their life energy." Molo held up the rock and pointed it around the room. "I can see everyone in the courtyard. The boys are busy at the forge. Felsic and his brother are out back. Arlin and some of the farmhands are gathered below the watchtower."

"Wow." Rinn suddenly remembered what Cat had said about Clive watching her. Apparently, she had been right all along.

"Now, do you know what I see when I look at Yallakh?" Molo's jaw tightened, and he held Clive firmly. Rinn nodded meekly. "I see thousands of souls, each one bound to a cursed tattoo on his body. And not just any souls, elf souls. His tattoos are made of elf blood. He murdered elves and stitched their souls to his body."

"What? Why?" Rinn was starting to feel sick.

"He uses their souls like armor." Molo spoke with the utmost loathing. "Elves are naturally resistant to magic, and Yallakh has thousands of their souls trapped in his tattoos. With that much armor he would be immune to almost anything. No fighter or mage could stand against him. If you recall, he resisted a direct blow from your spear."

"But, you beat him, twice." Rinn insisted.

"Yes, but Clive can see those souls, so I can find the chinks in his armor." Molo did not speak with pride, but with revulsion. Rinn sucked her thumb reflexively. She came to find a way to resolve the problem of the stranger trapped in her basement, but the more she learned the more confused her emotions became. She tried to speak, but she could not think of anything to say. The situation was worse than she could imagine: Yallakh was guilty of genocide.

"Nothing would please me more than putting that monster down, but I am not even sure if he can be killed." Frustrated, Molo rose and paced across the room, taking Clive with him. "Until we can figure out what to do with him, he'll have to stay sealed in that cellar." With a sigh he headed outside, back to his forge. Rinn sat alone on Felsic's stool, mulling over the murky situation. She looked up to the ceiling and wondered how much of the conversation Cat had overheard.

::

That afternoon, Marshal assembled all able-bodied fighters on the brown lawn behind the house, a collection of teenage boys and grown men plus Rinn, Cat, and a handful of dwarves. Marshal paced like a commander preparing for battle. "We live in dangerous times. We can be fairly certain that Clanmorris will return. Once the winter snows thaw, they can attack us in large numbers. We will have to be ready to meet them." He recounted the journey to the Duke of the Wild to bring back weapons. He left out Rinn's role in the affair and any mention of her abilities.

Molo brought out the arsenal and distributed weapons to everyone based on size and skill. Felsic and his brother Mafic chose hammers, the preferred weapon of the Dverg. The other dwarves selected pickaxes, confirming Molo's suspicion that they were Dvalinn, rock cutters. The humans mostly favored swords and shields, except Arlin who brandished a hefty mace. Marshal chose a new sword for himself and set aside the pilum spears for Rinn. Cat selected a pair of knives from the expedition, even though she could barely hold them.

After the meeting, the five Dvalinn dwarves approached Marshal. The oldest and tallest of the dwarves introduced himself. "I am Botrogen." He bowed his head to Rinn. "We thank the lady for our freedom. We see that you are in need of winter homes for these refugees. Let us build you proper dwarven lodges."

A young, eager dwarf interrupted. "We'll dig half the height into the ground. Our design uses far less wood and holds heat better in the winter. And we can build them quickly."

"Thank you, Beryl." Botrogen glared at the young dwarf.

A squat middle age dwarf muttered to himself. "Humans build houses as tall as trees and complain when they are cold in the winter and hot in the summer."

"That's enough, Marl." Botrogen shushed the grouchy dwarf and turned his attention back to Rinn and Marshal. "We will happily craft these homes, we have but need of tools to shape the earth."

Marshal pointed to Molossus. "Speak with Molo. He can forge you whatever you need." The dwarves were delighted at the prospect of giant-forged tools. Marshal introduced the dwarves to Molo and showed them around the forge. Rinn hefted her bundle of pilum spears and carried them back to the house alone, Cat had disappeared off somewhere. She deposited the load in her bedroom and wandered through the house. She never realized how large her home had become, all the walls had been repaired and each room properly roofed. Translucent glass windows and newly crafted furniture made the interior of the house feel cheery and comfortable.

But one dark place still haunted Rinn's thoughts, the pile of stones behind the building. Curiosity drew her there. She found herself staring at the rocks stacked over the cellar entrance. Rinn searched for Tomin, who was usually tasked with guarding the prisoner. She wondered where he had gone. Yallakh was too dangerous to be left unattended.

"I know you're up there." A muffled voice seeped through the rocks. It was overly sweet, like the taste of fruit on the verge of rotting. At first Rinn was relieved to hear Yallakh's voice, reassuring her that he was not a corpse rotting beneath her home. Then the realization struck her that she was talking to a slaver, a murder, a soul stealing practitioner of dark magic. Yallakh was the worst human being alive, but Rinn could not help listening to him. He talked casually in his raspy voice. "Did you know there is no water down here? I have to lick rocks just to stay alive. Did you know that?"

Rinn mustered her courage and squeaked out a reply. "Serves you right."

"Oh, a girl. How splendid." Yallakh's tone was amicable. "It was so tiresome listening to that old drunk complain about his lack of alcohol, considering my complete lack of water. And don't get me started on the experience of eating raw grain. How long have some of these bags been down here?

Some of the grain tastes like bad mushrooms. Of course, I can't see because there's no light."

Rinn was amused by his banter, but was immediately overcome with guilt. "That cellar is too good for you, you murderer."

"Maybe." The stones became quiet. Rinn decided the tattooed man must have returned to the depths of the cellar. She turned to leave but Yallakh's voice called out. "Your voice seems familiar—like we've met before. I get it now, you're that witch girl."

"I'm not a witch." Rinn insisted.

"But you are that girl." Yallakh sounded confident, even proud. "I knew you would seek me out eventually. That is a truly unique power you wield. How did you come by it?"

"Not talking." Rinn turned her back to the pile of rocks, ignoring it.

"Still, I'm impressed." Yallakh continued his casual conversation. "You fought me to a standstill, and that is very hard to do. If it wasn't for that cursed soul-stone I would have taken you with me."

"What's a soul-stone?" Rinn could not help herself.

"You're not a very good witch, are you?" Yallakh seemed amazed. "The damnable rock that giant carries. It is a soul-stone."

"Clive?" Rinn blurted reflexively.

"He named it? What an idiot." Yallakh was bemused, almost jealous. "But if you're not a witch, what sorcery did you use on the Margot? And how did she remove her ginj?"

"I didn't use sorcery on Cat. I freed her, and now we're sisters." Rinn knew she should just stop talking, but all the bottled-up emotions inside her would not be still. Her father could only tell her so much about her abilities. Molo was sympathetic, but also not very helpful. Right now, even though she was talking to literally the worst person in the world, Rinn had a glimmer of hope that Yallakh might help her understand her powers better.

"Interesting." Yallakh shuffled around below the rocks. "If you're the one who freed her you might be the only person alive who can remove a slave shackle. The Khuraak won't be happy to hear about you." Rinn felt the pit of her stomach drop. Yallakh laughed, his coarse voice echoing through the rocks. "You have nothing to fear from me, I'm not going to tell. I won't be going back to them anyway, not after losing their prized possession."

"You lost her?" Rinn's curiosity wrestled with the butterflies in her stomach.

"I was hired to guard that troublesome Margot." Yallakh fell back into casual banter, like a guest at a dinner party. "If you ask me, I think that little brat can turn herself invisible. She nearly slipped through my fingers many times. One day she was just gone." There was sadness in his voice. "I was sent to track her down, but she's fallen under your spell. Once a Margot tastes magic, they never want to leave." Rinn decided she had heard enough, Yallakh was just trying to confuse her, to drive a wedge between her and Cat. Rinn refused to feel pity for this monster. He must have heard her footsteps as she walked away, because he called out. "Do come back another time. We have so much to talk about."

Chapter 22

Frost covered the practice yard as Rinn trained with Bos and the other teenagers. She wore her usual sparring outfit, a heavy woolen dress and her dragon-feather vest. Molo supervised the session with Cat at his side eagerly pointing out everyone's missteps. Lutra was excused from training for tower guard duty. Bos traded blows with two other teens: Calder, the one with long black hair, who swished his sword fluidly, and Rury, the son of Brogan the craftsman, who had a quick wit and a quicker fighting style. He leaped in and out of combat like a dancer, thrusting quickly and then disengaging. It should have been effective, but his aim was terrible, and he frequently stumbled over his own feet. Watching the three boys train, Rinn realized the only thing Bos had going for him was his size and strength, but he used them effectively.

Marshal worked with a handful of adults who were awkwardly trying to form a shield wall. Rinn had never seen an actual shield wall in combat, but she was sure it was not supposed to look so crooked. Standing alone in the practice field, Rinn felt very much like the outsider. None of the boys wanted to spar with her, and Cat never took their practice sessions seriously unless she was sparring with Marshal. Rinn half-heartedly swung and thrust her pilum at the air, rehearsing the drills Molo had taught her. She was ready to give up and go inside when she spotted three teenage girls at the side of the practice yard watching her. Rinn did not remember seeing these girls before, but so many new people had come to the hilltop in recent days. She set down her pilum and cautiously walked over to them.

A round faced teen with mousy brown hair smiled at her. "Are you Rinn?" She had an excited gleam in her eyes.

Rinn answered timidly. "Yes."

"I knew it." The girl was a few years older and much more developed than Rinn. She was wrapped in a fancy blue woolen cloak with matching fur mittens and cap. She remarked to the two teenagers accompanying her. "See, isn't she adorable? I love her hair, it's so blond and curly. And I love her outfit. Look at that crazy vest she's wearing, it looks like it's made out of insect wings."

"They're feathers." Rinn said to herself.

The other teenagers were obviously sisters, they shared the same pimpled complexion, straight brown hair, and brown eyes. The older sister was several hands taller than the other girls. She wore a colorless dress and a drab woolen shawl. She eyed Rinn with suspicion. "What are you doing out here with the boys?"

"I'm practicing." Rinn replied defensively. "My dad wants me to learn to protect myself."

"Why?" The older girl frowned.

"Let her be, Dev." The mousy haired girl bounced as she spoke. "I'm Tristy. This is Feena and her sister Devnet. We love your house. This whole hilltop is amazing. You can see the entire valley from here." The older sister rolled her eyes.

"The other boys are using swords." Devnet was back on the attack. "Why are you the only one with a stick?"

"I don't like swords. I prefer spears." Rinn desperately wanted to leave, but the need to stand up for herself was strong. But each time she opened her mouth, the wrong words came out. Rinn was sure the last thing these girls wanted to hear about was her weapon preferences.

Feena, the younger sister, finally spoke. "Devy, don't you remember? Rinn and her father came to the farm and hunted grashels. They used spears."

"Really?" Tristy's curiosity was piqued. She turned to Rinn. "Are you and your dad hunters? Is this a hunting lodge?"

"No." Rinn backtracked. "My dad was a soldier. So was Uncle Molo. They used to be in the Legion."

"You're from Sevria?" Tristy's eyes popped open in shock.

::

That night at dinner, Rinn was the topic of conversation. New dwellings for the refugees had barely been started, so everyone continued to gather in the main building to eat. Little kids ran around the room wildly, and the adults crowded together at long tables or on the floor. The teenage boys Bos, Lutra, Calder, and Rury sat together at a side table. Rinn thought she heard them mention her name several times while they ate. The three girls gossiped together at another table repeating her name constantly. Rinn leaned over and whispered to Cat. "Can you hear what they are saying?"

The feline girl stopped licking her bowl and tilted her head, adjusting her ears in the direction of the teenagers. She listened for a moment. "Hmm."

"What?" Rinn tugged on Cat's shirt. "What is it?"

"The boys don't want us at combat practice." Cat looked puzzled. "I don't know why. I think pouncing on the boys would be fun."

"What about the girls?" Rinn insisted. "What are they saying?"

Can adjusted her head like a weathervane in a changing wind. She listened for a moment and then frowned. "Well that's not very nice."

"Cat!" Rinn squeezed her arm forcing Cat to wince. Rinn wanted to know what they were saying, but a group of grown men approached the table menacingly. Sheridan, the father of Tristy, led the group. He was tall and had the build of a plowman, all upper body strength. Rinn could tell by his demeanor that he was not happy.

Sheridan spoke loudly and the chatter in the room died down. "Good man Marshal, what's this nonsense I hear about you being an Imperial?"

Marshal finished chewing a bite of food before he looked up. "It's true that I lived and worked in Sevria for many years, but I was not born there."

"Bogs!" Sheridan slammed two hands on the tabletop and leaned forward. "We have no love for Imperials. Too many of our kin have been killed by their damnable Legions." Some men in the group grumbled their agreement. Rinn wondered how her father could sit so calmly in the face of such open hostility. Rinn's knuckles were white as she clutched the table nervously. Even Cat crouched down on her haunches, ready to pounce.

Marshal waited for the grumbling to die down before he responded. "I have no allegiance to the Empire. I came to the wilds with my daughter to live the simple life of a freeman away from the troubles of Sevria."

"The only Imperials who come out here are either fugitives or spies." One of the farmhands shouted across the room.

"So, which is it, man?" Sheridan locked eyes with Marshal. "Are you a fugitive or a spy?"

Molo rose up, Clive in hand and towered over Sheridan. The group of angry men backed up. Molo reprimanded them harshly. "You speak plenty when your bellies are full, but if it wasn't for this man, you and your families would be out in the cold starving. Show some sense and gratitude."

Hadwin came over and placed a hand on Sheridan's shoulder. "The giant's right. This is not the way to repay his hospitality. It's the Clan that brought us so low. This man is just trying to help."

Molo added. "You should be thanking his daughter, too. It was her idea to let you stay." All the faces turned to Rinn, who wanted nothing more than to slip beneath the table and hide. Cat took the opportunity to jump up excitedly.

"And she killed a dragon once—with a shovel." Cat bounced in her seat. Rinn actually slipped beneath the table and hid.

::

Rinn did her very best to avoid everyone the next day. During her morning chores, she locked herself in her bedroom, but she was discovered by her father. Rinn kept her head down and spoke to no one as she completed her morning chores. The Dvalinn dwarves had been diligently digging out the rooms for five new homes. The farmhands harvested wood and constructed timber half-walls. Farmers' wives weaved thatch for the rooves and sewed mattresses and blankets. Rinn was tasked with carrying baskets of supplies to the worksite. Along the way, one of the dwarves stopped her.

"Heard you killed a dragon." It was Botrogen, the leader of the Dvalinn dwarves. He carried a pick axe and was covered in dirt and rock dust.

"I don't want to talk about it." Rinn attempted to hurry past.

"It's quite an honor." Botrogen professed. "Many a dwarf long to be called 'dragon-slayer'."

"It's embarrassing." Rinn felt her face turning red.

"Don't shy away from your accomplishments, they make you who you are." Botrogen stood level-eyed with Rinn. He was the tallest of all the dwarves on the hill. "Every dwarf here owes you their life. You gave us the freedom we never expected. You should be proud of your gifts." Botrogen patted Rinn's hand. His touch was as rough as stone itself. "If any of those humans ever give you trouble, just let us know." He winked at Rinn.

Rinn should have been reassured, knowing that she had her own personal dwarven hit squad, but it made her feel worse. Now, she had to worry about the dwarves, Cat, her father, the teenage boys, the gossipy girls, and everything else that seemed to be going wrong lately. She threw down her baskets and sauntered back to the house deep in thought. Before she knew it, she found herself in a dark corner behind the house, staring at the pile of rocks tucked out of sight.

Chapter 23

Rinn stared at the stacked stones. She knew Yallakh was down there, alone in the darkness, living a half-life off rotten bags of grain and the moisture from the cellar stones. The walls of his prison were carved in rock, so digging out would be a formidable task, but if Yallakh could not die, Rinn suspected he would find a way out eventually. Rinn wanted to talk to him again, to be sure he was alive, and at the same time the idea appalled her. She wrestled with the dilemma until a horn sounded in the distance. Rinn sprinted to the courtyard, following the sounds of people shouting. Hilltop was in a frenzy with men and women running every direction. From the watch tower, Lutra sounded a second, long, shrill note on his horn.

Marshal grabbed Rinn's arm. "Where've you been? Go get your armor and bring your pilum. Meet me by the gate at once." He rushed off, bow in hand. Rinn saw Molo lumbering through the crowd, a great hammer slung over his shoulder. Rinn raced inside and pulled on her dragon-feather vest. For a moment she was embarrassed to wear it, worried about what the teenage girls would say, but she valued the protection it provided. Cat appeared behind her, startling her.

"Cat." Rinn gasped, holding her chest. "What's going on?"

"Some things are attacking hilltop." Cat's fur was covered in a layer of powdery snow, and her tail twitched nervously. Rinn thought she saw a tinge of blood on her shoulder, but it was hard to tell against the rusty shades of her fur. Rinn grabbed a pilum and dashed outside with Cat. The fighting men and the teenage boys were assembled at the main gate where Marshal was barking out instructions. Rinn sidled over to him.

"Only fighters with experience in the field will be coming with us." Marshal checked everyone's weapons and shields. "We need the rest to stay here and guard this gate. Make sure none of these beasts get into the village." Rinn thought it was interesting, the way her father casually referred to the hilltop as a village, but that was exactly what it was becoming. And now it was under attack. "Rinn, you and Cat are coming with us."

Rinn nodded, joining the assault party with Molo, Seoras, Hadwin, and Bos. The big plowman Sheridan was visibly upset. "You're taking these little girls into combat and leaving grown men behind?"

Molo slung his hammer over his shoulder. "Watch your mouth, big man. That little girl could easily take you in a fight." He smiled with his oversized teeth. "She could probably best me if she really tried."

The crowd of men murmured the words "dragon-slayer" and "witch". They uncomfortably stepped away from her. Marshal put his arm around his daughter, wrapping her in his warmth. He stared down the pack of unruly men.

"Rinn has seen more combat than any of you. She is an obvious choice. And Cat can track with skills that no human can match." Marshal moved the hunting party to the gate. The crowd of men parted as dwarves pushed them aside. Three of the dwarves stepped forward, dressed in thick armor and carrying heavy weapons.

Felsic spoke breathlessly. "We only had enough armor to outfit a few of our number. Take us with you, we know how to fight these floefangs." He and his brother Mafic were battle-ready, wielding spiked war hammers. Botrogen joined them, fully decked out in his own armor, pick-axe in hand. Marshal smiled at the newcomers.

"Your fighting skills are most welcome." Marshal hurried the hunting party through the gate and closed it tightly behind them. Rinn could hear Sheridan grumbling as the gate shut. Outside the palisade wall, the silence of winter gripped the hillside, only the whistling wind broke the quiet. The snow-covered hills looked blue in the early evening twilight. Rinn held her pilum spear firmly as the party advanced down the hill. Marshal moved Cat to the front of the line. "Okay, Cat. Which way?"

Cat sniffed the air and twitched her whiskers. She stared straight ahead for a long moment and then quickly spun to the right. "There." She pointed with her paw to the logging grounds. The party moved in a group down the hillside, crunching loudly through the ice-covered snow. Marshal and Molo led the way, following Cat's directions. Rinn kept close to her father. In the dim light, the logging grounds seemed especially eerie. Rows of tree stumps looked like tombstones lined up in a twilight graveyard. Rinn breathed rapidly and the skin on the back of her neck crawled. She could feel herself being watched. Without warning, Cat tackled Bos to the ground as a ferocious, snapping head burst from the snow exactly where he had been standing. The beast had a long muzzle, like a wolf, deep-set eyes, and sharp curved teeth. The entire creature was longer than any canine, white and lithe, like an enormous weasel covered in scales of shiny ice. The floefang leaped through the air and dove back under the snow, disappearing completely.

The dwarves closed ranks, standing back to back. "More are circling around us." Mafic, the heaviest of the dwarves, pointed to his left. "Get ready, boys. Here they come." Three frozen white heads burst through the snow, jaws opened for the kill. Mafic caught the first head with a satisfying blow from his hammer. He laughed heartily as the beast skidded across the snow. The other dwarves moved in for the kill. Felsic pinned down the body while Botrogen delivered a finishing strike. The other floefangs disappeared beneath the snow.

"One down little brother." Mafic bared his teeth proudly at Felsic. The group reformed their circle ready for the next wave. The floefangs broke through the snow randomly, sowing discord among the fighters. One head appeared several feet from Rinn, she stabbed at it with her pilum. She must have unconsciously spoken the magic words that enchant her weapon because her spear tip was glowing brightly in the twilight gloom. Her feeble attack missed the monster as it slipped past her, diving back into the snow.

The floefangs continued to attack randomly, diving in and out of the party, like birds of prey harassing a flock of doves. One head appeared just behind Cat, nipping at her tail. Cat jerked it out of the way just as the jaws snapped down. The floefang snarled at the Margot, who hissed back. Molo swiped at the beast with his hammer, but it had vanished beneath the snow. Marshal had to roll to avoid an attack from below. The beasts were too fast for Rinn to catch with her pilum, but an idea occurred to her, a way to slow them down. Rinn carefully watched the snow, trying to find any clue to where they would attack next. The floefangs were quick, giving opponents very little time to react. Several in the party were sporting injuries, a nip or a claw wound on their arms and legs.

Rinn tumbled away from an attack, rolling near dwarves. A white feral body leaped through the air at her. Before the dwarves had time to react, Rinn held up her hand and summoned her shield wall with a word. "Beorgan." Instead of picturing the wall around herself, she imagined a cage surrounding the creature. The floefang hung helpless in the air, caught in a sphere of glowing green triangles and swirls. It growled and bit at the barrier, to no avail.

Molo roared his approval. "Good work, Rinn." He reached through the glowing wall and caught the beast by its throat. With a sickening crack, it shivered and slumped lifelessly. Rinn let the shield dissipate, and a pile of ice and fangs scattered on the ground. Molo nodded his head in satisfaction, holding Clive. Rinn noticed that Molo was sometimes holding Clive and other times not, though he never seemed to pick him up or set him down. She wondered if Clive truly was a soul-stone like Yallakh had said. Rinn was not sure what a soul-stone was, but she decided to pay more attention to Molo and his mysterious rock.

It did not take long to dispatch the rest of the beasts, once Rinn had discovered how to trap them in her shield. The dwarves and men easily defeated five more monsters. The final floefang retreated into the forest, but Cat was able to sniff it out and the dwarves put an end to it. After the combat was over, Marshal gave Rinn a proud smile and a gentle rub on her head. He led the hunting party across the hillside, where a worker lay mangled in the crimson-stained snow. Marshal bowed his head, as Hadwin announced. "That's Gam, one of Arlin's men."

Molo related the story. "He came down to cut wood, and the floefangs caught him. The beasts were headed for town, but somehow Cat was able to lure them back into the forest. She saved many lives." Molo beamed at the feline girl, who danced around happily. Rinn and Cat returned to the hilltop while the men dealt with Gam's remains.

::

Dinner that evening was a subdued affair, the death of Gam weighed heavily on everyone. Solemn cups were raised in his honor and everyone ate quietly and turned in early. Rinn and Cat readied for sleep. They no longer slept on the same mattress, they each had their own decorated bed, courtesy of the Dverg brothers. However, most mornings, Rinn would wake to find Cat curled up next to her in bed. Apparently, Cat snuck into Marshal's bed from time to time, too.

On this somber night, Rinn stared into the darkness. "Cat?" She rolled over to face the feline girl who was snuggled under her thick blankets. "What do you see when you look at Clive?"

Cat thought for a moment. "Clive looks like a great big eyeball."

"I know, but it's a rock." Rinn wondered why she even bothered to ask.

"It used to be a rock." Cat smoothed her ear with a paw. "But now it's a big purple eyeball. It looks around and it blinks."

Rinn was taken aback. "How can it blink? It doesn't have eyelids."

"It blinks." Cat nodded. She snuggled deeper into her blankets.

Questions still burned inside Rinn. "Cat. What do you see when you look at Yallakh?"

"Ghosts." Cat yawned sleepily.

That made sense to Rinn. It matched the description that Molo had given. Rinn knew that Yallakh was a horrible person, but his entombment did not seem right. Rinn made up her mind. "I'm going to free him."

"I know." Cat mumbled as she drifted off.

"I'm going to free him tomorrow." Rinn said to herself. Cat quietly snored as she slept.

Chapter 24

R inn waited until midday, when everyone was occupied with their daily chores. Men were busy constructing community houses, women were collecting food and spinning thread, and children were tending to the farm animals. Rinn snuck outside alone and skulked down the narrow corridor between her house and the palisade wall. She arrived at the conspicuous pile of stones, and looked around for Tomin. She had not seen him in days, he was supposed to be guarding the prisoner. Rinn suspected he was off drinking somewhere, and she decided it was for the best that he was not around.

Rinn cautiously tiptoed to the stones. "Yallakh?"

A gravelly voice responded from below. "I am here."

"I have some things to ask you." Rinn hoped she sounded more confident than she felt. She had taken precautions; she wore her dragon-feather vest and carried her pilum spear in case Yallakh became violent. She also brought a full waterskin as a peace offering.

Yallakh's tired voice echoed from below. "It would be easier to talk face to face."

Rinn wanted more information before she would agree to that. "What would you do if I let you out?"

The tiniest bit of hope flickered in his response. "I would simply leave."

"You wouldn't harm anyone here?" Rinn eagerly awaited his answer.

The weary voice replied with resignation. "There would be no profit in it."

"What would you do to Cat?" Rinn rephrased her question. "Would you try to capture her again?"

"Why bother." Yallakh cleared his throat. "She'll just keep coming back."

"What do you mean?" Rinn's stomach knotted up.

"You're not much of a witch." Yallakh coughed. "When a young Margot binds to a source of magic, it's for life. Sorcerers exploit this to force lifelong servitude. You feed them magic and they're your slave." The words struck Rinn to the core, and she reeled in disbelief. Cat was not bound to her, she was free to do whatever she wanted. Rinn removed her shackle, treated her like a sister, an equal. Cat was not something she owned.

"You're wrong." Rinn yelled back in anger. "Cat is not my slave. She doesn't belong to me. She's my sister." From behind her, Rinn heard the sound of purring. She whirled around to see Cat slip out of the darkness. Cat grinned broadly, showing her little fangs. Rinn smiled to herself, warmed by the ties of family. She grabbed Cat's paw and squeezed it tightly. "Love holds us together, not magic."

Cat pointed with her other paw to the rocks. "So, what are you going to do with him?"

"I don't want his poison here any longer." Resolution welled up inside Rinn. "I'm going to kick him off our hill and tell him to never come back."

Yallakh's voice interrupted. "And how exactly are you going to do that? There are a few stones in the way." Rinn let go of Cat's paw and set down her spear. She balled her hands into fists as she focused, whispering her word of protection. Her barrier appeared, a tight sphere enveloping the pile of stones. When Rinn had fought the floefangs, trapping them in her shield, she realized she could move them around at will. With concentration, she slid the rocks inside her shield across the ground, and deposited them against the palisade wall. A cloud of dust and mold escaped the opening to the cellar. Rinn grabbed her spear as an emaciated Yallakh clawed his way out. He rested on the edge of the top stair, breathing in the clean air. Rinn hesitantly handed him the full waterskin. He accepted it and took long deep swallows, clear water trickling down his dusty face like drops of rain falling on a parched desert.

"You are a wonder." Yallakh handed the waterskin back to Rinn.

"Keep it." Rinn waved her hand dismissively. "Now, we need to get you out of here. The safest route is behind my house, away from the construction. Follow me and keep quiet."

Yallakh held a hand against a wall to steady himself as he rose. "Not to sound ungrateful, but why are you doing this?"

Rinn had been asking herself that question all night. She did not want to admit that part of her rationale was not wanting to have a corpse under her house. But the better part of her could not bear to see any person, no matter how detestable, cruelly imprisoned and left to die. Certainly, Yallakh had a lifetime of sins to atone for, be he could not do that rotting away in a cellar. Rinn did not know how to explain herself so she just shook her spear and whispered forcefully. "No more talking."

Rinn slinked down the back of the house with Cat trailing noiselessly after her followed by the dusty fiend dressed in strips of rotting cloth. Rinn cautiously rounded the corner of her house into broad daylight. Yallakh had to avert his eyes against the full rays of the sun. The three hurried across the courtyard to the shadow of the far palisade wall. They made their way to the main gate, but found Molo blocking their path, holding Clive in his right hand.

"What's this all about?" The giant man's expression was stern but not hostile. Rinn noticed that in his off-hand he held his forge hammer.

"We were hoping no one would notice." Rinn fumbled.

"You can't expect to move that many souls around without Clive seeing it." Molo shook his head in irritation. He raised his hammer over his shoulder. "How are you going to explain this to your father?"

Rinn answered meekly. "Does he have to find out?"

Molo tapped his head with Clive. "Rinn, think before you act. You're not a little child. This man is a plague. He's killed hundreds, thousands of people. Who knows how many more will die by his hand. Do you want that released out into the world?"

"He deserves a chance." Rinn blurted out.

"A chance to do what? Change?" Molo ground his teeth. "There is no redemption for monsters like him. He's a murderer and he'll always be a murderer." Molo reached out to grab Yallakh. Rinn noticed that Molo was no longer holding Clive, the rock had vanished. As Molo started to drag the emaciated prisoner back to the house, Rinn stopped him.

"Don't you have any regrets?" Rinn barred his way, not with her spear, but with her arms held wide. Her piercing gaze struck the giant. "Don't you want a second chance." Anguish tore through Molo. He hung his head as he dropped the prisoner to the ground. He rubbed his eyes with an oversized hand. Yallakh crawled away from the giant and huddled against the palisade wall. Everyone eyed each other nervously.

Molo broke the silence. "Okay, what now, Sigillum?"

At the mention of the word, Yallakh's eyes peeled open in fear. He shrank away from Rinn as if she burned like fire, like she was a deadly poison. He crossed his arms over his chest protectively and buried his face. "God magic." He stammered in terror. "Keep her away from me."

"That's right, demon." Molo lifted the pitiful man off the ground. "With a word, she could tear your soul right out of your body and your damnable tattoos would not save you. But she's decided to give you a second chance, don't squander it." Molo opened the back gate and hurled him through it. "Now, get out and never return. Clive can see you coming for miles, so don't think of trying anything. Take this one chance you've been given, you won't get another."

Yallakh fled down the hillside as fast as his withered legs could run, stumbling several times in the driven snow. Molo closed and locked the gate and took a deep breath. "Come on, Rinn. You have chores to do." He rolled Clive around in his hand. "You too, Cat." He escorted the girls back to the house.

::

Three days had passed since Rinn released Yallakh and no one had said a word about it. Surely her father must know by now. Rinn watched him send several farmhands into the cellar to clean it out. Rinn found the waiting infuriating, she wished her father would just come out and yell at her and be done with it. Instead, he carried on as if nothing had happened, and Rinn was expected to do the same.

Rinn found herself on a long bench sitting with the other teenage girls. They were tasked with washing the newly sewn fabric the farmer's wives had created. The builders had nearly completed the new community houses. Some of the families had already started moving into their new homes. As the main hall emptied out, parts of it had been slowly taken over as a winter workspace. Felsic and Mafic had a carving and painting zone set up in one corner. Brogan, the craftsman, had set up a leatherworking table, which stank fiercely. A group of women had commandeered a large area to spin thread and sew fabric.

The cloth-making ensemble was led by Tristy's mother, Ceili. She had a fiery personality to match her auburn hair. She squeezed her curvy figure into a festive dress with a high-cut hemline and a low-cut top. Among the seamstresses, she was the most talented, creating expertly tailored clothes that were both warm and comfortable. Everyone seemed to want an outfit sewn by Ceili. Rinn thought she behaved like an adolescent, prancing around as if she were high-born and spreading gossip about everyone. Rinn silently washed her bolt of cloth, ignoring the other girls on the bench. Soapy water sloshed onto the flagstone floor as she scrubbed. The girls prattled on about the most inconsequential things—whose shoes were prettiest, what was their favorite food, and which boy had the best hair.

Tristy leaned forward to tease Rinn. "Kill any monsters today?"

"Not yet." Rinn bristled. "But I'm thinking about it." She scrubbed her cloth harder without ever looking up. Ceili loomed over her, tapping her foot.

"Not so rough, dear." She had a high-pitched musical voice. "You'll tear the fabric." Rinn exhaled through her teeth and continued scrubbing, a bit less harshly. Ceili returned to gossiping with the other girls. Rinn wondered where Cat had gone, she excelled at getting out of work by simply vanishing. Rinn wished she knew how to vanish. She looked down at the piles of cloth left to clean and sighed. She privately wished for something to happen, maybe an attack on hilltop, and Tristy could be the first casualty.

Chapter 25

Rinn could hear the commotion from her room. She grabbed her cloak and rushed outside to see what was happening. Many of the hilltop residents watched the heated exchange. Marshal stood on the walkway built over the main gate and yelled down at a person outside the walls. A shrill voice answered back. Rinn could not hear well through the murmuring of the crowd. She waded into the throng and found Cat among the onlookers.

"What's going on, Cat?" Rinn squeezed next to her.

"It's one of those redhead bandits." Cat's ears darted in different directions and her whiskers twitched.

"How do you know?" Rinn strained to see through the gate.

"He smells like one." Cat winced and stuck out her tongue. Rinn wondered how she could smell the bandit through this thick crowd of people. There were definitely things about Cat that Rinn did not understand. She did not have time to think about it right now, instead she wondered what the bandit wanted. After all the damage Clanmorris had wreaked across the countryside, this idiot was putting his life on the line showing up here. To Rinn's surprise, Marshal signaled for the door to be opened. The crowd collectively gasped as the gate opened to reveal a dirty teenage boy with red hair standing in the snow. Behind him, being led by a rope, was Marshal's horse Bayard. Marshal took the reins of his horse from the redhead boy and led them both inside the compound.

::

"I don't trust him." Molo slammed his mug down on the kitchen table.

"He's just a boy." Marshal remained stoic. "A boy raised by a gang of thieves and murderers. Now he's looking for a way out. We should help him."

"How do we know he's no different than the rest of them?" Molo grumbled as he poured himself another ale.

"He brought back my horse." Marshal was resolute. "It's the first unselfish thing I've seen from anyone in the clan." Marshal turned his attention to Rinn. "What do you think?" Rinn found herself speechless, her father never asked her for advice. She suspected he just wanted her to agree, so he could outnumber Molo. But the possibility existed that her father was actually unsure and wanted her honest opinion.

"I haven't really met him." Rinn meekly offered as she washed out her dinner bowl.

"I could kill him for you." Cat appeared. "I'll bury him where he won't be found."

"Thank you, Cat." Marshal patted the eager feline on the head. "I'll keep that in mind if I need anyone murdered. Before that, I think we should give Rinn a chance to meet him, see if she can figure out what he wants."

"Why me?" Rinn squeaked, shrinking away.

Marshal tipped his mug. "If you were a teenage boy who would you rather talk to, a nosy adult or someone your own age?" Rinn decided not to answer the question.

::

More visitors arrived at the burgeoning town the next day. The flirtatious innkeeper Muireen had not seen patrons at her establishment for weeks and was wondering what had happened. She heard rumors about a new settlement upriver on a hilltop and so she came to investigate, and trade. Rinn was actually happy to see Muireen and her caravan of food and drink, but when the innkeeper discovered that the owner was Marshal, she was a little too excited. When she gave

Marshal an affectionate hug and a kiss on the cheek, Rinn remembered exactly why she did not like this woman.

Muireen's caravan wagons were brought inside the palisade wall, driven by workers from the tavern. The sides of the wagons opened to sell food and drink, and all the townsfolk lined up. Somehow, they found valuables that they were lacking when Marshal asked everyone to pool their resources. Rinn was annoyed, but the overall mood on the hilltop was so joyful that she overlooked her petty grievances. Marshal waited until most of the townsfolk had conducted their business before he took his turn. Rinn closely watched him as he approached the caravan. The innkeeper received him with sultry eyes and a broad smile.

"Hello, Muireen." Marshal stood rigid and tall, like a soldier.

"Oh, you remembered my name, that's good." The innkeep twirled her auburn hair around her finger. "Nice to see you again, Marshal. Are you here to trade?"

"Yes." Marshal added casually. "But that's not all."

"Oh?" Muireen raised an interested eyebrow.

"I want to make sure you are safe." Marshal rested an idle hand on his sword hilt. "This is not the best time to be parading a caravan loaded with food and drink through the wilderness. Clanmorris is completely out of control. They burned down most of the settlements out here. You are lucky to have made it this far alive."

Muireen tidied up the counters of her impromptu store. "Thank you for the concern, but a girl can take care of herself. The clan boys did pay me a visit, but after a few rounds of drinks, they merrily went their way."

"That's not all that we've run across lately." Marshal tried to make a dispassionate appeal. "Several days ago, one of our men was killed by a pack of floefangs in the forest. And now we've heard that slavers are operating in the area."

"Sounds like you don't want me to leave." Muireen laughed coquettishly adjusting the skirts of her dress.

"I think you should stay long enough for us to ensure that your route home is safe." Marshal was trying very hard not to get flustered.

"How long will that take?" Muireen grinned with one corner of her mouth. Rinn could not stand to watch another moment. She stormed off to find Cat or Lutra, or anyone who could take her mind off this infuriating woman.

::

Rinn pulled her cloak around her as she sat in the freezing watchtower with Lutra. The Dvalinn dwarves had enclosed the base of the tower in stone, stabilizing it against the harsh winter winds. Even though it was bitter cold, Lutra practiced his flute, tiny puffs of steam escaping his instrument as he played. He wore an outfit made entirely from thick brown furs. Rinn laughed to herself, if she added ears and a tail, he could almost pass as one of Cat's own kinsmen. Then the thought occurred to her, maybe he was dressed this way intentionally. She put the strange thought out of her mind and repeated her question.

"Have you met him yet?" Rinn poked Lutra through his furs.

Lutra stopped playing. "I haven't talked to him, but I've seen him. He mostly hangs out with the girls. What was his name again?"

"Sionne." Rinn heard it from her father first, but everyone in town seemed to be talking about him. He was a bit of an enigma, the refugees here had suffered grievously at the hands of Clanmorris, but Sionne was given a free pass because of his likable personality.

"My Dad wants me to talk with him, figure out why he's here." Rinn shivered under her cloak.

"Why doesn't he do it himself?" Lutra shrugged and resumed his flute playing. His melody was high and wavering but tinged with melancholy.

Rinn vented. "He seems to think it would be easier to get him to talk with someone his own age."

"Aren't you a bit young?" Lutra criticized between melodies. "That redhead boy has to be at least seventeen."

Rinn was indignant. "I'm not too young. I've grown a lot since last summer." Rinn reflected on her own words. Since coming to her new home, she had grown considerably. Back in Viburna, she had been a lazy, foolish little girl. She never helped out around the house, she had servants take care of all her needs, she spent most of her time playing silly games with other kids. Rinn was amazed at how much of her young life she had wasted. She shook off the afternoon chill and headed down the ladder. "I'm not too young. And I will find out what's going on with this Sionne." She descended the watchtower, determined to find him.

::

Rinn stumbled upon Sionne loitering in one of the newly finished community houses. "You must be Rinn." The redheaded teenager rocked on a stool as he smiled. His teeth were wide and not straight, his hair was an unruly mess, but his green eyes sparkled with life. "Heard an awful lot about you."

"Me?" Rinn pointed to herself. For some reason, Rinn had donned her new orange dress before she went out to find the boy. She washed her face and combed her hair though she could not understand why. Sionne himself was dressed like a slob, mismatched shoes and torn breeches. His fingernails were filthy, and his face had smudges of dirt on it. But Rinn only noticed his lively green eyes.

"Yeah, you." Sionne spoke in a voice too deep for a teenager. "Seems like everyone here has opinions about you. Half of the people think you are a witch, the other half a hero." He leaned forward and rested his chin on his fist. "So, which one is it?"

"What?" Rinn found it hard to listen to the teen without being distracted by his eyes.

"Which one are you, a hero or a witch?" Sionne grinned smugly.

"I'm not a witch." Rinn blinked, clearing her head. "But, I'm not much of a hero either." Rinn cast her eyes downward.

Sionne reclined against the wall of the community house. "Well, you have everyone here fooled. They all think you're one or the other. So, if you're not a witch and not a hero, what are you, Rinn?"

"What are you?" Rinn reversed. "You come in here like everyone's best friend, talking like you own the place."

"Whoa." Sionne sat up, interested. "Calm down, firebrand. I'm just making conversation."

"Want me to kill him?" Cat literally appeared from nowhere, claws wrapped around his throat. Sionne froze in an absolute panic. Cat leaned over and hissed in the boy's ear. The teenager stifled a scream.

"Cat, that's enough." Rinn pointed her finger accusingly and shook her head. Cat pouted and disappeared. Sionne jumped off the stool with a start, scanning the room. But he was alone with Rinn.

"What in the blazes was that?" Sionne demanded, rubbing his neck.

"That was my sister." Rinn smirked. "She's a bit over-protective."

"That's a damn grimalkin." Sionne backed away from Rinn. "You're in league with demons. You are a witch. Stay away from me, witch." Sionne invoked a gesture to ward off evil. Never taking his eyes off Rinn, he scurried to the door and stumbled out into the snow. After he had gone, Cat appeared, rolling around on the floor laughing hysterically. Her tail spun around in circles as she laughed.

"Very funny, Cat." Rinn plopped down, feeling very cross with her idiot sister. "I was supposed to find out about him, not scare him half to death. He'll never talk to me now."

Cat could barely speak through her laughing fits. "His face. Did you see his face?" She took several deep breaths to try to calm down. But she broke into conniptions of laughter once more.

"This is serious." Rinn insisted, awkwardly angry and amused by her sister's stupid behavior. She crawled over and put her arms on Cat's warm furry shoulders. "Calm yourself." After a few small outbursts, Cat was finally able to compose herself. Rinn stared her sister down. "Okay, fess up. How long have you been able to turn invisible?"

Cat seemed genuinely shocked. "I can't turn invisible." She sat up and, in a blink, she vanished. Rinn heard feline giggles across the room, Cat was perched high on a wooden roof beam. She waved down at her sister. With a pop, she reappeared right beside Rinn.

Rinn staggered backward in astonishment. "What was that?"

Cat just shrugged.

"How do you do it?" Rinn reached out to touch Cat, to make sure she was real.

"I don't know. I can just slip in and out. I end up wherever I want." Cat answered nonchalantly. Rinn was stunned by her sister's incredible ability, but a subtle fear rattled in the back of her mind. She feared that her magic may be unintentionally enslaving Cat, just like Yallakh had said. Rinn summoned the courage to ask the dreadful question.

"Cat, how long have you been able to do this?" Rinn nervously waited for the answer.

"Ever since I met you." Cat acted like the answer was obvious. The realization struck Rinn like a hammer, Cat was using her magic. Rinn refused to believe it, but the truth was evident. A sense of guilt overwhelmed her, she had not meant to force her will on Cat, but nevertheless it happened. And if what Yallakh said was true, Cat was bound to her for life, inseparably tied to her magic. Rinn was both terrified and relieved. She stepped outside in the snow to clear her head and look for Sionne, but he was long gone.

Chapter 26

"You are going to fix this mess." Marshal berated his daughter at the kitchen table, slamming his dinner down noisily. He fixed his eyes on Rinn who was desperately trying to hide herself behind a bowl of soup. Molo leaned against a corner, listening dispassionately.

"Why me?" Rinn feigned innocence. "I didn't mean for him to get scared."

"Well, he was." Marshal fumed. "And now he's leaving."

Molo idly commented to Clive. "Let him go. One less thing to worry about."

Marshal raised his hands in frustration. "He came here asking for help. I gave him my word, I told him no harm would come to him, and you threatened to kill him." Marshal pointed accusingly at Rinn. "Fix this!" He stomped out of the kitchen, leaving his uneaten dinner behind.

Molo bent forward. "Wish I could've been there." He softly punched Rinn in the arm. He headed outside, but before he left, he looked back and added. "Just do your best."

::

Bos and Calder were hammering out projects at Molo's forge. Rinn approached and warmed her hands by the fire. She shouted over the clang of hammers. "Have you seen Sionne?"

"Who?" Bos yelled back.

"The redhead boy." Rinn shouted. She wished they would stop working for a moment, but they never did. Calder dipped hot iron into a snowbank with a hiss. His long black hair was tied back into a ponytail, making him look older than he was.

"Try the furthest common house." He answered. Rinn waved her thanks and loped off through the snow. Clouds had been gathering since morning and heavy snows threatened all day. A frigid wind blew across the hilltop whipping the snow into small eddies. Rinn leaned into the wind as she crossed the courtyard to the community houses. She entered the closest house for warmth. Inside three teenaged girls glared at her.

"Shut that door." Devy commanded. Rinn pulled the door shut and fastened the wooden latch. She shook snow off her boots.

"What do you want?" Tristy sat on a stool while Feena combed her hair.

"Have you seen Sionne?" Rinn bravely asked.

"Haven't you done enough damage?" Tristy sneered.

Feena spoke timidly. "He's in the next house over." Tristy spun around and snatched the brush from her hand. Rinn waved a quick thank-you to Feena and rushed out the door. The snow was starting to fall in earnest, thick white flakes dropping so heavily that Rinn could barely see the next house only twenty paces away. She wrapped her cloak around herself and trudged through the snowfall to the adjacent community house. It was filled with people taking refuge from the storm. Rinn found Sionne in a back room stuffing his meager belongings into a haversack. She stood in the doorway, dripping wet from the melted snow.

"Go away." Sionne chafed. He pulled the drawstrings on his pack closed.

"You can't leave now. There's a terrible storm brewing outside." Rinn noticed for the first time how poorly the boy was dressed. His woolen shirt was thin and worn, his cloak was flimsy and too small. He did not even have actual boots, just thick socks with leather soles sewn to the bottom. Maybe he was desperate and in need of help, just like her father had said. Rinn felt extremely guilty for the way he had been treated. "Please, stay, at least until the storm is over."

Sionne slung his pack over his shoulder. "It's safer out in that storm than staying here with you."

Rinn barred the exit. "I'm sorry for what happened with Cat. She's actually not that mean, she just likes to joke."

"Well, it wasn't funny." Sionne huffed, pulling his cloak around himself. He stopped directly in front of Rinn. "Get out of my way, witch."

"I'll put a spell on you to make you stay." Rinn grinned wryly.

Sionne stifled a laugh. "I bet you would."

Rinn eased her arms down. "Maybe I am a witch. But if you went out in that storm and froze to death, I'd feel horrible about it. Stay, at least until the storm is over. I will make Cat behave."

Sionne lowered his haversack. "That thing has a name?"

"Cat is her name." Rinn admitted. "Actually, it's short for Catherine."

Sionne chuckled darkly. "You people are weird."

"You have no idea." Rinn smirked at him.

::

Rinn shared the table with her father, Molo, and the hilltop dwarves, Cat sat beside her. Dinner was a stew of some animal she could not identify, but with the right herbs it reminded her of roast pig. Cat had discovered Rinn's secret stash of catmint, apparently some time ago, and she sprinkled flakes of it on everything she ate. She was purring as she licked her soup bowl clean. Marshal raised a mug to the dwarves.

"A toast to the Dvalinn." Marshal announced. "Because of your excellent designs and hard labor, the citizens of hilltop will sleep warmly tonight. The community houses are an absolute success."

"Here, here!" Molo raised his gargantuan mug. In unison the dwarves tipped back their mugs and then slammed them satisfactorily on the table.

Botrogen, the eldest dwarf, spoke for the crew. "It's been an honor working with you fine folk."

"Except that moron Sheridan." Marl grumbled.

Botrogen ignored his sour kinsman. "We raise a mug to Rinn. Without her bravery, we would never have had the chance to cut stone again." The dwarves drank and slammed down their mugs in the usual manner. Rinn meekly raised her cup, her father had offered her a small bit of ale, but she declined, opting for juice. She was worried about mixing her Sigillum powers with alcohol. Cat licked Marshal's dinner bowl clean, oblivious to the toasting and revelry.

Molo reclined on his tree-stump stool and addressed Marshal. "Djurl has an excellent idea. You should hear him out." He motioned to the dwarf. "Go on, Djurl."

Djurl was the scrawniest of the Dvalinn dwarves. His shoulders were narrow and his hands small, but his deepset eyes were keen with intellect. "We dwarves hate to sit idle, even in winter. You have a stone cellar below the house, and with your permission, we would like to begin quarrying stones to create an escape tunnel. Just in case."

"Sounds reasonable." Marshal admitted. "But what will you do with all the stones you quarry?"

"That's the best part." Molo's eyes lit up. "Go on, tell him, Djurl."

"We're going to stack the stones behind the palisade, to create a wall within a wall." Djurl held his hands together, like two walls touching.

"That'll be a nasty surprise for those clan-boys." Molo patted the thin dwarf on the back. "Stone doesn't burn." Rinn actually found herself quietly giggling. She would love to see the dejected expressions on those Clanmorris raiders when they find a stone wall hidden behind the wooden palisade.

"When can you begin?" Marshal asked hopefully. Everyone was staring awkwardly at him. He looked down to find a sleeping Cat curled up on his lap, purring loudly. Everyone at the table laughed, including Rinn.

::

The snows tapered off the next morning, but much of the next few days were spent digging the hilltop village out. Narrow paths connecting the buildings were carved into the deep snowbanks. The lean-to animal shelter was ruined, buried under driven snow. One community building was given over to housing animals. The snowbound caravan joined the families in the remaining community houses. Muireen was not unhappy with her situation—she spent every moment away from her business with Marshal. And even though she doted on Rinn, giving her small presents from time to time, Rinn could not help but feel animosity toward the woman.

Rinn sat in her room, awkwardly mending winter clothes. Cat lay near their small fireplace, playing with the skein of yarn Marshal had purchased for her at the harvest fair. Rinn complained as she sewed. "I wish that woman would go home."

"Who?" Cat mused, her paws and tail tangled in yarn.

"Muireen." Rinn mockingly over-pronounced her name. "She spends far too much time with father."

Cat rolled around, further entangling herself in yarn. "I think she's nice. She makes really amazing food."

Rinn threw her sewing on the ground. "Of course, she does. She's an innkeeper, and that's where she belongs, back at her inn. Not here."

Cat cocked her head to the side. "Wouldn't you like to have a mother? I think it would be nice."

Rinn was appalled. "Catherine! That woman is not my mother. I have a real mother who bore me and loved me. And somewhere out there, so do you. Don't you want to find her?"

Cat licked her fangs in thought. "Not really. She'd probably scold me and send me to bed without dinner."

Rinn scooted next to Cat and tried to extricate her from the maze of yarn. She unraveled several twists around her tail. "Don't you want to know if you have any brothers or sisters? Don't you want to know your family?"

Cat seemed confused. "You are my family."

"Oh, Cat." Rinn wrapped her arms around her sister. Cat purred warmly, tail waving contentedly. Unexpectedly, her feline ears shot up, and she sniffed at the air inquisitively. Her lithe body snaked out of Rinn's embrace and the yarn tangles in one fluid motion. She continued to sniff at the air as she moved through the room.

"Something's coming." Cat followed her nose out the door.

"Cat." Rinn pulled herself off the floor. "Wait for me."

Cat's nose led them outside into the crisp noonday snows. Molo was already at the front gate, shouldering it open against the driven snowdrifts. Cat bounded over to the giant, Rinn struggled to keep up.

"You can sense it, too, little cat?" Molo patted the Margot on her head. She climbed up onto his shoulder and perched like a bird. Molo strode into the deep hillside snow, parting it like water as he walked, Rinn followed in his wake. She felt vulnerable leaving the compound without any weapons, but she trusted that Molo would not intentionally lead her into danger. Molo's trail led north, away from the hill and towards the evergreen forest. Wintery winds blustered, and snow swirled around the trees, sending pine needles flying. Rinn clutched her cloak tightly around herself and trudged on.

Molo and Cat ventured deep into the sparse, upland forest. Fortunately for Rinn, the snowfall here was less than in the rolling hills below. In the lighter snow, Rinn was able to catch up to Molo and Cat. Breathlessly, she begged for an explanation. "What's going on?"

"She's coming." Molo gazed far off to the north. On his shoulder, Cat paralleled him, ears and eyes trained the same direction. Rinn realized that Molo was not carrying Clive, which was very unusual.

"Who's coming." Rinn scanned the barren snowy highlands to the north.

"Geamradh." Molo spoke the name reverently as he walked into the coming snowstorm. Rinn had no idea what he was talking about, but she had no choice except to follow him. Molo's path led directly into the icy torrent howling in the distance. Rinn pulled her thin clothes around her as she shouldered her way into the biting winds.

Chapter 27

A ceiling of thick white clouds loomed over Rinn's head. She had passed through the whipping winds and fierce snows to a place of calm. The air was noiseless and still, and the crisp aroma of ice filled Rinn's nostrils. She walked hunched over, holding her hands close to her body for warmth, but her eyes were raised, transfixed on the scene playing out before her. A colossal figure was moving through the trees of the sparse evergreen forest. It was impossibly tall, Rinn got dizzy just looking up at it. The creature Molo called "Geamradh" resembled a snow-white doe massive in size and scale. It strode delicately over the pines on stilt-like legs. Its deerlike face had clear blue eyes and a stone colored nose. Antlers resembling massive oak trees grew from its head, adorned with pure white leaves.

Molo and Cat proceeded slowly toward the towering legs and Rinn anxiously trailed after them. As they neared the colossal creature, Molo fell to his knees in awe. Cat leaped off his shoulder and bounded across the snow on all fours, like an actual feline. She weaved dangerously between the massive legs as they glided through the forest like huge white tree trunks. Rinn could barely watch. Geamradh slowed and settled into a stationary stance. It slowly inclined its massive head sideways to see the creature frolicking below it. Cat raised her chin to the giant head soaring above her, she crouched down and wiggled her tail and behind furiously. She shot straight up, and with a pop she was gone.

"Cat!" Rinn cried out. She ran ahead, fearing for Cat's safety. Molo grabbed her arm from behind and held it fast.

"Wait." He pointed high into the air. "She's there." Rinn looked into the blinding, white winter sky and found her crazy, feline sister, a tiny speck dancing around on the back of the massive creature. Geamradh did not seem to notice or care. Its mammoth head rotated until its two blue eyes stared directly at Molo and Rinn. The colossal beast lowered its massive head downward. To Rinn, this felt like standing at the base of a mountain watching an avalanche head straight for her. Molo shrank back, raising his arms over his head protectively. Rinn gaped in awe, unable to move. The creature stretched out its gargantuan neck until its immense nose was even with Rinn. The giant nose snorted, nearly knocking Rinn to the ground. It gently nudged forward, touching Rinn in the center of her chest. Surprisingly, Geamradh's nose felt warm. It glowed a mellow blue and Rinn's chest responded with its own green aura. The colossal head rose back to its full height, whipping up wind and swirls of snow. The ground rumbled as its towering legs strode onward.

Rinn turned to Molo, her hand on her chest. "What was that?"

Molo sat on the ground, dumbfounded. "That was Geamradh, the season of winter."

"The season?" Rinn pondered the impossibility of a walking season. Suddenly, she remembered her sister. "Wait. Where's Cat?" Rinn squinted at the sky and found her, just a dot bouncing on the back of the enormous creature. Rinn waved her hands wildly. "Cat. Come back." Geamradh lumbered away veering north and east. Rinn shouted even louder and Molo added his own bellowing voice. Eventually, the tiny speck waved back. With a loud clap, Cat slipped out of the air, stumbling onto the icy ground. She laughed and laughed.

Molo grumbled. "Stupid reckless feline. You shouldn't have done that." Cat tried to get up but fell back over, unable to stand.

Rinn rushed to her. "Gods. Cat, look at your paws." Her front and back paws were icy blue and stiff. Molo lifted the frostbitten Margot off the ground and wrapped her in his cloak.

"Let's get you home before your paws fall off." He led the way back to Hilltop. Rinn cast one last gaze at the gigantic creature, taller than the tallest trees as it journeyed deeper into the mountains, and then raced through the snow after Molo.

::

Cat recovered from her frostbite, but she could not walk for days. When she did, she tiptoed painfully on bandaged paws. She lost the fur on the tips of her ears and the end of her tail, and at night when she slept, she whimpered painfully. Marshal made her a drink of bitter roots to ease her suffering. It did help her sleep, but sometimes it made her sick. Rinn suggested adding catmint with excellent results. Rinn stayed with her sister and nursed her back to health. Lutra called to visit as often as he could. He would play his flute to lull Cat to sleep.

One afternoon, when Cat was sleeping, Rinn wandered through the empty house, feeling lonely. Her father was out hunting, Molo and the older boys were busy forging weapons and armor. The Dvalinn dwarves were mining in the cellar and the Dverg brothers were busily trying to craft all the personal items demanded by the townsfolk. Rinn decided to brave the outdoors. Now that Geamradh had moved on, the stormy weather had ended, and sunny skies returned. The temperature was cold but without the same bite. Rinn sauntered over to the community houses.

Rinn was not intentionally looking for Sionne, but she found him. He sat near the hearth chatting with Tristy and her friends. Rinn was conflicted, she did not want to talk to Sionne and she especially did not want to talk to the teenage girls, but she found herself walking over anyway.

Tristy smiled mockingly at Rinn. "How's your pet?" The other girls snickered with her. If Rinn had been carrying one of her pilum spears, she would have murdered Tristy on the spot. Before she could think of something spiteful to say, Sionne scolded the trio.

"Play nice, girls." He seemed genuine until he turned to Rinn and added. "Don't mind Tristy, she's actually not that mean, she just likes to joke." Rinn recognized his sarcasm, she knew coming here was a mistake. She spun around without a word and marched out the door, slamming it behind her. As she stomped across the snow-covered yard, she was surprised to find Sionne following after her. "Those girls really hate you."

"The feeling is mutual." Rinn fumed.

Sionne chuckled as he walked. "According to them, you bewitch people in the village and steal their souls. They claim you magicked the god of winter to stop the snows." Rinn desperately wanted to defend herself, but she did not know what to say. Even her own father had a hard time accepting her story of her encounter with Geamradh. Rinn squeezed her fists in silence. Sionne babbled on. "They're also spreading rumors about you using your magic to release demons and slay dragons. I don't believe anything they say, it's all talk. They're just jealous of you and your Dad. He's like king of this hill, and some people resent his authority. But I don't think you're all that bad."

Rinn faced him and screamed out loud. "I'm worse than bad. I'm a horrible witch. Now get away from me before I rip out your soul."

"Whoa, girl." Sionne waved his hands defensively. "You are a firebrand." He rested a hand on his hip. "Don't be angry with me. I'm not the one starting these rumors. I don't believe any of them. I've never seen you do any magic."

Rinn rubbed her face, her hands were icy cold. "I don't know the first thing about magic."

Sionne was taken aback. "But you can do it?"

"I guess." Rinn sighed. "But I don't know very much. I've never even met a real witch."

"Really?" Sionne smirked. "I know one. She lives in the forest."

Rinn's curiosity was piqued. She knew she was probably making a terrible decision, but she felt she had to meet this witch.

::

"I don't think you should go." Cat licked her bandages. She had been sitting up in bed more often, occasionally moving short distances around the room, but she was far from fully recovered.

Rinn stuffed bread and cheese into a bag. "Sionne says she doesn't live far away. We can get there and back in a single day."

"What are you going to tell father?" Cat stared at Rinn with big blue eyes. Rinn could feel the weight of her concern.

"Nothing." Rinn stamped. "I have to go. Who's going to teach me magic? Dad? Molo? The dwarves? Yallakh was the only one who knew anything, and we ran him off."

Cat never blinked. "I just don't think it's a good idea."

Rinn sat down on the bed beside her sister. "Cat, half of the people on this hill are scared of me. An honestly, I'm scared of myself. What if I lose control of these powers? What if I hurt someone I care about? I need to go, to keep everyone safe."

"Then go." Cat gently, very gently, pushed her away. "Just be safe and come home. We need you here." To Rinn, these words filled an empty place in her heart. As Hilltop became the home to more people, Rinn expected that there would be more required of her, but it was the opposite. Muireen had taken over the cooking and cleaning. Ceili and the other women performed most of the laundry and mending for the town. The younger children helped out with the animals. The men worked on carpentry. The dwarves cut stone. But Rinn had no special skills, and she felt useless most days. To have her sister say she was needed was a salve for her wounded pride.

"Thank you." Rinn hugged her furry sister. She gathered her belongings and snuck out to meet Sionne at the town gate.

Chapter 28

R inn trekked through the snowy forests with Sionne. The sun shone brightly in a clear sky, warming the day. Rinn used her pilum like a walking stick, and Sionne whistled a happy tune as they traveled. Rinn could not see it beneath the snow, but she could tell they followed some sort of trail, the trees and underbrush had been cleared away from the path. Since leaving Hilltop, the pair had journeyed east toward the rising sun, into the highlands at the base of the distant mountains. Their path did not have many twists or turns, Rinn figured if she reversed course, she should be able to find her way back home.

"Do you want to stop for a bit?" Sionne offered. He toted a heavy haversack, which Rinn assumed he had filled with food and water.

"No thanks." Rinn hiked on. "Is it much further?"

"Not far." Sionne pointed ahead. "Just past that ridge." They followed the trail into the rocky hillside. With a flourish, Sionne helped Rinn up several steep, snowy inclines. She curtseyed politely as she cleared the obstacles. Rinn saw an ancient weathered tree on the crest of the next hill, and below it a small cabin. Giant roots of the tree covered parts of the stone hovel. Its thatched roof was draped in ivy and snow. A tendril of smoke rose from the crooked stone chimney. Sionne led the way, and Rinn breathed heavy with anticipation.

The door to the cabin was short and wide and appeared as old and weathered as the tree above it. Sionne confidently knocked three times on the door and waited. From inside, a creaky female voice hailed him. "Hold on, my dears." A latch was thrown, and the door slowly opened. Standing inside was a stout, older woman wearing a gray wool dress and a black shawl. She had friendly creases around her eyes and a pleasant smile. "Come in, come in. Warm up by the fire." Rinn followed Sionne into the cozy cabin, ducking under the low-hanging doorframe. The inside of the cabin reminded Rinn of a shed for drying herbs. Bundles of plants hung on every wall, and pots of every size were stacked beside a fireplace in imprecise piles. An over-sized table dominated the center of the room, cluttered with bottles and bowls. The old woman swung a small kettle away from the fire. "What can I do for you children?"

Sionne did not seem to take any offense at being called a child. "My friend was hoping to meet a real witch." He gestured to Rinn.

The woman cackled in delight. "You want to meet a real witch? You've come to the right place. I am Biddy, the forest witch." She hobbled over to a cupboard and removed several earthenware mugs. She sprinkled leaves into them and poured in hot water. She handed the pair of steaming mugs to Rinn and Sionne and prepared one for herself. Sionne eased down into a wooden chair with his hot drink. He motioned for Rinn to explain her situation.

Rinn inhaled deeply and then blurted out. "I want you to teach me how to use magic."

Biddy wistfully blew the steam from her own mug. "Child. You don't 'use' magic. Magic is life. It's in the plants and fruits, their bark and roots. Magic is everywhere."

Rinn grew frustrated. "I mean magic like spells and enchantments. Making swords glow, conjuring shields, making things vanish. Magic like that."

The elderly woman sipped her tea. "That's not magic, little lady, that's fantasy. Magic is boiling the right root to cure a fever or mixing beeswax and oil to sooth a wound. The kind of magic you're describing isn't real."

"Yes, it is." Rinn demanded, her temper simmering.

"You've been listening to too many fanciful tales of dishonest bards." The woman was not cross, rather quite calm. She added more hot water to her mug. Sionne smugly drank his own brew, waiting to see what would happen. Rinn had journeyed all this way only to be told magic was not real. Her patience gave out. She forcefully set down her mug and snatched a glass bottle and tarnished silver spoon from the cluttered table. She held the spoon at arm's length, and in a flash of green light, the spoon turned brilliant white. Sionne's eyes bulged as he watched Rinn slice through a glass bottle, top to bottom, using only a spoon.

"That is magic." Rinn handed the spoon to the witch. She could not tell who was more in shock, the boy or the witch. An unholy silence gripped the room. Biddy let the spoon fall from her hand and backed away.

"That's not magic, that's sorcery." She covered her heart protectively. "You must leave. Leave right now." She hobbled to the door and opened it. "Out. No sorcery here. Not here." Rinn felt guilty for upsetting the woman. She shamefully gathered her things and moved to the door. She glanced over at Sionne, who was still plastered to his chair in shock. Without a word, she left the witch's cottage. In a rush, Sionne grabbed his things and raced after her.

Rinn retraced her tracks in the snow. Sionne caught up to her but kept a good distance away. "What was that?"

Rinn shuffled her feet as she walked, never looking up. "That's who I am. I'm not a witch. I'm not a sorcerer. But I did kill a dragon. I can make magic weapons and shields. And apparently I can rip out people's souls."

Sionne gulped. "That's crazy." They walked on, an awkward silence between them. When they came to the rocky drop-off, Sionne suggested an alternate route. "There's a trail around these rocks to the south. It takes a bit longer, but it'd be safer. Don't want you falling down and getting hurt." Rinn appreciated his concern, she followed him across the ridge to a dense copse of trees. As they entered the shady growth, Sionne took off running. Ten red-headed men with swords stepped out from their hiding places. Rinn knew she had been betrayed. The ambush was perfect, she was completely alone. Neither her father, nor Molo, nor Cat knew where she had gone. She would have to face Clanmorris by herself. She let her pack fall to the ground and readied her pilum. The bandits spread out around her. Sionne was nowhere to be seen.

"Aosta wants her alive." The lead clansman reminded the others.

"She killed my brother." A burly bandit threatened to attack. His bushy red beard was flocked with gray, and his face was painted with black stripes. "This puke will get what's coming to her."

"Easy, Dolan." The head bandit edged towards the hostile man. "We kill her, and those hilltop people will be harder to fight." He put his hand on the man's sword arm.

The burly bandit pulled away. "I don't care. My brother will not be disgraced by a little girl." With murder in his eyes he advanced on Rinn, instinctively she activated her shield, a translucent dome of green spirals and triangles. The clansmen fell back several steps, murmuring about witchcraft. The leader warned them to hold their ground.

Rinn saw their resolve breaking, so she decided to act brave. "Let me go or risk your own deaths." She threatened with her pilum spear, but it rattled in her hands. They saw through her false bravado.

"Somebody put an arrow in her and let's go." The leader waved his hand. On command, one of the redheads unslung his bow, notched, and fired at Rinn. The arrow struck the barrier and ricocheted off. He fired a second shot with the same result.

"I can't get through, Hughes." The archer complained.

"Fine, swords then." Hughes, the leader, whistled to Rinn. "Girl. We don't need to fight. Drop your weapon and come out from behind that thing." He waved his hand in the direction of the barrier. "We just want to talk."

"No talk, she dies." Dolan was fueled by grief and hatred. He swung his sword at the green barrier and the blow glanced off, unbalancing him. He swung again, hacking away at the magical shield. Several other clansmen joined in, slashing at the barrier with their swords, sending green sparks flying. As they pounded away at her shield, Rinn felt a stabbing pain start to build in the back of her head. She realized her shield was not going to hold out forever. She needed to go on the offensive, but she was afraid. Her pilum glowed green in expectation, but Rinn did not want to kill.

The bandit archer was the first to cry out in pain as he was seized from behind. With a crack and soft thud, he fell to the ground, his neck bent at an unnatural angle. A dark shape stooped over and unsheathed the fallen man's sword. The clansmen turned to face their new foe, only to be efficiently chopped down one by one. In a matter of moments, the quiet copse of trees had become the scene of a massacre, six bandits ruthlessly slaughtered. The others fled in terror. The dark shape threw down his bloodied blade and stood at the edge of the glowing barrier. He considered the terrified girl curiously.

"You can come out now." The gravelly voice unmistakably belonged to Yallakh. Hesitantly, Rinn lowered her shield, it felt like a vice on her head had been released. Yallakh was still clothed in his rotting black wrappings, his cold brown and red eyes regarding her. "Some weapon you are."

Rinn did not know how to respond. She wanted to be grateful to Yallakh for saving her, but the sight of the mutilated bandits made her sick. She dashed out of the grove covering her nose and mouth with her cloak, refusing to look at the carnage. Once out on the rocky plain, she stopped and caught her breath. Yallakh slowly walked over, keeping some distance between himself and the girl.

Between dry heaves Rinn admitted. "I'm not a weapon."

"Obviously." Yallakh sat down on a frozen boulder as if the cold did not bother him. "What are you even doing out here?"

Rinn tried to compose herself, brushing off her winter dress and cloak and trying to wipe the snow off her boots. "I wanted to meet the forest witch."

Yallakh considered her response. "You're trying to find a teacher. That's not unreasonable. But, what I asked is, why aren't you in Sevria where you belong?"

Rinn was taken aback. Her father had told her that her life was in danger, that the Empire was not a safe place for her. Rinn had no reason to doubt him, but she also had no proof that he was telling the truth. "I don't belong there. The people in Sevria want to kill me."

"Why?" Yallakh crossed his legs casually and sat back on his boulder. "If you're a Sigillum, then you're the protector of Sevria. They should celebrate your coming with feasts and parades. You have your own palace."

Rinn acknowledged that she had no reason to trust Yallakh—the sting of Sionne's betrayal was still fresh. Yallakh was a slaver and murderer, but he was asking the right questions, things Rinn should have reasoned out for herself. She knew that her father was keeping secrets from her, but she never stopped to question his motives. Was going against the gods really in her best interest? Rinn said the only thing she could think of. "The Curia want me dead."

Yallakh's wrappings shook as he laughed. "Oh! So, Daddy is trying to play politics. This is going to be very exciting." He rubbed his hands together.

"I don't understand." Rinn shook her head.

Yallakh rose and paced around his boulder. "Every time the Empire gets in trouble, the gods send a protector, a Sigillum, to save the day. Gifted with divine magic, these women shield Sevria from conquest and disaster. But now, the threat is coming from the inside, and your Daddy doesn't want his little girl to get caught up in a nasty civil war, so he brought you out here." Yallakh stopped an arm's length from Rinn. "Did you know that being out here has probably weakened your powers?"

"What did you say?" Rinn stared at him in disbelief.

"You draw your strength from Sevria itself." Yallakh started walking away. "Can you imagine how strong your magic would be if you were still in the Empire." Yallakh strolled down the hill away from Rinn.

"Wait." She called to him. "Where are you going?"

Yallakh answered her without even turning around. "I'm taking you back home before you freeze to death." Rinn raced down the snowy hill after him, full of doubts, about her father, about her powers, and about herself.

Chapter 29

Rinn followed Yallakh across the snowy plains using her wasted spear as a walking stick. Even though she did not actually use it in combat, just imbuing the metal with her magic caused it to decay within hours. The setting sun dipped low on the horizon, sending streaks of orange across the twilight-blue snowfields. Yallakh pressed on, never tiring. He did not stop to eat or drink, and only when Rinn fell very far behind, did he pause. He would wait for her to catch up before resuming his unrelenting march once again. Rinn was surprised when he stopped in the middle of an open plain, motionless. Rinn scanned the horizon and saw the reason. Ahead, in the snow sat a single rider on horseback, her father.

The two men faced off, the soldier on horseback and the monster. For the longest time, they scrutinized each other, never talking or moving, just locked in a deadly staring match. Finally, Yallakh gestured to Rinn. "You'd better go." Rinn shuffled through the snow to her father, occasionally shooting a glance back at her villainous guide. He remained unmoving, like a statue. When Rinn came to her father, he pulled her up onto the saddle. The warmth of the horse felt amazing. Rinn hugged her father from behind. Wordlessly, the two rode off into the twilight, leaving the frozen stranger alone on the snowy plain.

::

Rinn's father had never shouted at her so brutally, she did not even know his voice could be that loud. "Alone. In the wilderness. With that murderer. Rinn, what were you thinking?"

"Yallakh was helping me." Rinn defended herself, suppressing her feelings of guilt. "He was leading me back home."

"You should not have been out there in the first place." Marshal yelled his reply. Molo sat patiently in one corner of the kitchen as silent as the rock in his hand.

Rinn continued her tirade. "It's not his fault. It's Sionne. He lured me outside. It was a clan ambush. They were going to capture me." Rinn quieted down to almost a whisper. "But they tried to kill me instead."

"Tried to kill you?" Marshal exploded. "Do you have any idea all the things I gave up just to keep you safe? Think about that the next time you decide to throw your life away."

Rinn felt sorry for herself. "It's not my fault. It's Sionne. He's the one to blame."

Marshal would not yield. "War is brewing out there. I will not have you caught up in it."

"Like the one in Sevria?" Rinn spoke with conviction. "Yallakh told me. He said it's the reason you brought me out here, out of the Empire."

Marshal stared at her in disbelief. He turned to Molo for reassurance, but the big man wore his I-told-you-so expression. Even Clive's single eye seemed to regard him smugly. Marshal surrendered. "Okay. Okay. There is truth in what he said. If you stayed in Sevria, if you had been found out, you would have been used as a pawn. Your life would be wasted fighting their useless wars."

"Who? What wars?" Rinn pleaded. "Who's fighting? Why won't you tell me anything?"

Marshal collapsed on a stool and rubbed his brow. "Sit down." He pulled out a seat for Rinn. She sat down timidly. "Rinn, all I have ever wanted for you is a simple, happy life. I wanted to spare you the horrors of war, something I am all too familiar with." He shifted uncomfortably on his stool. "Do you know what a Sigillum is?"

"A weapon." Rinn answered without hesitation.

"Yes, a weapon." Marshal nodded. "Sent by the gods to defeat the enemies of the Empire. But no one is attacking the Empire, it's falling apart from the inside. The Legions abandoned the cities they swore to defend. They gather in the west, preparing for all-out war. The power-hungry Curia raise their own private armies paid with tax money. And the Church is so mired in corruption and bureaucracy that it is powerless to stop the inevitable conflict. Sevria is doomed, and I don't want you to be there when it falls."

"But I'm supposed to be protecting it." Rinn's blue eyes were as deep as pools.

"You can't protect yourself from a handful of bandits." Marshal levelled the accusation against her, not harshly, just honestly.

"Only because I was afraid to kill them." Rinn answered meekly.

"What will you do when you face a Legion of soldiers?" Marshal posed the difficult question. Rinn grappled with the answer, but she did not have one.

::

A lone night jay chirped outside Rinn's dark window. She sat on the floor of her bedroom, watching the flames of her private fireplace. The wood was nearly spent, and the logs glowed an amber color. Rinn's chores were complete and she was alone with her thoughts. In midwinter, nighttime came long before bedtime. "Cat, what am I going to do?"

Cat reclined on her bed, wrapped in a thick woolen blanket. "Get more firewood?" She tilted her head sideways, hopeful.

"Cat." Rinn chastised. "What am I going to do about Sevria?"

"What's wrong with it?" Cat asked with half-closed eyes.

"It's all broken." Rinn explained the different warring factions in the Empire to Cat, who almost paid attention, but eventually lapsed into a gentle feline snore. Frustrated, Rinn

186

left to gather firewood for the night. She was rummaging through the woodpile in the main hall when the swarm of villagers burst into the house looking for Marshal. Rinn retreated into a corner and let the villagers pass. The crowd found Marshal in the kitchen. Chaos filled the room, women crying, men shouting and brandishing weapons.

Marshal raised his hands trying to control the turmoil. "Quiet! Everyone, please!" The noise of the crowd reduced somewhat. "What is going on here?"

"Our girls are gone." A woman wailed hysterically. It was Morven, the tall slender wife of Hadwin. She hugged Ceili, who cried on her shoulder.

"Someone stole our daughters. My Tristy is gone." Sheridan, the burly plowman, burned with hostility. "You have to find them, right now."

Molossus entered the kitchen door, holding Clive. "I can't find any traces of the girls. They must've left hours ago, and we didn't notice."

Sheridan's temperament worsened. "My daughter would not walk out into the cold in the middle of the night."

"It's Sionne." Rinn announced and all heads in the room turned to her. Suddenly, she wished she had not opened her mouth, but she felt compelled to explain herself. "He lured me away from town and into a bandit trap. He probably did the same thing with the girls."

"Where?" Sheridan stomped across the room to Rinn. "Where are they?"

Rinn shuddered as she remembered the copse of trees smeared with torn bodies. She did not want any of the villagers to discover that terrible place and blame her for the massacre. "They won't be there anymore."

Sheridan berated Rinn, grabbing her by the arm. "Then how do we find them? How?"

"I can do it." A limping Cat tiptoed into the room. The crowd parted to let her pass, Rinn moved to help her recovering sister. Cat smiled weakly. "I can find them." Rinn wiped the tears of happiness from her eyes, or maybe they were tears of sadness at seeing her sister in such a state. Molo joined them in the center of the room. He lifted Cat from the floor and cradled her in the crook of his arm, just like he would Clive.

"I will bear this little one." Molo declared.

Marshal addressed the crowd at large. "We leave at once. If you are coming, assemble at the main gate." Nearly the entire population of hilltop mustered at the gate. Nervous wives hugged their husbands and fretted over their older children. Bos, Lutra, Calder, and Rury represented the teenage fighters, along with Rinn. Sheridan, Hadwin, Brogen, Arlin, and several farmhands were the adult warriors. Felsic and Mafic added a dwarven component. Dvalinn dwarves do not travel quickly over long distances, so they stayed back to guard the hilltop. Rinn was dressed in her iridescent armor, and Cat was swaddled in blankets. Marshal and Molo joined the hunting party distributing weapons and shields to everyone. Rinn hefted a new pilum spear, it felt comforting in her hand.

"Let's get going." Sheridan brashly threw back the bolt on the gate.

"Wait." Marshal held up his hand. Like an officer getting report from his subordinates, he questioned Rinn. "Tell us about the bandits. How many men attacked you?"

"About ten." Rinn guessed, trying her best to remember.

"What weapons did they use?" Marshal continued.

"Mostly swords, a few with bows." The picture was coming clearer in her head.

Marshal asked his next question as professionally and stoically as possible. "And how many were left alive?"

"Less than half." Rinn answered honestly. The crowd gasped, boys and men backed away from the girl. The women made gestures to ward off evil. Rinn desperately wanted to clear her name, but she did not know how to explain

Yallakh's role in the massacre. She said nothing, silently suffering the townspeople's revulsion.

Marshal addressed the awestruck crowd. "Remember, our goal is to get the girls back safely. If we rush in with our swords raised, the girls are more likely to get killed." He stared exactly at Sheridan. "Control your rage. If there is a way to negotiate with the clan, we will do that. If that fails, then the sword, but only together and at my command. Is that clear?" The crowd grumbled in affirmation. "Okay, Cat. Lead on."

Molo pushed open the town gate while gently cradling Cat in his arms. Marshal slung a bow over his shoulder and mounted Bayard. The rescue party marched through the gate in a double file line carrying torches. Rinn lagged behind at the end of the file with the dwarves. Mafic, the good-natured Dverg, twirled his war hammer as he traipsed through the snow. Felsic, his dour brother, carried the torch.

"Are you sure your Cat can find these missing girls?" Mafic wondered.

"It should be no problem." Rinn admitted. "She has an excellent nose."

"Finding them and rescuing them are two different things." Felsic observed. "Who's to say they didn't leave voluntarily."

"Who would want to go with the Clan?" Rinn winced. "It's a pack of thieves and murders."

"They probably say the same thing of us." Felsic shrugged. Rinn chewed on that thought and realized he was right. To Clanmorris, Marshal and Rinn were the invaders. They moved onto their land and killed their men. Rinn was starting to realize that this might not have a peaceful resolution after all. She shivered in the cold, knowing that she would likely be forced to kill once again, and the thought of it terrified her.

Chapter 30

The rescue party trudged through the fields of midnight ice, freezing winds biting at exposed skin and snuffing out torches. Thick snowfall obscured their vision. The waning moon Sidus shed very little light, and the unseen moon Tenebra never had any light to give. Occasionally, Molo would stop to let Cat sniff at the night air. They would make slight adjustments in their course and the group would set off again. Marshal rode in wide berths, scouting the nearby areas on horseback.

Rinn contemplated her Sigillum abilities as she walked. She knew only a few words that tapped into her powers. 'Gifan' activated her acies, her enchanted weapon. She did not need to say the word, just think it. She had not tried enchanting other people's weapons. She decided at some point she should attempt it. 'Beorgan' activated her shield, a dome about four or five paces across. Rinn had figured out how to trap things inside her shield and move them around. Her father had taught her two other words, 'Ahebbe' and 'Onlithe', but he had no idea what they meant. Rinn had experimented with the words on different weapons and shields, but without any results. Once, she chanted 'onlithe' while holding her spear and the tip of the weapon broke off and fell to the ground. Some great fighter she turned out to be. Noises in the distance distracted Rinn from her thoughts.

Molo signaled to halt and Marshal rode to him. The two conversed for quite some time, and the order was given to extinguish the remaining torches—the rescue party was getting close. They trudged up a snowy embankment, Rinn used her pilum to navigate the steep climb. Even though they were short in stature, the dwarves proved to be very surefooted, easily beating the rest of the party to the top of the incline. When Rinn reached the dwarves, she could see an orange glow emanating from a canyon below. A large campsite stretched out along a frozen riverbed that coursed through the canyon floor. The gray stone walls that rose up on either side like cliffs flickered in the light of the campfires. Rock-shelf overhangs created ideal shelters for lines of tents pitched beneath them.

"What's the plan?" Molo leaned against his giant hammer. All the members of the party waited for Marshal's response.

"Those cliff walls are too steep and icy to climb." Marshal scratched at his thin beard. "We'll use that to our advantage. Lutra, do you have that flute you play?"

"No." Lutra seemed confused.

"That's a shame." Marshal hung his head for a moment. "It would have made a good distraction."

"You need a flute?" Mafic offered. "Find me a straight branch. My brother and I can craft one in moments." Marshal sent the teenage boys to find a suitable stick. While they searched, Marshal outlined his plan. He wanted to cause a distraction and attack the camp from a distance, drawing out as many warriors as possible. In the ensuing chaos, several party members would slip in and locate the girls. The teen boys returned with a perfectly straight pine branch. Mafic and Felsic began tooling the wood with impossible speed. While they worked, Marshal assigned everyone their tasks. In a short while, the Dverg brothers had constructed a perfectly smooth and beautiful six-holed, wooden flute. There was even a small bird etched into the shaft. Lutra took the instrument and played a sample note, a rich high-pitched whistle. He nodded approvingly.

"Everyone has their assignments." Marshal waved. "Remember, fight only when you have to, flee if you can. Our goal is to confuse the camp, not defeat it. Lutra, as soon as you get to the top, start playing. Molo will lead the assault from the opposite cliff. My group will infiltrate the camp." He gave the party the customary Legion military salute, which only Molo returned.

Rinn watched Lutra and the other teenage boys depart for the far side of the canyon. Molo led Hadwin, Brogen, Arlin, and the farmhands in the opposite direction. Rinn remained with her father, Sheridan, and the dwarves. Cat stayed behind, taking refuge in a snowy dugout created by Molo. He draped blankets over her hiding place to keep her warm. She curled inside like a hibernating hedgehog. Rinn patted her sister's warm fur and then pulled the blankets over her, kissing her head. "Good job, Cat. You found their hiding place. Now get some rest." Cat snuggled deeper into her blankets.

Marshal stealthily led Bayard and his team to the mouth of the canyon. Even though two bandit sentries stood guard, Marshal assured everyone that they could not be seen, the sentries' own torchlight would blind them to the darkness. Marshal silently mounted his horse and whispered in his ear. Time seemed to stop for Rinn as she waited in the dark and cold. After what felt like the length of the entire evening, she heard the call of a single note wafting on the night air. The note, turned to a melancholy melody. Rinn recognized the tune, remembering hearing Lutra practice this exact song in the watchtower. The notes rose and fell, harmonizing with the winter wind.

The sentries began to discuss with each other and hailed to other men in the camp. Before long, a group of raiders with torches gathered and set out to find the source of the music. Rinn anxiously watched the men depart, heading around the side of the canyon. After they had gone, Molo and his men lined the opposite clifftop, shouting and throwing rocks, rolling small boulders down into the canyon. The stones reverberated loudly as they ricocheted off the canyon walls. The general alarm sounded in the camp and dozens of men rushed out with swords and axes. They poured out of the mouth of the canyon past Marshal's hidden rescue party.

Once the horde of clansmen had passed, Marshal spurred his horse forward and rushed into the camp. Sheridan, Felsic, Mafic, and Rinn followed on foot. A sentry spotted them and loosed an arrow at the incoming rescue party. Marshal returned fire from saddleback. With several well-placed shots he downed one sentry and forced the other to abandon his post. Marshal rode deep into the canyon, while Sheridan and the dwarves moved tent to tent, looking for the missing girls. Rinn followed nearby, keeping guard. The tents were small domed frames with animal skins stretched over them, and most were empty. The few clansmen that were found did not put up any resistance, they were not fighters. Rinn grew nervous as she ventured deeper into the canyon, not finding any sign of Tristy or her friends. She could hear the sounds of fighting echoing down from the clifftops. Marshal led the search party down the narrow canyon to its end, a frozen waterfall hanging from the walls like one massive icicle.

Marshal whirled Bayard around and surveyed the campsite in frustration. Sheridan and the dwarves had searched nearly every tent, but the girls were nowhere to be found. Rinn heard a hollow sound, angry shouts from far away getting closer. Redheaded clansmen poured out of a dark cave concealed beneath one of the rocky overhangs. Sheridan gaped at the tide of bloodthirsty clansmen in horror. Marshal yelled for everyone to flee as he spurred his horse forward, driving him directly into the oncoming horde. He slashed with his sword as he rode through the crowd. The dwarf brothers pushed Sheridan onward, using their shields to break through the crowd. Rinn slipped behind them, stabbing right and let with her pilum. Together they carved a path through the wall of clansmen, but not without getting bloodied.

Rinn could see the canyon exit, but a line of clansmen barred their way. Marshal rejoined Rinn and the others, bleeding from multiple wounds to his arms and legs. Before the clansmen at the exit could attack, a pack of roaring teenage boys caught them unawares on their left flank. Mafic laughed as he dove into the fray, swinging his hammer wildly. Rinn turned back to see the redheaded horde rallying behind them. Unexpectedly, from above, a very large boulder came sailing down, scattering the bandits as it crashed to the icy floor. The canyon was filled with deafening echoes as Arlin and the farmhands called down from above. High on a clifftop, Molo readied another massive boulder. Mafic, Sheridan, and the teens got the better of the few bandits that blocked their way, and the embattled rescue party fled the canyon, hurrying to the clifftop to regroup with Molo and the others.

Sheridan berated Marshal as he ran. "My daughter's still in there." Marshal did not answer, he was struggling just to stay in the saddle. As Rinn ran from the bandit camp she was filled with remorse. They came to rescue Tristy and her friends, but the bandits had overwhelmed them. There must be over a hundred men in that canyon. Now the three girls were hopelessly trapped in the hornet's nest of enraged clansmen. Their failed rescue attempt only made things worse. Rinn started to cry as she ran.

"You can still save them." A sleepy, feline voice called out to her. Rinn stopped abruptly and looked around, seeing no one.

"Cat?" She called out to the empty night air.

"It's not too late." Cat's voice sounded like she was standing right behind Rinn, but when Rinn spun around, no one was there.

"Cat! Where are you?" Rinn shouted. "I want to rescue the girls, but I can't get to them."

"Yes, you can." Cat whispered in a dreamlike trance. "Are you ready?"

Rinn tightened her grip on her pilum, trying to steel her nerves. "Yes, I'm ready." The night unfolded, and Cat slipped out of the darkness behind Rinn. Cat wrapped her warm furry arms around her sister. Rinn felt like she was being pulled underwater, instinctively she held her breath and closed her eyes. A violent undertow buffeted her, but it was warm and bright. Even through her closed eyelids she could tell she was somewhere as bright as daylight. She felt impossibly squeezed and then, with a pop of her ears, solid ground appeared beneath her feet. She opened her eyes to see Cat slip back into the darkness. Cat mouthed "Good luck" as she vanished.

Rinn found herself inside a dimly lit cave. The irregular ceiling was so low Rinn could barely stand up. Moisture collected in turbid puddles that pocked the floor, the place stank of refuse and decay. Huddled in one corner were the three girls, dressed in filthy, torn clothes. Tristy was crying as Devnet held her. Feena, the youngest, sat alone, cradling her knees. Rinn rushed over to them, hunched down to avoid the low ceiling.

"Rinn?" Devnet gawked in disbelief, as if Rinn were an apparition.

"It's me, Devy." Rinn assured her. Tristy lifted herself from Devnet's lap. Her face was a mess with a large bruise on her left cheek and a black eye. She threw herself forward hugging Rinn and crying uncontrollably.

"Did you get captured, too?" Feena sobbed, looking up.

"No." Rinn denied. "I came to rescue you."

Tristy was so shocked she stopped crying. "You came to rescue us? Why? Why would you do that?"

"You needed help." Rinn knew she was doing the right thing, everything about it felt correct. No matter how poorly the girls had treated her, no one deserved this fate.

"There's no way out." Tristy sniffed pathetically. "We're trapped here."

"I have a key." Rinn held out her pilum with a wry grin. The spearhead glowed a faint green illuminating the cave. Rinn helped Feena up and led the three girls to the front of the cave. Iron bars blocked their way, but Rinn carved through them with her pilum as if they were made of paper. The girls watched in amazement as the metal bars clanked to the floor. Rinn faced the three girls instructing them in all seriousness. "Now, promise me, whatever happens, you must stay right beside me. Do not run. I will protect you, but I can't do it unless you stay close." Tristy and Feena nodded emphatically, Devnet was too shaken to respond.

Rinn crept down the cave corridor, past several empty enclosures. A lazy prison guard leaned against a wall, snoring. Rinn and the girls tiptoed past him to the main cavern. The main chamber opened into a massive room filled with bedrolls and crude furniture, but it was mostly unoccupied. A few stray men had stayed behind, reclining in their cots or tending meager fires. The four girls kept to the shadows as they moved around the perimeter of the room. Several passageways led deeper into the cave, but only one led out. Rinn could see the canyon floor in the distance and the campfires illuminating it.

"It's time to go." Rinn held up her pilum as she boldly led the girls out the cavern entrance into a canyon filled with hostile clansmen. The three teenage girls cowered behind her in fear. Redheaded clansmen hollered and jeered when they saw the four girls exiting the cave. A tall, muscular brute with a painted face confronted them.

"Going somewhere, little pretties?" He grinned with brown, cracked teeth, rocking his serrated axe menacingly. The clansmen shouted their encouragement as he threatened the girls. Rinn lowered her pilum.

"We are walking out of here." Rinn showed only absolute determination. "You will not stop us."

One of the bandits came up behind the large clansman and whispered to him. "Deel, that's the witch. She's the one who murdered ten of our men."

"Good, then I shall enjoy killing her." The burly clansman twirled his axe with a grin and advanced. He swung his wicked blade at Rinn, and she deftly sliced through the axehead with her glowing pilum. Clumps of worthless metal fell to the ground. Deel staggered backwards, staring at his empty axe handle. His embarrassment turned to rage, and it overtook him. "Kill her." He shouted. The horde of clansmen drew weapons and nocked bows.

"BEORGAN!" Rinn yelled in a voice that was more powerful than her own. She imbued her barrier with the unwavering need to protect Tristy, Devnet, and Feena. The shield that rose around her was thick, multiple layers of swirls and triangles. The barrier shone like daylight, many in the horde had to avert their eyes. Rinn walked forward slowly, steadily, deliberately into the center of the clansmen. Like water they parted as she passed. Deel berated his fellow warriors, goading them into battle. They fired arrows and slung stones at the bright green barrier, but they bounced off ineffectively. Rinn walked resolutely toward the mouth of the canyon. The girls huddled close to her as the clansmen launched everything they had at Rinn's barrier—knives, swords, rocks, spears, axes, flaming logs, but nothing would penetrate it. They yelled and cursed at the girls, but Rinn walked like a queen to the mouth of the canyon, impervious to the abuses of the clan.

As she moved, Rinn spotted Sionne's face among the hostile clansmen. She burned with the desire to go to him and make him pay dearly for his betrayal, but her duty to the girls came first. She thought she saw fear and regret in his eyes, but she carried on, ignoring the traitorous teen. She led the three girls out of the canyon and no one dared to follow her into the dark snows.

Rinn walked a good distance away, maintaining her shield as long as she possibly could, it provided their only light against the blackness of night. The four girls navigated their way to the edge of an embankment and Rinn finally let her barrier fall. She struggled to catch her breath and dropped to her knees in exhaustion. Feena held Rinn as she coughed repeatedly, struggling to breathe. After some time, Rinn recovered, but she felt weak and dizzy. Feena helped her to her feet, and Tristy clumsily attempted to support her other side. Together they labored through the snow, trying to find the others. Devnet trailed behind them, walking in a silent daze.

Chapter 31

Lutra found the girls stumbling through the snow. He rode across the wastelands on Marshal's horse, Bayard. Morning twilight had broken the darkness of winter night. When Lutra arrived, he slid off his mount and threw his arms around the Rinn. "Boldyn be praised!" He fought back tears. "We thought you were lost. Your father has gone mad with grief." Then, if having noticed the other girls for the first time, he stepped back in awe. "You escaped?"

"Rinn rescued us." Feena admitted honestly.

"How?" Lutra stared at Rinn, who slumped against Feena, barely able to stand.

"She appeared in our cage and walked us through the bandit camp untouched." Tristy hesitantly recounted the next part. "She used some sort of magic shield. Nothing could get through it."

"Yeah." Lutra agreed. "I've seen it." Tristy seemed baffled by his casual acceptance of Rinn's magic. He smiled at Rinn in awe. "You held off the entire Clan by yourself?"

Devnet spoke for the first time, in hysterics. "They threw rocks and knives and axes. They shot arrows at us. They shouted and screamed, they were going to kill us. Kill us!"

Tristy hushed her friend. "Quiet, Devy. We're safe." She folded her arms around her. Devnet wept openly.

Feena propped up Rinn. "She can barely walk. We need to get her to shelter so she can rest." Together Lutra and Feena hoisted Rinn onto Bayard's back. Lutra quickly mounted behind her to steady her in the saddle. He grabbed the reins and turned to Feena.

"The others are just north of here, inside the evergreen forest." Lutra turned his horse northwards. "The dwarves were making a fire when I left. Can you lead everyone that direction?" Feena nodded her head. "Perfect. I will drop Rinn off and return for you." With a snap of the reins, Bayard thundered off across the wastes.

::

Marshal lay on several blankets spread out across the snow, a broken off arrow protruding from his right hip. Molo was tending the numerous wounds on his arms and legs when Lutra arrived on horseback with Rinn. Cheers of joy welcomed him. Bos and Calder helped ease Rinn off the horse and settled her on the blanket next to her father and the sleeping Catherine.

Lutra excitedly told his tale. "She rescued them." He was giddy with excitement. "Rinn found the girls and walked them out of the camp using her magic."

Sheridan grabbed Lutra by both shoulders. "Where are they? Where's my daughter, boy?"

Lutra tried to squirm out of Sheridan's grasp. "They're coming this way. I couldn't carry everyone, and Rinn was in terrible shape."

"Which way, boy?" Sheridan shook Lutra vigorously.

"Calm down." Hadwin pried Lutra away from the burly plowman. "You rode straight here?" Lutra nodded slowly, steadying his head. Hadwin pointed to the horse trail. "Follow those tracks and you'll find your daughter."

Sheridan gathered the other teenage boys and took off down the horse trail at a brisk jog. The dwarves stoked the small fire with fallen tree limbs and dried pine needles. The heat of it lulled Rinn to sleep, and she wrapped a drowsy arm around Catherine, snuggling into her warm fur. As she drifted off, she saw her father reaching out to her in a daze, repeatedly calling her a name she did not recognize: Tabitha.

::

Rinn woke with a start in her own bed, Catherine snored softly beside her. The house was eerily silent, and daylight streaked through the brown glass windows of her bedroom. Rinn sat up feeling sore all over. She quietly climbed out of bed, trying not to disturb Cat, who was curled up with a contented smile. Rinn was dressed in her night shirt, so she pulled an old woolen dress over it and worn boots on her feet. She sleepily wandered through the empty house, her face smeared with dirt and her curly blond hair sticking out in all directions. She stopped in the kitchen to grab a bite of bread before she headed out, looking for everyone else. She slung her winter cloak around her shoulders and stepped outside.

The entire population of Hilltop was gathered in the courtyard. When the crowd saw Rinn they cheered loudly, raising their hands and shouting her name. Confused, Rinn started to creep backwards through the door, but she was pulled into the crowd by friendly hands. All the adults came up to congratulate and hug her. The teenage boys patted her on the back. Lutra danced around playing his flute, everyone calling him "Nightsong the Bard". Feena embraced Rinn warmly with tears of joy in her eyes. Tristy and Devnet curtsied to her politely. The dwarves individually came and stoutly shook her hand. Mafic laughed loudly, hugging her and all his dwarf brothers. Marl refused to be included. Rinn was thanked by people she did not even recognize. Small children ran up excitedly to touch her dress or offer her little treats before dashing off.

Molo stood at the far end of the crowd, towering over everyone. He waved Rinn over, and the crowd parted, making an aisle for her. She hesitantly moved forward, one foot in front of the other, uncomfortable as the center of attention. She tried to tame her unkempt curls, brushing them with her fingers. She wished she had put on her new orange dress instead of the plain brown one she wore. Even her boots were old and scuffed and in need of repair. Meekly, Rinn stopped before Molossus and waited. Felsic stood to one side of the giant, he winked at Rinn when she arrived. Molo raised his hands and the jubilant noise of the crowd was reduced to a low murmur. Situated next to Molo was a sturdy table. Unexpectedly, he lifted Rinn up and set her on the tabletop. The crowd cheered, but he hushed them once again.

Molo addressed Rinn in a loud official voice, like a herald. "Rinn Amali. There is not a person on this hilltop who doesn't owe you a debt of gratitude. You have been gifted with an amazing power, which you've chosen to use in the service of others. You have freed those trapped by slavery." The dwarves all cheered. "You have fought fearsome beasts." Hadwin and the boys cheered. "You have opened your home to refugees and defended them against the ravages of war." Several rounds of 'huzzah' went up. Rinn's face was redder than red, and her heartbeat thumped loudly in her ears. Molo continued. "And when three of our own daughters were taken from us, you went alone into the horde to return them to us." Boisterous applause rang out from the crowd. Sheridan cheering the loudest of all. Molo once again called for silence.

"It has been discussed and agreed by everyone here." Molo held Rinn's hand. "From this day forth, you will be known as Lady Rinn." The color blanched from Rinn's face. Felsic came forward with a wooden box and Molo helped him onto the table top. He produced the gold and gemstone necklace that Duke Kapros had gifted Rinn. He made his best effort to fasten the chain around her neck, but Rinn was a bit too tall for him. She leaned forward and helped him fasten the chain. Once the clasp was secured, the gems glowed a faint green. Molo raised his hand and announced. "I present, Lady Rinn, ruler of Hilltop."

"Wait. What?" Rinn jerked away from Molo. "I can't rule, I have chores to do." The crowd chuckled. Rinn waved in exasperation. "I can't be the ruler. What will my father say?"

Molo gently placed a large hand on her shoulder. "It was his idea."

::

"Lady Rinn, Lady Rinn." Cat sang as she pranced around. Her paws were almost completely healed; however, the fur on her ears and tail were taking their own time growing back.

"Stop saying that." Rinn was annoyed as she brushed out her hair. Since her so-called coronation, Rinn had become more self-conscious of her appearance. She only wore her orange dress, because it was the fanciest thing she owned. She scrubbed her fingernails and polished her boots. She chastised her feline sister. "Cat, quit goofing off and get your clothes on. We're meeting with Ceili and the dressmakers today. We have to look nice, they'll be expecting it." Cat made a face like she had just eaten a raw vegetable. Grudgingly, Cat crawled into her dress, the one with the slit cut for her tail. Rinn saw that it was already too small for her. Rinn wondered how quickly Margot grew.

"Can we visit Daddy before we go?" Cat begged.

"Sure." Rinn smiled. The two girls walked out of their bedroom hand in paw. They poked their heads into Marshal's bedroom. Molo had successfully removed the arrow lodged in Marshal's hip, but the wound was deep and would take some time to heal. Faithfully attending his needs was Muireen. Rinn had come to grudgingly accept the innkeep turned trader. She dutifully cared for Marshal, tending to his smallest needs, and he seemed to enjoy the attention.

"Daddy!" Cat bounded into the room and threw her arms around Marshal. He winced happily. Rinn hugged her father with more care.

"You girls look nice." Marshal said in a weak voice.

"We are meeting with Ceili today." Rinn brushed off the skirts of her dress trying to look regal.

"I see you're still wearing your necklace." Marshal sat up in bed. Rinn absently felt the gold chain around her neck, the stones glowed faintly at her touch. He smiled. "It suits you." He repositioned himself for comfort. "You're not still mad are you."

"I was never mad. Just surprised." Rinn insisted. "I'm only fourteen. It's not normal for adults to want my opinion."

"I'm sure you're doing fine." Marshal chuckled. Muireen brought him water, and he drank it, though his expression clearly indicated he would have preferred ale.

"Hilltop is really growing." Rinn excitedly told him about the new families that just arrived. Construction on a second round of community houses was already underway. Hilltop residents were working as hunters, carpenters, smiths, cooks, seamstresses, diggers, butchers, millers, and town guards. Most people bartered for their goods, but sometimes Imperial coins traded hands. Muireen's caravan left to reopen her tavern as a trading post. Once the spring thaws began there were even plans to clear and widen the southern forest trail leading to the inn and the main crossroad. Marshal listened to Rinn excitedly tell him everything about the growing town. Cat pretended to fall asleep several times. Eventually Rinn exhausted all her news. She hugged her father good-bye and left to meet with the dressmakers, dragging Cat along with her.

Chapter 32

Winter was gradually leaving. Melted snow ran down the hillside in rivulets. Rinn picked carefully through the courtyard, trying not to get mud on the hem of the new green dress Ceili had sewn for her. Rinn was slowly becoming accustomed to her daily routine as ruler of Hilltop. In the morning, she visited each community building to see if there were any needs. Feena accompanied her most days. She was only one year older than Rinn, and the two girls worked well together. Feena had a knack for organization. Also, she did not mind Catherine's childish pranks, she found them more palatable than Tristy's meanspirited attempts at humor. Rinn enjoyed the company, and the two girls talked at length.

"We have a team of scavengers leaving today, m'lady." Feena led Rinn to the new postern gate, constructed in the ever-expanding palisade wall. Even though Rinn had reprimanded her many times, Feena would not stop calling her "m'lady".

"Are they traveling far?" Rinn fretted.

"Just to the nearest farms." Feena assured her. "They should be home by evening."

"We should see them off, just for good measure." Rinn decided.

"That would be lovely, m'lady." Feena beamed. The two girls arrived at the wooden gate leading out of town. Six men had gathered for the mission, visiting nearby farms sacked by the clansmen and bringing back anything useful. Metal was highest on the list, because the smiths had exhausted their supply crafting weapons and armor. But with the impending arrival of spring, farming implements would soon be in high demand. The scavengers brought wooden sleds for hauling. Rinn advised them to remain clear of the forest and stay near the river. Arlin was leading this scavenging expedition and he reassured her that they would be careful. His men carried swords and bows, just in case. Rinn waved and wished them good speed as they departed.

Rinn was pleased to see the scavengers leave in such good spirits. "What's next?" She consulted her teenage advisor.

Feena looked at the notes she had scrawled on a slateboard. "The Dvalinn dwarves wanted to see you today. They should be down in their tunnels."

Rinn shuddered. She did not care for the cellar when it was just a cellar. But the dwarves had been mining rocks for over a month, who knew what could be down there by now. They had expanded the cellar into a permanent living quarter and tunneled deeply into the hillside. Rinn was unsure if she wanted to visit them. Not to mention the unsettling memory of Yallakh's time sealed in the same cellar. Rinn braced herself. "Alright. Let's go."

::

Rinn led Feena down the winding stone tunnel. It was astounding to Rinn that five dwarves where able to dig something so incredibly long in such a short time. The tunnel was flat and wide with evenly spaced depressions for torches. The walls were smooth, exposing the natural rock layers of the underground. Rinn and Feena travelled such a distance that they were not certain if they were even under the hill they called home. The tunnel gradually sloped ever downwards, never branching. Ahead Rinn could hear the clang of pickaxes.

"I think we're close." She tried to sound upbeat, hiding her own fears.

"Good." Feena walked half stooped over, even though the ceiling was more than twice her height. She clutched her slate board tightly. Rinn noticed her friend's apprehension and tried to make conversation to keep her distracted.

"I wonder how the dwarves make the tunnels so tall?" Rinn bemused. "I mean, they can't exactly reach that high." Rinn stretched out and could not touch the top of the vaulted ceiling.

"You dig down." A voice startled Rinn and Feena. Ahead, one of the Dvalinn bent against a wall, so completely covered in fine rock dust that he was perfectly camouflaged. "You start at the top and work to the bottom."

"Djurl." Rinn put a hand over her pounding heart. "I didn't notice you."

The dwarf seemed unconcerned. "Botrogen wants to see you. He's just ahead with the others." Djurl led the way down the corridor. The air was heavy with chalk and dust. Rinn and Feena covered their noses and mouths as they descended deeper into the tunnel. Rinn could smell moisture. She heard the dwarves ahead debating.

"If you dig here, you'll flood the entire tunnel." Botrogen was waving his arms furiously at the others.

"There are seven layers of bedrock above us." Larimar, one of the other dwarves, argued. He was muscular but thin, with a black and brown beard.

"If that river changes course, those shelves won't hold." Botrogen stamped the butt of his pickaxe on the ground.

"That could take centuries." Larimar complained.

Marl imitated Botrogen in a grumpy voice. "Never waste your time building tunnels that won't last."

"Exactly." Botrogen agreed. The dwarf leader noticed Rinn and Feena arrive. He hastily brushed off his mining clothes. With a bow of his head he addressed her. "Lady Rinn. Miss Feena. Thank you for coming. We have a matter to discuss." He motioned to several medium sized boulders, perfectly arranged like furniture in a sitting room. He set cups and a pitcher of water on a flat, table-like rock. Rinn held her cup in amazement, it was carved from a single stone, tooled as thin as ceramic. Botrogen poured her a glass of water. Rinn drank politely, but the water tasted like chalk. She remembered Yallakh describing the experience of licking moisture off rocks to stay alive. She tried to put him out of her mind.

"As you can see, we have harvested enough rock to complete the walls around Hilltop." Botrogen finished his glass in a few gulps. The other dwarves set down their picks and joined in a round of refreshment.

Feena spoke up. "The stone walls look amazing, hidden behind the wooden palisade." Botrogen smiled proudly and nodded to the other dwarves in satisfaction. Feena smirked. "Those clansmen are in for a nasty surprise if they try to attack again."

"About that." Botrogen set down his cup. "Our good dwarf Beryl has a crazy idea."

"Brilliant idea." Corrected the youngest dwarf.

Botrogen eyed him suspiciously. "We wanted to get your opinion, m'lady." Rinn listened as Beryl described the design of a new gatehouse to replace the wooden entrance. The building would be thick and wide with narrow windows and a walkway. But it would be a fake. A giant wooden door would be built against a fortified stone wall. The bandits could batter at it all day and the door would never budge. Beryl laughed at his own design, but the other dwarves were more skeptical. Botrogen begged Rinn's opinion of his insane scheme.

"I think it's fantastic." Rinn chuckled. Beryl beamed, and the other dwarves shoved him playfully.

"But how will we get in and out of Hilltop?" Feena questioned.

"Everyone will use the postern gate." Botrogen explained. "It's smaller and easier to defend."

"And if the scavengers come back with enough scrap, the smiths can fashion a proper metal portcullis." Feena deduced.

"I like it." Rinn admitted honestly. "This could save many lives. Excellent work everyone." Rinn rose and curtsied to the dwarves. Remembering the translation of a dwarfish phrase Felsic had taught her, she added. "You honor us with your labors."

"It is our pleasure, Lady Rinn." Botrogen and the other dwarves bowed deeply.

::

In the early evening, Lutra struck the watch tower bell twice, an alert signal. Rinn and Cat headed to the postern gate. The scavenger team was arriving. Rinn immediately noticed something was wrong, their mood was somber as they pulled a heavily laden sled through the gate. Rinn rushed forward, but Arlin, the lead scavenger barred her way.

"It's not a pretty sight, m'lady." Arlin cautioned. Cat held her nose.

"What is it?" Rinn stared at the ominous shape concealed under a tarp.

"It's Tomin." Arlin answered quietly. "We found him at his farm. Well, not him, but his corpse, frozen in the snow."

"How did he die?" Rinn insisted.

One of the farmhands came forward, presenting an empty jug. "He had been drinking, m'lady." Rinn's mood withered. Tomin had made great progress when he first arrived. He worked hard and stayed away from alcohol. But when he was tasked with guarding Yallakh, he was frequently missing. He had not been seen in quite some time, and no one noticed or seemed to care. Guilt ran through Rinn. Hilltop was becoming too large with too many people. Rinn could not keep track of everyone, but it was her duty to keep them all safe. She felt the need to talk to Felsic and Molo about Tomin.

Rinn found Molo at his home with Felsic and Mafic. Cat joined her, immediately grabbing Clive when she arrived. She rocked him in her arms and danced around the room. Molo just rolled his eyes at her antics. He nodded in deference to

Rinn. "M'lady. What can I do for you?" Rinn hesitated to bring up the bad news about Tomin, so she opened with a detailed explanation of Beryl's plan. Molo and Mafic found the whole scheme so hilarious they even made Felsic laugh. Rinn also explained the need to craft a metal gate for the postern entrance.

"Have the scavengers returned?" Molo asked, rescuing Clive from Cat. She pouted until she found a series of animal figurines Felsic had carved.

"About that." Rinn related the news of Tomin's death. She also voiced her fears about protecting the residents of Hilltop if she did not know who was living here. New people were still arriving; although, as the temperatures gradually became warmer, the flow of refugees had lessened.

"You need a census." Felsic suggested.

"What's that?" Rinn asked. Cat tried awkwardly to fix the figurine she had broken. Felsic snatched the pieces from her and worked on it himself.

"It's a list." Mafic completed his distracted brother's thoughts. "A list of everyone who lives here, sorted by families."

"The Imperium takes one every ten years, for tax purposes." Molo offered.

"Should we have taxes?" Rinn pondered.

"I don't think it would be a good idea." Molo confessed. "These rustic people highly value their freedom. They believe Imperials live under harsh laws, like taxation and servitude. They would leave Hilltop before they would agree to become part of the Empire."

"But what about the benefits?" Rinn argued. "Good roads, safe travel, and fewer bandits."

"To some, freedom to go where they want and do what they want is more important." Molo countered. "If you want to create a world for everyone, you have to respect many viewpoints." Mafic and Felsic raised their mugs in agreement. This was going to be more difficult than Rinn had originally thought. She did not know anything about the workings of government, especially on a large scale. Rinn concluded that she was going to have to study. She could read, but she was not the best at it. It occurred to her, Muireen had run an inn for many years, she would know about keeping track of things.

Rinn thanked Molo and the dwarves and took her leave, dragging Cat with her. She needed to find Muireen. Hopefully, she could teach her how to run a town.

Chapter 33

Rinn sat in her study quill in hand staring at the blank ledger page. The room had once been an extra bedroom previously used by Molo and more recently, Muireen. The former innkeep permanently moved into Marshal's room to provide him with care day and night while he recovered. He was healing, albeit very slowly. He took painful steps and practiced pulling his bow to keep his arm strength up. His appetite returned, and his color was improving, but he rarely left his bedroom. Rinn visited him each day to bring food or just to talk. Rinn valued her father's military knowledge and his keen ability to deal with conflict fairly. She came to him for advice on the subtleties of people management.

Muireen had begun teaching Rinn how to keep a ledger. Rinn's head swam when she tried to add long columns of numbers, but Muireen told her to keep at it. Rinn introduced Feena to Muireen and together the two became an unstoppable force of organization. Just in time, too. The warmer weather heralded the coming of the rustic feast day of Imolia, and the townspeople expected a celebration. Rinn did not know the first thing about the rustic religion, yet she was expected to host their most revered holiday. Rinn tasked Feena and Muireen to plan activities for the feast day. Rinn stared at the blank page in front of her. "Cat, what am I going to do?"

Cat appeared next to her. "About what?" She sniffed the inkwell.

"This festival." Rinn whined. "They want me to lead it, but I don't know the first thing about their religion." Cat attempted to dip a claw into the inkwell, but Rinn snatched it away from her. "Cat, are you even listening?"

"Festival." Cat bobbed her head. "Sounds like fun, like a fair. That was great fun. Until Yallakh showed up." Cat flattened her ears and stuck out her tongue.

"About him." Rinn proceeded carefully. "If I ever wanted to find him, could you do it?"

Cat made her I-ate-something-gross face. "No."

"But you found the girls across miles of snow." Rinn insisted.

"Tristy stinks from all that perfume she wears. It's easy to find smelly flowers in snow." Cat pinched her nose. "But, Yallakh smells like rot and decay. And this time of year, that's everywhere."

Rinn slouched over. "So, there's no way to find him."

"Clive could do it." Cat suggested, snooping around for something else to play with. Rinn realized she was right. Molo admitted that Clive could see Yallakh from very far away. Even though sense and reason scolded Rinn for considering it, something inside her desperately wanted to talk with Yallakh once again. She had questions that only he would answer.

::

News of the upcoming festival enveloped Hilltop in hope and good cheer. The community houses were tidied, and the barn swept clean. The townspeople busied themselves decorating the courtyard with pine branches and colorful ribbons. A pack of giddy children raced through the courtyard led by Seoras' youngest son Kelan, his broken arm long forgotten. The Dvalinn dwarves worked tirelessly to finish the artificial gatehouse before the festivities. Molo and the teenage boys collected enough metal from the scavengers to fabricate an iron portcullis for the postern gate. Ceili and her team of seamstresses churned out traditional festival garb, white scarves for women and red mantles for men. Parents made decorative hats for their children. Rinn braided a crown of pressed flowers for Cat adorned with sprigs of dried catmint.

Several days before the festival was scheduled to occur, Rinn was pleasantly surprised to see her father hobbling across the courtyard. He leaned on a cane with one arm and was supported by Muireen on the other. "Daddy!" Rinn rushed over to hug him.

"Hello, princess." Marshal smiled through the discomfort.

"I'm a lady, not a princess." Rinn corrected.

"Have it your way." Marshal hobbled toward a wooden bench, Muireen guided him to it. It saddened Rinn to see her father looking so feeble as he moved. She waited patiently until he reached the bench. He gingerly settled down with a sigh of relief. Cat slipped out of nowhere on the bench next to him. She peered up expectantly, swishing her tail. He grudgingly patted her on the head as she crawled onto his lap. He groaned in pain as she snuggled into his chest. "Good to see you, too, Catherine."

"Will you be coming to the festivities?" Rinn asked as she attempted to pry Cat off her father's lap. Cat stubbornly refused to move.

"Oh, he'll be going." Muireen pointed an accusing finger at Marshal. "Imolia is the celebration of rebirth and growth. It's a time of healing. If he wants to get better, he'll need to pay his respects to the spirits of spring." Rinn actually contemplated what the spirit of spring looked like. She pictured a colorful version of Geamradh, bedecked with flowers and green leafy antlers instead of stark white ones. The whole notion seemed ridiculous, so she pushed the thoughts aside.

Muireen bent down and gave Marshal a small kiss on the head. "Now that you've seen the decorations, let's get you back inside."

Marshal lifted Cat off his lap. He rose very slowly and with assistance. He wrapped an arm around Rinn and hugged her. "The town looks amazing. You are doing a great job."

"Thanks, Daddy." Rinn whispered through tears mixed with joy and sadness.

::

Rinn and the other teenagers busied themselves in the main hall, hanging pine wreaths and laurel. The smaller children made wishing ornaments to hang on the wreaths. Rinn even made a few ornaments herself, all of which had a triangle and spiral theme for some reason. The teenage boys goofed off playing silly games. Feena helped Rinn, while Cat climbed to impossibly high places to hang laurel. Tristy and Devnet quarreled in a corner, and Rinn could not help but eavesdrop.

"I won't finish it on time." Tristy whined. "Imolia begins at sundown the day after tomorrow, and I'm stuck here decorating."

"It looks fine, Tristy." Devnet replied sullenly. "He's going to love it."

"I can't give it to him like that." Tristy was mortified. "The trim is half done, and I haven't even added a lining."

Rinn and Feena secretly snickered at Tristy's shallowness. Devnet glared at them indignantly. "What are you girls laughing at?"

Tristy turned up her nose. "Ignore them, Devy. This is an adult conversation. They're too young to understand." Tristy and Devnet whispered on their own for a short while and then left. The older boys followed them out, leaving Rinn alone with Feena and possibly Cat, who could not be seen, but was probably hanging around somewhere. Probably. Rinn worked on placing the rest of her ornaments, but she could not shake Tristy's jab. Rinn was fourteen and she had never had a boyfriend. She told herself it was only because there was no one she was really interested in. Rinn was convinced that when the time came to find a match, she would be fine.

"Hey, Feena." Rinn interrupted her friend, who was poking sprigs of dried flowers into pine wreaths. "Are there any noblemen in the rustic lands?"

"None that I know of." Feena answered still heavily focused on her work. "Why do you ask?"

"I was thinking." Rinn admitted sheepishly. "If I am a lady, do I have to marry a lord?"

Feena giggled pleasantly. "Oh, m'lady. No one cares about that stuff out here. You're free to marry whomever you want." Feena narrowed her eyes slyly. "So, is there someone you're keen on?"

Rinn fumbled her own decorations. "Absolutely not." She blushed terribly. "I'm far too busy to think about anything like that." Rinn busied herself with arranging candles, tying knots—anything to distract her attention away from this conversation.

"Well, I think Tristy has a thing for Bos." Feena observed.

"Really?" Rinn wrinkled her nose. "Why?"

"He's big and strong. And I suppose he's not too bad looking." Feena conceded. "But he's not my type."

Rinn grabbed at the chance to turn the tables. "So, who is your type?"

Feena stared off in the distance. "Nightsong. He's dreamy. Beautiful and talented. I'd marry him in an instant."

"Lutra?" Rinn could not shake the mental image of Lutra dressed in animal skins. She even imagined Margot ears and a tail on him. She chuckled to herself. "Just so you know, he has a serious crush on Catherine."

"Really?" Feena frowned. She sighed, crestfallen. "I don't think I can compete with her. She's too exotic."

A voice from high up in the rafters called down. "You can play with Lutra, too, if you want. I don't mind sharing."

Feena blushed and Rinn laughed. "Oh, Cat. You're too precious."

The girls joked and talked for the remainder of the afternoon as they made final preparations for Imolia. Rinn had never felt so thoroughly content. She lived in a wonderful home, surrounded by friends, with a purpose and a role to play. In its own simple way, this could be the happiest day of her life. But her joy was short-lived. Angry, gray storm clouds gathered overhead, rolling down the mountains like an avalanche. Fierce winds tore through Hilltop, and by evening, all the outdoor decorations had been stripped away. House roofs rattled, and doors shook each time the wind changed direction. The townsfolk sought refuge inside the community houses fearing a major storm. The snow started shortly after nightfall, large, heavy flakes the size of flower petals. The town was soon buried, and with it Rinn's hopes for a joyful Imolia.

Chapter 34

S omehow, Rinn could feel the fury of the storm in her chest. The relentless snows piled higher and higher entombing everything in town. The doors of the main house quickly became snow-bound, forcing Feena to seek shelter with Rinn for the night. Cat was sent as a messenger to her parents, Hadwin and Morven, to let them know she was okay. Cat slipped into the shadows and was gone.

Feena lay on a bedroll near Rinn's fireplace. She bemoaned the situation. "It's bad luck to have snow on Imolia. It's an omen of calamity." Feena pulled the covers to her chin. Dark thoughts swirled through Rinn's head, she was sure that the colossal, snow-bringer Geamradh was nearby. She had half a mind to venture out into the storm and chase the cursed beast away, but Molo had told her that Geamradh was winter itself. Rinn could not even fathom the idea of picking a fight with an entire season. More terrifying would be the repercussions if she actually won—she did not want to be the person who murdered winter. The snows would come, and they would eventually stop. Rinn decided her job was to rally the people and help them weather the storm, not fight against it.

::

Rinn woke early and assembled her team in the kitchen. Feena, Cat, Muireen, and Marshal rubbed sleep from their eyes. Rinn poured everyone spiced cider from a boiling kettle, a delicacy intended for the Imolia festivities. Right now, Rinn could not think of a better use for it. "Alright. Let's get this town up and moving. First order of business, contacting the townspeople." She pointed to Catherine, who sniffed her mug suspiciously. She sampled it daintily with the tip of her tongue and made a sour face, she did drink hot beverages. "Cat, can you visit the community houses and make sure everyone is okay?"

Cat saluted like a soldier and vanished, spilling her cider everywhere. Rinn rolled her eyes and fetched a towel. "Next, we have to make contact with the Dvalinn dwarves. I assume they rode out the storm in their tunnels. The dwarves are our best chance of digging out of this disaster. After that, we'll contact Molo and company. We'll need his strength."

Muireen, Feena, and Rinn attempted to open the front door of the house, but the snow accumulation was too heavy. Marshal offered the excellent idea of removing the door pins and lifting the door carefully away from the frame. Once the door was removed, snow poured into the kitchen. Everyone scooped the fresh snow into pots and urns for drinking water. Sullied snow was sent to the wash sink. Rinn and company finished clearing the kitchen when Cat reappeared, slipping out of the air onto a chair.

"Been to all the community houses." She smiled.

"Good work, Cat." Rinn pulled a warm blanket from near the fire and wrapped it around her sister. The frosty Margot purred appreciatively. Rinn asked her. "Is everyone alright? Do they need anything?"

"Firewood mostly." Cat sat down near the hearth. "House number five has a clogged chimney—smokes up the place when they try to burn anything."

"Okay." Rinn made mental notes. "We'll start at house five before they freeze to death."

"What are you going to do?" Her father inquired, sipping his cider. Muireen sat close to him at the kitchen table, too close for Rinn's comfort.

"I'll try to carve a path to Molo's house and enlist his help." Rinn moved to the snow-filled doorway. "I have an idea I want to try out." She closed her eyes and tried to visualize the snow that blocked her way. She summoned her sphere-shaped barrier just outside the door, focusing it into a person sized area. With great mental effort, she pushed the sphere of snow away from the door, parting the snowbank as it slid forward. Rinn could not keep up the exertion for very long, but she did make a viable exit from the house. The others rehung the door while Rinn rested near the fire, the mental effort left her feeling tired and very cold. Muireen and Feena shoveled deeper into the snowbank, clearing a wider path. It was not long before they encountered Molo coming the opposite direction.

"You're up early." The giant man smirked, his grizzled beard was coated in icicles. They welcomed him inside and offered him warm cider, which he accepted gratefully. Mafic and Felsic, who lived with Molo, arrived a short time later. Together the team helped dig out the buried town. The chimney on house five was cleared first followed by several shattered windows and leaky roofs. The Dvalinn dwarves dug snow tunnels connecting all of Hilltop. Festival foods were delivered to each building to raise the general morale of the townsfolk. While everyone agreed that having a storm on Imolia was a terrible omen, they praised Rinn for doing a good job caring for the snowed in town. Rinn felt everything was going well until Muireen broke the somber news.

"We're running out of food." Muireen showed Rinn the nearly empty pantry off the kitchen. Much of the food reserves had been depleted making treats for the festival. In the community houses, food was also getting scarce. Hunting would be impossible in the deep snows. The situation seemed dire.

Marshal offered this advice. "We should send an expedition ice fishing."

Rinn raised an eyebrow. "What good would that do? Aren't the lakes all frozen?"

Marshal chuckled. "Only on top. All the fish are still there, alive, but near the bottom. Cut a hole in the ice and drop in a fishing line. It's slow work, but any food is better than none." Molo and some of the heartier men were elected to go. They took several dwarven pick-axes to break through the ice.

Rinn hugged each of the men as they left. She had faith that they would succeed, Hilltop would not be left to starve in the cold.

::

The next few days were exhausting for everyone. But sunny skies helped prop up the town's grim disposition. Paths were cleared and activity in Hilltop slowly resumed. The Dvalinn were given the arduous task of clearing the snows outside the town where the drifts piled high against the palisade walls. Lutra and Calder climbed the watchtower and swept it clear of snow. Hadwin, Sheriden, and the other men worked around the barns, caring for the farm animals that remained. Muireen dug out her remaining caravan wagon and attempted to open for business.

Most of the townsfolk knew exactly what needed to be done, so Rinn's leadership was not really needed. She moped around Hilltop trying to be helpful. The town's women spent their time indoors, cooking, cleaning, caring for children, mending clothes. Rinn found that two of the farmer's wives, Gallina and Morven, had set up a small infirmary, treating runny noses and minor cases of frostbite. Gallina had some knowledge of brewing leaves and making poultices. Rinn was impressed by their efforts and praised them verbally.

Rinn tried her hand at shoveling, but she tired quickly, it was exhausting work. Rinn visited the barns, but she realized she had no experience caring for animals and she was just getting in the way. She retreated to her house, past children sledding down snowdrifts and having snowball fights. Rinn quietly prepared lunch, and after taking food to her father and Muireen, she retired to her study. Too many thoughts jumbled in her head: the food problem, Clanmorris, boys, Sevria. But what vexed Rinn the most was uncertainty about her own powers. She knew she could do more, she would need to, she could not face the Empire with only a spear and a shield.

Rinn once again tried experimenting with the two words she did not understand. "Onlithe" just seemed to break things, totally useless. Rinn selected a small metal poker leaning by the hearth. She held it tightly and uttered "Ahebe". Once again, nothing happened. In frustration, she threw it across the room. The poker clanged against the far wall, but it did not fall to the ground. Rinn stared in amazement as the metal poker floated softly, like a feather, to the floor. With a gentle clink, it touched down. Rinn scurried over and lifted the poker and released it. It crashed down loudly, as if nothing had happened. Muireen cracked open the door.

"Everything alright?" She seemed honestly concerned. Unfortunately, Rinn responded with raucous, insane-sounding laughter. Everything was better than alright, Rinn had unlocked a new skill. She had no idea how it would help her, but the novelty was exhilarating. Rinn spent the rest of the day making everything in the house float. Muireen and Marshal were both impressed and confused. Cat found it hilarious, she begged Rinn to make her float, but Rinn was reluctant to use her newfound power on her own sister. However, armed with new abilities, Rinn felt unstoppable. She would unravel the meaning of "Onlithe" and every other new word she would discover. She would take on the entire Empire. Nothing would stand in her way.

A quiet knock interrupted her. Feena cautiously peered around the door. "Rinn. I think you'd better come outside." Feena nervously held her hands to her chin and chewed her knuckles.

"What is it?" Rinn set aside whatever she was floating.

"It's Sionne." Feena squeaked. "He's returned."

Chapter 35

Rinn walked through the postern gate, pilum in hand. Outside, Sionne stood alone in the snow, guarded by a wary Bos and Arlin. They were shielding him from Sheridan, who levelled every possible threat at him. Rinn raised her hand at the violent man as she walked past, and Sheridan's insults slowed to an eventual halt. Rinn lowered her forehead and creased her brow as she confronted the traitorous teen.

"Leave." Rinn uttered, restraining her hatred.

Sionne shivered in the cold, his thin clothes flapped in the wind and his socks were frozen to his feet. His head hung low, and he dared not meet Rinn's gaze. "I'm here to turn myself in."

Rinn did not flinch. "We don't want you."

"I know what I did was wrong, but I was starving." Sionne pleaded. "I came to accept my punishment. But first you have to listen to me."

"I don't have to do anything you say." Rinn smoldered, levelling her pilum at him. "By rights, I should kill you now."

"And I would not hold it against you." Sionne admitted. "But, please listen to me first. The clan is coming. The winter storm left us without anything to eat. Everyone thinks you have an endless supply of food."

"And who's fault is that?" Rinn yelled at Sionne, advancing ever closer with her pilum.

Sionne flushed. "Not me. Those stupid girls opened their big mouths, trying to bribe their way back home."

Rinn's anger could not be contained, the point of her pilum glowed brightly. "You blame the very girls you sold into slavery—just to fill your stomach. You are the most selfish and arrogant wretch ever born. We don't need your help. We don't want your help. If Geamradh was here, I would send her to bury you and your damnable clan forever."

Sionne bent low in abject terror. "Can you do that?"

"Leave." Rinn demanded, holding her pilum tip a hairsbreadth away from his chest. It burned white hot. Sionne gave Rinn one last pitiable look, but Rinn's resolve held. He turned and slowly trudged away into the snow. Rinn watched him go, shivering in his thin and torn tunic. Rinn hated him, but she also hated feeling like a villain even more. She left the postern gate trying to forget about the worthless traitor, but the pangs of guilt would not leave her. Rinn gathered up a bit of food and a warm cloak and gave it to Cat. "Go, give him this. It's more than he deserves." The feisty Margot slipped into the misty air and was gone.

::

The ice fishing expedition returned. The townspeople cheered as the party dragged their sleds laden with fish into the courtyard. It was not a bountiful haul, but it would fill empty bellies for a while. Rinn congratulated Molo and the other fishermen in front of the whole town. Afterwards, Molo pulled Rinn aside.

"We need to talk." Molo whispered, although his whispers were as loud as a normal person's speaking voice. "While we were fishing, I saw something."

"Let's meet back at the house." Rinn tried to be covert, but it was difficult to hide talking to someone the size of Molossus. She collected Cat and hurried home. Muireen and Marshal were out for a stroll, which was for the best, Molo entered and asked if they were alone. Rinn confirmed they were and latched the door.

"Clive saw him." Molo disclosed privately.

"Who?" Rinn kneaded her hands anxiously.

"Yallakh." Molo set his round rock on the table. "It's unmistakable. He's living in my old cave on the other side of the river." The gears began to turn in Rinn's head. She wanted to see the ex-slaver, and now she knew exactly where he was. She would have to fabricate some excuse to leave Hilltop. Molo grabbed her attention by slamming his giant fist on the table. "We have to drive him out. We can't have that monster so close to us." Molo was visibly shaken.

"We have bigger problems right now." Rinn countered. "Clanmorris is on the move. I was visited by that traitor Sionne, trying to weasel his way back into Hilltop. He claims that an army of clansmen are heading this way."

"He could be bluffing, trying to trick us to take him back. But he could be telling the truth. Cursed clansmen." Molo gripped Clive like a vice. "So, what became of Sionne?"

"I sent him away." Rinn felt guilty for rejecting him, and she was still unsure if she had done the right thing. She wanted to tell Molo that she had given the boy some food and a new cloak, but the giant's mood was so sour that she held her tongue.

"Good." Molo huffed. "There's no room on this hill for traitors."

::

The war council gathered in Rinn's study: Marshal and Molo, as the military advisors; Seoras, representing the townspeople; Botrogen and Mafic, representing the dwarves; Sheridan, representing the loudmouths; and Bos, who acted as unofficial captain of the town guard. Cat was present, too, lounging in the rafters. Rinn addressed the group as confidently as she could. "According to Sionne, the Clanmorris warriors have run out of food and are getting desperate. He says they are planning a major attack on Hilltop. They seem to think we have a surplus."

"How do we know this information is reliable? That boy can't be trusted." Sheridan bellowed.

"Even if it isn't, we should be prepared." Marshal countered, sitting on his stool. His mobility had greatly improved in the last few days, but he still used a cane whenever he walked long distances.

"We should weigh Sionne's words carefully." Rinn shuffled papers trying to look important. "He said he was turning himself in to pay for his crimes, which I don't believe. However, if things are actually going badly for the clan, it would make sense for him to try to come here, begging for a handout." Nods of affirmation spread through the room. The council began to debate contingency plans in case of attack. Rinn deferred to Molo and Marshal's military expertise to devise a defensive strategy. Molo prioritized finishing the false gatehouse and strengthening the walls around the town. Marshal recommended increasing martial training for the townsfolk. Rinn listened to all the ideas, but deep down she knew that for the survival of Hilltop, she alone was their greatest defense.

::

"Cat, can you help me sneak away?" Rinn whispered to her sister across their bedroom. From her bed, Cat shot her an expression that said is-that-even-a-question? Rinn explained. "I know where Yallakh is. I need to go see him." Cat wrinkled her nose. "If I leave on foot, Molo will see me. And he hates Yallakh."

"You should, too." Cat complained.

"I know." Rinn sighed, staring at the ceiling. "But there are things he knows. He worked with the clan for a while. Maybe he can help me figure out how to make these raids stop."

Cat shrugged. "When do we leave?"

"Tomorrow, before daybreak." Rinn pulled up her covers and closed her eyes. She knew she needed sleep for tomorrow, but the chaos in her head would not quiet down. She tossed in her bed, grappling with dark thoughts of war, the bandit massacre at the hands of Yallakh, and the cold, miserable Sionne walking off into the snowy wastes.

::

Cat shook Rinn awake the next morning, the twilight of dawn had barely arrived. Rinn stumbled out of bed and crossed the room, holding on to the wall for support. She splashed cold water on her face to try to shake off her night of poor sleep, and it helped, but only for a moment. Cat handed her a heavy woolen outfit and a traveling cloak. Rinn dressed and pulled on her boots, she selected a pilum spear from her personal stash, which was growing smaller. She signaled to Cat. "Okay, I'm ready."

Cat held onto Rinn's hands, like two girls playing a game. Cat inhaled deeply and pulled Rinn into the air. Because Rinn was calm and ready, she noticed everything. She was dragged by the sensation of an undertow into a new place. The room dissolved and was replaced with a wide, purple, groundless space, Rinn felt like she was falling through an endless sky. A warm glow bathed the area, and small yellow sparks swirled and eddied past her at impossible speeds, like tiny flocks of hummingbirds made of stars. In less than the span of a single breath, Rinn found herself standing in the snow at the bottom of the hill.

Rinn released Cat's paws. "What was that?"

"What?" Cat smoothed the fur on her head and neck.

Rinn knew Cat was not intentionally being frustrating, but she really tried Rinn's patience at times. "What was that purple glowing place?"

"Oh." Cat remarked casually. "I call it the Mist."

Rinn's curiosity could not sit still. "But what is it? Where is it?"

"I don't know. Not here." Cat tilted her head, one ear up and the other down.

Rinn persisted. "Can you go there anytime you want?"

"I guess so." Cat put a paw on her chin.

"How long can you stay there?" Rinn quizzed.

"I get kicked out if I stay too long." Cat admitted. "I'm not part of the Mist. That's how I move. I slip into the Mist and let it kick me out where I want to go." All this new information astounded Rinn. She used to believe dealing with people was the most complicated thing in the world. Now, she had to come to terms with her own supernatural abilities, the existence of walking seasons, and the realization that there were places outside of her own reality. Rinn was not sure how much more she could take. She shook her head to clear it. She had a mission, she needed to find Yallakh. She focused only on her task as she led Cat up the frozen river.

Chapter 36

R inn and Cat traipsed through the wooded snowfields north of the river. Rinn had a general idea of where Molo's cavern was, but she had never actually visited it. For some reason, Molo refused to let anyone come near his former home. Rinn had always wondered why, but she did not want to risk the giant's ire. Her yearning to see Yallakh eclipsed that fear, she would deal with Molo and whatever she found in that cave. The girls wandered until the morning sun was well above the mountains. Cat discovered a set of footprints, and the pair followed them into a gully between two steep hills. At the base of a deep fissure they found an irregular cave opening that resembled a dark, screaming mouth.

"This must be it." Rinn fretted to Cat. Cat sniffed at the air but said nothing. Rinn timidly led the way, on constant guard with her pilum spear. A small stream of water trickled from the cave mixing with the snow and rocks below. The mouth of the cave was taller than two or three Molos and overgrown with hanging moss. As Rinn ventured inside, she remembered the horrible place where Tristy, Devy, and Feena were held captive. The rock walls had a similar appearance, dull gray and dripping with moisture. She put the memory behind her and pressed on. Rinn suddenly realized she did not bring a lamp or torch, she wanted to smack herself for such an idiotic oversight. She whispered to Cat. "Can you see anything?"

"Rocks and more rocks." Cat's voice echoed off the cave walls. She sniffed at the air again. "But I do smell something. Something burning." Rinn gulped. Wordlessly, the two girls slinked down the dim winding corridor. Rinn could see an orange glow around a bend in the passageway ahead. As she crept forward, the cave opened into a high-ceilinged chamber spangled with thousands of glistening stalactites. In horror, Rinn realized the cave was filled with bones, not casually strewn across the floor, but meticulously woven into tables, chairs, and shelves. A massive bed of bones rested in one alcove and a fireplace crackled in another, its mantle crafted from the skulls of unrecognizable beasts. Grizzly chandeliers made of rib bones hung from the ceiling and horn torch-holders lined the walls. Reclining in the center of it all like a king, sat Yallakh on a giant chair of bones.

"Welcome." He spread his tattooed arms wide. "I was wondering when you'd show up." Cat hissed at him and bore her claws.

"Catherine, be still." Rinn calmed her sister. "We're here to talk." Rinn watched Yallakh rise from his bone chair, he was dressed in warm animal pelts over his usual black wrappings. His hairless head was exposed, revealing an endless landscape of miniature tattoos playing across his scalp and face. Rinn reminded herself that each image was inked in the blood of elves, binding their tortured souls to him. Rinn began to wonder why she came.

"It's so good to see you." Yallakh took several steps towards Rinn. "I was looking for shelter from these miserable winter storms when I found this place. I do love the decor." He twirled around in a winsome manner. He stopped abruptly and slumped over in an exaggerated sigh. "But it gets so lonely here. I desperately needed company, and you might be the only person in these detestable lands worth talking to." He smiled at Rinn, showing shiny bone teeth inked with tattoos. Rinn hated him even more when he poured on the fake charm.

"Save your false courtesy, Yallakh." Rinn backed up a step, keeping her pilum levelled at him. "I need you to answer some questions."

"It would be my pleasure." He bowed mockingly. Cat circled to the left, flanking him.

"You worked for the slave nation." Rinn struggled to remember the name of those people.

"The Khuraak." Cat reminded her.

"The Khuraak." Rinn repeated. "You know the locations of their bases."

Yallakh considered for a moment. "I may have visited a few from time to time."

"Could you lead a raiding party to them?" Rinn felt her courage rising.

"Precious girl." Yallakh laughed out loud. "You mean to take on the Khuraak all by yourself? They number in the tens of thousands. Their boats are as numerous as flies on a battlefield."

"Maybe so, but I mean to stop them." Rinn felt sure of herself.

"Stop them from what, being slavers?" Yallakh cocked his head. "That's who they are. People are their cattle. Slave trade is their economy. It is taught from father to son, written into their religion, ingrained in their very identity."

"I'm going to make it unprofitable." Rinn countered.

Yallakh reclined back onto his oversized bone chair smiling to himself. "Well, that would be something." He seemed to have accepted the thought, even enjoyed the idea of it. Rinn decided she had learned what she needed to know about the Khuraak, so she changed topics.

"What do you know about the Sigilla?" Rinn tried to ask casually. Cat shook her head, but the question was already out.

A snide grin crept across Yallakh's face. "Daddy's been keeping secrets from you. He doesn't want you knowing the truth."

"What truth?" Rinn had been unwittingly hooked.

"You're a killer." Yallakh said musically. "A servant of the Empire, born to a life of bloodshed."

"I am not." Rinn refuted shaking her pilum.

"Yet you come here ready to kill, along with your carnivorous pet." Yallakh scoffed. Cat slipped into the air and reappeared on the back of the bone chair, her claws wrapped around Yallakh's throat.

"I'm no one's pet." Cat hissed in his ear, then she vanished.

Yallakh shot up in his seat, rubbing his throat. "I seem to have struck a nerve." He repositioned himself in the chair to give the semblance of relaxation, but his hands stayed dangerously close to his knives. He levelled a stare at Rinn. "Why are you really here?"

Rinn blurted out the problem that was vexing her. "My powers are growing, I can feel it. I want to make sure I don't lose control."

"You don't want to hurt the ones you love, you mean." Yallakh corrected. "Do yourself a favor, war maiden, abandon them now. Your future can only be violence. Anyone who stays by your side will be drowned in the tides of war." The truth of Yallakh's words caught Rinn off guard. She realized how her father must feel, wanting to protect her from the horrors of warfare. Rinn was already racked with guilt over the injury he had received attempting to rescue the three girls. She would be devastated if anything should ever happen to him on her account.

"Rinn." Cat tugged at her sister's arm. "We should leave. Yallakh doesn't know anything but lies."

"I don't even know why I came here." Rinn felt more anger towards herself than the tattooed fiend.

"What did you expect? That we would be friends?" Yallakh's acerbic wit bit into Rinn. "We're killers. Society has no place for people like you and me."

"I'm nothing like you." Rinn spat back. "I thought I could help you, but clearly you like being damned."

"You're the one in need of help." Yallakh pointed out. "That's why you came." Tears welled up in Rinn's eyes. Before she could start crying, Cat grabbed her by the hand and slipped away. Rinn materialized outside the cave, in the snowy ravine between the two hills. Rinn could not hold it in any longer, she collapsed in a fit of tears. Cat held her close as she cried, swearing in a language Rinn did not recognize.

::

Rinn and Cat walked to the postern gate, Rinn's eyes were still red and puffy. They knocked on the gate, which opened for them. Molo was waiting inside, his arms folded in anger. "Where have you two been?" Rinn wanted to defend herself, but she did not have the mental energy to care. Molo did not even wait for a response. "Clanmorris has been spotted, nearly four hundred men heading this way. The citizens of Hilltop need you."

Pessimism soured Rinn's attitude. "Tell them to flee, get somewhere safe. This town is doomed."

Molo grabbed her arm. "You don't understand. They have nowhere to go, this is their home. They can't leave, it would mean the sword or the shackle for them. You're their only hope. They will stand with you, but you have to lead."

Rinn yelled at Molo. "I'm a fourteen-year-old girl with a stick." She threw her pilum to the ground. "Who are we kidding? I can't save anyone." Rinn started crying, startling Molo. She covered her face and ran inside the house.

Cat covered for her sister. "That monster Yallakh messed with her head." Molo cursed as Cat followed Rinn into the house. Rinn was set down near the fireplace and a warm mug placed in her hands. She felt numb to the passage of time, she watched the flickering flames blankly, clutching her mug, never taking a drink. People came and went, some even spoke to her, but Rinn never moved. The logs shifted in the crackling flames. Rinn remembered her childhood, sitting by the firepit in the courtyard of her house in Viburna. There was no snow, no monsters, no fear of attack. Her world was small and safe, the gardens of her home were surrounded by high brick walls. Even though she did not grow up with a mother, Rinn's world was filled with the love and devotion of her father. The household servants insulated her, doted on her with small treats and long walks through the marketplace. In her dreams, Rinn could hear her father's voice.

"Rinn, it's time to go." Blinking, Rinn looked up and saw her father, not the young vibrant figure of her childhood, but an older and scarred version of him, walking with a cane. "Rinn, the enemy is here. We need to go."

Chapter 37

Rinn let herself be led up the stairs to the roof of the new stone gatehouse. She had been outfitted in her dragon feather armor and a pilum spear had been placed in her hand. To the east and south, Rinn saw Hilltop surrounded by a sea of orange lights, hundreds of torches flickered in the twilight. The reality of war was starting to sink in: the town, her town, was about to be besieged by an army. They were hopelessly outnumbered—a town of farmers, dressmakers, and children against a bloodthirsty horde of warriors. She saw the dwarves in the courtyard below, fully decked in their unique armor, ready to fight. She felt guilty for freeing them from slavery only to die here. Townsfolk lined the palisade walls, armed with bows and spears. Molo barked instructions to villagers carrying large shields. High above in the watchtower, Nightsong played a hopeful melody on his flute.

Rinn searched nervously for her father, craving his protection and advice. He was far away on horseback commanding groups of men in the courtyard. He was still not walking well, so Rinn knew that the saddle was the safest place for him. Bayard would protect him. Marshal spied his daughter on the gatehouse and saluted. Rinn wanted to wave back, to call out to him, but she was gripped with uncertainty. She felt guilty for being on the roof, high above everyone else facing the dangers of battle. She knew the gatehouse could not be breeched, its fake wooden doors were set against solid stone as thick as thirty hands. Rinn did not want to be left by herself, but she was not alone. Feena guarded Rinn's left, awkwardly dressed in leather and chain armor, holding a long spear similar to Rinn's pilum. Her straight brown hair had been pulled back into a ponytail tied with a long green ribbon. To Rinn's right, Cat rocked back and forth on her haunches. She wore her own version of Rinn's iridescent dragon-feather armor which covered her forearms and head. Rinn wondered when Molo and the dwarves had time to fabricate it, but she was glad her sister was so well protected.

Bos, Calder, and Rury ascended the stairs, outfitted in stout armor and carrying swords. Bos saluted. "Lady Rinn. We are your official guard." The other two teenage boys joined him in a salute.

"Won't nothing get past us, m'lady." Rury winked.

Rinn felt her heart melt. This town was fighting, not because they thought they could win, but they were fighting for her. She was their only desperate hope. Rinn realized they would die for her, and she was racked with shame. She reached out and touched the boys. "Go. Tristy and Devy need you. I will be fine. Protect the town, protect those who can't protect themselves." The boys looked at each other, confused and conflicted. Rinn smiled at them sadly. "Go."

The three boys bowed deeply. "As you wish, m'lady." The boys reluctantly departed. Rinn knew she was making the right choice, they were more likely to get killed if they stayed near her. "You should go, too, Feena."

Feena shook her head. "My place is with you, m'lady. My life would have ended in those caves. Before you, it was not even worth living. You've given me everything, freedom, purpose, and friendship. I won't abandon you now." Rinn hugged her gently.

"Stay safe. No heroics." Rinn commanded, and Feena playfully saluted. Rinn turned to her feline sister and held her paws. "It will be up to us." Cat nodded in agreement. "If your powers really depend on me, then this might help." Rinn reached up to the gold necklace she always wore. She pried one of the stones away from its setting. The dark gem glowed green in her hand. Rinn held the stone tightly and concentrated, harvesting her desperate need to protect Hilltop. When she opened her hand, the stone glowed white. She delicately placed it in her sister's paw and the Margot's eyes lit up with glee. She licked Rinn on the cheek, which caused everyone to laugh. In the distance, ranks of clansmen warriors marched toward the town.

::

Deel, the tall and muscular leader of the army, rode on horseback to within earshot of the gatehouse. Egan, the bandit chief, accompanied him. He pointed Rinn out to his commander as they approached. Six burly clansmen rode with them, armed with large shields. Deel called out to the townsfolk assembled on the palisade walls. "People of the hill, surrender your town or be destroyed."

"Go away." Cat yelled back, which brought some chuckles from the townsfolk.

Rinn took a deep breath and summoned her courage. She would only get one shot at this. "Men of Clanmorris, we don't need to fight today. I know your people are starving, but this is not the answer. I would meet to talk with you about other solutions."

Deel postured in his saddle. "We don't make deals with witches." He raised his arm and half a hundred archers lit their arrows with fire. He signaled, and a volley of flaming arrows sped toward the town.

"Incoming!" A defender on the wall yelled. The townsfolk ducked behind the safety of the protective palisade wall as flaming arrows slammed into the wooden posts. Rinn could tell the clan was clearly aiming for the wall, very few arrows sailed above it and some stuck into the ground below it. Another round of arrows followed, dousing the posts with oil and fire. Soon, an entire section of the wall was engulfed in flames. The Hilltop residents stood their ground, shielding their faces from the smoke and heat. The fire spread until the wall on one side of the town was entirely ablaze, illuminating the night with its orange light. The bulk of the army maneuvered to the flaming wall, and as a large section of burnt palisade fell away, the clansmen cheered heartily. But in its place stood a stout stone wall hidden behind the wooden beams.

The townsfolk mocked the attackers as the confused clansmen looked on. Deel and Egan circled each other on horseback yelling and gesticulating. The palisade continued to burn away, revealing tall stone walls completely surrounding Hilltop. The clan regrouped, their leaders arguing loudly. Inside the fortress, spirits were high, the first ruse was a success, demoralizing their attackers. Mafic danced with Felsic and the other heavily armored dwarves. Marshal and Molo held the joyful citizens in check, this battle was far from over.

The enemy lines parted, and two teams of men hauled massive wheeled cages forward. Hulking, shambling shapes paced inside. Giant teeth bit at the bars, long black claws dug for freedom. Two men in crimson robes stepped out from the horde and paraded before the cages, gesturing in unison and speaking strange words.

"Are those sorcerers?" Feena hyperventilated.

"I guess so." Rinn was more curious than fearful, she had never seen anyone actually utilize magic other than herself and Cat. She studied the sorcerers' performance as they enthralled the beasts. Massive cage doors were opened, and two lumbering creatures shambled out, beckoned on by the robed figures. To Rinn, the beasts resembled huge, misshapen bears with front limbs the size of tree trunks and stubby, stunted hind legs. The beasts howled and tore at the snowy ground with their black claws. The army of clansmen cheered the monsters on with hoots and hollers from a safe distance away. The sorcerers urged the beasts toward Hilltop.

Rinn called down to the courtyard. "Molo. What are those things?"

The giant held out Clive and scanned the area. He yelled up to Rinn. "Those are Caedes—we called them rock rippers. They burrow into the sides of mountains. They could easily breech our walls." Nervous defenders readied their bows and spears as the beasts approached.

Rinn called out to the men on the wall. "Stay your weapons." Again, she hailed Molo. "Cat and I will tend to the beasts. Tell the townspeople not to interfere."

Molo yelled back. "Be safe, and watch out for the trenches near the town walls. They are filled with spikes and covered in snow."

"Thanks for the warning." Rinn called, waving appreciatively. Rinn turned back to the two girls on the rooftop. She gave Feena a withering smile.

"Be careful." Feena mouthed, worry in her eyes, and Rinn nodded.

Rinn reached out for her sister. "Okay, Cat, it's up to us. Can you get us down there?" Cat smiled without any signs of fear. Rinn squeezed her paws and the two girls slipped away. For the briefest moment, Rinn could see the shocked expression on Feena's face as she watched them disappear. A familiar undertow pulled Rinn through the purple mist, depositing her on the soft snow outside the town. She was approximately halfway between Hilltop and the enemy lines. The two beasts lumbered toward them.

Rinn readied her pilum. "Cat, do you think you could annoy those things? I want to lure them back to the enemy lines."

"It would be my pleasure." The Margot bounced.

"Stay away from the robed men, we don't know what powers they have." Rinn worried if the sorcerers could control the rock rippers, they might be able to ensnare Cat. Rinn grabbed her paw one last time. "I love you, Cat." Cat beamed at her and held up the little white stone Rinn had given her. She popped it in her mouth and swallowed. Her eyes glowed as they changed color from blue to bright green. With a wicked grin, she slipped into the night. Rinn looked around and found her on the back of one of the rock rippers. Compared to the bulk of the monsters, Cat was tiny. She drew a dagger and thrust it into the nape of the rock ripper's neck. The beast roared with irritation and turned its head, biting at the pest. Cat had already vanished, reappearing on the second beast. She slipped in and out with impossible speed, harassing the monsters, who howled in dual rage.

While Cat distracted the beasts, Rinn edged toward them. The rock rippers were larger than Rinn expected, at least as tall as the city walls. Their massive front legs ended in two black, curved claws, similar to a badger's. The monsters swiped at the annoying Margot pest. Cat slipped in and out repeatedly, never given the monsters a chance to touch her. Rinn advanced to within striking distance of the beasts, and that is when she noticed the blue aura surrounding their heads. It was the same blue that emanated from the slaver's shackles. Rinn was giddy when she realized she could actually see magic, but with it came the realization that she had no idea how to stop it. She could not exactly cut through an aura.

The lumbering rock-rippers clawed and bit at the feline mosquito that harassed them. In the distance, Rinn could see the two sorcerers watching expectantly. The warriors of Clanmorris jeered as the girls engaged the monsters. Rinn rushed forward, stabbing one of the rock rippers on its stunted hind leg, causing it to rear up and angle toward her. Rinn dashed past the beast toward the battle lines of the clansmen. The giant beast followed her like a kite. She raised her barrier as redheaded archers began to fire arrows at her. She ran straight into the horde of redhead warriors, the beast thrashing about wildly behind her. The clansmen scattered in fear.

"Cat!" Rinn shouted. Her sister appeared beside her. "Get me close to one of their heads." Cat grabbed her shoulders and the pair slipped away.

Rinn stumbled as she materialized on the nape of a rock ripper's neck. Its fur was as thick and tough as thorn bushes and smelled like a barn that had never been cleaned. But Rinn could see what she needed, the blue aura encircling the beast's head. She desperately hoped her idea would work. She raised her hands and cried out in a loud voice. "Onlithe." The blue magic hissed for a few moments before it flickered and dissipated. The rock-ripper shook its head violently, trying to reorient itself. Before Rinn could fall off, Cat grabbed her and slipped them back to solid ground. The beast blinked and snorted, wheeling its head around, clawing blindly at anything nearby. Clansmen ran in terror as the beast rampaged through their camp. The two sorcerers fled as well.

Cat jumped up and down clapping. "Let's do the other one."

Rinn leaned on her pilum trying to catch her breath. "Sure thing." Cat grabbed her and together they slipped into the mist.

Chapter 38

Rinn and Cat lay on the cold stone roof of the gatehouse, thoroughly exhausted and delirious with laughter. In the distance, two rock-rippers wreaked havoc through the enemy lines. Feena stood over the two girls, fanning them with the sleeves of her tunic. "That was incredible."

Rinn reached out for her sister, slap-happy. "Cat did all the hard work." Cat snickered in her feline way, too dizzy and tired to talk.

Feena offered Rinn a drink of water. "How did you turn those beasts back?"

"I know a word that's good at breaking things." Rinn rolled over, trying to keep her sides from hurting. "Apparently, it's really good at breaking magic." Rinn and Cat started laughing again. Eventually, the rampaging beasts were subdued, but at great cost to the invading clan, the bodies of many men bloodied the snow. The sorcerers were nowhere to be seen. Once Rinn had recovered, she was filled with the urge to see that her townspeople were okay. When she appeared at the edge of the gatehouse roof, the crowd in the courtyard and lining the walls raised a great cheer. Rinn was taken aback by their praise. She shouted down encouraging words to them, but also reinforced the need to stay vigilant.

Beyond the city walls, the clansmen began to regroup. Their army was weakened, but it was still more than three hundred strong. Deel and Egan hustled the men into a sloppy marching column and goaded them to the gatehouse. A wall of shields protected the vanguard. Behind them, a crew of twenty men lugged a large battering ram. Molo signaled to the archers to hold their fire until the time was right. The heavy ram was hauled to the gatehouse doors. Music wafted down from the watchtower, Nightsong played a comical funeral dirge on his flute. Defenders on the walls stifled snickers. Deel and Egan urged the ram-bearers forward, with a huge effort, the clansmen swung the massive tree-trunk into the doors. An earsplitting sound echoed across the hilltop, but the doors held fast. The clansmen battered over and over without success until the end of the ram was a splintered ruin, much to the amusement of the dwarves, Beryl in particular. Nightsong changed his tune to a bawdy tavern tune, the townsfolk joined him in song from the wall tops.

Frustrated, Deel called for axemen. Twenty men with double-sided axes stepped up and assaulted the wooden doors. Shield bearers vigilantly provided cover even though the townsfolk had yet to fire a single shot. The wood of the doors began to splinter and split. Inside the walls, Molo raised his giant hand signaling the defenders to be ready. The archers on the wall nocked their arrows and took aim. The axemen broke through the door, ripping away heavy beams of wood, only to find a thick stone wall behind it. Screams and curses of disbelief and frustration rippled through the vanguard. Molo lowered his hand and the defenders on the wall unleashed a barrage of arrows into the confused raiders below. Rinn and Feena threw rocks from the gatehouse roof. Chaos reigned in the Clanmorris column, men turned and ran, taking cover under their shields. Some clan archers returned fire with deadly accuracy at close range. Rinn was forced to put up her barrier to protect herself, Cat, and Feena.

Deel directed his troops to charge the town walls. Riding on horseback with a whip, Egan corralled those who attempted to flee. The bulk of the main force headed for the town. Hundreds of clansmen fanned out along the walls, protected by their archers. The raiders quickly stumbled into the spike-filled trenches. Caught off guard, many plunged onto the stakes concealed in the snow-covered ditches. Curses and cries went up, but the hazard did not waylay the horde for long. They picked their way safely through the spikes, hacking away with their axes and swords. The useless battering ram was rolled into a trench, effectively flattening the deadly spikes. Clansmen scaled the walls with hooks, ropes, or on each other's backs. Defenders repelled them with arrows and spears. One inventive group of clansmen began shoveling snow against the walls to form a ramp. Others joined in, piling the snow ever higher. The defenders on the wall were held at bay by clan archers who gathered around them. A hundred raiders worked together to build a snow ramp that scaled the town walls.

Once Rinn realized the walls were going to be breeched, she yelled to her father and Molo below. She quit the gatehouse roof and raced with Cat and Feena to the threatened section of their defenses. Before she could arrive, the first enemy warriors topped the wall. Marshal picked off several with his bow, but more howling redheads followed, pouring onto the wall tops with axes and swords held high. Most of the defenders ran, they were not professional soldiers. The few that did make a stand were hacked down by the redhead marauders. Rinn helplessly watched as Arlin, Hadwin's brother, was savagely run through by a clansman's sword. He fell from the wall, lifeless. The raiders reached the ladders and shimmied down into the courtyard. A phalanx of townsfolk attempted to box the raiders in using a shield wall formation. Marshal picked off several more clansmen with his bow before drawing his sword and charging into the fray on horseback. Heavily armored dwarves with hammers and picks waded into the mob. Molo swung his oversized club at the ladders, sending wooden rungs and clansmen flying.

By the time Rinn reached the battle zone, the horrors of war were on full display. The phalanx wall was overrun. The dwarves were surrounded. Molo and Marshal fought furiously but were drowning in a sea of clansmen. Rinn was standing on the edge of a nightmare, helpless men and women were butchered as she watched. Blood-thirsty clansmen beat at the doors of the community houses where the children and the defenseless were hiding. Rinn was watching the slaughter of her own town. Her ears rang, her lungs filled with heat, her heart accelerated to an inhuman speed. With a feral scream she raced forward, her pilum burning with white-green light. Nowhere in her mind did she think of saving her city or protecting her friends—she only thought of one thing: death. Clanmorris would suffer for this atrocity. Rinn would not stop until they were utterly destroyed.

Rinn exploded into the enemy lines with such speed she could barely see her own movements. She watched herself carve a river of blood through the raiders. She wished she knew how to use her pilum better, the killing was happening too slowly. She ripped through the clansmen surrounding her father and Molo, and annihilated anyone near the dwarves. Rinn found herself inside the community houses, executing any raiders who dared to enter. By the time she was outside again, her violence had turned into madness. Rinn felt like a rider desperately pulling at the reins of an out-of-control stallion. The carnage she was unleashing was terrifying. She was the scared little girl back in that awful copse of trees filled with blood and bodies, except that this time she was the killer and not Yallakh.

Enemy warriors fled in horror from Rinn and her deadly spear, climbing over each other like desperate ants fleeing a flood. Her father screamed for her, but Rinn could not stop, she had to keep on killing. Molo attempted to block Rinn's path, holding Clive, Rinn could see the magic in its purple eye, but she would not be waylaid. The word "Ahebe" passed from Rinn's lips, she became lighter and hurtled forward like a ballista shooting over Molo's head onto the stone palisade. She landed in the thick of the clansmen attempting to flee over the wall. She plowed through them with her glowing pilum, wetting the battlements with their blood. The few that fought back were splintered and skewered. Rinn realized that the metal of her spear was burnt and spent. She threw down the useless stick and bent over to pick up an axe, which burst into green glowing flame at her touch.

The remnants of the attacking force fled down the hillside. Deel and Egan were attempting to regain control over their scattering forces. Rinn felt herself propelled towards the two men on horseback, she leaped from the town walls and raced after them. Rinn saw Cat out of the corner of her eye, trying to get her attention, but Rinn could not stop. The urgent need to utterly destroy the clan leaders consumed her. She unwillingly crashed through the fleeing warrior horde, killing anyone in her path. Before she could reach the clan leaders, two sorcerers in crimson robes flanked her, chanting in unison. Rinn turned to face them, but found herself paralyzed, held in thrall by their magic. She could see the blue vapors emanating from them, thick cords that wound around her like ropes. Rinn breathed the word "onlithe" and the magic ropes fell away. The sorcerers stepped back, alarmed.

Rinn advanced on the robed pair with her axe. The taller of the two sorcerers quickly raised a hand and summoned a javelin of blue energy. He hurled it at Rinn like an arc of lightning. The bolt struck her barrier with a thunderous impact, throwing her backwards. Encouraged, the second sorcerer joined in, and the two alternated summoning and hurling bolts. Rinn was pinned down by the electrical onslaught. She gave ground not knowing how long her shield could withstand such powerful attacks.

Catherine slipped out of the night air behind one of the sorcerers and sank a dagger into his back. The warlock shrugged off the blow and cast a net of magic around her. Cat tried to slip away but she was held fast in his magical snare. Rinn could only helplessly fend off the barrage of bolts as she watched her sister struggle. A familiar pressure and pain in the back of her head warned her that her shield was failing. If only she had her pilum, she could hurl it at the warlock, but she had no idea how to throw an axe.

Seeing the two girls hard pressed, the clansmen began to regroup, forming a wide circle around the combatants, eagerly awaiting the outcome. Their numbers had diminished, but they were still a sizeable host over a hundred strong. They roared like spectators at a gladiator fight. Rinn spent her energy alternatively dodging and blocking magic bolts while trying to gain ground on the taller sorcerer. He wisely circled to match her movements, keeping a safe distance away. His partner finished weaving his magic net, effectively securing Cat to the ground and moved to rejoin the battle. Rinn knew her chances were slim if the two worked together. Her battle-rage was wearing off and she was beginning to feel drowsy and stiff, staggering as she moved. The fear of dying was the only thing keeping her awake. In the distance, she saw her father on horseback barreling towards her. She knew she had to finish this before he arrived, the sorcerers were too powerful for him.

"Stop it." A rock sailed through the air, hitting the taller sorcerer on the head. It distracted him but did not seem to do any harm. Sionne picked up another rock from the ground.

"Stay out of this, boy." The sorcerer growled.

Sionne threw another rock, which bounced off uselessly. "Leave her alone. She's just a girl." He scrambled to find more ammunition.

"She's a witch and she must die." The sorcerer conjured another javelin, sizzling with magic. Before he could throw it, a dark figure walked casually through the circle of clansmen and stepped between Rinn and the two robed men. Dressed in his usual black wrappings, Yallakh surveyed the destruction around him. With a flippant tone he addressed the crowd, Rinn in particular. "Did you really think you could spill this much blood without me noticing?" The two sorcerers eyed him suspiciously, magical bolts readied. Yallakh folded his arms and appraised Rinn. "This is quite a mess you've made. Maybe you're a better weapon than I first thought. But enough is enough. It's over."

Rinn wanted to cry. All was lost. She and Cat were defeated. Yallakh had sealed her doom. Hilltop would be overrun without her to defend it. She was so tired, she could not raise her axe to fight him. Cat squirmed helplessly beneath her magic net, hissing and clawing. The taller sorcerer pointed to Yallakh. "Leave us, demon. This is not your fight."

"Really?" Yallakh raised the tattoos over his eyes where his eyebrows should have been. "I've taken a liking to this girl. She's coming with me."

"Know your place, slaver." Deel muscled through the clansmen and into the circle. He stood with the sorcerers. "The witch dies."

"I think not." Yallakh licked his lips. Marshal arrived on his horse in time to hear Yallakh's proclamation. "This girl will not fall to the likes of you."

The two sorcerers hurled their magic bolts at Yallakh. The lightning splintered uselessly against the soul shield protecting him. Rinn could faintly hear the wails of suffering elves as the lightning faded. Yallakh drew two daggers and casually skipped toward the sorcerers. They attempted different offensive spells on Yallakh before finally turning and running. Unfortunately, robes are not the best clothing choice for speed. Yallakh overtook them and planted a dagger in each of their chests. He reached into their robes and yanked out a glass vial they each wore around their neck. He crushed the vials in his hand and the mages convulsed and dissolved into piles of ash.

In the distraction Yallakh created, Rinn crawled desperately to Cat. With great effort, she touched the magical netting and forced it to release with her word of breaking. Cat caught Rinn as she slumped to the ground. The confused clansmen watched the events unfold, not knowing what to do. Deel cried for an attack, but with the deaths of the sorcerers the warriors were reluctant to fight. A few archers loosed arrows at the girls. Rinn was too weak to summon her shield, but Marshal brought Bayard alongside his daughters protectively. Cat fretted as she held Rinn in her lap. She took three big deep breaths and slapped her paw against the side of the horse. Marshal, Rinn, Cat, and Bayard blinked out of existence. A panicked whiney could be heard as they vanished.

Chapter 39

Rinn could no longer hear the sounds of fighting. Her body was sore, and her head throbbed. She rolled onto her side feeling the hard, cold stones beneath her. She struggled to open her eyes, when she did her vision was dim and out of focus. Someone cradled her head in their warm lap. Rinn usually had difficulty remembering her mother's face but the feeling of resting her head in her lap seemed incredibly familiar. Tears filled her eyes as she attempted to call out. "Mom."

"She's awake." Feena's voice trembled with grief. "Help me! Help me get her up." Rinn felt many hands around her, helping her to stand upright. She wanted to walk, but she was too dizzy and lightheaded, instead she slumped forward. Oversized hands caught her and lifted her from the ground. Rinn was carried to a warm place and settled in a soft bed, thick blankets were layered over her. She almost drifted off to sleep until a shivering, furry shape was placed in bed next to her. Rinn groggily folded her warm arms around her bedmate and pulled her close. A heaviness overcame Rinn and she sank into a deep sleep. In her dreams, she was leaning out her bedroom window enjoying the warm night air in her hometown of Viburna. The golden glow of the marketplace illuminated her neighborhood. Fireflies leisurely mingled with the stars in the nighttime sky. The visible moon Sidus hung high in the sky, round and peaceful. The serene night was broken by cries of alarm as fires erupted across the city. Horse hooves thundered through the streets. Citizens screamed as buildings crumbled and fell. Towers toppled and steel rang out in the night. War had come to Viburna.

Rinn woke with a start. She was laying in her own bed next to Catherine who snored softly. Rinn was shocked to see the blankets and sheets were stained crimson. Her arms and face were covered in dried blood. In horror, Rinn fled the blood-stained bed. She checked herself for injuries, but she seemed unharmed. Her clothes and her hair were a ruin of dried blood. Rinn shook Cat awake. Her fur was matted in many places with red, but she seemed uninjured. Cat stretched herself awake and gave Rinn a curious look. Cat's normally blue eyes had turned a faded shade of green. She twitched her whiskers. "You look awful."

Rinn stripped off her blood-fouled clothes and tossed them into a basket along with the soiled bedsheets. She vigorously washed herself in a nearby basin, scrubbing her face, arms, and legs until they were sore. She attempted to wash her hair, but the ends were so tangled and crusted with dried blood that she had no choice but to hack them off with one of Cat's knives. Her curly blond hair was half its original length by the time she was done. Cat cleaned herself in her usual way. Rinn grabbed a new outfit for herself and threw one to Cat, who frowned at the prospect of wearing a dress, even though her favorite leather clothes were ruined.

Exiting her room, Rinn found Muireen casually sitting at the kitchen table with her father, who was sipping a mug of ale. "You're awake." His good leg and left arm were bandaged, but otherwise he seemed fit. He set down his mug and studied his daughter intently. "Are you okay?"

Rinn silently nodded her reply.

"Good, we need you outside. There's a decision only you can make." He reached for his cane and steadied himself as he rose from the table. He hobbled to Rinn and reached out to tousle her newly cut hair. "I like it."

Muireen opened a cupboard. "Do you girls want anything to eat?"

"This really shouldn't wait. There will be time for breakfast when it's done." Marshal opened the kitchen door into the bright daylight outside, Rinn and Cat had to avert their eyes. Muireen handed warm cloaks to everyone and lightly kissed Marshal on the cheek. "Be safe."

"No heroics." He smiled back to her. Marshal limped outside, Rinn and Cat following closely behind him. The courtyard was filled with activity as the people of Hilltop labored to reclaim their town. Rinn covered her mouth in horror when she realized what they were doing—stacking dead clansmen onto wooden carts like plague victims. The events of the previous night came rushing back, drowning Rinn in waves of guilt and remorse. All those bodies, those lives, were ended by her, she was the plague. Workers pushed carts full of corpses through rust colored snow to the postern gate where they lined up like a caravan of the macabre.

Gradually, the townsfolk began to take notice of Rinn. People kept their distance from her and whispered strange words. "Fury's wrath." "Chernok's flames." "God's handmaid." Some even made signs of protection when they saw her. Marshal led her through the courtyard past Sheridan and Hadwin who leaned on their shovels and watched her wordlessly. Rinn crossed near the Dvalinn dwarves who were clearing debris from the town walls. They stopped long enough to nod nominally in her direction before resuming their work. Yallakh had been right, Rinn thought. She was a killer and now everyone knew it.

Marshal led Rinn to the gatehouse stairs. He took each step gingerly, leaning heavily on the stair rail. Rinn helped him when she could. On the rooftop, Lutra sat playing his flute. He stood up when he saw Rinn and smiled happily at her. "Hey." Rinn tried to smile back, but she did not have it in her. Lutra waved to Cat who flicked her tail back and forth in reply. Lutra peered at Cat with concern. "What happened to your eyes?" She gave him a devious grin with her little fangs.

Marshal escorted Rinn to the edge of the gatehouse where she could see the entire countryside. Some distance away from Hilltop, unfurled across the hillside, were the remnants of the Clanmorris army—fewer than a hundred men huddled around meager campfires. They had no tents or shelter and did not seem to threaten the town in any way. Rinn looked on bewildered. "Why are they still here?"

"They can't leave." Marshal explained. "They don't have enough food to get home. Their leaders did not plan on defeat and left these men to starve." Marshal gripped the end of his cane tightly. "Yallakh came last night. He told me the clan leaders fled on horseback, abandoning their troops." Rinn was astonished that her father actually spoke to Yallakh, considering all that had happened between them. Marshal mused. "I think he was a soldier once, the kind who understood defeat."

"Those men don't have to starve." Rinn knew she had to find a way to save them. She was partly motivated by guilt over the slaughter of so many of their number, but she also could not sit by idly while helpless people suffered. "I need to find Feena. She knows our stores, she knows what we can spare. We will find the food."

Marshal's stifled his emotions. "I knew you'd make the right choice." He hobbled off leaving Rinn alone with Cat and Lutra. They were alternating making stupid faces at one another and laughing. Rinn interrupted their game and pried Cat away.

"We need to talk." Rinn escorted her sister back inside the house.

::

"I'm going." Rinn was dressed in her battle armor, which had been cleaned and repaired. She hefted a new pilum spear and a pack of provisions.

"Rinn, don't do this." Her father stood in the doorway, leaning on his cane. He had been through so much in the last year. He had fled Sevria to escape the ravages of war, but it found him anyway. Rinn loved her father, even though he was still keeping secrets from her, and she felt regret disobeying him, but this was her one opportunity to stop this bloodshed for good. If she did not go, the clan would regroup and lay siege to Hilltop again.

Rinn tried to reason with her father. "The remnants of Clanmorris are heading home. This is my chance to find out where they live."

"Send trackers." Marshal pleaded. "Bosky and his woodsmen could do it. Why does it have to be you?"

"I have to meet with their leader." Rinn was unwavering. "I mean to talk some sense into him. It's something the woodsmen can't do."

Marshal hobbled over and grabbed his cloak. "I'm coming with you." Rinn interceded, laying a hand on his arm.

"Not this time." She hugged her father. "You're still recovering from your injuries, old and new. You've seen enough war. I can manage this."

"You're not going alone." Marshal scolded her the way any desperate parent would.

"I won't be alone." Rinn opposed. "Cat is coming with me."

"As am I." Molo bent to enter the doorway, dressed in warm travel clothes, holding Clive in his hand. "I can track the clansmen without risk of being seen." He extended a large hand for Marshal to shake. "I'll watch over your daughter and keep her safe."

In resignation, Marshal accepted the giant's hand. "Okay, my friend. But you had all better come back safe." Rinn felt the warmth of everyone's concern for her, even after the atrocities she committed the night of the battle, she was still deserving of love. Her father sorted through her bag like an over-protective parent, making sure she had everything she needed. He offered to loan her Bayard, but ever since Cat had pulled the horse through the Mist, he was terrified of her. He snorted anxiously and bolted whenever she came close.

The sun was starting to set and Rinn was wanting to leave before the trail was lost. Molo, Cat, and Rinn headed for the postern gate. Feena and Lutra met them there, waiting with travel packs. Rinn rebuked them. "No. Not this time. You two are staying here."

Lutra flippantly ignored her. "I'm just going out for an evening walk. Nothing you can do about that."

Feena added. "And I'm coming along."

Rinn tried to explain. "This is not a game. We don't know how far we'll have to go or what we'll find when we get there. I'm not dragging you two into another warzone."

"You can't stop us." Feena grinned wryly, and Lutra gave her a satisfied nod. Cat hopped over and bopped Lutra playfully on the arm. The two laughed and played.

Molo bent over and whispered in Rinn's ear. "Maybe he could keep her distracted on the way." Rinn sighed heavily and nodded her head. She straightened her travel sack and gave her father one final hug before she exited through the gate, Molo following close behind her. Feena fell in line third, and Cat and Lutra trailed behind her, goofing off like children.

Chapter 40

P atches of spring grass poked through the snow, and sunlight warmed the late winter afternoon. Rinn and her party traveled quickly, following the straggling clansmen. At first, the horde headed east, directly to the snow-capped mountains. Rinn was worried about crossing the dangerous peaks in wintertime, but then the horde veered south, staying to the foothills. For six days and nights, they skirted the edge of the mountain range, until they came to a wide pass. Molo used Clive to cautiously lead the party into a hilly countryside nestled between two mountain chains. Chilly streams flowed from lofty peaks and burbled across the highland hills.

Rinn marched on, thinking how much easier this journey was than her icy trek to the mountain fortress of Duke Kapros. The winter chill had broken, and warm breezes promised spring's coming. Molo joked as he walked, teasing Cat. Lutra played his flute merrily. Everyone was doing well except Feena, who was not accustomed to prolonged travel and tent sleeping. The girls boarded together in one tent, with Lutra in another. No tent was large enough to house Molo, so he slept outside, usually under some tree. Rinn could not be certain, but she suspected that Cat may have snuck into Lutra's tent once or twice after everyone else had gone to sleep.

After a morning of hiking, the party arrived at a wooded ridge. Molo held up Clive and announced. "We're here." He scanned the area with Clive's purple eye and waited for Rinn's instructions.

Rinn lowered her pack and unslung her pilum. "How many are out there?"

"Thousands." Molo frowned. "Maybe tens of thousands." Lutra and Feena's eyes went wide. Cat played with her favorite skein of yarn, not seeming to care. Rinn faced her companions, attempting to pull her hair back into a ponytail, but she had cut it too short.

"This's your last chance." She appealed to her friends. "I have to go in there, but you don't have to follow. If you want to remain, I won't hold it against you." Feena bit her lower lip and shook her head no.

Lutra cast a glance at Cat before he stepped forward. "We're coming with you." The resolution in his voice was final.

"Okay." Rinn accepted it, they were in this together. She advised everyone to leave anything they did not need. The tents and travel packs were stashed between two odd trees and covered with leaves and brush. As the party departed, Cat held up a paw.

"I'll be right back." She skipped back to the hiding place and disappeared behind the two trees. A moment later she returned. "Okay, we can go."

Molo looked at her suspiciously. "What was that all about?"

"I marked it, so we can find it again." Cat sauntered by casually.

Rinn's face reddened as Cat walked away. She turned to Molo and whispered. "Did she just do what I think she did?"

"I don't even want to know." Molo stared straight ahead stoically.

Clive guided the party down the forest ridge to a wide valley cleared of trees. A woodland city sprawled out before them, hidden between the mountain ranges. Rows of timber houses with tall thatched roofs lined haphazard streets. The city was surrounded and subdivided by wooden stake walls, not unlike the palisade built around Hilltop. Watchtowers overlooked the entrances to the city, topped with thick thatched canopies. The area was abuzz with activity, common folk coursing through the streets pushing carts or toting wicker baskets as they went about their daily routines.

The party remained hidden in the tree line above the city. Molo scanned the area with Clive. "What do we do now, Sigillum?"

Rinn twiddled her spear in her hand. "I guess we go introduce ourselves."

Lutra was not convinced. "Shouldn't we sneak in, or something?"

"Why?" Rinn contested. "If we sneak around, they'll think we are up to something. They'd be more likely to attack us."

Feena chimed in. "But aren't we up to something?"

"Not exactly." Rinn had a mischievous look in her eye.

::

Rinn nonchalantly led the party to the nearest entry gate. She tried to casually walk into town and failed miserably. When a member of your party is quarter giant, it is hard not to be noticed. Redheaded townsfolk pointed and gawked as the huge man passed. Guards in the watchtowers called down.

"You there, stop." They had bows trained on the foreigners. The guards all had red hair; actually, just about everyone she had seen so far was a redhead. Rinn wondered if she should have colored her hair before she attempted to stroll into town. Then she remembered that Molo did not have any hair to dye. The point was moot now, the enemy was already alerted to their presence. Rinn tried a non-standard tactic.

"Hi." She waved happily. The guards cast confused looks at each other.

"State your business." One of the bowman stammered.

"I'm here to visit." Rinn replied, holding her spear behind her back. Cat scrunched her face dubiously. The baffled guards debated among themselves. Rinn motioned for everyone to keep walking.

The party almost managed to get through the gate before someone cried out. "It's the witch!" Chaos immediately followed. Rinn raised her barrier as the guards released their arrows. Feena clung to Rinn in fear, and Molo scooted Lutra closer inside the shield. An alarm horn blared as more arrows bounced off the green glowing dome.

Rinn turned to her sister. "Cat, can you find out where their leader is?"

"Sure." Cat stepped forward, ready to slip, but nothing happened. She tapped Rinn on the shoulder. "Um, Rinn. You have to lower your shield."

"Oh." Rinn blinked in surprise. She suppressed the barrier for a moment and Cat slipped away. A single arrow whizzed past her, before her shield was restored. Fortunately, it did not hit anyone in the party, but Rinn's nerves were rattled, she vowed to be more cautious. She moved the group down the main road into the heart of the city. Panicked townsfolk scattered as they approached, doors slammed, and windows shuttered. Members of the city guard mustered in the road ahead, two rows of archers with longbows. They launched multiple volleys of arrows at Rinn's shield.

Molo seemed concerned. "How long can you keep this thing up?"

"Against archers, for quite a while." She attested. "But not very long if they have magic." Rinn scanned the streets sourly. "Where is Cat?"

Feena reminded her. "She can't do that thing with your shield in the way." Rinn realized her friend was right. This was going to be more challenging than she first thought.

Lutra pointed to a rooftop. "I see her." Rinn saw her sister jumping up and down on the peak of a long building, waving her paws over her head. Rinn marched the group down a side road toward her. When she got close, Cat vanished and reappeared on a neighboring building, waving furiously. Rinn followed her sister through town, bewildered guardsmen chasing after her, constantly firing arrows. Feena and Lutra were shaken by the situation, but Molo was calm as he followed along holding Clive.

"Rinn." He placed a giant hand on Rinn's shoulder, stopping their progress.

"What is it?" Rinn asked, anxious to move on.

"Yallakh is here." Molo's expression was grim.

"Don't worry." Rinn reassured him. "I half expected it. It actually makes things easier." Molo did not seem convinced, but the party moved on, following their rooftop guide. The entire city was in a turmoil by the time they reached their destination, a circular three-story building near the center of town. An army of warriors assembled protectively in front of the structure, swords and axes drawn. They shouted jeers and taunts at Rinn and her party as they approached. Rinn frowned. "They're really making this much harder than it needs to be."

"How do we get past them?" Feena fretted. Rinn waved to her sister who was perched on the building just above the mass of warriors. She pointed to the men and pantomimed shooing them away. Cat nodded her head and jumped down from the building, landing behind the men.

"What is she doing?" Molo squinted to see.

A thunderous roar tore through the plaza, a deafening sound that shook the very ground. Warriors scattered in every direction, white with fear. Frightened clansmen fled to side streets and alleyways, dropping their weapons as they ran. On the steps of the central building, Cat sat on her haunches, licking her face.

Lutra stared wide-eyed in amazement. He stuttered. "Did you know she could do that?"

Rinn shook her head. "No." Her ears were still ringing.

Molo, unphased, urged them on. "Let's move before they regroup." The party ascended the steps to the building. Rinn lowered her barrier and squeezed her sister's paws as they joined up with her.

"Cat, that was awesome." She praised her with a hug. "You really scared them off."

"I didn't mean to." Cat moaned. "I was trying to make them chase me."

Molo ushered everyone inside the structure. "Whatever it was, it worked. Now, let's go." Inside the building, Rinn found a short wood-beamed hallway lined with ceremonial weapons and shields. The dark interior was illuminated by charcoal braziers. Rinn warily proceeded down the corridor with the rest of the party behind her. She relaxed her barrier, it taxed her more than she cared to admit. The hallway opened into a wide, circular room, the same shape as the outside of the building. Ornamental tapestries covered the windowless walls and iron chandeliers hung from the rafters, dripping candle wax. Armed guards wearing colorful violet sashes protected a heavy-set, elderly woman sitting on a large, high-back chair. Several maids attended her. Beside her, draped over his own chair, sat Yallakh. He gave Rinn a sanguine smile with his tattooed teeth.

"You got here quickly." He bemused.

The head of the woman's personal guard threatened with his sword. "We will defend our lady with our lives." The other warriors formed a tight group, ready to attack.

Yallakh turned to the elderly woman. "Aosta, let the girl speak." The woman on the high-backed chair leaned forward squinting, her plump cheeks creased with wrinkles. She studied Rinn intently, everyone in the room hanging in anticipation.

"I will hear what she has to say." Her ancient voice had a lively charm, low but musical. She rested her hands in her lap and settled into her chair.

Rinn took a stalwart step forward. She held her pilum in her right hand, not menacingly, but more like a staff or walking stick. She inhaled deeply, pushing down all her fears, she needed to have confidence in herself if this was going to work. "I am Rinn Amali, ruler of Hilltop. And I have come to help you raid and pillage."

The entire room was astonished, her own party most of all. Molo and Lutra actually took a step away from Rinn. Cat bounced on her paws with feline mischievousness. One person laughed loudly, clapping his hands in satisfaction. Yallakh stood up and applauded. "Oh, this is too good."

"Explain yourself." Molo grunted at Rinn.

"Trust me." Rinn hissed through her teeth. Murmuring filled the room.

Aosta adjusted herself in her chair. "Go on."

Rinn stated her case calmly, even though her stomach was in knots. "Hilltop is a town of farmers and fishermen. We know how to make food. But your attacks have left us starving. Your raiders burned our fields and killed our cattle, and now you are starving, too. You need us, you need the food we create. We are not your enemy, and we should also not be your prey." The entire room listened to Rinn, transfixed by her words, except Cat. She was completely distracted by blobs of candlewax on the floor.

Rinn took another deep breath. "There is something we do want: slaves." Everyone was even more stunned by Rinn's second statement. The room was filled with yelling and bickering. And that is precisely when Deel and twenty of his raiders burst through the doors, swords leveled at Rinn and her party.

Chapter 41

Tension seized Aosta's chamber as the three groups of warriors squared off. Deel and his entourage harried Rinn's party, who took refuge against one wall. Feena cowered behind Rinn, and Lutra stood behind Molo. Aosta's guard threatened Dell and his warriors, demanding that they withdraw. The three-way standoff remained until the elderly woman rose and scolded everyone like children.

"What is the meaning of this? How dare you raise weapons in my house?" She pointed a finger at Deel. "Stay your sword or face the trial." Deel and his men grumbled, but they sheathed their weapons. Egan and his raiders stormed into the chamber, ready to attack. Seeing the sour expression of Aosta vexing everyone in the room, he and his warriors timidly backed down the hallway. A hush settled over everyone and Aosta calmly returned to her chair. Yallakh watched the show with great interest, the tattoos at the corners of his mouth turning up in a sickening smile.

Aosta addressed Rinn. "Continue, my dear."

Before Rinn could begin, Deel blurted out. "Don't listen to this witch. She slaughtered hundreds of our best warriors."

The head of Aosta's guard reprimanded him. "There is no dishonor in dying on the battlefield, sword in hand."

Deel was incensed. "They did not die in battle. It was an unholy massacre. That girl, that one little girl murdered hundreds of our warriors with her own two hands. Don't be fooled by her—she's in league with demons. She's a curse, and she must die."

The men in Aosta's guard did not know what to do. Half of the guard kept their weapons leveled at Deel at his warriors, the other half turned to confront Rinn and her party. From the hallway, Egan braved a comment. "I saw her. I saw her in a fit of rage covered in the blood of our men. Deel speaks the truth, she's a monster."

Rinn held her spear tightly, trying to balance the precarious situation. If she left now, everything would be unresolved, and more battles would inevitably follow. In order to keep Hilltop safe, she would be forced to kill enough of Clanmorris until they could fight no more. She did not want that, she came to stop the blood-shed, not insure it. There had to be a peaceful way out of this conflict. She had been so sure coming here was the right thing to do, but this was an absolute mess.

Aosta brooded over the predicament. She studied Rinn with piercing, intelligent eyes. Everyone in the room awaited her pronouncement. An attendant brought her a goblet, which she accepted. The elderly ruler took a sip of her drink and then asked. "Is this true, girl?"

Rinn was trapped, she could not deny what she had done. She looked at Yallakh, who had predicted that her future could only be one of violence. Rinn wondered if society really did not have a place for a monster like her. She fought back tears. She had done the right thing, she needed to protect her people, no matter the cost. She wiped her eyes and steadied her resolve. "It's true." Then, she pointed at Deel accusingly. "But this moron attacked a town of farmers, women, and children with an army. We had no choice but to defend ourselves by whatever means possible. If anyone's to blame for the death of those men, it's him."

Aosta considered this. She turned to Deel, who was gobsmacked. She compelled him to answer. "Did you raise an army against the innocent? Did you order the killing of women and children?"

Deel stammered as he defended himself. "I was justified. Hughes tried to peacefully capture her, and she murdered ten of his men." Rinn shot Yallakh a nasty glare, he just shrugged indifferently. Deel continued. "I raised an army to bring her to justice. Everything I have done was by our laws."

Aosta weighed his testimony. "Do you have any proof of these accusations? Do you have any witnesses?"

Deel grinned. "I do." He barked an order to Egan and his men. "Go fetch the boy." A long time passed in the round chamber, everyone waiting in silence. Molo placed a reassuring hand on Rinn's shoulder, she reached out and touched it appreciatively. Feena and Lutra huddled together against a wall, overwhelmed by the proceedings. Cat had wandered off, poking at one of the glowing braziers with a claw. Deel bolstered his men with smug nods and reassuring clasps on the back. Aosta's guard remained divided, warily watching both parties.

Finally, Egan and his men returned, dragging with them the redheaded teen Sionne. He looked worse than when Rinn had turned him away at Hilltop's gates. Clearly, he had been beaten, probably for his disobedience on the battlefield. One side of this face was bruised and swollen, the whites of his right eye stained blood-red. His left arm was bandaged, and his clothes were a ruin. He kept his eyes downcast, refusing to meet Rinn's gaze.

Aosta spoke. "Boy. Were you with Hughes' men when they tried to capture this girl?"

"Yes, ma'am." He managed, even his voice sounded terrible, cracked and broken. Rinn began to feel immense guilt for the way she had treated him. He was a liar, a betrayer, a kidnapper, but he was a boy trapped in circumstances beyond his control.

Aosta questioned further. "Did you see her kill Deel's men unprovoked?"

"I heard the killing, ma'am, but I didn't see it." The beleaguered boy finally looked up, begging. "But, it wasn't her fault. Dolan attacked her, he wanted to kill her. He blamed her for the death of his brother." Egan shifted nervously in place.

"That's a lie." Deel reached out to strike the boy, but the guard intervened. Both parties tried to speak, to justify their actions, but the elderly woman waved a dismissive hand.

"Quiet. We do not have sufficient proof." Aosta spoke slowly without emotion. "If we come to an impasse, we must settle this with a trial."

Deel's jaw dropped, he shuffled back several steps. He squealed. "I will not fight that abomination. This is not justice."

Aosta replied dispassionately. "If she uses magic, we'll know that she cannot prove herself honestly, her life and the lives of her companions will be forfeit."

Deel reasserted himself. "You mean, I fight her, and she can't use her powers."

Aosta nodded. "Yes."

"Agreed." Deel held up a fist.

"Not happening." Molo muscled forward, in the face of the exuberant warrior. "I'll fight in her place." He stared down the clansman with a sneer.

"You do not stand accused." Aosta rebuked. "The girl must clear her own name."

Molo howled. "I won't stand by and watch a teenage girl fight a full-grown man. This is not justice, this is insanity."

Aosta was unmoved. "She has already admitted to the killings. Now we must see who carries the blame for their deaths." Deel folded his arms satisfactorily.

"You will regret this." Molo warned.

Rinn interceded. "It will be okay. If this is the only way to stop the bloodshed, I will do it."

"You can't fight this brute without magic." Molo pleaded with Rinn. "Don't do this. There has to be some other way."

"If this means that Hilltop will be left in peace, it will be worth it." Rinn was resigned to her fate. Thoughts of her old home in Viburna and the problems of the Empire were far away. Now, Rinn only wanted to give her father and everyone else who called Hilltop home the chance to live their lives without the constant fear of attack. If this was the only way to do it, she would willingly take the risk. Rinn calmly walked over to Cat, who was unraveling the threads of a wall tapestry. "Cat, I have to fight this man. If anything should happen to me, make sure the others get out of here safely." Cat peered at her sister quizzically, one ear up and the other down. Rinn gave her a big hug and parted with a wilting smile for Lutra and Feena. Molo tried to stop her, but she shook her head. He embraced her tightly and then let her go. Rinn walked to the center of the room. "I accept."

Deel made a derisive laugh. Molo seized his arm and yanked him aside. "Think you're tough, fighting little girls?"

"This is justice for all the men she slaughtered." He pulled away from Molo and proudly marched out of the room with his entourage. Egan and his bandits followed close behind like a pack of puppies.

The head of Aosa's guard addressed Rinn. "The trial will be held in the town center. For your safety, my guard will escort you there." Rinn and her companions fell in behind the guard as they left Aosta's chambers. Outside, people were lining the streets. Whispers and murmurs spread through the city like a toxic cloud, drawing redheaded men, women, and children out of their homes. Rinn was paraded down the main street past ordinary looking shops and houses with large thatched roofs. On-lookers gawked and pointed at the witch and her odd retinue: a giant, a half-cat, and two teenagers.

Rinn arrived at the center of the city, a large, irregular plaza of hard packed dirt covered in crushed limestone. The space was fronted by a variety of shops and lined by spectators and curiosity-seekers. Deel entered the plaza first, raising his arms and cheering, trying to get the audience to join in, but they were subdued—the trial was a serious affair. Rinn entered next, and many were shocked to see their war leader had been pit against a girl half his size. Rinn carried her resolve to the middle of the plaza and stood pilum in hand. Aosta was borne to the town center on a wooden litter, heavily decorated with carved animal heads and brightly colored canopies. Her guard delivered her to an elevated platform on one side of the plaza. Yallakh casually wandered in and sat down on the edge of the platform. Aosta addressed the crowd, and as she spoke, a thick-necked man standing at her side repeated her words in a bellowing voice.

"A trial has been called. Two witnesses stand before you accused of the deaths of hundreds of our warriors. One of them will take that guilt to the grave. These are our ways, this is our law." The crowd chanted in unison a dirge-like hymn. Rinn was astonished to see even small children joining in the rite. Deel strutted to the center of the ring and pulled a two-handed sword from its sheath, his men cheered him on. Rinn stepped forward to silence.

Feena cried out in a meek voice. "You can do this, Rinn."

Rinn spun the pilum in her hands, trying to warm up. She attempted to recall all her training, all the drills she practiced in the courtyard.

"Remember your footwork." Molo called out, as if he could read her mind.

The head of Aosta's guard stepped forward. He positioned himself between Deel and Rinn. "This trial determines your guilt or innocence. Any treachery will automatically prove your guilt and your life will be forfeit." He turned to Rinn. "If you use your magic, you will have assumed your guilt. Do you understand?" Rinn nodded in acknowledgement. The head guard cautioned Deel. "No underhanded tactics, poisonings, or tricks. You will fight fairly, or you will die." Deel scoffed and swung his sword around in preparation. The head guard stepped away. "The trial will begin now."

Deel grinned maliciously. "Get ready to die, little witch."

Chapter 42

The two combatants faced off in the central city plaza, surrounded by a somber crowd of redheaded spectators. Rinn was a girl of fourteen wielding a spear against Deel, a savage brute with a two-handed sword. Deel was twice the size of Rinn and built like an ox. The muscles on his upper body bulged as he stalked his prey. Rinn danced around deftly, waiting for him to strike. Rinn's companions held each other's hands as they watched. Yallakh observed everything with keen interest. Even Catherine was paying attention, watching her sister with wide green eyes.

Deel made his move first, swinging fiercely with his sword. Rinn dodged and used her spear to deflect the follow-up strike that immediately followed. Deel disengaged and strutted around the plaza, twirling his sword in a fit of braggadocio. He laid into Rinn once more, swinging widely. Rinn dodged the first strike and readied to block the next, but Deel's sword twisted in midair and his next blow came from the opposite direction, squarely cutting into Rinn's midsection. She was thrown across the plaza, skidding to a stop on her hands and knees. She coughed and spit out bits of crushed limestone. She rose up and leaned against her pilum, seemingly unscathed.

"What is this witchcraft?" Deel accused, pointing his sword.

"Dragon feathers." Rinn tapped the vest she wore.

Molo shouted from the sidelines. "She killed it herself."

Aosta nodded. "I'll allow it."

Deel growled and rushed the girl once more. She rolled away, but he was relentless, Rinn barely fended off a flurry of attacks. Deel's size and strength would overwhelm her, but she had the advantage of distance. She kept her spear directed at her opponent's face, forcing him to divert it before he could strike. Rinn aimed a few jabs at the man's legs, trying to slow him down. Deel was quick for his size and dodged the feeble attacks easily. He pressed her with several more savage strikes, and Rinn gave ground. She was already starting to tire, huffing loudly, whereas, Deel's breathing was calm and even. Rinn knew that if she did not end this quickly, she would not have much of a chance.

Rinn timed her strike perfectly, waiting for Deel to swing and then launching her own counterattack. She thrust straight at Deel's chest, aiming for his heart, but the big man caught the shaft of her spear in his left hand, holding it fast. Rinn was lost, she could not overcome his strength. Deel kicked her hard in the chest, flinging Rinn backwards. Her spear slipped from her hands as she sailed across the plaza, landing painfully on her side. Deel tossed the spear to his left and advanced on the fallen girl, ready for the kill.

Rinn could feel the maelstrom inside her. With a thought, this insignificant soul would be vanquished. She could tear the city apart like an unstoppable whirlwind, sparing no one. She could be an avalanche with the force of Geamradh, the very embodiment of winter. It was necessary for her to live on, no matter the cost, no matter what amount of bloodshed was required. Rinn fought it back. Even as Deel came for her, swinging his sword against an unarmed opponent, Rinn fought it back. She did not want to become the monster, she did not want to kill indiscriminately just to stay alive. Deel caught her with his blade, slashing through her left shoulder just below her dragon feather vest. Rinn cried out in pain, but she held it back, she would not destroy this city.

With blood pouring from her shoulder, Rinn rolled to Deel's left as he swung. She could see her spear, some distance away, and she sprinted to it. Deel gave chase, but she arrived first. She grabbed her weapon on the run, hefting it on her good shoulder. She knew she only had one shot, it had to count. As Deel closed on her, she turned and threw her pilum, just as Molo had repeatedly drilled into her. The tip caught Deel in the abdomen and sunk deep, but it was not enough, he did not stop. He swung his two-handed sword down, forcing Rinn to spin to avoid the blow, taking the impact on the back of her vest. The power of the blow sent her sprawling to the ground. As the bloodied warrior raised his sword for the kill, Rinn kicked at the shaft of her spear still stuck in his gut. Deel staggered back in pain, trying to remove the iron pilum. He needed two hands to dislodge the weapon, and he refused to let go of his sword. Rinn staggered to her feet and backed up a few paces. She ran straight for Deel and jumped in the air. He raised his sword defensively, but he could not stop her from stomping on the end of her spear shaft, snapping the wood. Deel fell to the ground in agony, coughing up blood. Yallakh clapped gleefully.

Rinn kicked the sword out of the fallen warrior's hand, and tipped him over with her foot. He lay on his back, bleeding out onto the plaza ground. Rinn retrieved his sword. Seeing the hate in his eyes and she felt pity for this proud man laid low. "You don't have to die today."

Deel spat blood. "I won't be beaten by you. I'll kill you, your family, and your whole town, damn it." With a single hand, Rinn plunged his sword into his chest and forced it down. Deel breathed his last. Rinn staggered over to her friends, clutching her bloodied left arm in pain.

Aosta rose and spoke. "All bear witness, the man Deel takes the guilt of the death of his warriors to his grave." The throngs of spectators began to chant in unison. Rinn spotted Sionne among them, watching her with his bruised and bloodied eyes. As Rinn neared the edge of the plaza, a shadowy figure sprang from the sidelines, knife in hand.

"Die, witch!" Egan screamed as he stabbed at Rinn's back. She did not react fast enough to defend against his sneak attack, but his blade never found its target. Egan was stopped mid-strike by a clawed hand reaching through his neck. He stared wide-eyed as Cat materialized before him. With a flourish she finished him off, raking his head messily from his body. What was left of Egan crumpled to the ground, lifeless.

Cat raised her bloodied paw to the sky. "Justice." She howled in her feline voice. The crowd joined in chanting the word in unison. Molo rushed over to Rinn, tending to her injuries. He bound her wounded shoulder with a cloth strip torn from his own shirt. Feena and Lutra stood close by holding their weapons out defensively. The head of Aosta's guard approached them.

"You have nothing to fear from us. This girl has proven herself innocent in the sight of all. Come, let us see to her wounds."

::

Aosta's chamber was packed with the redheaded leaders of Clanmorris. Rinn, cleaned and bandaged, was ushered into the room with her friends. The elderly Aosta sat on her high-backed chair, overseeing the proceedings. Yallakh sat on his own chair to her left. Aosta's guard signaled for silence and a hush fell over the room.

Aosta sat up in her chair. "Rinn, ruler of Hilltop. Twice you have been wronged by members of this clan. You have proven your innocence through combat and an act of justice." Cat smiled self-assuredly. "By your right, you may demand restitution. What would you have?"

Rinn breathed in deeply, this was the moment. Everything that had happened led to this exact encounter. The future of the Rustic Lands rested in her hands, and she knew what to do, how to make it right. Not just for herself and her friends, but for everyone living here. This was the reason she had been gifted with her powers. She knew this would not stop here, Sevria waited, and she was compelled to go.

Rinn addressed the entire room. "People of Clanmorris, you're an honorable tribe of warriors. I would never deny you your sacred and proud traditions. But in payment for the wrongs done to me and my people I have two demands." Yallakh leaned forward, listening eagerly. "First, in payment for the unjust war started by Deel and his men, you'll agree to never attack the citizens of Hilltop again. Instead, you'll turn your raiding against the Khuraak. They build secret outposts on your shores to engage in slave trading. They line their purses with wealth stripped from these very lands." She pointed to Yallakh, who held up his hands in feigned innocence. "This man can show you their hiding places and where they hoard their gold. Plunder their outposts, bring them to ruin, but deliver their slaves to us. Hilltop will offer food and supplies for each slave released to us." Yallakh giggled like a girl, giddy with excitement. He reached into his bandages and fished out a slender black key imbued with blue runes, holding it up for all to see.

The room was astir with shuffling and murmuring. Aosta signaled for silence and the guards relayed her order. Once the crowd had settled, the elderly woman spoke. "If it is as you say, Clanmorris accepts your terms. Hilltop will be protected under our laws." Molo laid a proud hand on Rinn's good shoulder, nodding approvingly. Feena and Lutra exchanged glances, impressed by Rinn's rhetoric. Cat could not be seen, Rinn suspected she was up in the rafters somewhere. Aosta continued. "And you have a second demand?"

"Yes." Rinn acknowledged. "In payment for the cowardly attack by the bandit leader Egan, I demand the surrender of one of your own. He'll be released from Clanmorris to accompany me and my companions home."

Aosta calmly asked. "And who might that be?"

"The boy called Sionne." Rinn wrestled with herself. Even though she hated this boy, she knew he would be held partially responsible for the death and disgrace of Deel. His life in Clamorris would be a misery. She could free him from that, even though he did not deserve it. The crowds parted, and the redheaded boy was dragged forward and flung unceremoniously at Rinn's feet. He stared up at her with his bruised and bloodied eyes.

"Why?" He mouthed. Rinn knew mercy was the correct choice. The boy would never be accepted at Hilltop, not after what he had done, so he would be forced to travel with Rinn into Sevria. Maybe he could find some way to redeem himself. Rinn offered him a hand, to help him off the floor.

Chapter 43

Hilltop glowed in the distance, lit by cheery bonfires. The orange light played off the shiny stone walls protecting the town. A bell in the watchtower rang out as Rinn and her party climbed the gravel path up the hill. After twelve days of travel and a terrible ordeal by combat, Rinn was finally home. At the postern gate, a mass of people waited to greet her. The townsfolk were still wary of Rinn and her unnatural abilities, but they could not contain their joy at seeing her safe return. Her companions were welcomed warmly. Lutra was reunited with his brother, Bos who had Tristy hanging off his arm. Bos gave his brother a firm handshake and a nod of approval. Molo was greeted by the dwarves who gathered around him, hugging his legs awkwardly. The children ran up to pet Cat's fur and play with her tail. Feena even received a half-smile from her sister Devnet.

Rinn entered last with Sionne, and a collective gasp rippled through the crowd. Harsh words and curses greeted the traitor. Bos moved protectively in front of Tristy, his hand on his sword. Others drew weapons. Rinn held up her hand. "Good people, stay your swords. This boy is under my protection. We will only be staying a few days before we depart."

Marshal limped through the crowd, leaning heavily on his cane. "You're leaving?" Muireen accompanied him, wrapped in a woolen shawl. Rinn moved to her father and threw her good arm around him, hugging him tightly. He returned her warm embrace. They held each other for a long time before Rinn let go.

"I'm going to Sevria." Rinn said plainly. "I am going to set things right." There was an adult-like determination in her eyes, an indominable spirit in her poise. Even though her left arm hung in a sling and her body was a mess of bruises, Rinn knew she would not stop, not until everything was as it should be. In her heart, Rinn knew this was her purpose, the reason she was gifted with her powers.

Like a typical parent, Marshal said. "Come inside and we'll talk about it."

::

The feast was meager, but joyful. Food was still scarce in Hilltop, but warmer spring days coaxed slumbering animals from hibernation, ready to be hunted. Spring greens sprouted in the valleys, and the ice on the rivers and lakes thawed and the fish began to nibble once again. The townsfolk gathered in the main hall of Rinn's home, celebrating the news that Hilltop was safe from Clanmorris attacks. Muireen opened the last kegs of ale and wine from her caravan and the townsfolk drank, danced, and made merry. Lutra provided much of the music with his flute. Rinn recognized that he was still playing the pine-wood instrument Mafic and Felsic hastily carved on the snowy plains, and it sounded amazing.

Molo hauled his tree stump chair over to where Marshal and Rinn sat. He lifted his mug to Rinn. "This girl gave us quite the scare." Molo recounted the story of how Rinn had faced Deel in one-on-one combat, without magic, and defeated him. Marshal listened to Rinn's accomplishments in amazement, every so often taking a drink to steady his nerves. As she listened to the tale, Rinn could hardly believe it herself, especially the way Molo embellished it. Cat bounced over and dragged Rinn onto the dance floor, mindful of her injured arm. Rinn found herself in the midst of a crowd of young people spinning and dancing. She joined in the revelry, letting months of stress and worry fall away. She took turns dancing with different people: Cat, Feena, Calder, little Kelan, and even Bos, much to Tristy's chagrin. Still, there were faces she knew were missing from the festivities: Rury, Arlin, the dwarf Djurl, and many others who had lost their lives in the battle with Clanmorris. Rinn mourned for them, and their families, but she took solace in the fact that she had spared their town from future conflict.

Exhausted, Rinn left the dance floor and slouched into a chair like a teenager. Looking around, she realized that Sionne was not among the party guests. She wondered if he was still holed up in his room, brooding. She reminded herself to take a plate of food to him, he'll need his energy for the long journey ahead. Rinn sat collecting her thoughts when an assembly gathered before her. Molo led the group, addressing her formally.

"Rinn Amali, we all are aware that you intend to travel to Sevria, to right the wrongs of the Empire." The giant man knelt down on one knee. "I am Molossus, I will be your hammer. I vow to protect you and help you carry out your mission." He added briefly. "Oh, and Clive will be coming, too." Rinn laughed and nodded to the big man.

Molo stepped aside and Lutra approached. He laid his flute at Rinn's feet. "I am Nightsong, I will be your bard. I vow to spread the stories of your heroics and selflessness." Rinn was on the verge of tears, but she nodded okay.

Feena came next, kneeling down. "I am Feena. I don't know how to fight, but I vow to help you in any way I can, to the ends of Sevria if need be." Rinn could feel the lump in her throat, and she sniffed as she agreed.

Cat bounced in. "I'm Cat." She paused for a moment. "And I'll be your Cat." Rinn chuckled and took her sister's warm paw. Cat grinned and backed away, green eyes sparkling.

Felsic and Mafic knelt down next. Mafic spoke for both of them. "Lady Rinn, you freed us from our bonds of slavery and our lives are yours. We will be your craftsmen, wherever your path leads."

"Someone has to keep that fancy armor in good repair." Felsic winked. Rinn accepted them, repeating a dwarven blessing Felsic had taught her. The two Dverg smiled and bowed.

Unexpectedly, Calder approached. He laid his sword at Rinn's feet. "I am Calder, son of Hadwin. I vow to be your blade, though I do not know where you go." Somewhat surprised, Rinn agreed. Calder rose and placed a hand on Feena's head. "Someone has to look out for my little sister."

Lastly, Marshal approached, solemnly without his cane. He could not kneel down, so he inclined his head in respect. "The day I have always feared has come. You are leaving for Sevria. I cannot stop you. I would not stop you. You were meant for this and I've been a fool not to see it." He reached into a small pouch that hung around his neck and fished out a delicate medallion. It was a dainty triangle decorated with wavy lines, and it glowed a faint green, not the exact same shade as Rinn's own magic, but similar. He handed the medallion to his daughter. "This was your mother's."

Rinn held up the small metal triangle in awe. "It's still glowing after all these years." Rinn could feel the warmth of her mother in the magic and tears streamed down her face. "How is this possible?"

Her father answered, barely bottling his own emotions. "She made this for me before she died. It's made of a rare metal that will never rust or tarnish."

Rinn showed the medallion to Felsic and the other dwarves who touched it in amazement. "Morton thrane." Botrogen said reverently. "You have to dig to the very bones of the world to find this."

Felsic observed. "This metal is as old as time itself." A collective gasp spread through the room. Rinn studied her mother's medallion, a perfect triangle, like the ones that appeared in her barrier. Inside, she knew that this shape had some deeper meaning, some specific purpose, but she had yet to unlock it.

Marshal continued. "That pendant is your key. It will prove who you really are: Sabrinn Sevralis, daughter of the Empire." The news came as a blow. Rinn knew the Sigilla were closely associated with the emperors, but she did not know she shared their bloodline. Marshal divulged one of his deepest secrets. "You've always known your mother as Lania, but her true name was Tabitha, the youngest daughter of Virago. Her husband, your grandfather, was Tarandus, the last Sevrian emperor."

::

Rinn sat in her bedroom for the last time, holding the two necklaces: the one that was meant for her grandmother and her mother's own medallion. They looked like they were part of a matched but incomplete set. Her mother's medallion was in perfect symmetry with the pendant on her grandmother's necklace. The green stones in the gold necklace were streaked with thin veins of white, and Rinn wondered if it was the same metal that comprised her mother's medallion. She carefully placed the two necklaces into a leather pouch and hung it around her neck. She wore her traveling clothes and her dragon feather vest, faithfully mended by Felsic and Mafic. She hoisted her backpack, filled with personal items: travel outfits, a new dress sewn by Ceili, bits of ribbon left over from Imolia, a figurine given to her by Felsic, bathing necessities, and a bedroll. The backpack was a bit heavy, but if she balanced it right, tolerable. Her left shoulder still ached, but the pain was lessening every day.

Rinn walked through her house, trying to remember what it looked like when she first arrived, a pile of stones resting on a flower covered hill. In one short year, she had witnessed the transformation of that hilltop into a bustling town. She loved her home, but knew that it was not really where she belonged. Her place was in Sevria, a country torn by war and intrigue. For whatever reason, it fell to her to set things right. Maybe it was the royal blood in her veins, maybe it was the will of a higher power. Rinn did not care or mind. This was her task, something only she could do, and she would not back down.

Rinn shouldered her pack and exited her house into the warm, sunny spring day. Her fellow travelers had gathered at the gate, along with Sionne, who stood miserably by himself. He was, however, dressed in suitable clothes and sturdy shoes, and he sported a new backpack. Maybe there was hope for him after all. Rinn marched down to meet them.

"Let's go find that missing Emperor." Rinn merrily called to Molo.

He chuckled. "Maybe what Sevria needs is an Empress." Rinn gave him a cross look as she headed to the gate. She met her father and Muireen. He needed a bit more time to recover, but he vowed to catch up with them on horseback by the time they reached the Vallum, the walls of the Empire. Rinn gave him a big hug and even spared one for Muireen. They said their good-byes and the party headed down the hill, bound for Sevria. Molo and Clive took the lead. Feena, Calder, and the dwarves followed in orderly rows with Rinn joining them. Cat and Lutra trailed behind, goofing off the entire way.

Epilogue

T he community at Hilltop continued to grow, expanding into a major trade center, a bastion of civilization in the Rustic Lands. Today, the city is known as Saorsa, the jewel of the east. Travelers from all over the world come to relish in her beauty. More than a million people call her home. In the heart of the city stands a solitary hill and on it the remains of an ancient fortress. You can still walk the castle walls and see the false gateway. Some claim you can even see the rust colored stains of ancient blood on the battlements. The stone house is a ruin once more, but its significance has not been lost. To this day, at least among the locals, the site is reverently known as Dunabrin, or Rinn's Castle.

Glossary

Language of the Sigilla

acies: magic focused into a blade or point
'ahebbe': word for 'float'
'beorgan': word for 'shield'
'gifan': means 'gift' used to summon an acies
'onlithe': word for release

Gods of Sevria

Aedis: god of ceremonies
Caminus: god the forges
Divum: goddess of the skies
Imbur: goddess of rain
Ingo: god of the mountains
Lucus: god of forests
Onrigo: godess of the oceans
Parma (*the Shield*): god of protection
Sidus: god of magic; also, the visible of the two moons
Tenebra: goddess of darkness; also, the unseen moon

Rustic Religion

Boldyn: the god of fire
Chernok: the god of death
Geamradh: the bringer of snows
Imolia: holiday of rebirth, first day of the calendar year
Samria: goddess of nature

Geography

Brigantum: island continent west of Edera, renowned for its high-bred horses

Edera: continent south of the Pernic Sea, its western half is the Sevrian Empire and eastern half an untamed wilderness

Egesian Sea: dangerous, narrow sea between Edera and Uurden Els, infamous for its pirates and violent seastorms

Murstein: northernmost region of Uurden Els, ancestral home to the dwarven race

Migalia: a savage archipelago just west of Sevria, the Empire launched a series of unsuccessful invasions to the islands

Pernic Sea: vast ocean north of Edera populated by hostile sea monsters

Roinn Mountains: snow-capped mountain chain across northern Edera

Sevria: a dynastic Empire in western Edera spanning more than 500 years of history

Uurden Els: large continent east of Edera, known for its endless inhospitable deserts

Viburna: Rinn's childhood home in Sevria

Creatures

Caedes: (rock-rippers) large, fearsome beasts that bore into mountainsides with their fierce claws

Feathered Dragons: (bobs) large, flightless reptiles covered with feather-like scales

Floefang: creatures made of living ice with snouts resembling a wolf and long, flexible bodies like a ferret

Grimalkin: demonic familiars associated with witches

Grashel: burrowing pests with spiny, poisonous quills

Margot: rarely seen humanoid race with feline features from the deserts of Uurden Els, known to exhibit an affinity for magic

Bibliography

It is my privilege to call attention to these excellent books that helped me craft the world of Sevria:

Complete Encyclopedia of Elves, Goblins, and Other Little Creatures, Pierre Dubois 2005
The Dragon Keeper's Handbook, Shawn MacKenzie 2013
An Invitation to Old English & Anglo-Saxon England, Bruce Mitchell 1995
Everyday Life in Medieval Europe 500-1500, Kathryn Hinds 2009
How to Draw Fantasy Art & RPG Maps, Jared Blando 2015
Every Xanth Novel ever written, Piers Anthony 1977 - present

Special appreciation to Orson Scott Card for his seminal guide: How to Write Science Fiction & Fantasy 1990.

Sneak Peek:
Volume 2: Words of Warfare

Chapter 1

W hen the forest ended at the base of the world's largest wall, Catherine was not impressed. Her whiskers hung low and her ears folded back in annoyance. She was a Margot—half feline, half human—a desert creature from the sands of Uurden Els. Her soul-sister Rinn pushed her way through the underbrush, spitting out bits of leaves.

"I think we've arrived." Rinn proclaimed as she spotted the wall. She squinted up at the imposing monstrosity that blocked out half the sky.

Cat tapped absently at the stones. "Who put this thing here?"

One by one, Rinn and Cat's friends emerged from the forest. They jokingly referred to themselves as Rinn's army. They were not much of an army: one soldier, a handful of teenagers, two dwarves, and a quarter-giant. But they were all loyal to Rinn, willing to follow her anywhere, even into the heart of a civil war.

The quarter-giant Molossus proudly placed a hand on the enormous limestone wall. "This is the Vallum, the eastern edge of the Sevrian Empire. One thousand miles of stone and engineering." Several of the teenagers whistled at the architectural marvel. It towered over Rinn's army like a cliff. At the top of the mighty rampart, miniature sentry towers dotted its lofty parapets. Rinn saw no windows nor doors, only stark, imposing wall stretching to the horizon north and south. For its size, the barrier had not been well maintained, chunks of fallen stone littered the forest floor and trees grew right up against the stones like weeds.

The traitorous redhead Sionne asked. "What now, princess?"

"Stop calling me that." Rinn chafed. Now that she was here, Rinn was unsure what to do. She spent the last half-year traveling through the Rustic Lands to the edge of the Sevrian Empire. She turned fifteen on the journey. She did not have much of a celebration, a homemade sweetbread cooked over a campfire and a round of singing. But she was surrounded by her friends and family, her favorite way to spend a birthday. In the last six months Rinn had changed. Her long blond hair was growing back. Her height had shot up so much, she was almost eye to eye with her father. Her skinny, girlish figure became more defined, her muscles tempered by daily hiking and hunting. Her friend Feena, who was close in age, had fully blossomed in the ways that turned boy's heads. Rinn's adoptive sister Catherine was even starting to show feminine curves beneath her fur. Rinn was frustratingly skinny and under-developed. She wondered if she was doomed to look like a bean-pole all her life. She set her worries aside, more important concerns were pressing, like how to get past this wall.

Rinn reached out a hand and touched the Vallum. Its yellow stones had been polished marble-smooth and pieced together without visible seams. Rinn recognized the craftsmanship—dwarven. And not just any dwarves, this wall was built by Dvalinn dwarves. When Rinn fled the Empire two years ago with her father, she had known nothing of dwarves or war or magic. Now she was coming home, well versed in all these things.

"The Dvalinn built this." Rinn observed.

Felsic and Mafic, the two dwarves accompanying her, scrutinized the colossal wall. Mafic, the more rotund and cheerful of the two, agreed. "Most certainly. Our Dvalinn cousins fit stone together so tightly not even water can pass through." The two brothers were Dverg, dwarven artisans skilled at delicate handiwork, completely unaccustomed to large scale construction.

"It's not very pretty." Felsic scoffed at the bland stone.

Rinn chuckled. With a rustling of branches, Rinn's father emerged from the forest on horseback. Last year he took an arrow to his hip and it never healed correctly. He remained in the saddle most of the time, which was challenging in the dense forests of the Rustic Lands. But he was a trained equestrian, and he navigated the wilderness with grace. Rinn asked him. "How far do you think it is to the nearest gate?"

Marshal peered down the length of the massive wall. "The gates are spaced every 50 miles. But we've been avoiding the main roads, so there's no telling how close the nearest one might be. If I could get a peek on the other side of the wall, I'd have a better chance of knowing where we were."

"I could go." Catherine raised a paw eagerly.

"I don't think that's the best idea." Molossus, the quarter giant, held up a hand to object, but Cat was already gone, vanished into the air. Margot did that—disappeared into thin air and reappeared at will. At least Catherine did that, and she was the only Margot Rinn had ever met. Rinn was not sure what other Margot were like, but in her mind they all behaved just like her sister.

"Where did she go?" Feena looked around, bewildered.

"Don't worry." Lutra reassured her. "She does that. She'll come back when she wants to."

"We'll camp here until she returns." Marshal announced. Everyone let their packs slide to the ground and plopped down to rest.

"I could really use a bathroom." Sionne eyed the Vallum suspiciously.

Lutra cuffed him on the back of the head. "Go find a tree."

Marshal organized a hunting party to scavenge for small game in the vicinity. He took Feena and her brother Calder along. Feena was learning how to use a bow, she had no talent for hand-to-hand combat. Her brother, however, was a natural swordsman. Lutra, the aspiring teenage bard, departed with the dwarves to forage for food. Felsic and Mafic had a knack for finding edible mushrooms, and Lutra always knew how to spot sweet, ripe berries.

Rinn stayed behind with Molo and Sionne. She was glad to have the giant and his curious rock Clive around. Sionne was a different story. She had saved him from certain death, but she did not trust him. He had betrayed her too many times in the past. He only came along because he had nowhere else to go, kicked out of his clan and shunned for life. Rinn offered him his only chance at redemption, not that he seemed to want it. Still, he had made an effort to clean up, he tossed his old threadbare clothes out in favor of a new travel outfit and he even bathed occasionally. His red hair stuck out in every direction like a bird's nest and his teeth were crooked and unwashed, but he was trying.

Rinn started digging a fire pit with a small shovel from her pack. The dwarves taught everyone how to make campfires that are invisible from afar by digging into the ground. A small side tunnel allowed air to flow under the fire and keep it burning. Dwarven fire pits did not make much smoke and were excellent for cooking. Molo ambled over as Rinn worked.

"Need any help?" The giant man offered.

Rinn wiped her sweaty brow. "I'm good. Just keep an eye out for Cat."

Molo held up Clive, his strange rock with a purple eye painted on it. He scanned the area with a frustrated grimace. "I can't see her, but she could be anywhere."

"She'll be back." Rinn promised, digging deeper into the ground. The foraging party returned with wild mushrooms and forest onions. Marshal and the hunters arrived some time later with a clutch of strange rabbits with long squirrel tails and bushy ears. The animals in the Rustic Lands always seemed peculiar to Rinn, yet most of them tasted perfectly fine.

"Any sign of Cat?" Marshal asked, dismounting with his catch.

"Not yet." Molo answered in a hushed voice. Rinn tried not to look anxious, but her sister had been gone a long time. Dinner came and went with no sign of the missing feline. As daylight faded, Rinn became seriously worried. She hugged her knees as she sat on the ground near the fire. Her father came to sit beside her.

"You can contact her, can't you?" Marshal said. The bond between Rinn and Cat went deeper than anyone suspected, but she was not ready to reveal that fact, even to her own father. Still, parents had secret ways of knowing about their children, at least that is how it seemed to Rinn.

"Yes." Rinn nodded. "I can contact her."

"I think it's time." Her father pressed.

Rinn grudgingly agreed. She rose up and cleared her head. She recalled the time Feena and two other girls from Hilltop had been kidnapped. A rescue attempt failed, and all hope seemed lost, but Cat spoke to Rinn in her mind and helped her locate the imprisoned girls. Rinn held on to that sensation as she spoke to the evening air. "Cat, can you hear me?"

Everyone watched Rinn in expectation. Several minutes passed, and Cat finally answered. Help me. I'm stuck.

A wave a relief poured over Rinn. "Cat, where are you?"

I'm on the other side of the wall. Cat moaned. It won't let me back through.

Rinn did not realize she was gesticulating wildly. Her friends could only hear one side of the conversation and they watched her curiously. "Cat, are you okay?"

I'm hungry. Cat noted.

"But are you safe?" Rinn could not see her sister, but she could feel her nod her head yes. It was unsettling knowing Cat's actions as if they were her own. She wondered how deep their magic bond ran, how closely their souls touched. "Stay put. I'll come get you." Rinn vowed. Cat sniffed and nodded again.

Lutra grabbed Rinn's hand. "Is Cat okay?"

Gently prying her hand away, Rinn answered. "She's fine. She's just trapped on the other side of the wall. For some reason she can't slip back through."

Molo wrinkled his bald head and scratched at his bristle-brush beard. "Why would anyone build a wall that lets magic in but not out?"

"They want to keep something inside." Felsic deduced.

"Or someone." Marshal furtively cast a glance at Rinn.

Oblivious to the implication, Rinn asked. "So, how do we get Cat out?"

Marshal responded. "I'll ride to the nearest gatehouse and go through."

Molo shook his head. "Too risky. Night is almost upon us and the nearest gate could be miles away." Holding Clive high above his head he scanned the wall, discovering nothing.

Lutra peered up at the Vallum soaring above him. "I don't think we have enough rope to go over."

The normally quiet Calder commented. "If you did, would you want to climb it?"

"No." Lutra admitted.

Rinn could feel Cat pacing on the opposite side of the wall, a disquieting sensation that made her feel frustrated and impatient. "We have to do something." Rinn blurted out. She stomped over to the Vallum and started to concentrate. A